Praise for Apricots and Wolfsbane

"Pull up the hood of your cloak, make sure no one is watching and prepare to learn how to become an assassin. The beautiful Lavinia Maud follows a secret quest for her own holy grail—a tasteless and odourless poison.

Its effects must take time enough to avoid suspicion, while she must find a dosage that allows a path for escape. In the meantime, she applies her deadly craft with breath-taking ruthlessness, as some don't deserve a painless death.

K M Pohlkamp's gothic story becomes darker as Lavinia's ambition leads her on a journey from which there can be no return. Her experiments are unhindered by concern for her victims, and she admits the poisoner's reward is the look of surprised understanding in the eyes of a doomed victim.

Written in the first person, the atmospheric undertones and fast pace make this a book which is hard to put down. If you like happy endings, look away now—and be careful what you eat or drink!"

—Tony Riches, author of the *Tudor Trilogy*

"This is not my usual genre, however, I enjoyed the novel immensely. The story kept me on my toes with the action and the plot twists."
—Lisa Orchard, author of *The Super Spies* and *The Starlight Chronicles.*

"I don't normally read historical fiction, but I am a huge fan of this book. Although rich in period detail, K.M. Pohlkamp's Apricots and Wolfsbane reads like a modern-

day psychological thriller. Fans of the Dexter series will love Lavinia, an anti-hero the reader simultaneously gravitates toward and cringes away from. In some scenes, Lavinia is so sympathetic, my palms sweat with anticipation, hoping Lavinia could escape every predicament she found herself in. In other scenes, my stomach turned in revulsion at the lengths the poisoner went through while stalking and attempting to murder her prey. This is a perfect book club novel—with enough interest and intrigue to keep everyone turning the pages and enough depth for a lively discussion afterwards. I can't wait for the sequel!"
—Megan Cassidy, author of *Always Jessie*, *The Misadventures of Marvin Miller*, and *Smothered*

"The talented new voice of K.M. Pohlkamp brings meaning to historical fiction. I was swept away in this haunting tale of murder, politics, confession and complicated relationships. After reading this tale of poison, revenge, confession and power, you will ponder the idea that everything—even the vilest murder—can be forgiven.

Pohlkamp has brought to life a piece of history that captivated me with its unique flavor. Lavinia Maud is a Poison Master who bit into my soul even as I prayed for her to stop."

—Robin Martinez Rice, author of *Imperfect* and *Hidden Within the Stones*

"Delicious. Apricots and Wolfsbane is a unique thriller packed with impressive research into historical poisons. Fast-paced, grim, and darkly funny, Pohlkamp's prose is intoxicating."

—Jessica Cale, author of *Tyburn*

Apricots and

Wolfsbane

K.M. Pohlkamp

Filles Vertes Publishing

Coeur d'Alene, ID

Filles Vertes Publishing, LLC
PO Box 1075
Coeur d'Alene, ID 83815
www.fillesvertespublishing.com

Publisher's Note: This is a work of fiction. Names, characters, places, and incidents are a product of the author's imagination except in the case of historical figures and events which are used fictitiously.

Book Layout © 2017 Filles Vertes Publishing
Cover Design © 2017 Broken Arrow Designs
www.brokenarrowdesigns.org

Apricots and Wolfsbane/ K.M. Pohlkamp. -- 1st ed.
ISBN 978-1-946802-02-6
eBook ISBN 978-1-946802-03-3

DEDICATION

To my parents, who taught me to dream.

To my husband, whose support makes my ambitions possible.

To Paracelsus, who coined the phrase,

"sola dosis facit venenum."

And Locusta, whose life inspired this novel.

Dramatis Personæ

Gaulshire

The Maud Household

LAVINIA MAUD — Poison master

ASELIN GAVRELL — Lavinia's apprentice

EDMUND GAVRELL — Aselin's brother

Peers

EDWARD AKWORTH — Baron of Camoy

TEDRIC JAMES PASTON — Earl of Gaulshire

AGNELLA EDITH PASTON (DARLEY) — The Countess of Gaulshire, widowed and remarried to Tedric as his second wife

ISABEL MARION PASTON (VACHER) — Former Countess of Gaulshire and Tedric's first wife, executed for treason

KELTON DARLEY — Agnella's son from her first marriage.

SILAS PASTON — Son of Tedric and Isabel

NICHOLAS VACHER — Viscount Gesbury, Isabel's brother, Silas's uncle.

COMMONERS

FATHER EUSTACE — Pastor of Marfield

HAYLAN MORYET — Magistrate of Marfield

MURIEL SALLAY — Kelton's servant

CRANSHIRE

GILES LANTON — Viscount of Matheson

SAMUEL "TUC" DARCY — Giles' food taster

CHAPTER ONE

The violent display of convulsions lasted longer than I anticipated.

With my boots propped on the table, I remember watching beads of wax roll down the candle, marking time between my victim's spasms. The brothel room was sparse, and the bed in the corner remained undisturbed. I had assumed the role of temptress that evening, but delivered a different climax.

I savored the fear on my victim's face as much as my own unlaced mead. The sweetness of both danced on my palate. His repulsive gagging, however, I endured with patience.

My target focused upon me. His hand shook, reaching out in a misplaced plea for aid. Instead, I raised my goblet in a final toast while he turned purple. He glanced towards his spilled glass, and then studied my face with new understanding. With his last remnants of life, he pieced together what I had done. Those little moments made the act so delicious. And as his body collapsed upon the floor, I added one more success to my mental tally.

Murder just never got old.

The scratching of my chair sliding across the uneven floor broke the sudden, serene silence of the room. Driven by curiosity, my boots echoed with each step towards my victim.

The man's eyes contained a lingering remnant of vibrancy despite the departure of the soul they once served. White froth percolated from his open mouth, overflowing the orifice to trail down his neck. It was not an honorable death, but my client had paid for certainty, not dignity.

Curious, I examined the large ruby on the victim's pointer finger which matched the client's description — an ornate setting with a coat of arms on one side of the gem and a mare's head on the opposite. The worked piece of silver did not seem important enough to procure my service, but as a professional, I had not asked for justification, only payment. Material significance so often motivated patrons to fill my coffers. I recognized the inherent sin, but I never judged a client's reason. I was not qualified to cast the first stone.

I did admire my victim. After all, he was a fellow criminal. I believed his talents as a thief must have been remarkable to pilfer the ring unnoticed from the finger of its owner. I often boasted of my own sleight of hand, but admittedly, I could not accomplish such a feat. Though in my defense, assassin clearly trumped thief.

After donning the black leather gloves concealed within the lacings of my bodice, I returned to business. I pushed the tipped chair out of the way and pulled on the ring, but my motion abruptly halted.

Caught at the knuckle, the gem did not budge.

I stared at his limp hand, dumbfounded, before a flame of focus burst through my body. How I craved and savored that rush. That high, and the feeling of power, motivated my ghastly craft all those years. Despite the stress, I never lost control of my emotions on the job. No matter the circumstance, I learned to remain calm and reason through any dilemma. That night was no different.

Grabbing the corpse's wrist in one hand, I pulled on the metal band with all my strength. Still, the damn ring did not move, even with my heel braced against his chest. But through the sound of my grunting, the unexpected scratching of a nearby rat interrupted my efforts.

The rodent stood tall on his hind legs, observing the entertainment outside his hole in the floorboard. What else could I do except laugh in amusement? There was something poetic about the meager creature being the singular witness to the growing farce, while beyond the chamber door, an entire brothel remained unaware.

But their ignorance would not last for long.

By God's nails, I was not going to degrade myself to play tug of war with a corpse, nor disgrace my spit to serve as lubrication. I retrieved the dagger from my boot and sawed through the bone of the blasted digit. In contrast, his purse strings cut with ease and the contained sum gave me confidence the proprietor would retain his promised discretion. Eager to depart, I cleansed the ring with the pure decanter of mead and left the contaminated gloves on the table.

I threw the finger to the rat.

Sheathing the dagger in the waist of my skirt, I returned to the main hall where boisterous music assaulted my ears, accompanied by drunken laughter. I added a meager sigh to the noise, surveying the sweaty, depraved crowd between me and the door. My eyes had long grown accustomed to the salacious activities occurring in every direction, but the obscene filth still violated my morals.

Keeping my head down, I managed to pass through the horde without gagging before one wandering hand grasped my rear. After a quick flash of my dagger, the drunkard relented. I longed to add to the rat's dinner, but still on the job, I could not afford a confrontation.

Humanity is a self-absorbed species. Throughout my career, I exploited that trait. The truth allowed me to disregard the number of potential witnesses within the brothel. No one would remember a plain maiden come morning and only the stewsman knew what occurred in the backroom. He smiled when he caught my glance. I gave the coin purse a gentle toss in his direction, glad the mess was now his problem. After retrieving my cloak from the hook by the door, I departed into the vacant streets of Marfield, knowing where I must go.

The air smelled of fresh rain, and above, grey clouds thinned. In my haste, my boot splashed into a puddle, wavering the moon's reflection on the surface and soaking the hem of my skirt. I did not care. The percussive rhythm of water dripping from rooftops paired with my excited footsteps over the cobblestones.

Ahead, a man lighting a lantern paused to behold my figure. I supposed I was dressed for entrapment. My sleeveless bodice was pulled low and tied tight, pushing up my bosom — and I had not worn a chemise underneath. The crimson ensemble complemented my brown hair left loose. I could sustain the role for the sake of the kill, but I would not indulge a bystander. Wrapping the cloak tight around my torso, I glared back as I passed.

The garment's velvet enveloped me in a familiar embrace of comfort. My father gifted the cloak not one year before he passed through the Celestial Gates. It was the olive color of wet moss, custom dyed to match my eyes. My marks often told me my irises sparkled like jewels, but those men were not the most poetic or astute. They all became unwilling test subjects with only one means to satisfy my desire. My smile broadened, recalling how well the thief had played his part.

But the sight of the looming church steeple subdued my arrogance in the space of a breath. A gust of cold wind conquered my excitement-induced sweat, and the call of the cross beckoned my heart. My conscience burned with the debt of transgression. I craved dispensation with every bone in my body and the complete essence of my soul. The sacred pilgrimage was the necessary second half of my routine and the singular act that kept me grounded all those years.

Entering the church sent needles into my back. An empty nave, especially at night, always humbled my heart. It was the result of intimacy, the crushing awareness of being alone within the House of God. Behind the far altar, His Lord's likeness gazed down upon me from the marble crucifix. For a moment, I swore the ruby ring around my thumb burned, challenging my gall for the first time that evening.

Reminded of my guilt, my gut threatened to collapse inward, but I endured, knowing internal peace was moments away. With a deep breath, I permitted the lingering, sweet essence of frankincense to burrow into my lungs; the woody aroma enveloped me in reassurance. Exhaling, I turned towards the confessional, ignoring the ominous aura of the surrounding statues cast within shadow. Their hard, grey eyes also glared upon me in judgment. I never claimed to be as pious as those Saints, but there are murderers amongst their ranks. St. Vladimir, for example. If the Church forgave him for slaying his brother and raping his sister-in-law, surely God had room for a poison master.

Closing the confessional door, I knelt before the wicker screen dividing the small, unlit chamber, and made the sign of the cross.

"Forgive me, Father, for I have sinned."

My familiar voice startled the silhouette on the other side of the partition.

"Lavinia." Father Eustace spoke my name with reserved dejection. "Again, rushing to the confessional will not exonerate such premeditated acts."

I continued despite not receiving an invitation, "It has been three weeks since my last confession."

"The confessional door is not a revolving stile, my child."

He demonstrated impressive wit, given the late hour, but I had suffered through his lecture before.

"I confess the sins of murder," I continued, "of theft and deceit. I am gravely sorry for these transgressions and the sins of my past."

The old man doubted my every word, but truly, the weight of the violation always resonated within. For many reasons, I was glad the act never became trite. The relentless craving to kill rooted deep in my bones, but I understood the sin.

Father's silhouette turned to face me through the partition screen. I knew the exact lines of judgement etched around his eyes without needing to see his face.

"If you spoke true, Mistress Maud, you would not already be thinking of how to improve whatever concoction you just administered. Admit it. I am right."

My knees waivered before resuming the ritual. "My God, I am heartily sorry for having offended Thee, and I detest all my sins because I dread the loss of Heaven and the pains of Hell…"

Father's preaching continued during my act of contrition, but I ignored the lecture.

"…but most of all because they offend Thee, my God, Who art all-good and deserving of all my love. Amen."

Constrained frustration emanated from the man who found himself lost for words. After a moment, he spoke plain. "Lavinia." His exhale conveyed his struggle. "I cannot condone such continued transgressions. I will no longer play a part in your cycle."

I admired the tactic — he tried to get through to me by withholding the grace of confession. As a renowned botanist himself, Father Eustace understood my passion for herbs and shared my curiosity for experimentation. We also both overflowed with perseverance. I thought he would never cease his attempts to redeem my soul, but I was not convinced it needed saving. I *was* remorseful. I believed the Gospels. For as much as I enjoyed the act, I regretted the result of every single death and atoned. I harbored a gruesome skill, but as my God-given talent, I felt an obligation to cultivate it nonetheless.

An awkward silence hung between us until I could endure no more. "I will recite ten Hail Marys as penance."

After sliding two gold crowns for indulgence under the partition, I opened the door to the confessional. Before I could depart, Father Eustace called to my back from the other side of the screen.

"What did you use this time?"

The hesitation in his voice brought a smile to my face. He wished to both know and retain his ignorance, but curiosity won the internal struggle. Under all the finery and robes, priests are human.

I turned on my heels to face him. My cloak flared from my silhouette with the slow, eloquent rotation. Even there, in the confessional, I could not suppress a hint of pride in my answer. The priest alone would appreciate the rarity of the tree I had acquired. My own eyes sparkled in anticipation as I left him with a final thought before departing into the starless night.

"We call them Beans of Saint-Ignatius," I said with uncon-
cealed pride. "But you were right about one thing — the more
concerning question is what I am concocting next."

CHAPTER TWO

From a fair distance away, the dim light of a single candle illuminated a window of my modest, cobblestone cottage. I was not surprised to see Aselin still awake, but the discovery widened my grin. Having made my confession, I reclaimed the pride I earned in the brothel, and she alone would share in my excitement. Above, rain clouds had dissipated, and I took advantage of the full moonlight to hasten my pace along the road.

My house and lands resided on the outskirts of Marfield, the largest city within Gaulshire. Nestled on the edge of the vast green hills of common English countryside, the location provided ample clients while facilitating discretion. A dark stone wall circumnavigated the perimeter of the grounds and struggled to contain my small jungle of shrubs and gardens. In select places, trees limbs had broken through the wall's aged mortar. My grandfather built the house with love, though he could not have envisioned the abode would harbor such a venture. My father would not have approved, but my grandfather would have appreciated my aspiring spirit.

The cottage comprised a single story with a cellar and thatch roof. Taller gentlemen often hit their hats on the exposed beams of the low ceiling, but I never had an issue. I did my best to adorn the modest structure with quality furnishings and add color to the dark interior — a navy rug in the main hallway, striped chairs in the parlor. Humble, but more than many had. I had been born within the walls, a few years before the turn of the sixteenth century, and now, I maintained my inheritance with pride. Not a speck of dust rested upon the furniture or a drop of soot beyond the hearth. When I returned home that night, I was pleased to see everything in order and straightened my sentimental goblet on the corner of the entrance hall table.

Behind, the wooden floorboards creaked with approaching footsteps. Aselin was a dedicated apprentice and an attentive servant. Her outstretched arms received my cloak and handed me a cup of hot cider with a curtsey. Aselin's body fidgeted with anticipation, but she withheld her barrage of questions until I unlaced my boots and sat in the parlor. Amused, I assuaged her inquisitive thirst and answered the most pertinent query first.

"Yes, it worked."

My reply fostered her smile of satisfaction. Aselin sat at my writing desk and wetted a quill in preparation. I waited until she found the proper page of my leather-bound journal before continuing.

"It did take a larger dose, per the Guild's warning," I resumed. "He drained half the goblet before I noticed the first twitch in his face. The small movements grew into uncontrollable, violent muscle spasms of the entire body. The convulsions persisted for a quarter of an hour and conveniently prevented speech. Near the end, he began to froth from the mouth — tiny white bubbles he could not swallow. I believe the final cause of death to be suffocation due to muscles tightening and preventing breath."

The scratching of Aselin's quill persisted for a moment to record my dictation. Errant strands of blonde curls fell into her face as she concentrated. The bags under her eyes confessed physical fatigue, but passionate curiosity kept her mind sharp at the late hour. She visibly processed the poison's effects as she reread the notes.

"Thus, it is similar to your acid of apricot," Aselin conjectured.

I shook my head, "No. The acid first brings unresponsiveness, *then* convulsions." Again, I could not hold back a grin. "He was very much aware of his fate."

I recounted my trouble with the ring she now examined, and Aselin gave a vile, cackling laugh of amusement. She fingered the strange characters engraved on the inside of the band, presumably the reason for the ring's worth.

"This seems to be a cipher." Aselin looked up with her eyebrows furrowed. "Who do you suppose employed the thief?"

Her question struck me — my mind did not think of such things. I had assumed the thief stole it for his own gain, but Aselin always saw the bigger picture. With the strange markings inside, most likely her assertion was correct.

But the answer was not our concern.

"I did not have time to ask between his gags." I eyed my apprentice as I mocked, unwilling to acknowledge her valid thought. "Surely someone will be disappointed, but you must learn to be comfortable with unanswered curiosities. We rarely learn the effect our profession has on the fabric of the shire, but we can find fulfillment knowing we have altered its course."

I did not waste a further thought on the silver band. With my story complete, and Aselin's questions answered, she closed the journal with an exhale of disappointment.

"I wish I could have seen it." Her shoulders slumped with the admission I already knew.

She was, in many ways, the daughter I would never have. It was for the best. To raise a child and carry on my business would have been impractical. And Aselin was everything I desired in an heir. However, back then, shy of ten years my junior at fifteen, she had no reason to rush. I would not risk sending her on an assassination until I was sure she was prepared.

Standing, I walked towards my apprentice with empathy. The freckles she tried so hard to cover were apparent through her fading powder. "I know, Aselin." I cupped her cheek within my hand and gazed into her blue eyes. "I know. Soon. You are nearly ready."

She would be ready before I was comfortable with the notion and to avoid further discussion, I changed the subject.

"Did Edmund receive word regarding the castorbean plant?"

Aselin shook her head in reply. "I am sorry, Master."

Now it was my turn for disappointment.

The Guild, my circumspect ring of likeminded alchemists, traded rumors of a potential new poison source, though no one had yet isolated the toxin. I knew, from the depths of my soul, I could break the bean's secret — if I could get my hands on the plant. My contact claimed to have dispatched a courier with a seedling, and I was eager to hear of its progress north.

"Well," I resigned, "then I suppose he is free to deliver this ring on the morrow."

When I took Aselin as an apprentice, her brother, Edmund, became a convenient errand boy. In time, he took over household duties, allowing me to devote full attention to my craft. Edmund loved his sister so much, he followed her into my sanctuary of crime against the screaming protest of his conscience. I could only guess what lie he told himself before falling asleep each night, but his loyalty had never faltered.

For being twins, Aselin and Edmund shared little in common. Aselin loved the game as I did — the challenge to see what could be extracted and distilled, the satisfaction of cultivating a precarious plan to fruition. I detected that predisposition the first moment we met. A year after my father passed, I became the sole witness to Aselin's meager attempt to filch an apple at the market. Despite being successful, the girl lacked finesse, and it was a matter of time before she got caught. But something about her temperament sang to me. Confident I could polish her natural instincts for my benefit, and I invited the orphaned siblings into my home.

My Great Aunt's protests were vehement and immediate. She served as my guardian at the time, but it was my house. After I reminded her of that fact, with a threat I was ready to back, she wisely declared me of age and left. It was unclear if she suspected the illicit activities I ran under her nose, but to my amusement, she departed with haste.

I enjoyed having Aselin look up to me. Having someone to mold and inspire gave me increased purpose, and over the years, she became a co-conspirator. Aselin provided a loyal cohort to brag to after a successful night's work. But I also valued her intellect. I was certain we both spent that night dreaming of ways the Ignatius bean formula might be improved.

The spring sun burnt off the humidity of the previous night's shower. The plants in my gardens behind the cottage presented a bright green hue that sparkled with dew. Since my stores of the fruit seed dwindled, I was relieved to see flowers blooming on the apricot trees near the back wall. However, today's task was to harvest aconite.

Upon opening the wooden gate that partitioned off my virulent growths, I stumbled on the corpse of a hare that must have sampled too many leaves of hemlock. The fate served the rodent right for having the nerve to dig under my fence. Thankfully, it had not damaged the plant's fragile, infant white buds. I buried the animal at the foot of a shrub, amused with the thought its body would fertilize the same plant that killed it.

To the left, the blue flowers of aconite captured my attention, and I cupped a blossom within my gloved palm to admire its beauty. Better known as "wolfsbane," one of the bloom's petals forms a cylindrical helmet around the rest of the flower, giving the plant its English name, "monkshood." The delicate petals contrast with the lethal potential of merely touching the plant's leaves. In many ways, I strived to be the embodiment of the flower.

Beyond the stone wall in the stable, Edmund's horse nickered as the boy prepared a saddle to deliver the ring. I had presented the object in a velvet sack with no background except its intended recipient, and he did not ask. Over the years, we had fallen into a delicate dance of lack of detail. Edmund was the one who chose to maintain ignorance, and I supported his delusion as a welcomed aid to discretion.

Picking up the shears, I harvested the glossy, segmented aconite leaves before overhearing the murmur of Edmund's unexpected conversation. The familiar second voice warmed my heart like the first sparks of a fire, but the realization of my appearance smoldered the flame. My hair was a mess of snarls and sweat pulled up under a wicker sunhat, and my simple violet frock was suitable for toil, not captivation. To my dismay, by the time I closed the garden gate to conceal the plants, Aselin was already announcing my guest. I only had time to wipe dirt from my face.

"Madam, Magistrate Moryet is here to visit."

Without the aid of wardrobe, I relied upon charm. Setting down the basket of clippings with my gloves beside the gate, I crossed the yard to embrace Haylan. My body conformed to his frame with such precision God must have built me for that purpose. Over breeches matching the chestnut color of his hair, he had worn my favorite, long suede jacket that accentuated his height. His trimmed beard added to his distinguished semblance and tickled the top of my head.

"Haylan, how have you been?" His presence always gave my tone a lift of brightness.

He returned the embrace with warmth and kissed my forehead before speaking, "I hope I have not interrupted your gardening."

I could have listened to his baritone voice forever. "Never. No call of yours is ever undesired."

He smiled once more, this time showing his pearl-white teeth. The singular dimple on his left cheek struck my affection like a dart.

"And the same to you, Lavinia. You know you are family to me."

So the dart had been poison-tipped, but I hid my grimace.

In truth, he was like family, just not in the way I desired. After my father died, Haylan took it upon himself to check on me regularly. While I did not need the oversight, I would not dissuade his attention.

My father had served as Marfield's magistrate for twenty years. Haylan had been his apprentice, and we grew together, often exploring the halls of the gaols without permission. As a result of his training, Haylan had learned several of my father's behaviors I naturally inherited — attention to detail and unquenchable curiosity. When my father passed, the Earl had an obvious choice to fill the vacant post. But the appointment and legacy should have been mine. As a woman, that was not possible, and perhaps one of the reasons I rebelled by seeking the opposite path.

Aselin returned with a tray of sage water, sliced lemons, and a small plate of biscuits. I gestured towards the table on the back patio with as much allure as I could muster. "Would you please join me for a small refreshment?"

Haylan nodded and led me with a hand placed at the small of my back. He pulled my chair out for me before he took his own. "I was in the area and could not pass the opportunity to make a call. I do apologize for interrupting your herb harvest."

I kept a questioning look from my face for the second it took me to understand his presumption.

"There is no need for an apology. You will have to stop by for braised chicken when the marjoram is dried." I looked up through my lashes as I spoke, only to find him picking dirt from his fingernail. Frustrated, I turned to his favorite topic of conversation. "I hope it is not unfortunate work which brings you to this side of town?"

He sipped his drink before shaking his head. "No, but there was a murder in the brothel last night."

I swallowed my own sage water without a skipped beat. "The poor girl," I said, making the sign of the cross.

Haylan expectantly shook his head. "I am sorry for the omission. It was a patron it seems."

"Ah, well bless his heart the same." I could not pass up the opportunity to pry, "Do you have any leads?"

To my relief, Haylan shook his head. "No. The stewsman found the client this morning on a bed in a back chamber. He assumed the poor man suffered heart failure resulting from the evening's activities, but that would not explain why the corpse was missing a digit on his right hand. The cut looked fresh."

"Missing only a finger?" I furrowed my brow into a convincing curious expression while swallowing annoyance. It seemed the stewsman had grown lazy. Next time I would not waste a full coin purse on meager aid.

Haylan nodded. "I received notice a ruby ring was stolen, some symbol of membersh—"

I visibly saw Haylan bite his tongue before redirecting his thoughts. I knew there were limits to what he could share, and given what I withheld from him, I did not press.

Haylan shrugged. "I mean, perhaps there is a jewel thief emerging."

"Marfield is a large city," I observed. "It is understandable to desire commonality between a stolen ring and a dismembered finger, but without further cause for connection, it is wishful thinking." By the same logic, given the vast number of ruby rings, I deemed a connection between our two clients unlikely.

"Your father would have said the same thing." He shook his head in abrupt apology, "I am sorry. I did not come to talk about business. I should not be bringing up such subjects anyway. I hope you will forgive my lack of manners."

My laugh was filled with genuine amusement. "Haylan. You know I am accustomed to such conversation from my father. Being older does not mean we cannot talk about the same things from when we were children. I am the one woman in the shire to whom those topics are not insulting."

His eyes sparked with his smile, unveiling the bewitching dimple. "True, but we are not naïve children in your father's gaols anymore. You are a lady now."

And he was such a man…

Haylan set down his half-eaten pastry and assumed a more serious expression. "You are aware the whole town knows you dismissed your Aunt?"

I failed to suppress a laugh. "I should hope so, it has been six months now. Though, I would not say dismissed. She returned to her own manor. I am a grown woman and have no need for a guardian."

"It is improper for a woman to live by herself."

"I have Aselin and Edmu—"

"Lavinia, you know what I mean," Haylan cut me off with a compassionate tone. "I promised your father I would look after you. It is time you started seeing suitors more seriously. Or if you prefer, perhaps take the habit."

My heart craved a single suitor, and he considered me a sister. In his own way, Haylan unknowingly poisoned my heart with each visit, but I craved his attention, any attention, too much to relay the pain he caused.

I contained my thoughts with a sigh. "Why is it a woman has so few options?"

"Do you have a third to propose?" His finger tapped the glass as he offered the rhetorical question.

Evidently "poison assassin" was not an obvious alternative.

"No," I sighed once more. Eager to end the barrage, I lied. "I promise I will give your words thought."

Haylan smiled and finished the biscuit in a single bite before standing. "Good." He reached out his arms. "Come here, Lavinia."

I did. His embrace allayed my frustration. If he had asked, I would have considered giving up my budding career for him, and only him. I searched his blue eyes, longing for an inkling of hope before he broke away too soon.

"Lavinia, you know I wish the best for you."

"I do, Haylan."

He adjusted his hat and nodded, indicating readiness to leave. I escorted him around the cottage and through the front gate of the stone wall. He looked so gallant on his brown horse. With my mind caught in a web of wishful desire, I watched his proud silhouette ride away until it dissolved into the distant rolling hills.

Love is an uncontainable vine that roots in the essence of one's soul. Its thorns pierced my heart, but I vowed to coddle the sprout until it bloomed.

CHAPTER THREE

The moon phased black with no further word of the brothel corpse. I expected nothing less. Society cared little for the fate of a thief. He was a man, same as the King, but his caste and profession diminished him in the eyes of those with power. No crown, wealth, or alliance can remove frailty from life. Everyone reacted to my poisons the same.

Humanity also harbors greed. Many of my patrons coveted wealth, and I admit I did not mind the spoils that came with my success. But mastery and power fulfilled my lust. Everyone craved something. Along with ambition, each of the seven sins ensured a steady flow of patrons to my door. Some wished to hasten the death of a rich relative, others dreamed of revenge. The reasons did not matter, but I enjoyed their stories all the same. I offered an unparalleled solution for a multitude of problems. I changed and ended lives.

And one patron forever changed the course of mine.

I had established my workroom in the cottage basement long ago since my Aunt could no longer climb stairs. When she departed, I kept it there for convenience and ease of concealment. Somehow, over the roar of the fire roasting ground apricot seeds and Aselin scrubbing pestles, I heard Edmund answer a hollow knock on the cottage door.

I lowered the protective cloth from my face and listened to the conversation above in the foyer. The caller was a messenger, who unlikely knew the contents of the letter he delivered. Moments later, Edmund presented me with a piece of parchment and one of my signal coins.

The round, bronze circle featured an engraved wolfsbane flower, embedded with a chip of topaz. The coin was indeed one of my markers, indicating this new client to be a trustworthy referral. The short accompanying note contained a generic request, but the signature made my stomach drop.

The Baron of Camoy summoned me to a meeting at Blackhaven Tavern the following evening.

A baron!

Of course, back then, Edward Akworth was still a baron. The fact my enterprise reached such rank fanned my pride. While the author of the note gave me awe, the lack of details piqued my curiosity — and Aselin's.

She took the letter from my hands as her face lit, imagining the possibilities. Her fingers stroked the inked words which stirred her ambition. Looking to me over the parchment, her eyes pleaded the wordless request.

The time had come to include her in the details of my business, and I rather liked the imagery of attending to a baron with an apprentice in tow. For my own amusement, I posed the rhetorical question. "Would you like to accompany me on this call?"

The girl exhaled with unbelief. "Thank you, Master!"

"Lady Maud, no, please…" Edmund wasted no time inserting his objection.

In our excitement, Aselin and I had forgotten his presence in the room.

I turned to regard the young man whose hazel eyes begged with love and worry, but they would not pierce my resolve. He sheltered himself from the cruel realities of the world, and I feared innocence would be his downfall. At least his sister possessed the wisdom to study the game, though I doubted she would be able to protect them both.

"Aselin is old enough to make her own choices, the same as you," I lectured. "You cannot protect her forever, and it is not she who needs protecting. If this is the path of her calling, then we must help her walk it. Sufficient training is the best advantage I can give her against the risks."

"But Mistress…"

"Do you not remember the time she dropped my signal coin in front of the baker? How I had to cover for her wretched excuse? Look how well she now lies as a result of my guidance."

Edmund's pale reflection flamed red. He glared, flustered at his sister before turning on his heels without further word.

I called to his back as he climbed the steps, "Edmund, I will not conduct such a meeting uninformed. I want you to inquire into Edward Akworth and his house with discretion. See what you can uncover including his enemies, his allegiances, and his desires."

Reluctant obligation motivated his answer, though he did not afford me the courtesy of turning back around. "Yes, Madam."

Aselin buzzed with excitement throughout the following day. I remained a perfect example of composure, for her sake, while savoring my own internal rise of anticipation. Though to her credit, Aselin adopted a professional semblance the moment it was time. Even through her mask of youthful folly, her demeanor perfectly suited deception. She just needed a little guidance. Aselin was a rough-cut gem, and I polished each facet with diligence, shaping her into a ruthless assassin. One day, I knew she would sparkle.

But I was still Master, and there would be no confusion with the hierarchy of our roles. For the appointment, I wore a black velvet bodice over an embroidered red skirt. I assigned Aselin a simple, tan overdress.

The tavern was crowded with chairs, leaving little room to walk past men guzzling ale. Meandering through the disarray of tables, my skirt brushed against one breedbate who glared in response. I paid him no heed, leading the way to the backroom per the summons. Aselin was not so bold. With her hesitant steps, she was only half way through the crowd when I saw her cheeks flush from a drunkard's advance. I shook my head at her innocence, she needed the job as much as I did. When she caught up, I focused with a deep breath and then pushed aside the sheer drape segregating a private parlor. The curtain's tassels of glass beads swayed with a soft clatter announcing our presence.

The Baron of Camoy sat tall in a wooden chair, fingering his tankard. His red hair and freckles did not satisfy my desire for the rugged masculine, but I could see how another would find appeal. Under a navy brocade vest, loose shirt lacings hinted of the well-toned chest waiting beneath. Appearance aside, surely many desired to enrapture the Baron for station alone. But widowed childless by the sweating plague not a year after his marriage, Akworth refrained from courting publicly. Edmund had uncovered several rumors as to why, but nothing concrete.

"Good day, Baron of Camoy. I am Lavinia Maud." After setting down our extinguished lantern, my curtsey dwelled deep and deliberate. "I am humbled you would call on me personally, and honored for the opportunity to serve. This is my apprentice, Aselin Gavrell. You have my assurance of her confidence."

Despite the deliberate plain dress, the Baron licked his lips at the sight of Aselin. I now know he has a penchant for blondes, but such a reaction to Aselin was not an isolated occurrence. For all my skill and achievement, I envied her in that regard and in the moment, only professionalism suppressed my flame of jealousy.

To his credit, Akworth's focus did not detour long; his reputation as a shrewd businessman held true. Through trading goods, he had accumulated wealth and a wide net of contacts, both foreign and domestic. Given his vast connections, the fact he had selected me for this assassination stroked my vanity. Several assassins in Marfield alone would have accepted such a client. As such, my pride swelled as he rightfully turned his attention back to my direction.

"Mistress Maud, thank you for coming." He gestured towards a chair across from his own. Aselin sat behind me on a bench against the wall before the Baron continued. "You come recommended by my peer with esteemed credentials."

Mentally, I raced through my list of clients to guess who provided the referral, though I resisted the urge to prod. The signal coin he presented provided sufficient proof, and I respected the privacy of my patrons.

"Thank you for those kind words, my Lord. I take great honor in my perfect record." I retrieved the coin from my handbag and handed it back. "You may return this to your friend or pass it along as you see fit."

Akworth accepted the coin with a nod. "I suppose we ought to proceed."

"Of course." At least one aspect of my curiosity would not be starved. I appreciated his direct nature, though I also found it intimidating.

By the time patrons built up the nerve to contact me, most had dwelled on the notion for weeks. Even with their minds decided, I often sensed hesitation in their voices, and insecurity in their hearts as they struggled with the reality of their requests.

The Baron of Camoy taught me to play the game at a higher level.

Sitting back in his chair, Akworth's demeanor remained casual, as if we discussed the weather. His expression harbored no insecurity, and his voice did not waver. This was not his first hired hit, but I never would have anticipated the mark he called.

"I would like to acquire your service for the target of Lord Matheson."

My lips parted, but somehow, I withheld my gasp.

His voice remained bored as if our meeting was a trivial delay to his evening. "He would be the easiest target of those blocking my tariff proposal in the Upper Chamber."

I swallowed hard, unsure I had heard correctly. I tried to keep the tremor out of my voice, "The *Viscount* of Matheson?"

His eyes bored through me. "Is there a problem?"

I never read people well, but even I understood there was no ground for refusal. At this point, the Baron had taken me into his confidence, and given his casual attitude towards the request, I had no doubt he would act to ensure my silence if I did not remain supportive. Luckily, he had picked the right assassin.

"No," I responded without hesitation. "No. I am only surprised."

I had never served a peer before, let alone assassinated one. Thieves, cheating wives, disloyal bankers, are one thing. But a peer… That would test my skills beyond my experience. Could I keep calm in front of such nobility? Could I gain the necessary access? Could I get out unseen? But the greater question remained — could I accept the risk that came with targeting a viscount?

"It has come to my attention," Akworth continued, oblivious to my insecurities, "his steward seeks to hire for the scullery. I will provide papers of recommendation and false identity. The rest will be up to you."

"Aye, my Lord." With my head still spinning, I responded before I had processed his words. At least he had already solved the problem of access. I could work the angle of a scullery maid.

"It is not lost upon me what I am asking of you, Mistress Maud." Akworth set down his tankard, sitting forward to focus upon me. "Your growing reputation assures your capability, but for the additional complications and risks with this mark, I am willing to triple your standard rate."

This time I managed to keep my mouth closed. *Triple.* After the initial shock, my youthful arrogance and ambition took over. The prospect alone suppressed all reservations, and now he offered to fill my coffers! All lingering doubt vanished from my mind. I imagined lining my workroom with new flasks, ordering a silk gown that would daze my beloved Haylan. Biting my cheek, I concealed my raging excitement and retained professional dignity.

"Very well," I calmly accepted with a naïveté I did not realize at the time. "Do you have a preference in the method? Do you desire something quick or painful?"

"Giles Lanton is an honest gentleman with a lovely wife and three boys. There is no need to cause undue suffering." Akworth reached into his pocket and produced a sack of coins along with an envelope. "I understand you require half up front?"

"Yes." I accepted the papers and purse. The weight of the coins reinforced the risk, but it parched my thirst even more. Standing tall, I addressed my new client. "I will not let you down, my Lord." I curtsied, sensing Aselin mimic my motions behind. "I will be in contact when the task is complete."

After receiving his nod, I led the way back through the crowd and out of the tavern into the narrow, unpaved street. Without a word, I lit the lantern and proceeded through town. As my boots ground the gravel beneath, the weight of the assignment manifested, and insecurity blemished my thrill.

I had accepted a *viscount* for a target.

Aselin, however, could no longer contain herself. Between the echoes of our heels, she begged with innocent wonder. "Can I see it?"

Pausing under the overhang of a jetty, I waited for a link-boy to pass. I regarded my apprentice with my hands on her shoulders, concerned by the steadfast wonder in her eyes. "Aselin, if you ever had reservations, you need to excuse yourself now."

"Nobility does not scare me," she replied with even more arrogance than I possessed. "A viscount is man, same as a thief. You know murder is all the same in the eyes of God."

I paused from the nerve of her reply but chose to feed on her excitement, allowing myself to enjoy the moment with her. My elation reemerged like the first tentative stars above, daring to shine where even the sun forfeit. I now had the caliber of mark and patron which had aroused my fantasy for years. Upon my pillow, I never dwelled on the risk which accompanied my ambition, but by day, the peril could not be disregarded. Reality is always more bitter than dreams, but the sting proves we are awake.

"Very well." I passed the coin bag into her eager hands, my awareness heightened to be in the night street with such a sum.

Aselin peered inside for a moment with silence, needing to see the coins to believe. She returned the purse to my bag, and as we walked, I watched the risk dawn on my apprentice.

"Master Maud, are you afraid?"

Her sudden change relieved the teacher within; she did grasp the gravity of the commission. We left the crowded rows of closed stores in the heart of the city, turning onto an open path to my cottage. Away from curious ears, we could now speak more freely. I gave my speech for her benefit, though allowed the words to fill me with reassurance as well.

"I have waited a long time for such an opportunity to capture prestige. Such chances in life are rare. When these moments arise, you must take them, regardless of consequence and regardless of risk. Aselin, if you are not willing to gamble everything, then you should not be in the game."

Her eyebrows tightened as she processed the thought. I later coached her regarding inscrutability, but that night I challenged a different facet of her development. "Do you have a method proposal?"

Aselin answered quickly, without thought. "Apricot acid fulfills the client's desire for a painless death, and we just harvested leaves."

Disappointed, I shook my head. "The plan must anchor around how to gain access to the Viscount. Choosing a poison is easy once we know the method of delivery. The Viscount will have food tasters, a constant entourage, and be too wise to be seduced or trust a new member of his staff. That is the puzzle we must unravel."

One which, I boast, did not take me long.

The rat on the left convulsed so violently the metal cage shook on my workbench. The rat on the right was already dead.

Aselin watched over my shoulder with an excitement that paused her note taking. "It worked!"

I consulted my pocket watch the moment the second cage settled. "The seed extraction is three minutes faster." My own smile widened, seeing the dead rat had validated my hypothesis — an acid extracted from the apricot pit carried more potency than one purified from the leaves.

Setting down my quill, I relished the moment.

Since meeting with the Baron of Camoy, I had contemplated ways to fool the Viscount's food taster. *Sola dosis facit venenum.* "The dose makes the poison." The adage, originating from a Swiss German peer of mine, was a rather succinct, poetic way of expressing the essential fundament of my craft. He wrote, correctly, "All things are poison, and nothing is without poison." Even water can be toxic if too much is consumed. Of course in my trade, for the sake of concealment, logic dictated preference for a smaller portion of a higher potent mixture.

However, making a more potent extraction was not a trivial task, and that afternoon, I advanced the state of my craft. I later shared my results with the Guild through our coded correspondence, and the breakthrough increased my reputation. But the one person I longed to tell had died years prior. Pascual would have been astonished by the results, and his memory took me back.

Fleeting flashes of recollection invaded my mind. Faint memories from my mother's slow funeral procession, an image of her casket being lowered into the ground. However, I recalled my father's eyes from that day with detail, full of anguish and confusion, but predominantly fear. He looked down upon me, lost, unsure how to raise a daughter alone, unable to answer my questions of "why." He simply explained that the brightest candles always burn the shortest.

Not knowing better, he gave me a boy's education, and I grew indebted to his indiscrimination. His job often required attention at odd hours when my nursemaid was unavailable. In his mind, a tutor was as good as a nurse. And when faced with no other choice, he would head to the gaols with me in tow. Of course, the prisoners provided more entertainment than my rag doll, and if we kept our conversation through the bars quiet enough, my father never knew.

When I was near fifteen, my father obtained a Spanish spy. King Henry wished to flaunt the capture privately to Philip as an act of good faith, and the sluggish pace of international correspondence kept Pascual in custody far longer than most. My father ensured officials he could safely incarcerate the man. Throughout those months, Pascual beguiled me with vivid descriptions of magnificent frescos, mountains of gold in Spanish vaults, the beauty of his people and boasts of how his country's ships had discovered the new lands of savages.

Of all the things I could have inquired, I chose to exploit his knowledge of poisons.

I did not sleep for days after the first assassination he recounted. The concept of brewing a lethal extraction felt like a mythical power. Being not blessed with abundant beauty, or male gender, such knowledge gave me the capability to influence society and gain notoriety through intellect. I recorded every recipe Pascual could recall, every description of useful plants, every rumor and postulation. Pascual told me how to contact the Guild, and in return, I provided him with enough hemlock to end his life before the worst interrogations.

My father's anger shook the cottage after hearing of Pascual's death. He was the most coveted prisoner my father had ever captured and by failing to make good on his assurance, my father lost his best chance to increase his station. Despite the efforts of my father's entire staff, no one uncovered the cause of Pascual's death. Father Eustace counseled my father regarding the unfairness of fate, and that day marked the start of my own lying.

As for the Viscount — I knew my new apricot seed toxin was more potent than a leaf extraction, and the stronger poison would require a smaller dose, decreasing the risk of detection by the Viscount's food taster. However, I did not know what dose was lethal.

Proportioning was always a difficult matter. Toxicity does not scale linearly. I had a well-established scale for the apricot leaf acid and assumed the same curve would apply to the seed extraction. I had fed the rat one-third of my normal serving for such a weight and achieved impressive results. I normally tested my poisons on the small vermin I could catch with snares, but with the increased risk of this target, and the additional resources of my increased earnings, prudence necessitated a more sizable test subject, which required more toxin.

I broke the husks of dried apricot seeds with a nutcracker and patiently carved out the soft, inner meat. Throughout the night, Aselin and I tended to the kernels boiling in ethanol, stirring with trained eyes to ensure the mixture bubbled as required. Entrenched within the cellar workroom, we were oblivious to the moon's passing. When I finally stood up from the crucible, the distant song of the morning birds startled me.

I often lost myself during a purification, consumed by the alchemy and unaware of the passage of time. I found a calming peace in the elaborate meditation of measuring additives with precision, constantly working the bellows to maximize the temperature of the furnace, and the utmost attention to avoid my own contamination. The following day, debilitating exhaustion took root in my stiff joints, but I had a small pan of acid crystals drying under the noon sun and an inflated sense of pride.

Per my instruction, Edmund had fetched a goat from the market that morning. When he returned, Aselin measured the dried powder as I supervised over her shoulder: one-third of the normal dose for the sixty-pound goat. Edmund excused himself with disgust as his sister mixed the toxin into a serving of kitchen compost. To the sound of Edmund chopping wood in the background, Aselin and I clanked our glasses of ale and watched the goat devour his delicacy with a pocket watch. Minutes later, the goat fell sideways unresponsive, convulsed, and then passed. I could not have been more elated. The toxin proved more potent and passed every test.

I was ready for Lord Matheson and his food taster.

A few days prior, I had received the letter I waited for.

After months of dead-end searching, I had finally located a reliable carrier willing to bring a castorbean plant from the Mediterranean Basin. I arranged for Edmund to meet my contact in four days' time beyond of the northern boundary of Cranshire, our eastern neighboring shire. The timing allowed him to accompany me to the Viscount's estate in Matheson, the center city of Cranshire. A woman traveling such distance would be curious, but if chaperoned by her brother, she would be forgettable.

Aselin nearly threw a tantrum when I told her she would keep the estate while we remained away, but her presence provided no benefit to the journey and increased risk. After all, someone had to tend to my gardens.

Before departing, I did make a fine marjoram-brined chicken for Haylan as promised. In return, he agreed to check on Aselin while Edmund and I made a pilgrimage to the Cathedral in Matheson. Haylan never questioned the story or indicated a moment of doubt. The fact I deceived the magistrate, a detective trained to uncover fraud, boosted my confidence prior to the job. If I had given him reason, he would have dissected my lie out of professional honor and concern for his near-sister. Instead, he ignorantly kissed me on the cheek, promising a custard tart when I returned.

With two concealed portions of my apricot seed powder, and a few other extractions as a safeguard, Edmund and I departed at sunrise on a clear July day. The roads were dry, and the horses kicked up clouds of dust with each step. The monotonous, endless fields of green provided little feedback of progress, and without stimulus, the steady rhythm of my mount threatened to lull me to sleep.

Unfortunately, Edmund did not diminish the boredom. His idle commentary of scenery and politics failed to hold my interest. Conversational art always eluded him. Instead, I used the time to polish my cover story. I had worn an old, faded work frock, but cheap attire alone would not provide sufficient disguise. Unable to unlearn decades of etiquette and posture missing from the lower classes, my story would have to provide sufficient justification.

My mount, Sullivan, however, seemed to enjoy the long journey. My father gave him to me for my ninth birthday as a colt.

Sullivan's brown, dull coat matched the ordinariness of the animal, and despite his stunted conformation and gait, he rode comfortably enough.

In contrast, Edmund's mount, Onyx, had a glossy black coat and an impressive presence. Edmund took immense pride in the horse and had purchased him with several months' wages. More than a tool of transportation, Onyx became Edmund's confidant. And the horse was not going to speak, so if Edmund needed to confess his uneasiness to the beast, I had no reservations. We both maintained our outlets of confession.

We made efficient time and spent the night in a small inn west of Morfet Forest, which covers the border between the two shires. Overnight rain had made the path damp, but since it was a well-traveled road, I did not fear to leave a trail. The forest comprised of broadleaf trees with enough conifers sprinkled for contrast. The well-established fungus growths called me, and I wished I could have harvested samples for experimentation. Regretfully, I never had a chance.

We crossed the river into Matheson that afternoon. The Viscount's estate stood proud on a hill, overlooking the city. For a moment, I commanded Sullivan to hold so I could behold the structure. Despite being modest for a castle, the vastness dwarfed the largest cathedral of my experience. The sheer magnitude was overwhelming and served as another reminder of the hazard of this mark. With a last breath of decision, I commanded Sullivan onward.

At the wall of the estate, Edmund presented my papers to a guard, which did most of the work for his part of the lie. The guard escorted us through the castle to the steward, who rambled on in gratefulness for the presence of such an experienced servant. Akworth had penned quite the exaggeration of my skill, but

I only needed to uphold the ruse for a couple of days. I gave Edmund a kiss of departure on the cheek and wished him fair travel. We had agreed to meet back at the inn in a fortnight, and I expected to beat him there.

By my troth, I swear I never worked so hard! As a low member of the yeomen class, I was accustomed to performing my own household labor, but the relentless schedule of a servant threatened to break my body if it did not find relief. My hands cracked the second day from washing so many dishes. My entire body reeked of lye, and the odor lingered in my nostrils at night. At my fastest pace, I slowed the scullery. Luckily, my peers blamed my incompetence on disorientation while I learned the layout of the household. They also believed my cover story that I had previously been a nurse and could not spend another day raising rich, ungrateful feather-heads.

The scullery and office of ewery shared staff, which aided my plans. Adding to my fortune, the steward noticed I carried myself with grace, spoke properly and observed the finer rules of etiquette — attributes that bolstered my false pretense as a former governess. Therefore, on the fourth day, no one objected when I offered to serve the Viscount his afternoon cider.

Lord Matheson passed each morning with sport, dedicating the rest of the day to his business affairs with reluctance. For the sake of concentration, he preferred cider instead of ale with his afternoon refreshment. Per given instruction, I brought a pitcher to the kitchen to be filled, then placed it alongside a fruit and cheese plate on a silver tray. With everything prepared, I took the platter to the Viscount's office and waited outside the door for the food taster.

The taster arrived minutes later. A near decade older than myself, yellow skin mixed with oversized butter-teeth made him a curious sight to behold. Clothes struggled to hang with dignity over his scrawny frame. I had seen him in the back of the kitchen a few times and wondered how he had drawn the short straw of his post.

His eyes gave me a slow, once over as he approached. "You are new," he spit in a rude, short tone.

To honor my guise, I replied with complete politeness. "Aye, Sir. Hired four days ago. My name is Mable Bassett. It is a pleasure to meet you."

"Hmm." He gazed upon me as if I were dinner prepared to satisfy his salacious appetite. "Samuel Darcy, but everyone calls me 'Tuc.'"

I never inquired the origin of the nickname. I decided not to make a personal connection with the Viscount's taster in case he became a necessary casualty. But given his rudeness and wandering eyes, he failed to give me a reason to spare his life. I pulled the chemise of my uniform higher and discounted Tuc before placing my hand on the brass handle of the Viscount's office door with focus.

I needed to gather information prior to administering my poison, and thus that day, my intentions remained honest. Nevertheless, my heart still fluttered within. With a deep breath, I prepared to meet the man I had been hired to kill.

CHAPTER FOUR

L ord Matheson sat with his back to the door, deep in concentration. His broad shoulders towered over the chair that
looked too small to be comfortable. To each their own, I
suppose. The deep maroon of his doublet complemented his fair
coloring. Well-tailored, his clothes were simply styled, though fabricated of velvet and furs. He indeed flaunted his wealth, but in a
muted manner compared to the rings and jewels of his peers. I
assumed comfort motivated the choice. The man clearly wished
to be in the forest rather than behind a desk, signaled by the paintings of hunting scenes and old crossbows adorning the walls. But
the family portrait hanging over the unlit hearth caught my attention. The masterful portrayal highlighted Lady Matheson's
common beauty and the strong fatherly resemblance of his three
sons.

Refocusing my attention halfway into the room, I froze, realizing too late I did not know the required protocol. Should I break
the Viscount's concentration, or leave without word? Would a
former governess know? I glanced towards Tuc, who made no
indications. Without another option, I relied on instinct.

"My Lord?" I kept my voice polite and hesitant. Full of nerves,
I confess it was not an act. "Your afternoon cider."

The Viscount turned in his chair and broke into a smile upon seeing me. "Ah, you must be the new scullery maid."

My heart skipped a beat, surprised he even knew of a new hire amongst his staff.

I learned over the years not to harbor preconceived notions. Surely, those who met me did not suspect they stood in the presence of a ruthless assassin. Still, there are social protocols that supersede expectations. Even with an open mind, I did not expect a *viscount* to blatantly disregard social castes within his household. So when Giles Lanton stood to address me with a polite nod of his head, I almost dropped the platter. My head spun, wondering if something had given away my ruse. Even still, the caste of my true identity fell far below his rank.

"Good day Mistress…" He looked to me with expectation.

"Mable Bassett, my Lord. It is an honor to be under your employ."

The Viscount gave a small smile. "Mable, I appreciate your kindness, but there is no need for stuffy formality here. Respect and politeness are sufficient. This is my home; I would like it to be comfortable for my family and my staff."

"Yes, my Lord."

I saw his gesture, indicating to place the tray on the corner of his desk. But looking down at the cluttered mess, I could not discern where. Balancing the tray with one hand, I used the other to push aside parchments, quills, and random knick-knacks to clear space next to a cluster of half-burned candles in pools of melted wax. Without doubt, this was a man's sanctuary.

The Viscount nodded, satisfied with the selection on the tray. "But there is no benefit to ignoring prudence."

The Viscount looked to Tuc who poured himself a sample of cider. The taster smelled and swirled the goblet, as one might a fine wine. He took a sip, chewing the liquid in search of foreign notes before giving a nod of approval. Tuc then sampled a few grapes and bites of cheese as well.

"Do you find your accommodations adequate, Mable?" Lord Matheson asked between his bites of grapes.

"Yes, my Lord," I spoke true. I had prepared myself for, and expected, much less. The Viscount's attentive care for his staff further demonstrated his character.

"If you have any reasonable needs I expect you to communicate them to the steward, understood?"

"Yes, Viscount."

"Good." His smiled broadened before turning back to his work.

I understood the unspoken dismissal and gave a curtsey before departing the office. Tuc led the way out and then strolled in his own direction down a separate hallway, only to turn back with a lingering inspection of my frame out of the corner of his eye. I paid the man no heed and once alone, released a breath I unknowingly held.

Of course, the Viscount had to be admirable. The Baron warned me, but I had not expected such generosity. The Viscount governed in benefit of the common good, which incited distrust from his self-serving peers. He indeed had his enemies, making employ of a food taster not superfluous. Whoever filled the title upon his death would not be as considerate, but gracefully, that would be someone else's concern. I intended to complete the job. The Viscount's temperament towards his staff only made my task easier, and I felt no guilt in exploiting that trait.

However, the food taster proved an oddity I could not comprehend. Due to the natural conflict between our roles, Tuc kindled my interest more than most men. I wanted to know whom I battled. Over the following day, I casually inquired about him, curious to discern the level of his skill.

To my surprise, I learned many citizens of Matheson coveted Tuc's post. Given the potential risk of being a food taster, the Viscount insisted on filling the job with volunteers. Interested applicants applied from the servant caste of the city and finalists were subjected to a rigorous interview and training process. The candidate prevailing a concluding contest won the post. In return, the Viscount lifted their family from poverty. He gave them a small manor in the rear of the estate, and an annual salary beyond what they could have dreamed.

With his family's future secure, Tuc's cold chip seemed futile. So often those who receive fail to appreciate their blessings, always wanting, condemned to bitterness, and never satisfied. His job had risks, yes, but from what I gathered, none of Matheson's tasters had ever died from their duties.

I wondered if that truth would hold.

I also learned Tuc made his rounds with the maids — a pastime that aided my information gathering. Even with all the gossip and eyewitnesses, I refused to believe the scrawny man could be so well endowed.

Whatever the reason, it seemed I piqued Tuc's interest in return. As I folded a sheet, I caught him examining me from behind. His hand repugnantly lingered upon my waist as we passed within a narrow storage closet. I hoped persistent disregard would deflate his arrogance, but I should have known neglect would only strengthen his resolve. I refused to let Tuc, or any gossip, divert my concentration. I played a higher game and did not have the capacity for frivolous concerns. And with no further information to gather, I focused on selecting Lord Matheson's last day on Earth.

I decided to complete the task two days later when cloudy skies signaled impending rain. If I slipped the poison before the storm began, the rain would erase my footprints and impede any pursuit, if required. I did not anticipate my departure would be on such terms, but I did not mind the additional safeguard. "Mable" had come to serve Lord Matheson, a beloved Viscount. If he were found dead under suspicious circumstances, no one would question a former governess' concern for her own safety in such an estate. I intended simply to resign.

Based on the test run, I was confident I could slip the toxin to the Viscount after Tuc tasted the cider. The tactic decreased the risk of detection, and if the opportunity did not present itself, there was always tomorrow. Knowing I could take multiple attempts at the mark inflated my confidence, and while not graced with abundant beauty, I could be lavishly charming.

On the selected day, most would guess the hours prolonged with insecurity. On the contrary, time flew as I savored the anticipation. Inside, I reverberated with exuberance, contained by my honed skills to remain unmemorable. During every chore, the small vial of the apricot seed acid bounced within the pocket of my apron, reminding me of my secret. As I walked, I grew giddy each time I sensed the toxin's presence against my thigh. Riding my personal intoxication, never had I scrubbed, hauled water, or polished with such efficiency. My peers expressed satisfaction with my gained proficiency. In some ways, I had fallen into the routine of my labor, but knowing I would soon be back home in comfort made the toil easier to bear.

So once again, when I volunteered to serve afternoon cider, there were no objections from the staff. With everything in place, I made my way to the Viscount's office for the final time.

The impending moment before taking out a mark was always a spiritual experience. I possessed the most personal knowledge about the victim that remained beyond their own awareness. What could be more intimate than knowing the time and place of another's death? In a way, it was also unfair. What gave me the right to know more about their life? It was like the Heavens had shared a secret, that God had chosen this moment and selected my hands to carry out His will. I was humbled to be His hand-maid.

And I would let not anyone, especially an ungracious food taster, degrade the sanctity of the act.

As I expected, Tuc's demeanor stayed cold as he waited for me outside of the closed office door. "You again?"

"Yes," I replied with more politeness than he deserved. "It seems most of the scullery prefers to avoid the annoyance of drying and freshening up for presentation to his Lordship."

"So, the new maid gets the bother." He rocked on his heels, attempting to look down my chemise at his apex, but I merely turned away.

"It seems so," I said, my focus undeterred. I opened the office door with a racing heart, eager to finish this mark for so many reasons.

As a man of routine, the Viscount again toiled with his back to the door before I interrupted his concentration.

"My Lord, good afternoon." I gave a polite curtsey to his back, which he turned around in time to see complete.

"Ah, Mistress Bassett! It is good to see you again." The Viscount set down his quill and rubbed his eyes, recovering from the toil of staring at the array of numbers strewn across the desk.

"You as well, my Lord. I do hope you are in the mood for sausage and bread that just came out of the oven." I set the tray on the corner of his desk and stepped back for Tuc who meticulously performed his duty. Even my own mouth salivated from looking at the plate.

"Yes, I savored the aroma the moment you entered. Mother Abney is a fine baker." After receiving a nod from Tuc, the Viscount spread butter on his own slice of bread and took a bite. "Have you meet Catherine yet?"

"In passing, my Lord." My eyes scanned his desk with discretion, searching for a topic of conversation. "But I have enjoyed her baked goods. She has a gift for her craft."

Lord Matheson sipped the cider and picked up the quill once more. When Tuc turned to leave, I enacted my plan.

"My Lord, if I may be so bold, may I ask what work keeps you in your office every afternoon?"

Upon hearing my question, Tuc rolled his eyes, gave a quick bow, and departed. I smiled inside, knowing I had judged his character correctly.

Finally, I had my mark to myself.

The Viscount looked up in genuine surprise at the question but permitted my curiosity with grace. "Reviewing draft laws for the next parliament session, complaints and requests from citizens, budgets my advisors wish approved."

I walked around the desk towards him such that I stood between my mark and his pitcher of cider. Picking up a piece of parchment, I examined it with a veil of naïveté. "All the numbers... It is quite dizzying."

A little part of me died inside; clearly, the document was a tax roll.

The Viscount laughed. "Do you read, Mable?" He took the parchment from my hand before indulging in a bite of bread.

"Oh no, Sir," I lied. "I have never had the need."

He nodded, picking up his quill. I understood the subtle hint.

"I know you are busy. Thank you for indulging my question, my Lord." I took the goblet from the table by his side. "The least I can do is refill your glass."

I turned, placing my back to him. In a well-practiced motion, I retrieved the vial from my pocket, opened it with one hand, and dumped the toxic contents into the goblet. I then partially refilled it with care not to dilute the dose. With the small vial concealed between my fingers, I set the now tainted goblet back at his side.

"Thank you, Mable." He took a large gulp to wash down his bread and turned his attention to the pile of parchment.

"Have a wonderful afternoon, Sir." I curtsied and departed after his nod.

My heart continued to pound as I closed the door behind; my head swelled with pride. I had poisoned a viscount! With a deep breath, I reined my excitement. There would be time for celebration when the job was complete and until then, I needed to maintain cover. The effects would manifest within minutes and distance provided deniability. I pocketed the empty vial and made my way back to the scullery to await news, dreaming about the castorbean seedling waiting with Edmund at the boarder inn. I would have the prized plant in my hands that night.

Now, time dragged on.

Fifteen minutes.

Thirty minutes. I could not stop watching the minute hand's slow progression around the clock in the scullery.

An hour. Then two.

Each chime of the distant Cathedral bells felt like a knife in my back, and still, no word of concern came through the estate.

Someone should have checked on the Viscount by now.

With a deep breath, I reminded myself to stay calm. I had seen him drink the tainted cider. He would have fallen unresponsive, convulsed, and died of suffocation without drawing attention. In time, his death would be noticed.

With my thoughts distracted, the steward had to ask me twice to bring up a pail of hot water to Lady Matheson in her chamber. After receiving a quick chide for daydreaming, I offered an apology and complied. I could endure this service a few hours longer and concealed a barrage of profanity in my mind.

The weight of the large, wooden bucket challenged my capabilities and encumbered my progress though the estate corridors. Each step seemed a risk I might spill the scalding water. However, as I rounded a corner, the sight ahead caused me to forget the bucket and stop cold in surprise. With the abrupt motion, I lost control of the weight and tumbled back on my behind. The pail crashed to the floor with a fantastic spray. I never admitted the shriek I produced as hot water rained down upon me. Panicked, I pulled the wet fabric away from my skin as staff rushed from every direction, summoned by the commotion.

But my eyes focused on one person.

There, ten yards ahead, was a healthy, much alive Viscount.

CHAPTER FIVE

Thank God, the resulting commotion covered my shock. The circumstance also provided a plausible explanation for my stupor.

Servants scrambled with towels to soak up spilled water from rugs, wipe down walls and amongst the mayhem, a few even remembered to ask if I was all right. I dismissed their concerns, wary of the attention. I also tried to preserve dignity. I was fine anyways, physically at least. The layers of my uniform protected my skin from the worst of the heat, and in truth, the rug had taken the brunt of the spill.

My own concerns focused upon the incriminating empty vial resting in the pocket of my soaked apron, but I soon realized the ridiculousness of my fear. I wanted to both cry and laugh; what did an empty vial matter when my mark remained alive?

Torturing my wounded pride, Lord Matheson walked towards me through the crowd of servants. "Mistress Bassett, are you alright?"

"Yes, I…it is fine." I could not gather my wits, let alone form a coherent sentence.

He should not have been there. He should have been dead for heaven's sake!

I averted my eyes, feeling a swell of frustration rise like a kettle about to boil over. Of all the times to fail… The humiliation broke my heart, strained with shame. Praise the Lord my failure was private — my own taunting was burden enough. However, my half-dressed state provided a visible embarrassment. I had pulled my skirt hem improperly high to get the hot, wet cloth away from my skin. My bodice sat tilted around my torso. I did my best to ignore judging eyes, and with a few deep breaths, I regained control.

"I am fine," I managed to get out, before attending to my cover. "I am truly sorry for the disruption, Sir."

My slow words emphasized the fabricated regret. Mayhap I had been playing a servant too long, but even in my flustered state, the expressed concern for the Lord's household sounded genuine. Lying had always been one of my gifts, but the moment tested every ounce of my skill. "I apologize for the mess, for the rug, for the disruption. I will make sure it is dried out and if…"

"Mistress Bassett. Please, it is alright." The Viscount looked down, cutting off my apology. "It is just water."

If only my concern comprised solely of spilled water.

I took another deep breath. "Yes, my Lord."

"Sarah, please fetch another pail for my wife." The Viscount directed the request towards a pale maid who nodded and left towards the scullery. He then eyed the rest of the gathered crowd. "I believe everyone has tasks to attend to?"

Servants dispersed with his word. While the surrounding attention and fuss had sparked discomfort, being alone with my failed mark was worse. In my mind, I spoke to a ghost. My stomach tangled in knots, fearful he would confront me at any moment.

Had he sensed the poison and not finished the glass? Had he lost his thirst? With every fiber, I desired an explanation and the inability to inquire infuriated me as much as each breath he inhaled above.

"Mable," the Viscount paused, waiting until he held my attention. I looked into his face searching for the faintest symptom, any lingering clue to my puzzle as he continued. "Take a few minutes, go change your uniform, and relax. There is no duty so pressing it cannot wait."

When he offered his hand to help me stand, a small pain of guilt grew in my gut. For the love of God, I had just tried to kill him. The emotion felt foreign and indistinguishable at first, but I would not deny its existence. Even at that moment, his unequaled kindness touched me. The world would be a better place if men of his character steered the helms of our society.

But in such a world, I would be unemployed.

"Thank you again, my Lord," I replied, lost for what else to say.

"Think nothing of it," he said with a final smile. "But, if you will, you could do me a favor: Ask the kitchen which orchard provided the apples for the cider today."

My stomach dropped, spinning the wheels of my mind with concern. "Yes, Viscount?"

"The juice featured a peculiar bitter note I enjoyed. I think it could make an interesting ale."

Relief washed over me as I held back laughter. "Of course, my Lord!" With a quick curtsey, I departed for my quarters.

Once the door locked behind, I began hyperventilating.

My mind processed incomplete thoughts in an unorganized whirl of conjecture.

He *had* tasted the poison, I watched him take a sip myself. He even said he enjoyed the flavor. It was possible he lied, but such games did not fit his personality. The Viscount valued loyalty. If he suspected me, I would be in custody.

Therefore, his remark about the taste must have been genuine. And if he enjoyed the cider, he must have finished the glass.

I doubted he had a supernatural constitution.

There was no known antidote for the apricot acid.

So how? How did the Lord of Matheson still live?

One explanation remained, though my heart would not consider the answer.

After unproductive laps around the small, otherwise vacant servant's chamber, I fell back on the bed, finally admitting the singular plausible explanation: my dosage had been wrong.

I had only tested to the weight of the goat. I had assumed the scaling curve of lethal dose per weight for the apricot pit extraction was the same a poison isolated from the leaves. Clearly, the presumption was false. Yes, the pit concoction is more potent, and while it requires less toxin to be lethal than the leaf extraction, I had not given the Viscount enough.

I cursed at my ineptitude. I had gone through all the trouble to create a more potent toxin I could slip past the taster and not even used it in such a ploy. Given I had found a way around Tuc, I should have dumped my most toxic extraction into the damn cider. It had been arrogant to try a new poison on such a risky target. I vowed to test all future new extractions on unfortunate souls before utilizing them on the clock — but of course, that lesson did not solve my current predicament.

Staring at the ceiling from the bed, I accepted the reality of my situation. My mark remained alive, and I needed to improvise a backup plan. Plagued by failure and demoralized confidence, the burden seemed insurmountable. I also feared the risk of hasty plotting without proper contemplation. Frustration resonated deep in my core until it blossomed into resentment. Yes, I blamed the Viscount for not dying.

Filled with anger, the mark became personal.

As I changed out of my wet uniform, a new plan formulated in my mind. Since I now prepared a second attempt on the same mark, I no longer gave priority to the victim's comfort. His generosity be damned. Focused on revenge, I refused to use my remaining apricot seed acid and instead, envisioned a more heinous death. I vowed he would be a corpse within days if I had to force belladonna down his throat.

Still resounding with angered resentment, my mind woke in the morning lacking the capacity for all other thought. I no longer noticed body aches from labor. My mind numbed to the steward's orders, blindly following his instructions. Fueled by anger, I scrubbed a linen so hard against the wooden washboard I scraped my knuckles, causing them to bleed. I still did not care. My mind was preoccupied with the singular fantasy of a dead Viscount.

Several members of the staff attributed my aloofness to embarrassment. A few of the scullery maids tried to assuage assumed guilt by reminding me it was only water. Others refrained from speaking to me out of genuine frustration. Even if the spill was simply water, the soiled rug still had to be aired or the dyes would bleed, and the surrounding walls washed to remove dried water spots. A servant's work is hard enough without one of their peers increasing the task list. I began making amends by volunteering for additional tasks, but my motivation was not pure: my generosity laid the groundwork for my second assassination attempt.

Polishing silver was one of the most hated duties in the manor. At first, I did not understand why: few tasks could be completed sitting down, and it did not require the brawn of hauling water. But by the end of my first place setting, my fingers ached, and the polish made me lightheaded. The communal hatred was indeed justified. Thus, the appreciation I earned by taking over the chore brought me back into good graces with my peers. More important, the task provided the perfect cover.

The customary euphoria of anticipation I came to savor before a job was replaced that fated day with impatient irritation. I had to finish this mark to restore my record. Everything would continue to feel off balance until I succeeded, as if fate was askew due to the Viscount's extra breaths of life. But every assassination required a sharp mind, focused on the task and free of emotional burden. It was the only way to control risk. Details made or condemned a job. Three days after my failed attempt, I thought I had regained enough emotional control to try again.

Sitting in the back of the scullery polishing place settings for dinner, I put my plan into action. Through the door, I could see the butler pacing, continuously checking on my progress. Indeed, I was running out of time before dinner, but I deliberately worked slow. After the third poke of the butler's head through the door, I took a leap of faith.

"Unless you want to serve silver with spots or grab a rag yourself, you will have to be patient." My words came out with more rudeness than I intended. I should have recognized my tone as a sign I was not completely focused.

The butler's eyes narrowed, returning my discourtesy. "Dinner is in thirty minutes, and you are already late."

"I am well aware and suggest your distraction is only causing further delay." I took my eyes off the silver platter to stare the man down. "I will bring the silver to the dining room myself in five minutes. Does that satisfy your schedule?"

The butler scoffed but left without complaint; he could not chide me for taking pride in my work.

Within the candlelight, my reflection gleamed off the knives and chargers, however, a particular goblet and bowl had enjoyed special treatment. Camphor oil made the inside of both vessels shine with a reflection so remarkable I felt genuine pride for my toil. The oil would make a beautiful polish — if it were not toxic.

The polished silver gleamed on the wooden servant's cart I pushed to the formal dining room. The wooden wheels squeaked, drilling through my ears as I traveled with haste to meet the agreed schedule. Since I ran late on purpose, I did not have time to make two trips. I had piled everything I could onto the cart, carrying the spoons and knives in the pockets of my apron.

When I arrived, the room was a flurry of activity. Concentrating on their own work, none of the staff paid me a second glance. I joined in the toil, arranging the silver and discreetly taking care not to spread the contamination within the Viscount's vessels to the others. The camphor oil would taint the Viscount's food, but would not be detected by the food taster who served himself from the communal platters.

Once the table was set, I stepped back with an exhale to gaze upon the silver settings reflecting light from the chandelier above. The vessels gleamed as a symbol of my resilience. I could taste the satisfaction of victory, sweetened by days of anticipation. For a moment, I entered my own world, letting the French influence of the room carry me away in a moment of relief.

The room's decor was clearly persuaded by the feminine pref-
erences of Lady Matheson. A hand painted gold, floral pattern
embellished the walls above the chair rail and inside panel inlays.
Candelabras rested upon side tables, each adorned with blush
flowers. At the far side of the room, a white canopy above the
hearth featured the Lanton House seal. Adding to the ambiance,
pink hues were cast into the room through the large windows on
the side of the hall. The sun began to set over the city of Matheson below.

The kitchen staff interrupted my fleeting tranquility, entering
with military precision. Aroma of roasted quail watered my mouth
as I eyed the plates of buttered rolls and vegetables. The green
beans reminded me of my own vegetable garden and God willing,
I would be back to my cottage shortly to tend to them.

On cue, the family entered the room to find their seats. I had
seen the Lantons together only once before. The three boys ran
in with their arms extended with pretend flight, though one look
from their mother ended the imaginative birdcalls. The Lady, as
expected, exhibited pure grace, so much that she borderlined un-
interesting. Lord Matheson arrived last. He gave his wife a quick
kiss that seemed to break through her rigid demeanor. He then
tousled the hair of each of his sons before taking his place at the
head of the table.

I watched content, aware that I was the sole person who knew
the routine occurred for the last time. I had selected who would
die or live at that table. I could have killed them all, and perhaps
it would have been more merciful. Instead, the boys would grow
up fatherless, and the woman would wear black for months. Even
if she remarried, she would never find such love again. I almost
regretted my ruthless choice of toxin, but still haunted by my previous failure, my resolve fortified and my lips formed a sly smile.

Tuc entered quiet, dutifully minimizing his disturbance. He gathered a forkful from every platter onto his plate and sampled quickly for the sake of the waiting family. His face squished together after one bite he struggled to swallow. My heart skipped a beat before the youngest boy chuckled. Lady Matheson glared, but the Viscount just smiled, providing me with relief.

"After all this time, you still cannot stand my mother's pickled cabbage recipe?" There was a twinkle of amusement in the Viscount's eye.

Tuc washed down the bite with a gulp of mead. "It has the same strong twang as always, my Lord."

"Precisely as it should!" The Viscount loaded his plate with the purple strands before reaching for soup.

After departing with a bow, unneeded servants followed Tuc's leave. I trailed at the end of the line, delaying enough to see the Viscount drink mead from the goblet and slurp broth from the bowl. Symptoms would begin soon, and a hesitant smile broke across my face.

Of course, I had been down that path before.

With the waiting game resumed, I walked behind the other maids as slow as permissible without drawing attention. My ears strained, listening for the first hint of success. It hurt to breathe through the desperate prayer I mumbled.

Minutes later, the Lady's scream pierced from the dining room.

If angels had parted the Heavens and cast down in anthem, the sound would not have been as sweet.

The dining room doors burst open, and a butler frantically called for a doctor. Seizures had begun. I guessed the Viscount had minutes left.

The manor degraded into confusion. Staff ran to provide aid, some to satisfy curiosity. Murmurs of poison echoed through the halls, and ahead, several guards took Tuc into custody to my immense pleasure. All around me, maids were terrified, and the steward pleaded with his staff to settle.

"I cannot stay here, Sir!" The panicked plea of one maid perked my ear, and I turned to witness the exchange.

"Sarah, please," the steward pleaded. "We must not jump to conclusions."

"Do you suspect the Viscount's health has suddenly turned? Do you believe this is not poison?" She searched the steward's eyes for a remnant of hope, but he delayed too long. Tears fell from the maid's eyes. "I cannot stay!"

I could not believe my fortune and took advantage of the opportunity.

"Myself as well, Sir." I placed a towel into the steward's hands with dramatized fear. "Say what you will about my former bratty charge, this never happened in the McCalister household. I came to serve the Viscount, but not at such risk."

"Mistress Bassett..." The steward called to my back before being distracted by yet another crying maid.

Through biting the inside of my cheeks, I prevented the smile on the verge of appearing. Without further word, I donned my cloak, grabbed my meager bag of personal effects, and departed through a servant's door into the night.

As I headed to the stables, my boots pressed into the soft ground, moist from the previous day's rain. The last wisps of sunlight dissipated, turning the skies dark under a black, oppressing blanket. Damp, fresh air filled my lungs that did not exhale relief. I could not relax, not until I had achieved distance and made my escape.

Messengers on horseback furiously passed by along the path from the manor. Dirt sprayed from hooves struggling to answer their rider's call for haste. While most paid me no concern, their speed embodied me with a chill of worry. Around the estate, soldiers seem to stand a little taller, and more guards were at post. I should have anticipated such a response to the Viscount's death — The thought immediately hardened my heart with fear, I lacked proof the Viscount had even died. He might be on the floor in the dining room, holding on to lingering life, or surviving on account of my unknown folly. Preoccupied with uncertainty in the memory of my first failure, I failed to notice one approaching rider.

"Madam, where are you going at such an hour?" I caught the attention of the third mounted guard who halted my progress near the edge of the property. Disdain filled his words from a height that towered over my frame.

"To town, Sir. I have to get away from here," I replied, shaking in an act of deception. "I will stay the night in town with a friend."

No words or ploy could have prevented the next moments. The man remained on edge from the events transpiring in the manor and I bore the brunt of his panic-sparked duty. The guard gazed down upon me from the horse with intense examination before dismounting. My shoulder ached from the sudden force in which he grabbed and locked my arm behind my back. His free hand patted my body and stopped over the pocket of my apron. I recognized the smile of satisfaction as he pulled out a silver spoon. I had worn such a victorious expression only moments before, and now, my stomach dropped with the realization I had forgotten to leave the spare cutlery.

"I think it is more likely you chose to take advantage of the chaos and betray the Viscount." He spit the words into my face.

Staring at the spoon, my fear was no longer an act and anxiety tingled through my body like ice.

"A mistake, Sir! I am so sorry, I forgot I carried them, and with all the night's events, I had to get out of there as you must understand? Away from the poison!"

My face recoiled from the unexpected slap.

"Do not play dumb with me, wench. I imagine your 'friend' will pay a pretty copper for such fine silver."

I tried to run, but instead, found myself forced face down against the damp gravel. Small pebbles embedded into my stinging cheek. The loud call of the guard's whistle pierced through the emerging twilight and rang in my ears. He took pleasure vigorously searching my person, under my skirt, up my chemise and bodice. He ripped off my olive cloak, and I never saw it again. When reinforcements arrived, they dismissed the dried poisons in my bag as seasonings, but the few pieces of silver contained in the apron sealed my fate.

A stupid detail negated an entire plan of brilliance. Haunted by the mistake, I detached from reality as they wrangled my limp body. Rope cut into my wrists restrained behind my back. The men threw me into a barred wagon and whisked me off through the unfamiliar streets of Matheson. Over the rutted road, my bound frame bounced against the wood, bruising my skin containing marred pride. Beyond the bars, the city flew by and candlelit windows blurred into yellow streaks through my drowning vision. It all happened fast, faster than I could process. A breath later, the wagon abruptly halted, and I found myself thrown upon a damp, dirt floor of a cell.

Without words from the guards, the sound of the slamming cell door reverberated within the stone walls. The echo jarred my mind back into the truth of the situation. The gaols had been my childhood playground, but from the other side of the wrought iron, my child's wonder disappeared.

Worse, I still did not have proof my mark had been made. Ironically, my thoughts worried about the Viscount's fate more than my own. I wished I would have waited to verify his death instead of taking advantage of the chaos. If the poison failed a second time, I no longer had access.

I stared at the grey stone with an exhale of unproductive regret. I should not have attempted a second assassination so soon, not with my mind frazzled. And in the silent solitude, I found the courage to admit my circumstance: for the first time in my entire career, I had been caught.

I logically knew the risk of my profession, but never believed it could happen to me. *Me*.

The surrounding solid stone drove home the circumstance. The walls of my cage seemed to press inwards, and amidst the darkness, I struggled to prevent my mind from collapsing.

Regardless of what story I told, I had been caught leaving a viscount's manor with the Lord's silver. No one would question the word of his guard. If my false papers held to the detailed scrutiny, the trial's only purpose would be to hand down a sentence. And I knew what it would be.

In my youth, I had seen a man whipped once. For days after I heard his screams. Every time I closed my eyes, I saw red drops flying like dew from the whip raised over his bare back, blow after unrelenting blow. His skin hung from his tattered frame like birch bark.

Paralyzed by the thought of whips upon my flesh, I tried to envision the long, grotesque scars upon my own beautiful skin. Never again would I wear a chemise with bare shoulders. And I could not begin to imagine the pain…

Of course, I had seen murderers hung, too.

I should have felt blessed to be arrested for theft.

My mind fought the logic, unwilling to praise God for the guard's mistake. I could not find grace in the blessing I had been bestowed. Theft over murder — that was, if the Viscount had died. The uncertainty eroded my remaining strength. But other than for the sake of my pride, the truth did not matter.

How could *I* have been caught?

The internal dilemma drove me mad, and my frustrated screams echoed within the stone walls until I collapsed with exhaustion. My spirit cracked until it shattered, leaving my body to decay from fear upon the cold cell floor I still refused to acknowledge.

CHAPTER SIX

A faint tap on the cell door broke my sleep. The inadequate pile of hay kept my slumber shallow, but given the contents of my thoughts, I found it surprising I slept at all. I suppose days of labor had taken a physical toll.

Sitting in response, the bright light coming through the bars blinded my vision. I tried to shield my eyes, and when my arms did not respond, I remembered they remained bound behind my back. My shoulders throbbed from the restraint. My raw wrists stung, and any motion caused the rough rope to dig further into the sensitive skin. But pain was the least of my worries.

With my eyes forced shut from the light, my ears focused on the soft click of the door unlocking. The fire of panic flared, unable to discern why they would come for me in the middle of the night. Without an explanation, I leapt to the worst conclusion my ploy had been uncovered. They would need to know what I gave the Viscount if they hoped to spare his life.

My body trembled, curled into a ball, listening to the approaching footsteps with bated breath. Unable to withstand the ignorance, I peeked through one eye with tentative curiosity. The approaching light shined down upon me like the scrutiny of

Heaven's final judgment. With my fragile psyche, I swore my visitor was an angel. But as my eyes adjusted, the blinding orb focused into the image of a lantern, held by an ordinary man outlined behind.

"Lavinia Maud."

My stomach dropped, hearing my true name spoken in a whisper.

"Yes, I know who you are," the voice continued.

The man held the lantern to his face. His patterned wrinkles conveyed an expression of unnecessary seriousness. I understood my predicament well.

He set the light on the stone floor, and the lantern handle fell against the iron casing with a hollow clank. My confusion only increased when the man sat beside me, leaning against the far wall of the cell. I struggled to grasp the intent of this visitor, unable to discern what angle I should play. Thankfully, he spared me the burden of further speculation.

"We share the same employer, you and I," he began.

With only one person he could mean, Akworth's face flashed in my mind before he continued.

"In luck for you, he has a vast network of spies and is unwilling to risk the chance you will not keep quiet tomorrow."

"Sir?" My stomach tightened in prayer, hoping he did not mean to silence me permanently.

"All you need to know is that I am here to take you to freedom. However, the Baron has a price for my service, and you either accept or decline now."

Freedom? My mind wondered if I had heard correctly; my heart yearned for the comfort of his offer. Luck had never been present in my life, though I realized this moment was no different. Luck would have come without conditions.

"A price…" the words stuck in my parched throat. For a man who had hired an assassin as composed as ordering a meal, I grew unnerved by the compensation Akworth might require.

The man nodded. "You are in his debt. He will call on you at a time, and place, of his choosing. You shall not contact him while you wait, but know you will murder his next mark for free."

It all seemed too good because it was. I never imagined he would name such a mark, but youth gave me a naïve perception, and I lacked another option. The man offered to lift me from the jaws of Hell, and I had no position from which to negotiate.

He was indeed my angel.

"The Baron still wishes to contract with me? Even after this…complication?"

The man nodded. "You poisoned a viscount, Lavinia. Such an act should not be understated. You proved yourself."

The stroked flames of my pride triggered a smile. "My freedom in exchange for a hit? That is all?" Seeing his nod, I agreed without hesitation. "Of course. But is the Viscount dea…"

The man silenced my question with a glare and a finger to his lips. Frustrated, I complied, focusing on my life for the moment. He motioned for me to turn around, and then cut my bindings before helping me stand. I followed him and his lantern out of the cell, struggling to grasp my fortune.

On the way out of the gaols, my rescuer threw my cell key onto a desk occupied by a singular night guard. Relaxed with his feet upon the desk, the official barely grunted, enchanted by the stack of gold crowns within his palm. I assumed the bribe covered whomever else would be necessary to keep quiet. Though in a few days, no one would remember a suspected thief.

Outside, cold air pricked my skin. I never felt so alive. The distrust I harbored over the surprise rescue, the unbelief of my circumstance, it all vanished with a gust of night wind. It had been a dire situation, more so than I could admit moments before. My shivering frame erupted with goose bumps, but my soul rejoiced on fire as we made haste to the edge of town. I lacked all personal effects and a cloak, but I possessed freedom. I promised never again to take that gift for granted.

Under the moonlight, I could see my rescuer's age. His beard contained more hairs of grey than brown, and his frame slouched past its prime. However, he still towered a foot above me, and his prominent ears protruded out from his head in a unique profile I will never forget.

When we passed the last city structure, my eyes discerned the silhouette of a mount, colored dark as night, waiting for me while bound to a tree. The man placed a black blanket around my shoulders and helped me on the steed before handing me a purse with the rest of my fee. I stared at the bag of coins dumbfounded, swallowing so many questions with reluctance.

The strange man turned to depart, but I called to him with desperation. From the depth of my bones, I could not remain ignorant to one query a moment longer.

"Forgive me, my Lord, but I need to know. Is the Viscount dead?"

"I just broke you out of prison! You should be fleeing with full speed, and yet you linger to know if you made your mark?" The man gave a hearty laugh and then shook his head. "You indeed have the heart of an assassin, do you not?"

"Well?" My curiosity built on the verge of bursting through my composure like water through a weakened dam.

"Yes. He had seizures during dinner last night and was pronounced dead hours later. Well done, Lavinia. The Baron *is* pleased, despite the complication."

I was an amateur compared to the Baron. Likely the others who served him shared the experience evident within this man. For my own assurance of my patron's disposition, I had to ask again. "And he truly harbors no disappointment?"

"Truly. The Baron is preoccupied with his thief's failure to deliver some mare cipher. The news of your success brought him much needed joy. Now go!"

My mind itched at a curious connection being made, but not needing to be told twice, I let the fleeting thought dissipate.

I left Matheson and my strange savior behind, never having learned his name. With the night wind at my back and joy in my heart, I rode as fast as I dare push the unknown steed. My victorious laughter joined in duet with the night wind and with each stride from the horse, my justified vanity grew.

I had done it. I had killed a peer.

In arrogance, I forgave myself the stupidity with the spoon and basked in my own glory.

I had killed a viscount!

Killing yeomen and common folk seemed trivial now; I had risen into a station of my own. Nobles may shape our society, but I had proven I could shape them. I dreamed of what I might accomplish with my new proven power and to whom the Baron might pass my token. My clientele would grow, and I craved the prestige that would follow.

I rode hard, westward, until the trail faded into a light path at the tree line of Morfet Forest. Dense foliage blocked the sparse moonlight, and I could not even see my hands in the darkness. I might have trusted Sullivan to continue into the wood without light, but I rode an unknown steed. Forced to dismount, I walked the horse several hundred yards into the woods and found shelter under a tall oak far from the trail.

As I tied the horse to a branch, my mind turned to Sullivan. He had been a simple beast, a mode of transportation, but in a way, I had left a teammate behind. Perhaps one day, one of the Viscount's children would ride him through fields dotted with bluebell. I found perverse pleasure in the thought: the newly ascended Lord Matheson, riding on the horse of the woman who murdered his father. It was a shame few would know the irony.

That was the frustrating aspect of being an assassin. Failures were public, often too public, while successes could never be touted. A criminal must be their own source of praise, but at times, the solitude became exhausting. I longed to take credit for the Viscount, for the world to know what I had accomplished. Not many possessed the skill and the cunning to kill such a mark — I doubted many even within my own Guild. But I had, and the flames of pride kept me warm through the rest of the night. I dreamt of Haylan's awaiting custard tort, of Aselin's eagerness to hear my story, and focused on my castorbean seedling to ward off insecurities from the debt I now owed.

After hours of light sleep, my body responded to the morning with sluggish fatigue. My head pounded in a daze, but anxiety focused my efforts. I had a sufficient head start over any pursuit, and I feared to squander my advantage with further delay.

With the aid of a low branch, I mounted the horse who complied with patience. My stomach growled in protest, and my lips cracked dry. In contrast, the world around was covered with morning dew. The smell of wet wood permeated the air, and a light layer of moisture covered my blanket.

"We are almost there," I whispered into the horse's ear and patted the damp hair on the bridge of its black nose. "I promise you oats and rest if you will run half-a-day more."

As the first fingers of sunlight reached through the trees, I resumed the flight. The weary horse began a slow trot but found proper motivation after a kick of my boot heel. Hours later, I assumed we must have crossed the shire border, but the milestone did not bring the relief I anticipated. I longed to see the inn, to see Edmund, to see my new plant, and to recapture my identity.

The forest cover kept the morning heat at bay. When we broke through the tree line in Gaulshire, direct sunlight drained the remains of my fortitude. I struggled to keep upright on the mount. My thighs ached from the mis-sized saddle. My hands chafed raw from gripping the reins too hard. My body held nervous tension I refused to acknowledge, but motivated by fear, I proceeded on.

When we reached the inn that afternoon, we both looked worse for the wear. The mount's hooves dragged across the dirt path with each step. My windblown hair had tangled with leaves, and my skin possessed a second layer of fine dust. But the relief of seeing the structure rejuvenated my spirit. In contrast, I noticed Edmund's frame slump when my silhouette came into view. We had both passed the last few days in a surreal world: mine of harsh reality, Edmund's in escape.

"Madam," Edmund mumbled out of duty and nothing more. With obvious reluctance, he stood up from his game of dice on the porch to help me off the mount. "Where is…" he began, eyeing the strange, black horse, but halted the question after seeing the look on my face. His eyes took in the disarrayed sight of my appearance, and his tone shifted to one of surprising genuine care. "Mistress Maud, are you alright?"

"Yes. My journey had unexpected complications but proved successful. And yours?"

"I have your package, my Lady," Edmund reported with dejection as he handed me a skeleton key. He knew what the plant would be used for, and regretted his part.

I refused to let him diminish my excitement and gave him the reins of the steed in return. "Excellent! Please take…" I paused, unable to choose a pronoun since I remained unsure of the mount's gender — I had never thought to look. "…the horse to the stables. I will wash up and meet you at dinner."

I did not wait for acknowledgment, I could not. With aching legs, I stumbled towards the inn and found the room indicated on the key. I had to see the plant more than I needed to eat or rest. Beyond the door, its roots called to me through the soil now only one room away. My weak fingers fumbled with the key as I cursed the fickle lock. After several attempts to wiggle the bolt, the door finally opened.

There, on a little table in front of the window, stood my plant in all its radiant glory.

She was an infant seedling; her precious stalk extending mere inches above the potted soil. The glossy, dark red leaves featured hints of purple and sparkled in the sunlight through the window. I caressed their magnificent saw tooth edges, delighting in the soft, white mark left across my finger. The plant harbored a singular, developing red flower with luscious ovoid spikes beginning to extend from the blossom.

But where was the bean?

With a sigh, I regained control of my impatience. She was a baby; my beauty would bear beans in good time.

"I promise to nurture you," I whispered, willing the plant to prosper. "You will be among good company in my garden." I laid a gentle kiss on the budding flower and made sure the soil felt moist. Only then did I tend to my own condition.

It took a hard scrubbing to clean the layer of dirt from my skin. Shedding the servant uniform for a proper dress made me feel anew. Once I had styled my hair with an embellished clip and pacified my craving stomach, everything seemed as it should be, the remaining physical reminders of my near-failure finally discarded.

Edmund escorted me home the following day with the castorbean cradled in a satchel around my shoulder. Aselin fawned over the seedling and savored every word of my tale. The fact she did not hold resentment from being left behind made me proud and proved her growing maturity.

Safe within my cottage, my last concerns faded. Nothing could be done to pay back my debt at the moment, and I preferred not to dwell on the unknown. Sheltered from whatever plight would befall *Mable Bassett*, I believed Akworth's interests meant he would quell any lingering trail.

But the pride, the achievement, *and the sin*, all belonged to Lavinia Maud.

Morning bells rang from the church steeple the following day as I stepped foot into the empty nave. An orange hue of rising sunlight spilled through the stained-glass window, casting rainbows upon the ornate tiled floor. I blessed myself with the sign of the cross, and holy water dripped from my fingers to my modest bodice.

In the front pew, Father Eustace worked the beads of his rosary in solemn meditation. I hesitated to disturb his prayer, and stood behind the man, undetected by his elder ears. When his fingers embraced the bead starting the next decade, I rested an impatient hand upon his shoulder. The wooden pew creaked as the black-robed priest turned to meet my humble gaze.

"No." His singular word resonated through the nave.

A knot swallowed down my throat. Fear prevented me from accepting the old man's answer. "Father?" My voice cracked.

"No, I will not hear it." His eyes bored into mine while he stood. His robes billowed as he stepped towards me with confidence I did not know he possessed. "I assume you are here for a confession?"

"Yes, Father."

"And do you have a new sin to confess or more of the same?"

My silence provided sufficient answer.

Father Eustace spit the words with disgust, "I cannot, in good conscience, bestow a sacred sacrament on one who treats it with such apathy."

Light spilled through the window behind, illuminating the edges of his figure. He swelled with the fire of the Holy Spirit, and I had not felt so small since childhood. But his degrading presumption insulted my faith, and I would not stand for it, not even from a priest.

"Apathy?" Anger flared within my small frame. "How dare you suggest I hold such disregard for the confessional. How dare you doubt the weight I feel lifted, the peace I obtain through the sacrament."

"If your heart possessed true regret, you would learn." Father Eustace's fury reverberated through the nave. His fists shook in frustrated rage while spit sprayed from his lips." You would stop these heinous acts against your brother!" He swallowed, looking over his shuttering shoulder before lowering his voice. "Murder is a sin, Lavinia. A mortal sin. It does not matter if you have a talent for it. Your concoctions are *not* Divine inspiration. Have you ever considered it is the Devil who works through you? That Evil holds your soul in its grasp? You are the Devil's handmaiden,

Mistress Maud, and I will no longer participate in any delusion otherwise."

I struggled to breathe through the weight of his accusation. My body felt hard as a statue, my heart turning to stone to be denied the grace of my own faith.

What could I say? What recourse did I have?

Shock fueled my anger. Who was this man to deny a parishioner confession? Inside, a desire bloomed to use my talents to relieve the priest of his responsibility. The brief thought resounded like a call from my Savior to purge His Church of such evil. Clearly, this shepherd lacked the ability to lead his flock.

"Very well." My chest remained high, filled with the confidence of righteousness. I chose the principled path and departed without further word.

Alone outside, my heart loitered heavy with sorrow having been denied confession.

But the priest was not my Savior. Therefore I did not need him.

The cemetery behind the church featured a stone grotto dedicated to Mary, a shallow cave protecting a white statue of the Queen with flowers. Decades of burnt candles lay her feet with a continual presence of smoldering incense maintained by the Sisters. There, I began my new tradition. Kneeling before the Holy Mother, I made my confession. I gave thanks for the circumstance of my escape, for the success of my second poison, and the young seedling now thriving in a pot outside my cottage. I inhaled the spiced air within the grotto, and after finding peace at the feet of Her statue, I left redeemed.

I gave little thought of my debt to Akworth as I turned twenty-five late in the summer. Haylan graced me with a visit to mark the occasion. Receiving him in the parlor, the damned dimple of his smile melted my heart. My cheeks roused to the same color as the blush daffodils he presented with a soft kiss upon my cheek. He must have gone through immense trouble to find such quality flowers late in the season.

"Haylan, they are beautiful." My tone sparkled as bright as my eyes.

Sweet aroma emanated from the blossoms as I handed them to Aselin to fetch a vase and plates for the custard tort which fulfilled his promise. Once the parlor door closed giving us privacy, I motioned for Haylan to sit in a chair opposite of my own. I crossed my heels, placing my hands on my lap with demure, perfect posture.

"Did you have a nice pilgrimage?" He placed his hat on the table and poured himself a goblet of mead from the jubbe before serving the tort.

"I did. The carvings adorning the cathedral are amazing. You must visit sometime," I lied with ease. "Though you may have seen a new mount in the stable? Sullivan broke his leg during the journey and had to be put down, the poor beast. I was fortunate not to have been thrown when it happened. He took care of me to the end, lowering himself under the buckled leg with grace."

"Oh, Lavinia," Haylan put down his plate, focusing his attention on me. "I am so sorry. I know he had been with you for a long time."

I nodded. "Father, and now Sullivan not two years later. It seems I am fated to lose those I love. You had better not join that list." Haylan smiled as I looked up through my lashes, "I hope you know how much your company means to me."

"And you, to me." Haylan's smile turned playful. "You did not think I only brought flowers and tort for your birthday?"

To my surprise, he pulled out a small, flat blue box with a white satin ribbon from his pocket. The mystery kindled my glee. We exchanged small tokens every year for such holidays, but this fared well beyond our normal gifts. I accepted the box, speechless for a moment. "Haylan. You are too kind."

Masking my impatience, I slowly untied the ribbon and removed the thin cover to reveal a gold chain with an ivory pendant of a hedge bindweed flower. The gift indeed met my concealed expectation. The delicate carving captured the eloquence of the true blossom, its thin edges mimicked nature with stunning craftsmanship.

"My God." I looked up to my love with astonishment. "Haylan, it is beautiful."

He smiled broadly. "I know how much you love wildflowers."

I handed him the chain and kneeled to present my back. He fastened the necklace behind my neck as I fingered the pendant.

"Thank you, Haylan."

I retook my seat and smoothed my dress. In the sudden solace, I noticed he took a deep breath before changing the subject. I should have anticipated there was reason behind the elaborate gift, but at the time, love blinded my perception.

"Lavinia, have you thought about my question?"

I looked down for a moment, knowing exactly which he meant. He intended to bring this up again...

"Yes. I appreciate your concern and I am aware of the societal expectation, but I question why I should bow to perceived pressure? Despite my faith, the habit is not an option. I have not received such a calling."

Haylan gave a slight laugh. "I assumed as much. I hope you might make use of the necklace to pursue the other course."

I restrained my exasperation. Flaunting his gift to court another would have been near adulterous, but I spoke the words he wished to hear. "I wish suitors were lined up at my doorstep, but that is out of my control."

Haylan pressed, "Is there no one whom you desire?"

My stomach fluttered, and my mind raced. Did I dare?

I bit my bottom lip in contemplation. Truly, my hesitation was ridiculous. I could easily kill a man but could not confess my feelings to this one. Realizing the irony in that moment, I summoned the inner strength required to take a leap.

I chose my words with care, keeping my voice considerate. "There is one who has captured my heart. A handsome man of integrity, cunning. I have had a fondness for him since childhood, but he regards me with the love of a brother."

Haylan must have suspected, but never had I expressed my desires so blunt. Now, he could no longer hold reasonable doubt or dismiss unspoken signals.

Silence extended in the room as I both heard and felt my heart beating rapidly. I gazed upon him, waiting. The anticipation threatened to crush my soul.

But too much time passed before his response, and my heart fell.

"Lavinia," Haylan finally spoke plain, unwilling to acknowledge my confession while his eyes conveyed a deeper sympathy. "You should know I have started courting Mary Clements."

And there it was.

The true reason behind the gift. I had left myself unguarded and been stifled by love's dangerous toxin.

I retained composure for the sake of what remained of my pride. "The poet's daughter," I whispered with an exhale, before finding the courage to look up at the source of my breaking heart. "She is a fine match."

Unfortunately, I meant the words.

Haylan's face blossomed with a radiance I had never before seen. He obviously loved her.

"I appreciate those words, Lavinia. You must know you will always have a special place in my heart."

Unable to speak anymore, I nodded.

I rose, signaling an end to the visit. I wanted to be alone. I wanted to fall into a realm of despair I would never expose to my beloved Haylan.

"Thank you for the pendant. It is a thoughtful gift I will cherish."

With mercy, Haylan accepted my hint and finished his last bite of tort. He gave me an embrace that lasted longer than usual, one of sorrow and empathy. He knew he caused me pain, but ironically, he alone could help me heal. My heart laid in his hands.

"I will visit later in the week." He restored his hat to his head. "Perhaps we can further test your new mount."

"Perhaps." I opened the parlor door and walked him through the foyer.

"I am sorry, Lavinia. I promised your Father I would take care of you in his absence. He never had a chance to arrange a match for you, but I promise I will in his name, when you are ready."

I nodded once more, wishing he would just depart. He must have sensed my longing and left without further word. Closing the door behind, I retired to my chamber without explanation to Aselin or Edmund.

Days before I had fled a cell only to be caged yet again. In Matheson, I had almost lost myself to fear. Now, grief threatened to rip apart the fabric of my cognizance. My heart agonized, my battered soul crushed. I could not discern how I would ever be whole again. Abandoned, my fingers caressed the flower pendant above my bosom streaked with tears. And on my knees, I found the strength to grieve for what never truly was.

CHAPTER SEVEN

I hid my grief from Aselin and Edmund and poured my anguish into my work.

After the excitement of the Viscount's murder, dispatching my next client's inconvenient wife proved a letdown. The mark did allow me to make use of my excess stores of belladonna; I simply delivered the berries to be baked into her birthday blueberry pie. While easy money, the plan had not provided the training opportunity I desired for Aselin.

Aselin oversaw the care of the castorbean seedling with vigor, harboring as much excitement for the prospect as myself. Once the young stalk matured strong enough, we planted it in the concealed garden behind the cottage. The plant grew at a phenomenal pace, towering over our heads by the end of summer. To reduce the risk of losing the singular bush, I ordered Aselin to start a few new plants from cuttings. We also learned to prune the plant with rags tied around our faces to ward off coughing fits.

But despite our best tender care, the plant failed to produce a single bean.

I interrogated Edmund with vigor. I doubted the meek boy had it in himself to cross me, but switching plants would have been a crafty way to prevent the murders he abhorred. I could not fathom where he would have obtained a different plant that matched the Guild's description, but out of prudence, I had to rule out the possibility. Aselin latched onto my questioning with fury, and her unrelenting pressure brought tears to Edmund's eyes as she held him against the wall by his collar.

"I swear Ase! I did not tamper with the plant. I did not switch it!"

Aselin let go of her brother. His shaking body slid down the kitchen wall into a pitiful crumble of limbs on the floor. She perhaps...no, she *is* more suited for this profession than I am and I regarded her intensity towards her own kin with a teacher's pride.

But if Edmund had not tampered with the plant, then where were the beans?

My contact insisted I had the right seedling. I tried different soil, variable watering regimens. I experimented with artificial shade and fertilizers. Perhaps Father Eustace would have known, but I could not turn to him.

Out of options and full of desperation, I regarded the growth with new eyes one afternoon. The plant's branches limped heavy from the weight of oblong, spiny pod fruits. I plucked one and took care slicing it open with a pruning knife. Inside, the red pod contained three oval seeds that were light brown with dark streaks. My laughter roared so deep I scared a group of birds in a nearby tree.

The three seeds resembled beans.

The fruit pods the plant produces are not a bean, not in the classical definition. But given the appearance of the seed, I discerned the name to be representative or mayhap a translation confusion. Either way, I finally had my "beans." And lots of them.

Aselin and I experimented with various methods to purify the inner meat of the seed, and indeed, our standard processes proved inadequate. However, rodent tests showed mixtures of the bean's meat were lethal in large doses, and the results provided sufficient motivation to pursue unlocking the promised, tasteless potency.

Even with the excitement of the castorbeans, those fall months were clouded by the debt hanging over my head. I detested not knowing how Akworth would demand retribution, and the unknown obligation infuriated my desire for control. As the sun began peaking lower in the sky, I feared I would be under his grasp for years. Mercifully, he dispatched a summons towards the end of September for my apprentice and me.

Aselin and I met the Baron of Camoy in the same chamber of Blackhaven Tavern on a crisp morning. This time, I dressed plain as a symbol of my humble appreciation. A tan coif concealed my hair and matched the linen kirtle with a cream undersmock. Upon entering the back room, I swallowed pride and knelt before the Baron.

"My Lord, I appreciate the generosity you have bestowed upon your servant. She is here by your grace and that fact is not lost on her."

The Baron smiled, placing a finger under my chin to lift my eyes towards his own. The lace cuff of his sleeve protruding from his velvet coat tickled my neck.

"You dispatched a difficult mark without drawing attention to my House. You did not break cover or reveal my participation, even when incarcerated. That is loyalty and nerve beyond what I expected from a woman. I take care of those who take care of me, Madam Maud." He paused for punctuation. "Now please," he indicated to the chair across from his table. "Join me in a drink to our success."

Exhaling with relief, I gave a small smile, and took the indicated chair. Aselin once again sat discreetly behind me on the bench. Despite wondering about the contents of her thoughts, I could not look at her. I wished Aselin had not seen me debase myself before the Baron. As her Master, I suppose it was my responsibility to teach humility, and the client must be pleased above all others. Still, I preferred when she revered me.

At least Akworth seemed satisfied. My mouth watered, watching him fill a second goblet of wine. *Wine!* It was a luxury I did not have the privilege to enjoy often back then. Accepting the offered goblet, I swirled the liquid and detected subtle notes of cherry in the released aroma. Well crafted, the wine's smooth, distinct legs held a depth of sub-flavors. The selection indicated the Baron did mean to celebrate, and the realization eased my concerns.

"Did the act make way for the results you desired in parliament?" I inquired, attempting to provide enjoyable conversation.

The Baron responded with a short nod. "I expect the bill will pass this fall."

The moment of relaxation had been fleeting. Clearly, he wished not to dwell on the subject and as before, got straight to the point. Akworth's tone turned serious as he set down his goblet.

"Now, with regards to your debt, Mistress Maud. I have decided to pass your token to another. You will serve her as well as you have served me."

Her?

My imagination ran rampant. A woman! Instantly, I harbored awe for this new client; not many women cared for this game. I felt the pull of sisterhood to the unknown stranger.

"I hope you play chess?" Akworth asked. After seeing my nod, he continued, "My horse-litter is waiting to take you both to a game. You will find suitable attire in the coach."

I never grew accustomed to the Baron's abrupt tendency. Why he had bothered to summon me when such a short message could have been written in the original letter? Perhaps he wanted to feast on my humility. Perhaps he wanted to look into my eyes once more, to convince himself I remained the correct assassin. After everything that happened in Matheson, I did not blame his insecurity; I would have wanted the same.

Maybe he wished to make his pleasure clear after the complication. If that was his reason, I remained grateful. The support of a man with such prestige bolstered my confidence. I wondered if he knew my first attempt failed. Even with the vast network of spies I learned he employed, I doubted he could have known, and I was not going to tell him.

I placed my goblet on the table, also turning to business. "And dispatching of their mark fulfills the debt owed to my Lord?" I repeated, needing to be sure.

After his affirmative nod, Akworth rose and opened the back door of the chamber.

I stood with a polite curtsey and a smile to my patron, determined to keep him on my client list for the sake of my coffer. "Then as you wish, my Lord Baron. I will not let you down."

"Be sure you keep that promise, Madam Maud."

The warning gave me internal pause, but I kept concern from my face. I looked toward Aselin who followed my lead out the discrete backdoor of the inn.

We emerged into the back alley where an unmarked black horse-litter waited. The sight paused my steps, never had I ridden in such luxury. The coachman opened the door, and when I regained my presence, he held my hand as I led Aselin into the coach.

Once the horses began their trot, I opened the box, finding two gowns which took our breaths. I appreciated the first clue of my new patron. Whomever Akworth's peer was, she was high class, and I quivered with anticipation.

I selected the crimson gown for myself — it better matched my coloring — leaving the pale green garment for Aselin. Together, we helped each other change and tie bodice strings, taking care not to wrinkle the delicate fabric. The soft, tightly weaved textile caressed my skin. Hand embroidery adorned every inch of the silk embellished with beads that sparkled in the sun. Both garments were works of art in fabric. I never would have guessed my wardrobe someday would rival those pieces. That first taste of luxury teased my desire.

"Where do you think we are going?" Aselin's asked, giddy with childlike excitement.

I had not a clue but joined in her thrill without concern. Taking turns, we combed out each other's hair with our fingers and marveled at such splendor. For a moment, we were two girls playing dress up until professionalism restored my focus. I had always dreamed of this caliber of clientele, but after the complications with Lord Matheson's murder, pangs of doubt dampened my excitement.

I was not sure what I expected, but I never would have guessed my debt would be passed. The fact Akworth would not be selecting the victim made my stomach tighten with uncertainty. It was the first time I had been forced to work for a client I did not choose and target a mark I did not approve. On rare occasions, I did decline a job. For my own safety, I avoided serving as an intermediary between rival hordes. I refused to murder children and once declined to assassinate a nun. But now, there were no bounds to whom might be named as a target. The unknown patron could name anyone: a duke or royal, mayhap another as-sassin whose skill would prove insurmountable. Whomever they declared, I remained honor-bound to fulfill the kill.

When I thought I might fall nauseous from anticipation, the grey stone of a castle emerged in the distance, reaching up into the clouds as a tall fortress of prestige. I recognized the purple and red banners billowing from spires in the fall breeze, but I could not accept the reality.

"My God…" The soft expression of unbelief escaped my lips as I regarded our attire with new understanding. Aselin's blue eyes opened wide, gleaming like sapphires.

As we approached the estate, an unusual half-hexagonal room caught my attention. South facing, floor to ceiling windows stood out from the stone facade, and a diverse collection of contained greenery captivated my attention through the glass panes. To have such a sanctuary to grow plants! The prospect almost gave flight to my imagination, but now was not the time for such distrac-tions. Dismissing the thought with reluctance, I regained focus on the task at hand.

The coach pulled up to the estate's covered receiving porch, and a regal attendant helped us disembark. The emblem on his long jacket was indeed the purple and red crest of House Paston, the Earl of Gaulshire.

Stepping out of the coach, I felt like royalty. In all my life, that moment was the closest I came to the unreachable experience. My gown eloquently flared from my frame, the elaborate trim on my dress rivaled the molding of the porch's cover. Surrounded by wealth, I daresay I looked like I belonged. Despite all my nerves, my heart believed I did.

A butler escorted us through ornate hallways deep into the heart of the estate before arriving at a pair of tall, white doors trimmed with gold paint. My mind raced, analyzing the possibilities of who might be inside. If challenged, from the location alone, I would have guessed a lesser lord, or perhaps even the Earl himself. The client could have been a group or a singular representative of a hidden faction. Mayhap a military leader. All of those possibilities would have been more likely. But Akworth had said the patron was a woman. Even at that moment, I could not produce a single, viable conjecture.

After the butler opened the door and announced our presence, I took an expectant step inside.

"My Lady, Lavinia Maud and Aselin Gavrell."

I recognized the figure at the far end of the long parlor — any yeomen would. Countess Gaulshire, Agnella Edith Paston, sat in a high back armchair. Aselin and I immediately offered a curtsey. I did not try to contain the smile that crossed my face; I could not have been more thrilled with the patron.

With inhuman grace, the Countess floated across the floor towards our position. A snood adorned with pearls gathered her loose blonde curls and matched the multiple strand necklace around her neck. The soft, olive color of her skin complemented her hazel eyes as if a master painter had carefully selected the colors from a divine palette.

"Good day, Madam Maud, Madam Gavrell." The Countess looked towards the butler who closed the door, leaving us alone, and then turned her attention back towards me. "I have been looking forward to this meeting since I heard of your…shall we say, talents?"

"Thank you, Countess. I am truly honored, and surprised, to be invited into your home."

"The honor is mine," the Countess offered with grace. She retook her seat and indicated we should do the same.

Lady Gaulshire's warmth matched the brightness of the parlor. Sunlight illuminated the room through multiple high windows along the side. Subtle detailing of cream hues adorned pale-yellow walls contrasting vibrant potted bouquets meticulously constructed of local blossoms and ferns. Hung paintings featured women with parasols, gardens, and serene lakes I longed to visit, though I could not imagine such breathtaking features existed in reality.

The sight of the marble chessboard, however, caught me by surprise.

I assumed the notion of a chess game was a cover, or mayhap a euphemism. Certainly, Akworth viewed me as a pawn in his larger, strategic game. Dwarfed by my surroundings, I vowed not to be swept up in the majesty, nor power of the Countess. I would be the unassuming rook, waiting in the corner for an opportunity to strike for my own benefit. I would not squander the opportunity to rise in social status through serving such a client. So, if my Lady actually desired to play chess, I would oblige.

The Countess continued, "I admit my surprise and intrigue when I learned the Baron's…helper…servant," she swallowed, saying the word in a near whisper, "*assassin*, was a woman. In many ways, I am glad for it."

I smiled, touched by her unease. "God gave men power, but He gifted women with cunning."

The Countess laughed, and for the first time, relaxed her porcelain mask of perfection. "Amen! I have a feeling we will get along well, Madam Maud. May I call you Lavinia?"

"It would be an honor, my Lady."

"Then you must afford me the same courtesy. If we are to discuss something as intimate as…the use of your talents, it seems fitting we should at least be comfortable enough to use given names."

"As you desire, my Lady — Agnella." I offered the quick correction seeing the seriousness of her expression.

"I prefer to maintain a first-name basis with all of my ladies, and we are here to play chess after all." The brightness of her cheeks gave away the insecurity she tried to conceal. "Edward informed me you also had a female apprentice. I thought a nice afternoon with three women would be less conspicuous than conducting an audience with one."

The Countess' use of Baron of Camoy's given name in our presence startled me and shed light on what might lay under the surface of this exchange. Clearly, she found the notion of murder uncomfortable and tip-toed around the subject, as an awkward child dances with their feet on their father's shoes.

"I do appreciate your company," Agnella offered, again off-subject. "My husband has been moping for months, searching for some lost heirloom from his father. He is constantly misplacing things, and I find tending to my plants only occupies me for so long."

I wondered if the Countess was always this verbose or if the condition was a manifestation of nervousness. It seemed I would need to address the question looming over the room. I decided to ease her pain as I set my own pieces on the board.

"All I need to begin my service is a name. I do not require justification, nor your participation. You can be as knowledgeable or as distant as you desire."

Agnella ignored my remark and opened the game with her knight, a choice as bold as hiring an assassin. I followed with a more standard response of a nearby pawn.

I was adequate at chess. I understood the function of the game and could hold my own if required. But I struggled to predict my opponent's moves far enough in advance to counterattack. I thrived in details, not big picture strategy. Chess played too long for my attention, and by the end, I would have rather seen my king tipped over then continue through fatigue. The Countess would have found a more worthy opponent in my apprentice.

However, time passed with ease in the Countess' presence. A master of conversation, Agnella made us feel comfortable and appreciated. As the game progressed, I turned my focus from the checkered board to unraveling the puzzle that was the Lady of Gaulshire.

For a while, she ignored my suggested topic of conversation. Instead, we discussed the weather, gardening and then progressed to the less mundane topic of politics. She had taken my bishop when she summoned the courage to return to the true question at hand.

"How do you do it?" she asked without context, focusing on the chessboard, unwilling to make eye contact. I understood the game gave her a welcomed distraction of comfort, such that she could pretend no other reason existed for the audience.

"That depends on several factors," I began. "The method of delivery, how much discretion is necessary, and the amount of suffering the client wishes to impart."

I sensed Agnella shudder the slightest amount.

"But why poisons?" she inquired. "Would a knife not be easier?"

I shrugged, seeing Aselin fidget in the chair beside us while watching the game. "That option is less clean and discreet. Poisons also level the playing field; as a woman, I never need to overpower a male target. Murder with poison is also a perverse paradox. Often poisons are placed into food or drink and the unknowing victim, of their own power, consumes the item. In effect, they commit suicide.

"Some assassins say poisons are a dishonorable way to kill, but I will pose the question: Is murder ever honorable?" I paused for thought as my knight took her rook. "I say it can be when it is done with reverence. There is an art to it. And certainly, sometimes, it is for the greater good. I especially take pride knowing my own extractions, a substance I purified with my own skill and intellect, brought down the mark. Anyone can buy a sharp stick from a blacksmith and stab someone in the back. Few can create the poisons in my repertoire."

Agnella looked up from the board to make eye contact for the first time. The awe in her eyes enflamed my pride. "You make your own poisons?"

"Of course, my Lady. I enjoy the challenge. I am currently working on a new purification that is said to be odorless and tasteless, but no one in my Guild has unlocked the exact formula. I intend to be the first and expect such an advancement will allow me to finally ascend to the rank of Fellow."

To my delight, her intrigue had been captured. "There is Guild for…poison making?"

"Yes." I nodded. "Though clandestine, for obvious reasons."

Agnella pondered the thought for a moment, distracting her concentration. Her next move of the queen left her bishop unprotected. "What is your favorite poison, Lavinia?"

"Wolfsbane," I replied without hesitation, ignoring the opening she provided in mistake. "Also known as aconite. It is said that Emperor Claudius was poisoned by his wife, who placed aconite leaves into a plate of mushrooms. Even back then, women knew how to work the angles afforded to them. I simply find the blue flowers beautiful. There are not many blue petals in nature, and I embrace the notion something delicate can be so formidable. Poisoning can occur simply by touching the plant's leaves."

"And yours, Madam Gavrell?" Agnella looked beyond me towards Aselin.

I did not have to turn around to know the sinister smile that formed on the lips of my apprentice. I also already knew her answer.

"Hemlock, Countess," Aselin began. "It is a small white flower, indigenous to Europe and South Africa. It was used by the Greeks to kill their prisoners, including Socrates. The plant's symptoms are uniquely heinous. Death comes from paralysis: the victim is conscious, but their body does not respond. Respiratory systems shut down, and they endure waking asphyxiation."

Lady Gaulshire's mouth opened silent, failing to generate a response before turning attention back towards the game.

After minutes of silence, she finally offered her order.

"My husband loves mushrooms."

Her eyes gave away what she feared to speak aloud. My heartbeat and breath held still, waiting for confirmation. I had wanted to increase the station of my kills, but this… A moment of doubt weakened my resolve as I hypothesized the missing pieces Agnella refused to acknowledge. My breath offered a silent prayer to God I assumed wrong.

Uneased, each word came from me as its own thought, "Is he the mark?"

Agnella moved her queen to challenge my own. "When Tedric's first wife was found guilty of treason, it cast a long shadow on their son, Silas. After we married, Tedric agreed my eldest son from my first marriage, Kelton, would be named heir. But that stands as long as we do not have a male son of our own."

She rested her hand on her abdomen. "The midwives say I am nearly three months along."

She sighed deep, sitting back from the chessboard. "I love Kelton, I will not see him displaced, even by my own offspring. If he is to remain next in line…"

I completed the words her tongue trembled to say, "The title must pass before the succession is altered."

Agnella nodded.

The Countess's love for her son inspired my awe: she loved him more than her husband. I understood a mother's love to be strong but never before had I seen such a display. To go to such lengths for him…

But could *I* do it?

First a viscount, and now the Earl of my own shire? If I had not been in debt, and if I had been wise, I would have walked away. But I overflowed with ignorant pride. I reminded myself everyone is subject to my poisons, earl and beggar alike. It was within my right to decide who lived and who suffered. A noble title did not provide sufficient antidote nor deterrent.

Still, I could not resolve one remaining piece of the puzzle.

"If I may, Countess. Why would Baron of Camoy sponsor this mark?"

Agnella blushed to which I nodded in reply. "I see." My early assumption proved correct. Clearly, they engaged in an affair.

Despite the complication that had occurred in Cranshire, I knew I had earned the Baron's trust. But this information shocked my core. To admit adultery to a commoner… And after the scandal with the first Lady of Gaulshire, it seemed foolish for the Earl's second wife to engage in such treasonous actions. Though love is a strange and powerful force that shapes this world as much as the ancient glaciers carved the valley and hills. I understood its calloused venom as an assassin captivated by a Magistrate.

The fact that Agnella and Akworth took me into their confidence set my heart ablaze. One hint of an affair, or the notion of my employment, could have destroyed them both. It would have been easy to expose them to the Earl. Too easy. In my wildest imagination, I could not have dreamed of such power over two nobles. And despite the fear, despite all the logic, poisoning Lord Gaulshire prevailed as the more attractive path.

I never apologized for what I was.

But with the mark named, I quickly surmised a strategy.

"In this case, I would suggest a private dinner party. Perhaps the Earl, yourself, the Baron of Camoy, and his two visiting cousins? As you said yourself, an audience with both of us is less conspicuous than one. Having heard your husband enjoys mushrooms, I will present him with a basket of delicacies from my region. Since it is autumn, death cap mushrooms are in abundant bloom. They have large, fruiting bodies, pale green in color with white gills. Sharing resemblance to Caesar's mushrooms and straw mushrooms, I am confidence your kitchen staff and food taster will not know the difference. Only a botanist trained in fungi would be able to distinguish them apart.

"Unlike most poisons, their potency is not reduced through the cooking process. Portioning is key in my trade. Your food taster will not be harmed from a single bite, but consuming a proper portion will be sufficient to cause death in a week, long enough to ensure no connection to our dinner."

"A week?" Agnella stirred in her chair. "How will he…"

"The symptoms are delayed two to three days," I explained. "They will start with stomach pain, diarrhea, nausea, and vomiting. Signs of liver damage will emerge, jaundice, delirium, falling sickness, and then deep sleep. He will die from subsequent failure of the heart."

"Is there not a faster way?"

"To avoid suspicion, this is my recommendation."

I watched the Countess' eyes in those telling moments of decision. This would be a turning point in her life and one of the most difficult choices she would ever face. I felt honored to bear witness to the moment.

Agnella stood with a sigh. "A dinner party then. So be it. I will make arrangements with the Baron. How long do you need?"

I stood as well, following her lead. "At least a week, my Lady, to gather the necessary ingredients."

She nodded, leading us to the door. Before following, I rearranged the chess pieces to place my own king in checkmate, lest a servant should examine the board. But my client remained distant, still struggling with the notion despite having declared her intention. Far too often, my patrons required as much attention as their marks, but I knew how to calm a nervous client.

I took her hand within my own and looked the Countess in the eyes. "You are a strong woman, Agnella, to make such a bold move. I admire your courage and conviction. I am sure you have pondered the dilemma for months, having already come this far. That is an indication you are making the right choice, so do not permit doubt to cloud your heart in the final hour. The hardest part is complete, and I will take care of the rest."

I gave a deep curtsey with a smile. "Until next time, my Lady."

It took all of the Countess' strength to nod in reply before opening the door. After Aselin and I entered the hallway, Agnella wasted no time shutting the door behind. I wonder how long she contemplated alone in that room. Though whatever consideration she endured must have been productive, for there were no immediate signs of doubt when we next met. For her sake, I hoped she would not come to regret the choice.

Gathering the mushrooms proved an easy task we completed in a singular afternoon, even given the number required for Tedric's legendary plump size. I had expected as much and hid the true reason for requesting a week to prepare. I meant what I said, two visiting cousins would be less conspicuous than dinner with one unknown lesser Lady a week before the Earl passed. But I did not want Aselin's first assassination to be such a risky mark.

I now had a week to give her training a giant step forward.

.

CHAPTER EIGHT

"**I** know!"

Aselin raised her voice, punctuating her assertion with tense fists. After a deep breath, she caught herself and corrected her tone. "You have shown me a dozen times, Master. I have practiced."

I produced a sigh any mother would recognize. Within the narrow, concealed alley, I checked her hand technique once more. Indeed, the position of her fingers well concealed the small, metal vial between her thumb and index finger. We both knew I stalled in reluctance, warranting her frustration.

It was a bright afternoon, one of those fall days stolen by the last remnants of summer. Representatives from every faction of Marfield society crowded the market. The vendors were as diverse, and their colored awnings dotted the otherwise monotonous city streets. Noise from the crowd compounded upon itself; each merchant yelled louder than their neighbor to attract patrons from the stream of curious eyes. The clamor filtered into the alley where I gave Aselin last minute instruction. Sweat beaded upon my brow, though not every drop was caused by the sweltering sun.

"Alright," I conceded. "Only the stakes are so high, Aselin. You do understand what would happen if you were caught?"

Her head nodded in silent reflection. Her eyes conveyed the deep understanding I hoped she possessed. It was the bitter reality of my profession. But no one in this world, not king or queen, nor merchant or assassin, grasps for power without accepting risk onto themselves.

My anxiety swelled for Aselin. I worried she might not find the act as glorious as she dreamt, that the reality and finality might prove too bitter to stomach. Murder was easier plotted than performed. There was no going back, no opportunity for restitution. To be an assassin required more than apricots and wolfsbane. The career demanded determination, courage, ingenuity, and most important, self-assurance. Aselin possessed the cunning, but the next moments would prove if she had the gall and stomach. I prayed she would not regret the experience.

With a deep breath, I led the way from the secluded alley and joined the main bustle of the market. Tense and focused, my mouth did not even water from the prevailing sweet aroma of smoked boar as my undeterred eyes searched for a target. Selecting a mark provided a new pulpit of power, deciding the fate of each unsuspecting wench and lad as they passed. The thrill was different than my normal flavor, but one which suited me all the same. The experience helped me understand the mind of my patrons.

As I searched, we strolled through the lines of vendors, buying a few items for our pantry, and blending into the crowd. The plums for sale within one stall called to my palate, deep purple and plump. I inspected each fruit with care, intentionally drawing out the process. Beside me, Aselin knew I tested her patience. Her hands fidgeted, but to my satisfaction, she did not protest.

I desired a target who would not cause too much trouble, but someone who might give Aselin pause to kill. Someone with a weakness she could manipulate, but not a mark of her own choosing. I dismissed the mothers outright — I was not heartless. The elderly and children would not have provided a worthwhile test. I could not condone killing for killing's sake and that day held a higher purpose, requiring a suitable victim. I wanted to give Aselin the full experience, to know if she would be a liability with the Earl of Gaulshire.

I decided early it should be a man, someone near Aselin's own age. That selection gave her an angle to play and a mark that could not be outmuscled. Almost all the targets on a job are male anyways, a man made the experience more practical.

Across the street, a lad lifting crates of chicken eggs from the back of a wagon caught my eye. Snags tainted the light fabric of his shirt, stained with sweat that also glistened on his muscular arms. He worked alone, but not in an isolation that would make Aselin's job overtly easy. As a fine specimen of masculine youth, it would also take every drop of the poison in Aselin's vial to bring him down.

For her first kill, Aselin selected my extraction of the St. Saint-Ignatius' bean. I had talked Aselin through the purification process, coaching over her shoulder as she prepared the toxin now ready within her possession. Her choice contradicted my expectation, but I followed the logic. Each poison had its own benefits and challenges; each assassin selected the toxin which best complemented their strengths and circumstance. My Ignatius bean extraction was colorless, though bitter. The delay between consumption and the onset of symptoms was short, which would provide immediate proof she had passed the test, but little time to achieve distance. Once consumed, the lad would experience violent convulsions and eventually pass from asphyxiation when his muscles grew too tense to permit breath. Some say death occurs from exhaustion brought on by the duration of intense spasms, but I knew otherwise.

"The man behind your back, with the red handkerchief tied around his neck," I described low into her ear. "At the egg stall with golden, short hair."

Aselin did not flinch or show any readable sign. After a moment, she regained our stroll before glancing in the indicated direction and nodding. "With the white shirt and brown breeches."

"Yes." I turned, regarding my apprentice with pride. "You can do this, Aselin. You are ready and well-practiced. Trust your instincts, maintain a path for escape and…"

"…always ensure deniability," she finished in unison, anxious. "Yes, I know." Aselin took a deep breath and then looked into my eyes in a genuine moment I've never forgotten. "Thank you, Master. I will make you proud."

With a nod, she departed before I could respond.

I browsed through squares of embroidery from one vendor's cart and watched her approach the mark. My nerves flew higher than if I had been executing the assassination myself. My mind analyzed the situation for how I might solve the puzzle. The obvious answer was the water vessel unguarded during his trips between the wagon and the stall. I would have slipped the toxin into the open jug as I walked by. But discretion was not Aselin's style. She preferred to target the head of the snake.

I laughed to myself, watching her pull down her bodice and give her breasts a lift before approaching the lad — not my preferred technique, but one she pulled off without flaw. Even from a distance, I could see she had the boy charmed within moments.

My eyes rolled as she placed a hand on his bicep, wondering if she delayed for her own amusement. We discussed the mistake in depth later. An assassin should not be memorable. It is best to get in, take care of the job, and then achieve distance from the scene.

After several minutes of flirtatious conversation, she asked for water and accepted the open jug. Aselin took a large sip to decrease the remaining liquid and then allowed a man walking past to hit her arm.

"Excuse me!" she called, permitting the momentum to turn her back to the egg vendor. Because I watched closely with knowledgeable eyes, I saw her dump the contents of the vial into the water with her back still turned. She then rotated to face the mark, talking with grand gestures to dissipate the powder through the water. I admit the delivery was well done. Flamboyant compared to my style, but well-executed all the same.

The man took the jar and helped himself to a long gulp that nearly drained the remaining water, wiping his lips on his shirtsleeve. With thanks, Aselin politely parted and continued on her way.

She had done it. My smile burst with pride.

I set down the piece of embroidery I pretended to examine and moved through the crowd in her direction. A minute later, a crash resounded from behind my back, followed by the screams of several women with egg yolk in their hair. I glanced behind as the crowd's attention focused in unison on the lad convulsing on the dirt street. A woman's wail of anguish followed, piercing the ears of everyone in proximity. A coif covered her tight grey curls as she cradled the lad in her arms, screaming for a doctor. Even if one had happened to be nearby, nothing could be done.

Aselin's pace paused as well, but she did not turn around when I caught up to her. Her eyes hosted an eerie, distant hollow while she held her breath. After several tense moments, she regained her stride.

"I killed him." The admission escaped her lips with bated breath, intended for herself more than my ears.

"Yes, you did."

I will never forget the perverse smile that formed on her face. How her eyes blazed with the light of triumph.

"Would you like to go make confession?" I offered.

She turned to me with a cold expression, suggesting I had somehow belittled her moment of victory with the ridiculous question. "Why?"

"Do you remember your first?"

Aselin retained quiet isolation that evening, so the sudden question surprised me, though I welcomed the indication of her self-reflection. As the night passed, I had noticed the event affected her more than she let on. She did not even touch her favorite stew Edmund served for dinner. I feared how she would feel in the morning and tended to her delicate state.

"Of course." I placed a cup of warm cider into her hand and sat in the chair in my parlor. "Though, I am ashamed to admit vengeful spite motivated the act. He did not deserve to die. In fact, I did not even know his full name when I slipped mandrake root into his soup."

I exhaled in thought, looking down at my hands with contemplation. I did not wish to tell the story, but she had a right to hear and perhaps, I had a duty to recount.

I settled into the chair while deciding where to start. Her reaction in the market had scared me. How did she not feel an ounce of sin? I realized the moment was a rare opportunity to reach her. She needed the lesson.

"We harbor a skill of great power, Aselin. I am honored to pass it down to someone so worthy and capable. But if I can teach you anything, it is to use the knowledge wisely. Do not miscomprehend, I understand the elation. I love the power that comes from administering a poison. I love watching someone struggle and knowing the pain came from my own hands. I crave that moment of exhilaration when the last breath of life disappears from their failing body.

"But to kill without cause or justification belittles our call as assassins. We must always wield our art with care and honor, or we are no better than the common criminal."

Without further fanfare, I recounted my story and told her the truth as best I could.

I was fifteen. Pascual had just committed suicide and my dreams danced with fanciful thoughts of poisons and assassination. The knowledge, and its potential, burned inside me. It consumed each waking moment. I hunted for plants matching Pascual's descriptions in every field. I could not eat a bite without searching for foreign notes.

And I searched for an outlet to fulfill my grisly urge.

The warm summer sun kissed my face as I gathered wildflowers up on Chesbrook Hill. The wood anemone bloomed large and the pyramidal orchids sparked within the handpicked bouquet. I missed her deeply, my mother. She used to make me crowns of cow parsley, so I included some in the bundle as well. With my labor of love complete, I began my weekly visit to her grave. I planned to share with her my thoughts of seeking a career as an assassin. Hers was the only safe console, and my dangerous admission would be swept away by the wind.

On the way, a brute bumped into my side hard while walking the other direction. The flowers flew up into the air, and damaged petals fell upon me like colored rain. Anger flared in my heart as I turned on my heels, shouting at the man.

"How *dare* you!"

The sneer on his face stopped me cold. His slow, deliberate steps back towards me accented his challenge. "And what will you do about it, wench?"

I swallowed, staring at his dirt-laden face and plain grey attire. He towered over my frame. Terrified, I choked on the words I longed to say.

He snickered at my silence. "I thought so."

His laugh echoed through my head. I had been on a tipping point, and he pushed me over. Glaring at his back, my eyes squinted with hatred as I made a quick decision: he would be my first.

After allowing him to escape a safe distance, I followed the breedbate, stalking my prey. My heart beat rapid, every sensation and instinct heightened as the world collapsed to only him.

He wound through the streets to a tavern near the outskirts of town. From the personal and lewd interaction with drunks and the bar staff, I gathered he frequently visited the crowded establishment. After he had sat at a table, a barmaid brought over a bowl of soup and a glass of ale without even being asked.

That night, I told Haylan the story of how I had lost the bouquet. He gave me a quick hug, counseling me not to bother myself with a drunk, and that no good would come from dwelling on an accident in the city. But I could not let it go — not with the fantasies bombarding my every breath. Haylan had no inkling of the deep desires festering within my heart. He had not heard the stories Pascual told. And every time I closed my eyes, the drunk's smug face flashed before me. The man's laugh haunted my dreams and reaffirmed my decision.

I made my plans in secret. I had my target and a location, but I needed the means. That night, I began the exquisite endeavor of selecting a poison for the first time.

I did not have the garden or the resources back then, but mandrake can be found in fields with dedicated persistence. The plant is also called "Satan's apple," or "gallows man," due to the root's similar structure to human form. Some folklore states mandrake only grows under the gallows where the semen of a hanged man fell to Earth, but in truth, it can be found naturally. Even Genesis 30 recounts that Ruben "found mandrakes in the field."

Having selected my poison, locating the plant became my personal quest. Day after day I searched. My skin grew tan from exposure to the sun. My back cramped at night from staring so long at the ground. With desperation, I even consulted Father Eustace where I might find mandrake leaves to make an ointment for my father. Using his tips, I canvassed the shire's terrain, and after a week of persistence, I discovered a small cluster.

I had been wandering so long I questioned if the plant was a mirage. After rubbing my eyes, I stared at the purple flowers extending from the clusters of rough, large leaves. With tentative, outstretched fingers, I convinced myself the growths were not remnants of my dreams. I took the fact I located mandrake as a sign of divine permission. I had searched with patience and been rewarded for my faith.

I dug up two of the precious growths, transplanting one to my garden where its line still thrives. The roots of the other I washed and boiled with care. For two nights, the precious cargo in a small glass jar weighed down my satchel as I watched the tavern from a nearby street corner. On the second, my mark returned.

The man had been a permanent part of my thoughts for weeks, but I took a bet he had not paid me another thought since that day. As such, I entered the tavern with my head uncovered. He, and several others glanced in my direction, but gave me no heed. I chose a table diagonal from his own, and after a wench had delivered his soup and ale, I waited for the right moment.

When his ale was half consumed, another barmaid came down the aisle of our tables. I stuck out a discreet toe far enough to cause her to trip. The tray of goblets flew from her hand causing an amber spray across the room with the bulk landing on my mark. The muscles of his back had tensed before he rose in anger that built like a storm cloud. I jumped from my seat, wiping ale from my own dress, and moved out of his way towards the careless wench.

Profanity reverberated through the small tavern with a volume that rattled the chest. Every set of eyes locked onto the mark whose anger I had knowingly inflamed. And while he towered over the cowering bar maiden, I slipped the cubed root into his soup.

"Baines!" The bartender called over the commotion. "Enough!"

The proprietor walked forward with a strong presence and lent a hand to the wench. He then stood between her and his patron, daring the man to test him. "Your dinner is on the house, alright? Certainly, that will make up for an innocent slip."

Baines. I was not sure if that was his given or surname until it was engraved on his tombstone, but somehow knowing the name made him a person more than a monster. A moment of doubt flashed through my mind, but the poison already waited.

Baines gritted his teeth in a quiet moment of tension before retaking his seat. Over the next minutes, dull chatter restored throughout the tavern. My nerves subsided, and to my own enjoyment, I watched Baines eat every last bite of soup.

Towards the end of the bowl, he started to pucker his lips. His face scrunched as he examined the ale. Consuming mandrake will affect the taste buds, even water will taste moldy. I could not imagine the effect it had on the cheap tavern alcohol.

Next, thoughts become cloudy as dizziness and nausea set in. Over the following minutes, Baines lost control of his movements. His hand tipped the goblet as he reached for another drink. His pupils grew larger than their irises, causing impaired vision. In his confusion, Baines cried out for help, but his slurred speech proved incomprehensible.

Once again, the tavern focused on his table in the middle of the crowded room. He stood, visibly shaking, and then collapsed into a deep sleep from which he never woke. Screams and chaos consumed the tavern. Several bystanders rushed to his aid, and after laying a vail of a few pence on the table, I swiped the tipped goblet from Baines' table before taking my cue for a quick exit.

Outside, I marveled at my own capabilities. I had done it. I killed a man on the first try without mishap!

With a firm grip around my metal souvenir, my mind clung to the memory, desperate to prolong the glory. I analyzed the order of his symptoms, deducing what occurred in his physiology: the physical manifestation of my dominance. Skipping away from the tavern, my heart raced with an unyielding smile. I was forever transformed, as if I had been awakened. Murder proved *easy*, mayhap even natural. I savored the power, and my soul basked in exorbitant pride. Every inch of my body tingled with a fire I promised to never let extinguish.

And then the church bells tolled.

The world crashed around me. Darkness consumed my essence. In an instant, my heart hardened with festered shame, the sin extinguishing the last morsels of lingering hubris.

I killed a man.

And for what? A scattered bouquet?

I could not own up to what I had done, not yet. My hate turned towards Baines who had made me do it. Deep down, my conscience recognized the misplaced blame, and after a night of failing to sleep, I could no longer even pretend to believe the lie.

I killed a man, violated God's sixth commandment, and one path existed to forgive the sin I feared would swallow me.

Father Eustace fell speechless that day in the confessional. I sat on the other side of the partition for at least twenty minutes after my trembling tongue released the admission. I dare say the shock of the sin struck him as much as the identity of the sinner. Even through the partition, he knew me. Among the usual rants of deceit, lust, coveting and missing mass, my confession stood apart. Unable to put together a worthy sermon on the spot, he mumbled something about the seriousness of the act, the need for reflection and penance, and then continued with the rite, forgiving my sin.

Inside, I felt made whole once more. Father Eustace had forgiven me, which meant God had as well. I had killed and been restored as if cleansed once more by the Holy Waters of baptism. Is that not the foundation of the faith?

I came to believe the entire trial had been divine planning. That God gifted me such skill so I might carry out his will. Isaiah 49: "The Lord hath called me from birth; He hath made my mouth like a sharp sword; he hid me in his quiver as a good arrow; He said to me: You are my servant." God had shaped my talent to wield for His use. Surely Baines did not hold God in his heart, and I was humbled to serve my Lord.

They buried Baines in the same cemetery as my parents. I never found peace with that fact, which is why I salted his gravesite every week. He deprived my mother of flowers, and I made sure nothing would grow for him in return.

After that first murder, the following week proceeded normally. The unexpected commonality reaffirmed my innate capacity as a new itch began to fester. I craved the thrill. The power, the satisfaction, the entire journey, and premeditation. I now knew the solution to satisfy my vicious thirst, and my father's gaols contained all the guidance needed. A year passed before I had the opportunity to indulge again. My client list started with freed prisoners, but over time, it grew to so much more.

Within months of my first contact, the Guild responded to my efforts to reach them. That fall, a hooded man shoved a crimson envelope in my hands as I walked home from the butcher. The fact some clandestine group knew my identity terrified me to the point I considered turning in my mortar and pestle. But the honor also elevated my self-confidence. Responding to an account of my kills, the leaders of my chosen craft deemed me worthy enough to contact. Me, a then twenty-two-year-old girl. The Guild offered to share brewing secrets, exchange contacts for ingredients and with their help, my business grew beyond expectation. I became part of something important.

Having told Aselin the complete story, I walked over to the table in the entryway where I kept Baines' metal goblet. Aselin fingered the cup with new understanding. After her first murder, she did not experience the spiritual regret that had consumed me. She listened to my tale, but beyond the pride of accomplishment, she could not relate. In a way, Aselin had it easier; she was spared the guilt of our profession. But I also worried for her soul. Whatever the justification and rationalization, murder is murder, and the Lord's teaching is clear on the path to redemption.

"I understand your point, Master Maud," Aselin offered, running her finger around the rim of the cup. "I have no desire to kill just to do so. I understand the risks and truly such peril would not be prudent without the promise of substantial benefit."

I nodded with a sigh. "There is that, too," I agreed before regarding her one more time in consideration. "Do you now find yourself ready to kill an Earl?"

Her eyes beamed like prisms. "Yes, Master."

And so, we began executing my plan.

CHAPTER NINE

Edmund did not speak to me for several days.

I wondered how Aselin broke the news of her first assassination, but the tension between them proved he knew. Edmund emphasized his silent defiance by placing Baines' cup in the drawer of the entryway table. Of course, I restored it, only to find the cup in the drawer the following morning. Other than our new game, Edmund decided to carry on as if nothing happened. The poor boy... I tried to maintain a routine to support his chosen false reality, but the house tensed with preparations for the upcoming dinner party.

The morning of the job, Akworth's messenger delivered finery required for the ruse and beyond our capacity. Basking in the memory of such luxury against my skin, Aselin and I tore through the parcel packaging with excitement. This time, a parchment note dictated wardrobe assignments. My dress featured forest green brocade, hemmed with gold stitching. After his punctual arrival, Akworth placed a coordinating emerald pendant around my neck and twirled me with my hand above my head. His judgmental eyes examined my frame, and he produced an audible smirk of satisfaction as I completed the rotation. He viewed me as his creation. He had pulled a low poison maker from obscurity and left no credit for the assassin.

Aselin pinned her hair up in curls with a borrowed gold barrette matching her silk gown. Each sleeve buttoned with pearls and the thread used for the ivy-patterned embroidery glistened with inexplicable brilliance. I followed the logic of Akworth's wardrobe assignments but eyed the auric gown with envy. Akworth's inspected Aselin with a kiss upon her hand, and instead of tolerable acceptance, his face radiated with lust. If we were not having dinner with his mistress, he might have had other intentions, but he maintained propriety as he led us to the waiting horse-litter.

We departed for the Earl's estate, the three of us, enduring restrained conversation prolonged by societal expectation. I could not discern if the Baron of Camoy resented being entangled in this event or appreciated the opportunity to have dinner with his love. Knowing him, likely both. But his eyes repeatedly glanced at the basket within my hands.

"May I see them?" The Baron proposed his question with an expectation of compliance.

"Of course, my Lord." I lifted the lid of the basket to reveal the half-dozen mushrooms wrapped in a satin green cloth.

He unexpectedly reached to examine a cap.

"I would not," I cautioned, pulling the basket away in time. "Touching one outright will not kill you, but it could make you sick. They are best handled with gloves."

I folded the satin back over the mushrooms and restored the lid as he withdrew his hand. Strain once again befell, and I noticed the Baron's fingers repeatedly intertwine before he tipped his hand.

"Agnella told me you know of us," he resigned.

I smiled, comprehending the reason for the Baron's unchar-acteristic tension. "My Lord, the glimmer in her eye at the mere mention of your name gave you both away." I saw Akworth gleam through the low light in the coach but guessed at his greater con-cern. "Your secret is safe with us, of course. We would never betray a patron."

With an exhale, Akworth finally relaxed. "I know. You proved your loyalty in Matheson, and I trust your word regarding Madam Gavrell."

"Your confidence is an honor, my Lord," I responded with Aselin nodding beside me, "and Aselin's loyalty is absolute."

Reassured, Akworth sat back against the coach cushion. His beloved would be his in a week or two, and they could soon begin a public courting. A period of mourning would be expected, though I doubted they would wait longer than necessary with Agnella's condition. They shared a genuine love, for only true pas-sion would be worth such a high stakes gamble. I envied them, and how could I not? I could have been fulfilled with half as much passion from Haylan. But wary of coveting the blessings of an-other, I dismissed the thought of my love. And after seeing the glimmer of hope in the Baron's eye, I could not resist prodding.

"Is it yours?"

I half expected a tirade in response for overstepping my bounds, but instead, a smile of pride grew on his face.

"I hope so, very much."

His response brought a smile to my heart. Tonight, two lovers would unite, and I rejoiced in that holy honor.

This time, the estate's grandeur did not incite my awe, my mind focused on the job. The Earl and Countess received us in a former parlor. The room was intimate and small though brim-ming with ornate detail intended to impress, or perhaps, intimidate. But with the basket I carried, no amount of wealth would dismantle my dominance. That night, I was the one with power.

Kindly stated, Tedric James Paston, the Earl of Gaulshire, possessed a plump frame. The gold buttons of his tunic stretched tight, and it seemed they might pop at any moment. His eyes featured a unique grey color, so dull they were almost haunting. The unique feature suited him just fine, and the gentle twinkle in his smile appealed to my sympathy as he bestowed pure love upon Agnella. He had no eyes other than for her. He received us properly, but his gaze left his wife only as long as necessary to be polite. I longed for Haylan to regard me with similar eyes, wondering how Agnella could throw away a deep affection most of us will never know.

Tedric had met Akworth twice before, but they greeted each other with formality. From watching the exchange, I learned the Baron of Camoy could act. He greeted the Countess with the utmost respect that almost convinced me he barely knew the woman. The discovery gave me pause, knowing he had likely used those skills during our interactions. What did the Baron hide from me? I did not have spare capacity to worry while on the job, and for the night, I pushed the thought aside to focus on my mark.

Aselin and I gave a deep curtsey when Akworth introduced us as distant cousins. Since we had already been to the estate under our true names, we felt it unwise to now don aliases, but I longed for the security of one.

"My Lord, I had the great honor to play chess with your wife a week ago. Her intelligence and cunning are as refined as her beauty. I am now grateful for the opportunity to dine in your presence, as well."

Tedric nodded. "I hear you gave her a run, Mistress Maud."

I smiled. "The Countess is too kind, my Lord." I looked towards Aselin who held out the basket. "In appreciation for your generosity this evening, we have brought a basket of local mushrooms cultivated on our land for your table. The Countess spoke of your Lordship's love for mushrooms and hope you will be delighted by the rich, earthy flavor of our tribute."

Aselin opened the basket and pulled back the satin cloth to reveal six caps. Tedric's eyes lit as he removed one and held it towards the light. The pale green rim around the white bulb showed prominently in the yellow glow of the candle.

"Thank you for your thoughtful gift, Madam Maud and Madam Gavrell." He placed the mushroom back in the basket. "How do you recommend my staff prepare them?"

Aselin answered as we had practiced. Their toxicity would not decrease with cooking, but I hoped to encourage minimal handling from the kitchen staff to avoid spreading illness. "My preference is a simple sauté preparation in butter and light salt."

"I concur, my Lord," I offered in support. "An intricate recipe would mask their unique flavor."

"Very well." Tedric accepted the basket and handed it to a servant to take to the kitchen. "I look forward to tasting such a thoughtful gift."

With that, the Earl took a seat within the parlor and invited us to do the same. Though as soon as his rear touched the chair, he immediately rebounded up.

"Oh," Tedric spoke with a hearty chuckle. "Dear, I have found my spectacles!"

Agnella rolled her eyes while her husband held up the found treasure. Aselin and I exchanged a glance, remembering Agnella's complaint Tedric frequently misplaced his possessions.

Pre-dinner conversation tested Aselin's patience. Her hands once again fidgeted within her lap. I glared at her in silent warning, and she held together thereafter. Agnella started out brilliantly but unfortunately did not fare much better as time passed. The glow she embodied when we first met was replaced with a solemn expression. The men became too consumed with conversation of fishing to notice, but I worried Agnella might crack under the pressure. When she started pulling at her gown with a small bead of sweat on her temple, I intervened. I also could not pass the opportunity.

"Countess," my polite interjection paused the conversation. "I saw the most curious room from the road as we approached: floor to ceiling windows that appear to be made for growing plants?"

"My grow room?" the Countess asked, eager for the distraction.

"A *grow room*," I repeated to myself. "Would you be so kind to offer us a tour?"

A wave of relief restored a smile to the Countess's face. "A splendid idea." She kissed Tedric on the cheek and then excused the three of us saying we would meet them for dinner.

The moment we left the presence of the men, I whispered in her ear with a hand on her back, "You are doing well, Agnella. It is almost done."

She nodded with an appreciative smile, relaxing her shoulders as she led Aselin and me down the hall.

"The grow room was a gift from Tedric," the Countess explained. "He knows I hate seeing my precious seedlings wither with the cold. It is a unique design inspired by a monk from Glastonbury Abbey that allows me to tend to plants throughout the year. Not all fair well throughout the winter, but enough prosper to assuage the indulgence."

Inside, my own anticipation flickered to behold an entire room dedicated to the growth of plants. The chamber was a testament to ingenuity lifted from my dreams. An array of windows provided a near half-circle view of the estate's back courtyard. When we arrived, the final fingers of sunlight protruded through the windows, and the flourishing leaves savored the last moments of light.

Overwhelmed by the vast array of ceramic pot filled shelves, my attention shifted between the plants, tantalized by the curious growths around me. The Countess attempted to provide order to my examination.

"The plants are arranged by the amount of water needed, such that the top plants require less frequent access," Angela explained with pride. "That was my own addition."

I nodded, recognizing the textured leaves of sage on a higher shelf, knowing they prospered in well-drained soil.

"It is clear the room is well thought out, my Lady," Aselin offered.

Agnella smiled, soaking in the complement like the dirt of the pot she watered with a metal can.

A pleasant mix of sage, fennel, rosemary and bay laurel combined to tantalize my senses within the warm, humid air. The impressive size of the purple, vertical flowers of betony next caught my attention since the plant is known to be slow-growing.

"This dear must have been flourishing for some time," I remarked, cupping a flower in my palm.

The Countess looked up from a pot of cumin. "Oh, yes. Betony is Tedric's favorite herb for the headaches induced by his advisors. I ensure we always have ample supply, but I will not miss having to fuss over the thing."

I smiled, pleased to find my patron's resolve restored. Seeing me wipe my glistening brow, Agnella laughed, nodding towards the blazing hearth.

"I usually do not tend to my plants in a full gown." She poured a little water on three rags and handed a moist cloth to each of us. "I take pride caring for the plants myself, but the servants keep the fire lit throughout the winter months."

With the sunlight retreated for the day, Agnella began closing the thick window shutters meant to retain the day's heat. I assisted, following her lead, as I admired the array of orchids and medicinal plants amongst the collection: hyssop which suppressed chest phlegm and soothed bruises, chamomile which aids digestion. But even with my expertise, I was embarrassed I could not name them all.

"Agnella, what are these clusters of pale pink buds?"

"Comfrey," she responded, amused, "used to heal inflammations and help set broken bones." After setting down a watering can, she looked towards me with a twinkle. "I suppose your expertise lies in plants of a different classification."

I laughed, appreciative of her excuse on my behalf. "Aye, my Lady."

After my question, Agnella found it necessary to thoroughly explain each of the plants. I love herbs, but the detail in which she talked tried even my patience. Akworth had told me the Countess passed time through gardening. Indeed, every growth showed meticulous pruning. My own garden existed from professional necessity, but the Countess's provided escape. Perhaps her hobby would no longer be necessary when she and Akworth could be open.

While I fawned over a sprig of lavender, a servant called us for dinner. Agnella immediately choked on nerves as she swallowed.

Again, I came to her side. "Are you having doubts, my Lady?"
She shook her head.

"Then you have nothing to fear. We have done our job well.
Now, let us start your liberation."

Framing the act in such a manner appealed to her conscience:
a liberation, not a murder. I noticed her back straighten as she led
the way to the dining room.

Upon our entrance, Lord Gaulshire pulled a chair out for his
wife before taking his place at the head of the table. The Baron
of Camoy sat to his right, taking care not to eye Agnella. I took
the setting next to the Countess in case she needed further assurance, leaving the chair next to Akworth for Aselin.

The table brimmed with delicious preparations: spiced quail,
apples, cheese, fresh bread, and green beans. To the Earl's side, a
small bowl of steamed mushrooms had been sliced and prepared
with flecks of a green seasoning. I could not distinguish the herb
from the aroma, and of course, I did not try some myself.

A servant came to the Earl's side and took a bite of everything
on the platters, including a thin slice of mushroom. I held my
breath, watching him chew the death cap, and suppressed a smile
at the taster's nod of reassurance. Eager, Tedric offered a short
prayer of thanks and pronounced it time to dine. I watched him
pick up the bowl of mushrooms and close his eyes as he inhaled
the aroma.

"Splendid, Madam Maud, Madam Gavrell."

I smiled. "I am glad, my Lord."

"Shall we each take one?" Tedric placed one sliced mushroom
on his plate and then held out the bowl in offering.

Agnella's eyes flicked with fear.

I did not miss a beat. "That is a generous offer, my Lord," I
began with a light hand over my heart. "But we gathered them for

you, and it would please me if you enjoyed the delicacy. It is a small measure of our appreciation for your generous hospitality this evening."

The rest of the table nodded in agreement, and Lord Gaulshire smiled. "Very well. I admit I am pleased by your insistence." He placed the remaining five caps on his plate piled high with generous portions from every platter.

I had not expected Lord Gaulshire to partake in such a massive feast and for a moment, I questioned if the dose would be lethal given the volume of his meal. Aselin connected with me, no doubt sharing the same thought. I took a breath of relaxation and gave her a subtle nod. Six caps were double a sufficient dose, even for a man of Tedric's size. I recognized my doubt rooted in the memory of Lord Matheson, not logic. Regardless, nothing else could be done at the time.

The meal proved delicious, as I expected it would be, and the wine flowed freely as it should in such an opulent household. Agnella struggled to eat and pushed food around her plate. No one else seemed to notice, or they assumed she suffered from morning sickness, but it didn't matter. Before the feast concluded, the Earl had consumed six death caps and was in a jolly mood. The evening concluded with pastries, toasts, and compliments for my mushrooms that grew more exalted with each goblet of wine.

When it was time, we followed Akworth's lead to end the evening. He laid a gentle kiss on Agnella's offered hand, and the singular spark in their eyes was the one moment I noticed between them the entire evening. I understood how caged they both felt, restrained passion threatening to burst through polite reservation. My own heart suffered in similar constraint and I never denied my envy. The end of their trial neared while my own plight with Haylan might never be pacified. After Akworth separated from his love, Aselin and I also offered our gratitude before departing for the horse-litter.

Moonlit fields passed outside the coach window as the Baron unfastened the emerald broach. Aselin placed the gold barrette into his waiting satin pouch as well. The dresses became patron gifts, but the jewels held far too much value.

For a moment, I had lived a dream: dressed in finery on a high-value assassination. The removal of the necklace signaled an end to the perfect evening. Wishing I had indulged in the moment, part of me regretted wasting the night worrying about Agnella. Yet, I stayed true to professionalism and shepherded my client through one of the hardest moments of her cushioned life, and for that I was proud.

"Your performance this evening lived up to your reputation, Madam Maud."

Akworth's unexpected compliment as we arrived at my cottage focused my attention to the Baron. Restraining my smile, I nodded in acknowledgment. "I am grateful my patron is pleased. Thank you again for your confidence and a wonderful evening."

I exited the horse-litter after Aselin as the Baron proclaimed his final warning to my back.

"I will be pleased when I hear rumors of the mushroom's effects. Until then, I would not rest comfortably."

I nodded once more and swallowed, hearing the words, but my step did not hesitate. The Baron's need to assert his authority did not waiver my confidence. I made my way towards the cottage choosing to trust myself.

As soon as the door closed behind us, Edmund rushed to embrace Aselin. He held her head against his shoulders, running a hand through her hair.

"Oh, thank God!" He exclaimed, pushing her out at arm's reach to make sure no harm had befallen his sibling.

I rolled my eyes. "It was a dinner party, Edmund, not a hunting expedition."

Normally Aselin would have shunned his concern, but tonight, she laughed and permitted his overzealous examination. "It was amazing, Edmund! The estate, the jewels, the berries they must have brought in from somewhere south."

"You should be proud of her, Edmund. She did well," I stated for Aselin's benefit more than the lad's. "She maintained polite conversation, played her part, and never gave away our cover."

Aselin nodded at my approving smile and then focused her excitement towards me, the only one who would understand.

"My Master! The exhilaration of every bite." Her eyes were wide as a child on Christmas. "How the four of us shared a secret and watched him happily eat poison."

Again, I smiled. "It is even more fun when you are able to gloat and watch the results."

Aselin laughed as she spun in her gown. "And you, my Master. It is an honor to watch you at work. How you demonstrated just enough demure to gain trust, how you knew the exact moment to excuse Agnella. I watched you close the entire evening and I never once saw the faintest of signs."

"Unlike your fidgeting?" I teased.

Aselin flopped into a chair, the volume of her skirt overflowed the seat. "I am sure you were not perfect on your first assassinations."

"No," I admitted. "But I meant what I said. You did well, and I am proud, Aselin."

Four days hence, I received an unsigned letter, but recognized the handwriting to be from the Baron:

Gastrointestinal pain began yesterday, delirium today.

"It should not be long now," I added, passing the note to Aselin.

Edmund read over her shoulder. "God have mercy on him."

"Indeed," I agreed, making the sign of the cross. Consumed with piety, I ignored Aselin's rolling eyes.

That Sunday after mass, I offered a silent intention for the Earl's weakened fortitude. The flame of my offering candle danced upon the wick as I knelt in devotion. I prayed for success. I prayed for the love I unchained between my patrons. And I prayed for deliverance from their threats of failure.

Days later, Aselin and I harvested the last crop of beans, flowers, and leaves from the protected garden when distant church bells began to toll off schedule. We looked at each other confused, trying to discern the rationale.

Edmund scoffed, stating the answer obvious to him. "The Earl is probably dead."

Aselin cackled first, but her laugher proved contagious. I dropped my basket of clippings, and she removed the rag from her face. We danced as two giddy children, frolicking together in the yard and holding hands in a spinning circle.

"You did it," Aselin exclaimed.

"We did," I said, arresting our rotation. "I mean that, Aselin."

She smiled, squeezing my hand.

Indeed, a few hours later, a knock sounded from the door. Edmund received a wooden box from the courier and brought it to me in the kitchen. The dovetail joints were a symbol of fine craftsmanship, and the lid featured a bright oak inlay contained in dark-stained cherry. While the box proved its own work of art, the contents took my breath.

The emerald pendant and gold hair barrette we borrowed that evening laid under a parchment note. This time, the writing gave away a woman's hand. The author had to be Agnella.

I know this job fulfilled a debt, but please accept these tokens of my appreciation.

I gifted the barrette to Aselin. She had worn it on her first official job and deserved to have the keepsake. But the large, precious jewel was mine. Held up to the window light, the emerald illuminated with an inner glow. Each facet compounded the luster and reflected back my gaze of accomplishment. I will never forget that moment. Years of risks and toil were brought to fruition. I thought of every failed extraction, every mark who had played a part to prepare me for this assassination. No one would deny it now; I had risen into a new station of my craft. I had killed an Earl without any complications, and my heart gleamed brighter than the gem.

However, despite all the achievement, a cloud of reservation loitered over the victory. My mark was dead, and now I needed to finish the job properly. For me, that meant confession. I wished Aselin would have joined me, but I respected her choice. Faith cannot be genuine if it is forced.

My heart ached as I passed the church. Dried, brown leaves crunched along the path under my boots as I walked to the grotto in back. I must have sat on the nearby stone bench for an hour, staring at the steeple, wondering if I dare ask Father Eustace once more.

I had passed down knowledge to another, united two lovers, and cultivated my God-given talents, but the priest's limited view would see poisoned faith. Surely, the love of two people brings more to the world than the early demise of one — not like Tedric would have lasted long with his girth anyway.

Wind rattled the remaining leaves on the branches above. I decided if Father Eustace did not find my remorse genuine, then I should not waste my time. I turned to the stone grotto to face the statue of the Queen Mother. Carved in a somber expression, her eyes cast down, forever weeping for her castaway Son.

"He is not castaway by my heart," I whispered. "Please do not forsake me in return."

A bitter wind billowed through the grotto causing the devotional candles at Her feet to dance. A reminder the fall yielded to winter in a reluctant abdication. For all my sudden rise and success, a nagging concern took root in my gut. Over the past seasons, my career had blossomed like a spring flower. I hoped my rise would also not wither and die as nature surrendered to the chill of winter.

CHAPTER TEN

News of the Earl's passing moved through the shire faster than the sun traced the sky. By the afternoon, interest had already progressed to the next rumor. Tedric had relative youth and decent health, making his death a surprise to Marfield. Still, he had been a passive leader, rarely utilizing his authority, so most residents remained indifferent.

That was, except for the magistrate.

Yes, I suppose his post carried an expected responsibility to inquire into the death of a ranking peer. But fie! Why did Haylan have to be so damn good at his job?

Mayhap I was too arrogant. To be honest, I simply did not think things through. I was a mere low-level common poison assassin, flirting with an elevated game. My marks were usually discarded and often dismissed out of the belief that their lives justified their unnatural deaths. But I should have expected such a high-level death would be investigated. I had the capacity to prevent the whole mess, and I failed. And if I had thought through that fact, I could have prepared Agnella.

Akworth relented and told me the story after my third request reduced to begging. He gained nothing from lying, and the distinct pleasure he reaped from recounting my downfall motivated truth — at least from his perspective. Agnella had struggled with her decision to hire an assassin. She could not even say the word "murder." Therefore, I was not surprised she flustered when questioned.

"Lady Gaulshire, to your knowledge did your husband have any enemies?" Haylan posed the query as gentle as possible, accepting a goblet of ale from a servant as he sat.

Agnella shuffled in her chair. "Of course! My husband is the Earl of Gaulshire."

Haylan exhaled with patience. "Anyone who gave specific cause for concern? Who might benefit from his passing?"

The Countess squirmed as her eyes flashed to Akworth standing quietly in the corner of the room. "No one confessed a scheme to me if that is what you are asking." She raised her voice in defense — her first mistake. "If we knew of a plot against Tedric, we would have arranged for increased protection."

Haylan raised his hand in a silent apology. "Of course, my Lady. I apologize and only ask as part of my duty." Seeing Agnella relax, he continued. "I have a few more questions if you will permit: Do you remember Tedric being exposed to anything out of the ordinary which might explain his symptoms? Did he pursue game off trail during a hunt and perhaps contact virulent growths? Could something he ate have become contaminated?"

The Countess swallowed. Why was a simple "no" so hard for her to say? Sweat began to glisten on her temples. Looking away from Haylan, she paused too long. "I… We employ a food taster." She cleared her throat. "I eat from the same platter nearly every meal. There have been no indications of anything abnormal."

Haylan sat forward in his chair, his suspicion piqued by the telltale signs of a lie. His heart must have raced. He could not have expected the routine interview to take such a turn, but my father had prepared him for such situations. Remaining quiet, he patiently baited his witness.

Uncomfortable, Agnella rambled to fill the unnerving silence as she had during our chess game. "Given Tedric's pain and symptoms, the physician said his stomach had fallen ill. He summoned the Bishop for a blessing. The physician drained Tedric's blood. Leeches, salves, minerals, he tried everything."

The magistrate's soft voice was enticingly smooth. "But what caused the pain, my Lady?"

Unsure how she would respond, Akworth wanted to intervene but could not tip their hand. From his corner, he painfully watched his love's eyes water, he said he heard her throat tighten.

"My Lady," Haylan continued. "I beseech thee to convey whatever lingers upon your tongue. Even the smallest bit of speculation may prove useful to ensure the security of the Shire." He looked into the Countess's eyes. "Lady Gaulshire, I suspect you know what caused the Earl's illness."

A tear rolled down her cheek as she glanced to Akworth once more. Receiving his nod, she continued with a voice so soft Akworth guessed her words.

"She said she would poison me if I spoke," Agnella's voice waivered.

Haylan's eyes widened. "Who?"

"The assassin," Agnella voiced, exasperated. "She blackmailed me into a dinner invitation. I did not know why." The Countess spoke with rapid speed. "If I knew her intention... I never dreamed she would... I thought she just wanted dinner for an audience with Tedric. She brought these mushrooms. Poor Tedric loved mushrooms. She insisted he need not share with the table. And when he fell ill, I suspected, but it was too late. I fear for my safety. You must understand, I am with child!"

Inside, Haylan must have fluttered with anticipation. Capturing the Earl's assassin would be the break of his career, the break I deprived my father of years ago. Haylan harbored ambition, same as myself. He would have recognized the opportunity and tasted the potential.

The magistrate took a deep breath, pausing to allow the Countess to settle. His words poured with genuine care towards the woman who now held the key to his career. "I do understand my Lady, I am here to help. We can make this right and bring this woman to justice." He knelt before her, taking her hand within his. "I need you to tell me everything you know, any contacts she might have mentioned. Details of each meeting, her appearance, description of the mushrooms."

Agnella exhaled, reassured once more by Akworth's nod from the corner. "Of course." She bit her lip, looking into the magistrate's eyes with insecurity.

"Let us start with a name. What name did this woman provide?"

The Countess swallowed. "Maud. Lavin — Lavinia."

Oh, how I wish I could have seen his face! The shock that must have occurred to Haylan's head and heart, his descent into a cloud of confusion and doubt. *Lavinia?* It is not a common name. *Lavinia Maud?* The girl he had grown with, his sister of other blood? The daughter of the late magistrate himself? Haylan made Agnella repeat it again to be certain.

Haylan completed his examination, but the clues could not have made sense. What would a common yeomen woman hold against the Earl? How could she have gotten so tangled in politics beyond her reach? With questions swirling in his head, Haylan did what any investigator would: follow the one lead he had, no matter the insanity.

Aselin and I were away meeting a potential new client the day Haylan came to investigate. I intended it to be her first solo job — with myself taking half of the earnings of course. If I had been home, perhaps I could have redirected Haylan's inquiry. After all, his heart did not want to believe the lead anyways. But as fate would have it, I was not the one who answered the door.

Edmund, of course, invited Haylan inside without second thought. He was a close family friend, and understandably, Edmund craved male conversation. The lad would not have held reason to suspect imminent confrontation.

And Edmund could lie as well as his sister, a trait that would surprise anyone acquainted with him. I knew he had the capacity, but I thought our interests were aligned since silence also shielded Aselin. But his true loyalty did not lie with me, and when confronted, he protected her by ensuring the blame fell at my feet.

Edmund gave me up in an instant.

He took a bewildered Haylan to the cellar room where I purified my extractions. While Edmund did not possess technical knowledge of the instruments, he explained them in enough detail to increase suspicion. He guided the magistrate to the fenced "herb" garden. Haylan had no interest in plants but knew of one botanist who would be able to identify clippings and tie the loose ends of the investigation together.

I was told Haylan waited for Father Eustace to finish the current decade of his rosary before interrupting the prayer. With a single glance, the priest knew the clippings in Haylan's hand and panicked as his worst fears came true. With the magistrate before him, the priest faced a crucial choice.

"Drop those right now!" The priest's voice echoed through the empty nave, save for two choir boys who later told me the story.

Haylan looked at the stems of leaves in his bare hand with confusion.

"They are poison, boy!" Father Eustace hit Haylan's arm hard enough for the clippings to fall to the tiled floor.

The rattled magistrate looked up to the priest with blossoming anger. "Do you know where they came from?"

Father Eustace responded frankly, "All sorts of plants grow in the forests and fields."

"But *these* plants," Haylan pressed, his words quivering in fear of the answer. "Are they native to the region?"

The priest swallowed.

"I took these from Mistress Maud's garden," the magistrate continued. "Did you know she cultivated such plants?"

Father Eustace stepped back, throwing his hands to guard himself. "I cannot…"

Haylan pressed forward, closing the distance down the aisle between the pews. "You can and you must. I have witness testimony of serious charges against Madam Maud. As a botanist, can you discern any innocent reason why she would have these growths? Are they medicinal?"

This is where the stories diverge in detail, but I believe Father Eustace tried not to say anything further. His veins bulged as his mind split in dilemma. A simple word to the magistrate would stop my killings, but he would be betraying the confidence of the confessional. He had to decide in that instant which tenent he valued more.

And Haylan relentlessly pressed. Despite the evidence, he refused to believe his Lavinia contributed to such a scheme. He needed to hear the words spoken, and he had youth on his side. With his heart shattered and anger inflamed, Haylan grabbed Father's shoulders and shook the old man.

"I am the Magistrate of Gaulshire," his voice thundered through the church, ringing within the structure. "You will answer my questions or face prosecution as an accomplice to murder!"

Whatever happened in that nave, I will never know, nor perhaps do I wish to. I feared such knowledge would taint my memories of Haylan. But both boys say the confrontation ended with Haylan towering over the weeping priest prone on the floor.

"Please, understand I was bound by the sacrament," the priest whimpered. "What could I have done? I have lost track how many times she confessed the mortal sin."

Haylan had heard enough. Gathering the clippings in a handkerchief, he left without a word and obtained a warrant for my arrest from the Justice of Peace.

Edmund did not disclose Haylan's visit, and I never would have known to ask. That evening, I had found it unusual my instruments on the workbench sat in disarray but saw no need to inquire. With a shrug, I placed my cup of sage water upon the workbench and toiled with the castorbean into the late hour, unaware.

Haylan later said my case was the easiest investigation he had ever undertaken. I had not covered my tracks, and the truth had unwound from Haylan's leads like a ball of loose yarn. For all my gifts, I had fatal flaws as well. I trusted too completely and failed to see the long game. I simply had not expected to be betrayed by

Father Eustace, nor to be so easily given up by Edmund and Agnella.

But another also felt betrayed.

I answered the door late in the afternoon the following day and found unexpected tears in my strong friend's eyes.

"Haylan, what is wrong?" I regarded him with genuine concern, unknowingly inviting my captor into my home.

Aselin and Edmund's curious footsteps approached from behind. I later wondered if Aselin knew, but I never thought to ask.

"Aselin," I ordered, "fetch some ale and biscuits."

"That will not be necessary," Haylan quickly corrected. He took off his hat and placed it on the table near the door, knocking over Baines' goblet. I noticed a curious red rash upon his hand, but the inexplicable pain within his eyes required my immediate attention. Haylan curiously remained silent for several moments while he chose his words. In my naïveté, I hoped his tears were on account of his courtship ending with Mary Clements. My heart leapt to my throat with the possibility he might confide in me. Of course, that was not the case.

"Did Edmund tell you I came by yesterday?"

I shook my head not wishing to interrupt his tale. My answer took him by surprise.

"I know what you did," he finally spoke, choking on the words.

"I am sorry?"

So, he did not wish to talk about the Clements girl, but in my arrogance, I still had not put it together. Part of my mind was composing a lecture to Edmund for forgetting to disclose Haylan's visit.

"The Countess said you gifted the Earl with strange mushrooms. Yesterday, Edmund showed me your…room, downstairs. And the garden…"

My stomach dropped. A fire of fear ran through me as if my spine was tinder.

To my dismay, Haylan continued, "And Father Eustace identified the clippings I took from your garden, breaking the seal of your confessional."

"Haylan, please," I interrupted, inferring the cause of his rash. "Why not have a seat? I will fetch a salve for your hand, and then we can sort out this misunderstanding." My mind raced, trying to discern how those pieces might alternately fit together, but he never gave me the chance.

He shook his head, pulling his coat sleeve down to cover his rashed, clenched fist. "Lavinia, no. Do not make this harder than it already is."

A tear rolled down his cheek, resting for a moment at his dimple before sliding down his chin. Haylan flashed the arrest warrant pulled from the breast of his jacket.

Before I understood the circumstance, he pinned me against the wall. The physicality surprised me. He either took no chance or had lost control of his emotions. My face was pressed into the plaster from his shoulder, the small of my back held firm with his knee. My wrists bruised from the force with which he grabbed and positioned them behind my back in chains he had concealed under his coat.

Haylan continued with the process through sniffles, and I swore his voice cracked. "You are under arrest for the murder of Tedric James Paston, Earl of Gaulshire."

I glanced at my servant and my apprentice, who both watched without a word. Aselin stared in shock, but Edmund stood boastfully stoic in a way that terrified my core. In that moment, I realized the same streak that ran through Aselin manifested in her brother. I had underestimated him for years.

A wagon with bars had pulled up outside my cottage. Haylan dragged me to the wooden cart without another word, and I endured my second ride to the gaols in a handful of months.

But this time was different.

This time, my heart shattered, and the shards labored my breath. I could not breathe.

This time, I traveled to my father's gaols, my childhood playground. I barely comprehended being imprisoned in Cranshire, this eluded my capacity.

Twilight peaked when we arrived. Most of the staff had left for the day, and to his credit, Haylan escorted me to a back cell himself. He pulled me along the vacant hallways with a firm grasp around my upper arm. Now that we were on Haylan's turf, and not at my estate, confidence returned to his posture. His steps were purposeful, and my own reluctant shuffle struggled to maintain pace.

Haylan assigned me the most private holding, away from other offenders who might taunt, or witnesses who might gape. I wondered if I had been afforded such privilege as a woman or a lifelong friend. Either way, no one else saw me enter the prison. It then occurred to me he may have picked the distant cell so we could talk. He unfastened my chains and entered the cell with me, closing the door behind.

I stood tall looking at Haylan, waiting for him to speak first. My stubbornness irritated him. He wished for me to beg forgiveness, or better, provide some elaborate plea of innocence he could use to set me free and end this horror. But I possessed too much arrogance and vowed to show the man who refused me that I bore no regret. I stared him down, waiting him out.

"Did you do it?" Haylan's direct question conveyed emotional exhaustion; he had to get to the point.

"What do you believe?" I challenged, trying to withdraw what evidence had been compiled against me.

"God's death, Lavinia, I do not know! Until yesterday I would never have... But after seeing your supplies and Father Eustace..."

"Which led you to what conclusion?" I questioned once more in a comforting tone.

"That Lady Gaulshire's story has merit. That you poisoned the Earl of Gaulshire!"

I did not move, standing straight to gaze back at the magistrate with a vacant expression.

"I will ask again, did you do it?" Haylan's eyes filled with tears, pleading with me to provide some shred of logic to unravel the nightmare.

"Did I kill the Earl?" I tested him, remaining strong as I answered the question honestly. "No." I saw an ember of yearning ignite within his eye. Remembering the pain he had caused me with the news of his courtship, I extinguished the fleeting hope without mercy. The assassin within took over. "No, I did not spoon the mushrooms into his mouth. I did not hold him down or force him to consume the fungus. He ate them willingly, even eagerly."

"But you gave him poison mushrooms, Lavinia!" Haylan shouted, aggravated.

"He never asked if they contained poison and I refrained from offering that detail."

"That does not matter!" His voice echoed through the chamber as anger broke through. I never discerned who sparked the fury: himself for having uncovered my scheme or myself for having committed the acts. But after a moment, he gathered his composure and asked the more difficult question.

"Why?"

Haylan's word hung between us. This was the question I had been dreading, the one I had no notion how to answer.

I could not condemn Akworth, not if I had any hope he might be mad enough to save me twice.

I could not reveal Agnella's motive. The Baron loved her and implicating her would be worse than revealing Akworth's part in the plot. I also did not know what lie she told to save herself from suspicion.

For the first time, I broke my stare, turning away in search of clarity. I doubted I could put my thoughts in a manner he would understand, but I owed Haylan enough to at least try.

"Haylan, my father handed you a profession, one I would gladly have taken if I could. What legacy did he leave me? What future do I have to choose from? You said it yourself, 'wife or habit.' And the one man I would consent to marry has no interest."

Haylan raised his finger. "Do not dare blame this on me, Lavinia."

"I am not," I retorted, quick. "But you have to understand my limited choices. So do not criticize me for pursuing my own trail. I have a steady source of income, I control my own destiny."

"By murdering?"

"That is what *you* call it." I exhaled and watched my breath form a small cloud before I looked down at my hands. The cold of the cell permeated through my dress and now threatened to invade my bones.

"Not just me, Lavinia." Haylan retrieved the blanket from the mattress and draped it over my shoulders. "The Justice of Peace, the King, society, the Bible!"

I did not offer a response.

His chest fell as he looked to me, his eyes swelled with tears he refused to let escape. With a gentle hand, he reached out to finger the petals of the flower pendant I wore around my neck, the delicate piece he gave me. I knew what he thought. He wanted to ask how I could have done this to *him*. But even now, he spared me that pain. The action conveyed enough.

Haylan's hand withdrew, and the magistrate took over, trying to put the puzzle together. "How did you even come in contact with the Countess?"

"She did not know beforehand," I quickly lied to provide obligated cover. "Rumors stated she was unhappy in her marriage and I provided a way out trying to win her favor."

Haylan shook his head unable to comprehend. "But that does not answer my original question: why?"

I turned away once more, fearful I had already said too much.

Haylan pressed, "How many acts have you committed? How did you even learn to make such atrocities? How could you defile your father's name, after everything he stood for?"

That crossed a line, he dared to invoke my father. My fists tightened in frustration as Haylan continued, relentless.

"Why? Lavinia? Why would you ever commit such a heinous act?"

I could not further withstand the interrogation and snapped with inflamed range, letting the blanket fall to the floor. "Because I wanted to!"

My temples throbbed as I glared back at the man I loved. It hurt to see myself diminished in his eyes, to know I broke his heart, to know he would condemn me regardless of everything. In that moment, I wished to cause him the same pain, and so, I continued.

"Because it is the one time where *I* am in control! *I* decide who lives and dies. *I* decide how much they struggle, how long they will convulse until they suffocate on their own vomit, or waste away a prisoner inside their own unresponsive body. With my own hands, I make the poisons which pollute their blood. My own creations. Ideas from the mind of an underestimated woman.

"Why do I kill them? Because I crave the thrill of planning the act. The anticipation, the skill and bravery it requires. I covet that instant they realize what is happening, what I have done. The sweet fear in their eyes. The desperate pleas which follow; because while I may be the one who poisoned them, I am the sole witness to their pathetic cries. How I live for the moment the last wisps of life leave their body. The flare of elation when their final breath is exhaled, and my victim degrades to a pile of flesh."

I stopped for a moment to catch my breath, my voice turned sinister as I pressed closer to Haylan, driving home the last nail.

"Why do I kill them? Because I can."

At that moment, the "Lavinia" Haylan held in his heart perished. My own heart broke, seeing hatred form in his eyes. The seconds of exhilaration from my speech had not been worth the pain I caused us both. Without further word, Haylan left me alone in my cell.

I had lost him forever.

Chapter Eleven

That night, in a rare moment of weakness, I let myself cry. My eyes swelled. My cheeks were streaked with dried salt. My bodice was striated with wet lines.

Since the rough, chiseled stone walls proved cold to the touch, I huddled against the wooden door, unwilling to touch the foul mattress. There, coiled into a ball, I liberated my tears. I do not know how long I grieved, but when I gained enough control to stop, my chest and throat ached.

Releasing the emotion proved calming and subsided the whirlpool of confusion spinning in my head. Only after I had cried myself dry could I start to make sense of my thoughts by considering them one at a time.

Haylan.

My dear Haylan... Now, it was my turn to finger the pendant, grateful he had restrained from ripping it from my neck. I regretted my tirade. Haylan did not deserve those words, nor the disregard I gave him. It was a moment of selfishness, birthed from my inability to handle the cascade of emotions.

What would I say when we next met? Would he hear or ever believe an apology? Of course, that all depended on what he now thought of me.

Did he still see me as a sister?

For years I had loathed the label, I now prayed it held true.

Did he see me as a common criminal?

Was his pain so great he would detach from our past? I feared I would become nothing more than another prisoner in his gaols. Perhaps it was foolish to hope, but it did not seem possible. I doubted Haylan could discard me. He might hate me with every fiber, but I would not be forsaken.

More likely, he was still in shock.

The complexity of the situation would require time. I tried to place myself in his shoes. He must have felt betrayed. He must have considered me lost, and I worried he might blame himself.

My father had asked him to look after me, and under that guidance, I had veered down this path. I had chosen this life long before my father perished, but Haylan did not know that. Regardless of his temperament when we next met, I needed to tell him he did not hold fault for my choices.

Though, mayhap, it was better if he discarded me.

Given my life was likely forfeit, I cared more about his mental state than my own. If it would save him from anguish, then I wanted him to cast me aside. Perhaps he could preserve our good memories. Perhaps my rant made it easier for him to let me go. And with that thought, my own guilt subsided.

One thing I did know with certainty: I still thought the same of him. I loved him, even at that moment.

I loved every part of him: the cunning which had unraveled the clues with speed. His ideals that had set his moral compass against his heart and prevailed. Haylan had stayed true to himself, despite everything.

And he had not betrayed me. I did realize that. If anything, not arresting me would have betrayed my father's legacy, everything he bequeathed to Haylan, and that would have hurt more.

My fists clenched with the thought. I still resented that Haylan had mentioned my father, and I refused to ponder his question of what my father would say. I obviously abstained from that line of thought because I already knew. My father had devoted his life to a justice I disgraced. I was the one who betrayed his legacy, but at the time, I could not admit the fact. Self-centered, I viewed murder as my right.

Instead, the invocation of my father turned my thoughts towards the years I had lost with him — the singular injustice of my life. While he had outlived my mother by well over a decade, he still died too young. I missed my father every day. What I would have given for his hands to cup my face one more time, to feel the security of his presence, to see the love in his deep brown eyes. He would have loved me still, despite everything.

I wonder, if he had lived longer, if I would have been on a conventional path. Haylan was right about one thing: my father would have seen me properly wed. He would have worked tirelessly to ensure a fine match, to raise a dowry, to secure the best future he could.

But what future would that have been?

Once I had killed Baines, I could not have stopped. The ecstasy tasted too sweet, and my appetite proved insatiable. Marriage vows to anyone other than Haylan would have been a lie. Tending to a home would have been its own prison, and even at that moment, I preferred the one with stone walls. I had taken a risk and did not regret my decisions. To make a choice is to live. I had followed my calling, embraced my gruesome passion, and the freedom of that knowledge transcended the cell bars.

My cell was large compared to the one in Matheson. The air smelled musty, and I assumed the freezing room had remained uninhabited for some time. Pulling the blanket tight around me, I clenched it so hard my knuckles turned white, but my efforts failed to ward off the unbearable chill. My body shook, rattling the cell door against the jam. In desperation, I curled on the tattered mattress, praying it did not have fleas. At least it kept my body away from the stone floor.

Throughout the night, I stared at the door, willing it to open. Where was my guardian angel with his lantern? My eyes had been fountains hours before, and now, they turned dry from staring. I laid on my side, waiting, praying for the two wrought iron latches to bend. I wondered if this night watch could also be bought with sacks of gold. My father would never have given in to such bribery, but I could not say the same for his men. Regardless, most of his men were long gone, and Haylan had unlikely amassed the same loyalty amongst his staff.

As the night progressed, my hope faded. Unable to sleep, my mind raced with contemplation. I thought of Aselin, hoping she might now pray for me in my hour of need. I thought of Agnella, wondering if she had found peace. I thought of Akworth who had started everything. Who had believed in my skill and laid down the challenge. And when I finally put it all together, I laughed aloud.

I had been so stupid! It became obvious then: the Baron had played a long-game for his love. Matheson had been a trial run for Akworth's real target, the Earl.

If I had failed with the Viscount, he would have found another way to pass his bill through the House — if there even was a bill. If I happened to take Matheson out, then it sweetened the real goal of testing an unknown assassin. My performance in Cranshire had been sufficient for Akworth to trust me with the biggest gamble of his life. But two jobs, and two trips to prison did not provide a convincing record. And now that he had a clear path to Agnella, Akworth no longer required a low-level poison assassin. I challenged myself to think like the Baron, to see the entire chessboard and the revelation manifested in one conclusion.

There was no rescue coming.

That night, I learned to step back and examine the larger picture. To think multiple moves ahead. I could plan every minute detail of a job. I could reason through the most difficult refinement and extraction. But I did not possess the strategic mind of Akworth. Nor of Aselin, for that matter. At least that night, I began to try.

Even with the new perspective, I could not discern any angle to aid my current predicament. If Agnella had given me up, then Akworth would as well. Father Eustace and Edmund seemed ready to testify against me, if not eager. Nothing could be gained from denial and, given the seriousness of the crime, confession would not result in leniency.

I could not tell the whole truth: that I worked for Akworth and Agnella. Whatever their testimony, Akworth would be sure they matched, and my word would not hold up to two peers. And above all, I valued my honor. Even if I had been used, they were my clients, and I would not betray them. My own stupidity left the trail which exposed us all; they had not turned me in by their own will.

I resolved not to betray Aselin, either. Edmund would have protected her, and she would have lied for herself. Nothing could be gained from revealing her part in the plot. The fact Haylan only arrested me remained a good sign Akworth and Agnella also planned to spare her. If Aselin could carry on my legacy, in a way, I would live on through her works.

But where did that leave my own fate?

I laid awake the entire evening, pondering, unable to identify a viable angle. My mind wasted in unproductive thought until the delivery of bread and broth marked the morning's arrival. The guard did not speak while he set the tray on the floor, but his eyes made sure I was still present. He probably had not even realized my gender in the flow of his routine. I ate slowly in my cell, listening to the wind beyond the walls. The broth warmed my core, and the restoration of strength filled my heart with resolve.

I knew what I must do.

Having made my decision, I began to accept my fate. I would go down on my own terms. My testimony would drop the jaw of every witness in the hall. I would provide detail of each murder, going back to Baines and after. Their eyes would grow, realizing how long I ran unchecked through the shire. Hell, I would even take credit for Lord Matheson. Word would spread of the deaths by my hands. While I had been caught, the score tipped heavily in my favor. One loss would barely blemish my record of unbridled death.

I vowed someday, bards would sing poems of the Poison Mistress from Gaulshire.

I practiced my speech until I achieved perfection. The stone walls became the jury. The door, the Justice of Peace. I closed my eyes, inhaling strength and bravery. I envisioned the shock in their eyes and craved the gasps that would rob the room of air. My pride blossomed, swelling within my chest. I was ready for them.

But where were the guards?

Once I finished composing my speech, the unknown hours passed slow, and my body grew restless. What was taking so long?

This had been a straightforward case, especially given the magistrate himself had collected the evidence.

Leaning against the wall, I resumed my watch of the iron hinges. Over half the day passed before they finally creaked open.

My heart fell to see anyone other than Haylan. A man I did not recognize entered the cell and did not even bother to close the door behind. Though in truth, we both knew I could not outrun nor outmuscle him. He looked at me with expectation, and after a moment of silence, I was not sure what he wanted.

"Get up, wench," he ordered. "The Earl of Gaulshire wants to see you."

CHAPTER TWELVE

The Earl of Gaulshire?

Flashbacks of Matheson clouded my judgment. I had already killed the Earl. It was the very reason I was in the cell! My mind processed the confusion until I understood the guard meant the *new* Earl, Agnella's son.

The Justice of Peace should have been the one to hand down my sentence, but I suppose, given the personal nature of the crime, the new Earl would want to do it himself. Near to my age, Kelton Darley was young for an Earl and would need to expeditiously prove he could fill his step-father's legacy. Bringing the late Earl's murderer to swift justice would be a good first step.

I stood tall before the guard. This moment started the role I had chosen to play. A captured criminal, yes, but one who had nothing except pride for her victories.

The guard did not have the patience for my game. He pushed me against the wall, much the same as Haylan had the day prior, and bound my hands behind my back with rope. By a tight grip around my forearm, he led me through the empty corridors of the gaols to a waiting wagon outside.

Relief washed over me as we left the city limits of Marfield. The undeveloped hills were easier to accept than curious eyes beyond the bars of my cage. The green grass had degraded to brown with winter's first snow, and the trees were as barren as my heart. Fighting trepidation, I reconsidered how to play the upcoming exchange. It was one thing to be smug, but another to do it in front of the son of my victim. I understood the pain of losing a father.

Kelton would play the grieving son, despite the fact Tedric was his step-father. He would have to show remorse out of obligation, but I doubted it plagued his heart as much as he would let on. The thought reestablished my resolution as the wagon passed through the estate gate. If I could maintain defiance in front of the man I loved, I could do it in front of Kelton Darley.

We proceeded passed the receiving porch and around the estate to a stark rear entrance. The top of the door's brass handle was discolored with wear, and the weathered wood splintered along the hinge. A small, cracked window was inset into the door. This part of the estate was not meant to be seen, and I reasoned my visit was covert.

Perplexed by the thought, I missed the guard's command to exit the wagon, and he pulled me through the small opening by my elbow with force. If I was not meant to be seen, then Kelton did not intend to brag about my quick capture. My mind raced, trying to discern what net the Earl attempted to cast. Yesterday's lesson flashed fresh in my mind. Reexamining the situation from every angle, I still failed to develop a single theory.

The guard led me through narrow servant corridors, past overcrowded boarding rooms, piles of laundry waiting to be washed, and hooks holding various brooms. The wooden steps creaked beneath my boots as we ascended to the second floor of the manor and into a small office at the top of the stairs.

The room appeared to be in a form of organized chaos. Some walls featured paintings paired thoughtfully with items that must have held significance to their owner. Other walls had empty nails and sideways tapestries. A stack of crates stood in the far corner with leather bound records half filling the open, top box. I deduced we stood in the new Earl's former office, assumingly half-relocated to a more appropriate room.

A small, framed oil painting of Agnella on the bookcase caught my eye. She was escorted by an attractive man, too young to be her first husband. Before I could further examine the portrait, the guard dragged me to the far side of the room as footsteps approached from the hallway. Anxious blood thumped against my temple as I refocused on the door.

"Leave us," the man commanded as he entered the room.

My guard recanted in protest, "My Lord, she is a confessed murder..."

"I said, leave us." His voice remained calm but this time, resounded firm with unwavering authority.

The guard gave me a quick glance unsure, but followed his instructions, closing the door behind as he exited.

The man was the same from the painting. He had Agnella's long, oval face with a delicate nose and brown eyes matching the color of his short hair. The worn leather of his boots needed desperate polishing, but the purple tunic looked too pristine not to be new. I assumed his wardrobe was symbolic of his current state of adjustment to the sudden ascension. Like mine, his life was in the midst of upheaval, and I wondered if he had been part of the plot.

"Lavinia Maud." From his tone, I remained unsure if he asked or spit my name in disgust.

Regardless, I maintained a tall posture, daring to look him in the eyes as I offered the expected polite curtsey. Though with my hands still bound behind my back, my action lacked the grace I wished to convey.

"I presume I am in the presence of the new Earl of Gaulshire?" I offered more of a smirk than a smile. "You have your mother's allure."

Kelton scoffed, walking towards me, critically analyzing. His curious lack of resentment or anger struck me. I had just killed his step-father. If he cared, there should have been an iota of malice, and he did not even attempt to make a show of it. I had guessed correctly. The Earl reached out and ran a finger along my chin, maintaining eye contact as he attempted to rattle me. Inside, I only laughed, willing to indulge a game of nerve.

"I am not what you expected, am I?" My challenge hung in the air between us, and my correct assertion seemed to startle the man.

"No. I expected my father's killer to be more…" He broke off, unsure of the word.

"Menacing? Older?" I offered, toying with him. "Less demure?"

"Yes."

He walked around me as I stared forward, permitting the examination.

"If I were any of those things, I would be less successful in my profession."

The Earl exhaled as he finished his lap to stand before me once again. "I suppose so."

For several moments, we maintained a silent game of chicken before I took control. "Ask me what you want to know."

He turned, breaking our stare, and took several paces away before addressing me again, "Why?"

I smiled, having guessed the question. Unable to relate to my urges, everyone always wanted to know *why*. "I am sure the magistrate gave a full report."

"Yes, but I want to hear it from you."

"It is rumored your step-father no longer pleased your mother. I wished to earn her favor by providing a way out." Unsure he bought my lie, I elaborated. "Birth handed you prestige and the inheritance of a title when your mother wed. For us on the bottom, we have to take risks to rise so high in one lifetime. I took a premeditated gamble. Yes, your mother mourns, but do you believe it is out of anything other than obligation?"

Kelton did not respond but continued his pacing. I maintained my still, tall posture, hoping my unexpected behavior would throw his guard.

"She did not want this," he finally offered. "Yes, Tedric did not fill her heart as much as my father, but she would not have wanted *this*."

I swallowed, suppressing the desire to demonstrate I knew better and maintained the secrecy of my client. "Then I misestimated, my Lord." I bowed my head in respect. "I spent my risk on the wrong mark, and I am gravely sorry."

The Earl turned, surprised by my words in a way I did not understand. After a moment of consideration, he spoke again, "They say you have been an assassin for several years. Who has kept you employed all this time?"

"The world is full of men whose ambitions exceed their station. Assassination is an easy answer to precarious rivals or inconvenient husbands. My clients are numerous and diverse, but, on my honor, I will not betray their identities."

Kelton's eyes narrowed, and he stepped forward, making his challenge. "Even so, I do not believe you would take out an Earl on your own accord. Give me the name, a name of even one person with whom you conspired, and I will release you free this day."

I bit my lip, reading his face and weighing my options. The offer came unexpected and made little sense. What would he say if I gave up his mother? Or Akworth? Why would he free a confessed murderer? Unless he thought I represented the bottom of a vast conspiracy against his family or a greater threat loomed. Both options seemed farfetched, but a sudden stroke of inspiration flowed through me. Perhaps I could begin to plot this game of chess after all.

I could think of one other reason. For once in my life, I put the pieces together correctly in time. The line of questioning, and his behavior, only made sense if he already knew.

I shook my head, defiant, and lied poor on purpose. I wanted to pass this loyalty test in spite of the truth. "I acted alone."

The force in which he slammed my body into the back wall knocked the wind from my lungs. My head fell back and hit the corner of a frame, leaving a small spot of blood on the plaster.

Kelton's anger resonated through the room as his fingertips dug into my shoulders. "I know the Baron had a part in this. You will speak the truth to me!"

He slammed my bound body against the wall once more. My dazed mind raced, but I stayed true to my ideals. I had made up my mind in the cell last night when I had had time to contemplate. It would be foolish to change course under forced pressure.

"I used the Baron to get to your mother!" I shouted back into his face. "He did not know, he is innocent."

Kelton stared into my eyes as I breathed heavily. After several breaths of his own, he let go of my tense frame. With the sudden withdrawal of support, my feet did not find their footing in time to prevent my body from sliding to the floor.

Kelton stepped a few paces away as his face unexpectedly softened. "My mother said you were trustworthy. I needed to see for myself." His hand rummaged through his pocket before he tossed a coin in my direction. "I know the whole truth, that my mother asked for your assistance."

The coin clanked as it hit the ground on its edge, bouncing towards me and spinning before it came to rest. The embedded topaz chip glimmered like a ray of hope. The engraved wolfsbane flower shined within the bronze.

"But what I do not understand," the Earl shook his head in confusion, "is she gave you up to the magistrate. Why did you not reveal her part in the whole plot?"

I believed he questioned my motive with sincerity, unable to fathom the act of selflessness. I looked up to him from my crumpled position on the floor and spoke from the heart. "She was my client, my Lord. It is that simple."

He laughed in exasperation but unsheathed a knife from his calf. "From everything my mother has told me, I do not understand where you choose to draw your lines of morality, but we are thankful for them." He turned me around and sliced the bindings around my wrists.

I regarded him in shock before accepting his outstretched hand of assistance to stand.

"You have proven your loyalty to the Baron," Kelton continued, "in Cranshire and again last night. So I will make you an offer, Mistress Maud. This one is genuine but comes without room for negotiation. If you choose to decline, my guard will take you to the Justice of Peace who will hand down a sentence of execution."

For the first time, my voice trembled, faced with yet another illusion of choice. "What is your offer?"

"From this day forward, I will be your sole client. Akworth be damned. You will live in a small cottage on this estate and take no visitors. You will accept whatever mark I declare. I expect absolute loyalty and discretion. If there is even a whisper of your endeavors or connection to my house, you will be executed. In return, you keep your life and will live in the comforts to which you are accustomed."

My head spun. A few months ago, this would have been a dream. To have such a patron! I would no longer need to worry about finances and could devote my time and attention to my extractions, to perfecting my craft. But now, when the offer came as blackmail, it felt like a trap.

But for Kelton to make such an offer, he had to have a mark in mind. Afraid I trotted on unstable terrain, I prodded with care. "Does my Lord have an intended mark?"

"Yes," Kelton stated with a tone implying the stupidity of the question. "Otherwise, I would have made your execution public and taken credit for bringing down my father's murderer. Instead, we will contain the rumor and release a public statement of death from a burst appendix."

I nodded. "And the identity of the mark?"

Kelton's patience waned. "I said no negotiation. Your answer, Mistress Maud?"

My mind remembered a similar conversation with Akworth's man. Once again, I did not have a choice. I bent down and picked up my signal coin, holding it out to my new patron. "Yes." Inside my stomach knotted. "Yes, of course."

The Earl nodded, taking the coin. "Good. Are we clear on the terms of the agreement?"

"Yes, my Lord," I answered again, unable to deny oncoming nausea. Nothing about the arrangement felt assuring.

"I assume you read and write?" He retrieved a piece of parchment and quill from a box in the corner. Seeing my nod, he placed the items on the empty desk and motioned for me to sit. "Make a list of everything you need to continue your work."

I stared at the parchment, afraid I would forget an item, but then realized the potential. No one else in the shire, save Aselin, would know the difference between genuine need and the greedy desire of a poison maker. I sat at the desk and started writing a long list of my wildest desires. With the conversation turning to my craft, my uneasy stomach settled.

"Most of the equipment I need exists in the cellar workroom of my cottage. However my stores are currently low, and many things will need to be acquired new. Mortars and pestles, a grinder, funnels, blotting paper, thermometers, scales, tweezers, full reserves of lye and acetone, cheesecloth, crucibles, appropriate glassware and a forge. I will need a workbench, isolated from the rest of my living quarters. Aprons, mouth coverings, gloves." I wrote the items as I spoke and more, my quill scratching against the parchment in a flurry of motion. "I had finished harvesting the seeds from my poison garden a few weeks ago. They should be recovered along with my poison stores, for that collection cannot be rebuilt. I will need pots to start seedlings, a protected place to plant in the spring — unless . . ." my eyes glittered with the possibility.

"Unless what?" Kelton seemed unamused by the growing list.

"Unless your mother could spare space in her grow room? That would allow my plants to gain a head start over the natural growing seasons."

"I will speak to her. What else?"

"Live vermin for test subjects. My journals." I paused trying to think of what else I could desire. "I am sure there are items I am forgetting at the moment."

The Earl exhaled, taking the list from my hand. "We can speak of other needs as they arise. In the meantime, I will send someone to your estate to fetch these items and procure the remaining supplies."

I nodded. "My Lord, the exact supplies I will need first depends on the selected poison for your mark, which of course, depends on their identity."

Kelton muttered and paced before taking a seat on the corner of the desk. He examined his hands in contemplation, deciding to fully take me into his trust. He was a mother's boy. Without his mother's assurance, I doubt he would have disclosed the mark so soon.

"I assume you know Tedric's first wife, Isabel, was found guilty of treason after she conspired with a French agent. Their son, Silas, never faced charges for the same crime, but enough rumors circulate for him to be disgraced in the eyes of many."

I nodded, already familiar with the politics. "What do you believe?"

"What I believe does not matter," The Earl responded without heart. "He is the firstborn of the Earl of Gaulshire, and many see him as the rightful heir, despite my father's edict after his second marriage. Silas has a blood claim to my new title."

"Does he intend to seek it?"

"That also does not matter." Kelton continued without hesitation. "You will dispose of him before he has the chance."

I swallowed.

At least now, I knew.

"I cannot rule with him looming in the background," he offered without prompt, "with another option readily available, the moment I slip or am forced to choose between two sides. His presence strangles my authority."

I smiled inside. Like his mother, the Earl had found it necessary to provide justification. Since his words were more for his benefit than mine, I bolstered his line of thinking. After all, I had a new patron to cajole.

"I agree, my Lord. You are wise beyond your years. For the stability of our shire, your authority must not be diminished. You cannot serve your subjects if your attention is divided."

"Exactly." Kelton smiled, relaxing.

I welcomed my patron's newfound ease which lightened the mood in the room, even as my head still ached from being slammed into the wall.

"Do you have a preferred method, my Lord?"

"Silas and I are on cordial terms, nothing more," he offered. "Now that I have been named Earl, I expect that will degrade. Do you have anything tasteless, something that cannot be detected by any means and acts with a delay? A poison that assures there will be no connection to me?"

"That would be the Holy Grail of my trade, would it not?"

I looked down at my feet wondering if I should even bring up the possibility. This was a risk, but it would buy time in case the Earl meant to discard me after Silas. My prideful arrogance also took over, and I still held faith, from the depths of my soul, I could purify the bean.

"It is believed such a poison could be purified from a plant nicknamed *Palm of Christ,* more commonly referred to as the castorbean. It is said a poison could be made that is tasteless, colorless, and odorless. This summer, I obtained a plant, and its seeds are part of the stores your men should retrieve. However, no one has been able to make a sufficient extraction. I am in the midst of my own experimentation and remain hopeful, but the recipe remains elusive."

Kelton's eyes lit with the possibility. "Do you think you can discern how to make such a toxin?"

"I am confident in my abilities, my Lord. Though I can offer no promises of a schedule."

"Six months," Kelton stated quick, sending a pain of nervousness to my gut and confirming his ignorance regarding my craft.

"My Lord..." My protests were silenced by his immediate hand.

"I expect results in six months. You shall resume your research immediately. It will be less conspicuous if Silas does not die so soon after my ascension anyways."

My mouth hung open in dismay, my mind appraising the feasibility with rapid assessment. Six months. At least the deal provided six more months to live — if discretion could be maintained.

"My Lord," I questioned with hesitation, "how many know I am here? How many know the truth?" The Earl's face turned somber. I almost felt guilty for removing his peace so soon after it had been obtained. "I ensured the group remained few in number. Myself, my mother and Edward," he counted on his fingers. "The guard who brought you here, Magistrate Moryet..." His voice broke off in thought.

I added to his list, "The magistrate obtained evidence from Father Eustace who knows my true profession. With your permission, I will ensure the priest is silenced. What about the guard, my Lord?"

Kelton shook his head. "Loyal to me, I am not concerned."

"And the magistrate?" I held my breath unsure how I wished him to answer. If Haylan had pledged conspiratorial allegiance to Kelton Darley, the tenants I held dear would have collapsed. But if Haylan was not already in on this scheme, his grave waited.

The Earl shrugged. "I met him yesterday. Do you know him?"

Did I know him? I laughed inside at the cruel irony. "I do, my Lord. Well."

My tongue tingled, resisting to speak the words which would set Haylan's noose. But my mind harbored no doubt of what needed to be done and not liking the fact did not change its validity. I swallowed, bit my lip and then proceeded before my mind could change. "The magistrate cannot be threatened or bought."

I exhaled as the world continued to collapse around me. In some way, I suppose I always knew we would be pitted against each other, Haylan and I. My choice of profession guaranteed this course. Now that the moment arrived, my heart crushed like ice under a wagon's wheel. But one person mattered to me more than the soul for which my heart craved: above all, I would protect myself.

With that thought, I summoned the courage to continue. "If he knows you are sheltering me…"

Kelton nodded. "Then relieve him of his post."

The command came too surreal to process, so I did not, but I could not keep despair from my face.

"Is there something wrong, Madam Maud?" The Earl challenged.

"No." I swallowed. "No, my Lord."

"Good. Anyone else?"

"My apprentice and her brother know the magistrate took me into custody, nothing more. They will not be an issue as they will stay silent to protect themselves. However, my apprentice would increase the speed with which I might unlock the castorbean's…"

"No," Kelton cut me off before I had finished enunciating my thought. "I am not bringing anyone else into this. And my mother said the girl brought her unease."

Despite the disappointment, I understood the basis for Agnella's impression. Aselin's company would have been welcomed during my long, solitary endeavor, and her experience would have been an asset, but I lacked a position from which to negotiate.

"As you wish," I resigned.

The Earl stood up with expectation. "Anything else, Mistress Maud?"

"No, my Lord Earl."

Kelton made his way to the door of the room. He turned towards me as if to say a final thought, but then changed his mind before departing.

Alone at the desk, I buried my face in my hands. In a matter of moments, I had ensnared myself in a fine-tangled mess, promised to deliver a poison that might not exist, and vowed to kill the man I loved.

CHAPTER THIRTEEN

The new Earl of Gaulshire proved his determination to obtain the ideal poison. Within minutes of our meeting, two men requested detailed descriptions of the items to be retrieved from my house. I described each article with as much detail as possible, but given their looks of confusion, I had little hope it would all be delivered.

The guards obtained the supplies under the ruse of gathering evidence. Edmund and Aselin granted them entrance to my home while pleading ignorance towards any of the equipment. Since Kelton's men were without knowledge and assistance, their performance exceeded my expectations. They missed a few thermometers and vials, but the boxes they delivered the following morning contained most of the list, including my full poison stores, seeds, and journals.

My new cottage overlooked a small pond that froze over after the first snowfall. The abode was smaller than my own estate, though of finer quality. When I first stepped foot into the house, my boots left impressions in a thin layer of dust. Occasional cobwebs caught my face as I examined each room. The air had a mustiness which gave me a cough that first night, but with open windows, it aired out fine.

Kelton dispatched a servant to assist with the cleanup; a young, shy bellibone who ended up with the permanent task of my care. Other than Kelton's routine checks of my progress, Muriel Sallay became my lone connection to the outside world. I was grateful for her company during those long winter months. Together, we made the cottage a suitable dwelling, but Muriel saw to the little details that made it a home. I woke to the smell of fresh bread most mornings, the soft sound of her singing filled the room as she cleaned, and each evening, she pressed a gown in preparation for the next day — and I mean gown. My provided wardrobe consisted of Agnella's old things, but the previous season's dresses were a luxury I savored.

Muriel was about a year younger than Aselin but meek as an abandoned baby bird. During those first few days as we scrubbed the cottage, she barely said a word not required for the task. It became evident she did not know who, or *what* I was, so I could not discern the cause of her intimidation.

Muriel and I could not be more different. She dreamed of tending a home, raising children, and waited for her father to find her a suitable match with the patience expected from my gender. As she swept my borrowed cottage, she lost herself in an imaginary world. She would go on to achieve that dream, but for the time she remained under my employ, I sought to give her a backbone to stand up to her future husband.

Muriel's initial intimidation transformed to awe as we set up my "laboratory." After some prodding, she conveyed her understanding that I was on the verge of discovering a new medicine and the Earl had provided the cottage to allow me to focus on my research. Bless her heart, Muriel was naïve. The fact that a female embarked on such an important endeavor of discovery struck the poor girl with dumbfounded admiration. Her misplaced reverence made me laugh, but I harbored no hesitation to portray the hero she desired with desperation.

Under the Earl's ruse, I taught Muriel how to tend the forge, grind seeds, monitor thermometers and read numbers well enough to operate a scale. At times, it reminded me of the first days with Aselin, though it took far longer for Muriel to provide more aid than hindrance. I offered to teach her to read, but she insisted she had no use for such a skill. In return for what knowledge I did share, Muriel taught me skills her mother had passed down, skills I should have learned from mine: how to prepare a proper stew, to bake a loaf of bread with a crispy crust and soft inside, and the finer points of embroidery. Her companionship kept me sane.

At night, when Muriel returned home, the circumstance poisoned my self-confidence. Each passing day increased the pressure of the Earl's deadline. Never before had I been plagued with such doubt. While I could withstand the moments of weakened self-faith, the looming dread of my next mark haunted every breath. I saw Haylan in every shadow. I heard his voice in the winter winds.

Why? Lavinia? Why would you ever commit such a heinous act?

Gratefully, I was never tormented by the memory of my marks. It is a dreadful condition reported by several of my peers. But thoughts of Haylan brought nightly tears to my eyes, and I understood their suffering for the first time.

It had been several weeks since I pledged allegiance to Kelton, and I could not delay much longer. Haylan had to wonder what became of me. I needed to contain the knowledge before his inquiries spread. He was a man of honor who respected authority, but Kelton's orders would only quench curiosity for so long. Each night, I gazed into the crackling fire of the hearth, attempting to summon courage to plan the necessary task. I prayed. I reminded myself of the logic. I knew the necessity. Still, Haylan was the first mark I questioned if I could kill. In my cowardice, I decided to deal with the priest first.

My borrowed mount struggled with the bitter cold during the half-hour ride into town. Agnella's old cloak proved warm, but I still longed for the comfort and familiarity of my lost green one. Flakes of light snow hung in the air above, indistinguishable from faint stars. I had not returned to Marfield since being carted away in the barred wagon. Inadvertently, the night of my revenge ended up being Gaudete Sunday.

Throughout town, pink candles flickered in windows. Seeing the hung wreaths and garland should have warmed my spirit, but guilt grew where Christmas joy belonged. Distracted by my research, I had not prepared for the Lord's coming, and now, Advent was almost over. But there would be time for penance later. Ignoring my longing, I focused on the task.

Since it was late in the evening, Father Eustace would be alone in the rectory. The path towards the home hid behind the church, providing cover as I approached. The tall, two-story structure featured a river rock facade with a brown, thatch roof. Vines grew up the rock and entwined with a stone cross hung over the front threshold. I had visited the rectory enough times to know the layout and used that knowledge to select the optimal entry point in the rear. With a deep breath of mental preparation, I placed my hand on the door handle and turned.

Hitting an unexpected stop, the knob did not rotate. I stared at the door, surprised to find it locked, but shrugged. The discovery did not dampen my spirits, it only slowed me down.

Father Eustace had become hard of hearing in his old age. Still, the sound of my torsion wrench within the bolt gave me pause. It had been some time since I picked a lock. I learned the skill from one of my early prisoner patrons as payment for his mark. Thankfully, the old rectory lock opened easily. With my hand around the ice-covered knob, I waited until a gust of wind howled before turning the handle again.

Once inside, I lowered the hood of Agnella's old velvet cloak. My skin tingled from the sudden warmth of the room, and I paused for a moment, allowing my fingers to regain feeling. From my post in the entryway, I could see the priest's back, reading in his chair by the hearth.

My cloak lowered to the floor without sound. Underneath, I had worn a plain smock with no undercoat to ensure my movements stayed as silent as possible, but the fabric of my skirt still rustled more than I desired. I shuffled my feet in approach, unwilling to lift a sole and risk the sound of a single footstep against the old floor boards. Making my way forward, ever vigilant, I continued until I stood a foot behind the unsuspecting priest. In position, I retrieved a small, metal vial from my pocket, and with held breath, dumped its contents into the goblet on the side table. After a careful step back, I waited, still as a statue. Moments passed, then minutes, measured by the crackling fire. I began to wonder if the old man had fallen asleep. When I thought I could not wait the duration of another breath, the priest turned the page and reached for his goblet.

My heart pounded in excitement, struggling to contain volatile eagerness. The thrill scratched my ghastly desires on the verge of bliss. My entire body tingled, desperate for the indulgence but agonized by prolonged expectation. I needed to hold on a few moments longer.

As Father Eustace brought the metal goblet to his lips, I nearly burst with anticipation. My eyes beheld the spectacle, unable to blink. The metal was so close to his flesh... My God! The pleasure of that moment, it lingered in ecstasy...

An instant later, liquid burst from his lips in a fantastic spray as he coughed. My rise climaxed, thrilled with the response. The old man found his feet with more speed than I would have wagered and he looked at the goblet in confusion. That was when he noticed my figure in the corner of his eye. His body froze from the fear I hoped to incite. I could not have asked for a better response.

Answering his wordless gaze, I stepped one pace out of the shadow. "I trusted you, Father, and you broke my confidence."

The priest's focus returned to the goblet with new understanding. His hand stiffened, the whites of his eyes were evident in the dark room. For a man who believed in Heaven, I found it ironic he seemed petrified at the thought of death. Father's eyes began to water as he set down the goblet with a shaking hand.

"You broke the sanctity of the sacrament first," his voice wavered. "I could not lie to the magistrate."

I shrugged, my voice smooth. "You chose one sin over the other, but it is still a transgression. It would have been wiser to cross the magistrate than the assassin."

Father Eustace placed a hand on the chair's arm to brace his trembling frame. "Wh... What did you give me?"

"Tsk, tsk," I toyed with glee. "The botanist does not recognize the flavor?"

"Please... Lavinia..."

I laughed and shook my head, donning my cloak to leave. "Anise, Father. All you will suffer is assaulted taste." I sighed, turning to him with a sudden cold expression. "I forgive your trespasses, just as you should have forgiven mine. Betray me again, and next time the additive will not be so benign."

For a moment, my eyes barreled into his, punctuating my threat. Before he could respond, I departed back into the night from whence I came.

It had not been a killing, but God the result tasted as sweet. I longed to watch the priest through the window, to behold the complete cycle of whatever emotions he would endure. Father Eustace should have counted his lucky stars I remained devout, despite the poor tending I received from my priest. I could have done it, we both knew it. That knowledge made me feel more powerful than if I had. Every day he would linger, knowing he lived by my merciful grace.

One loose end had been tied but the other still unraveled with dread. I grew ashamed of my reservation. Mayhap I was not the fearsome poison assassin I claimed.

Haylan had not hesitated to arrest me. It had pained him, yes, but he did not refrain or stall. He had performed his duty in our twisted fate. In effect, he had condemned me first. He knew the sentence that would be handed down and had no reason to believe I would be saved.

So why, after everything, could I not now condemn him in return? For years, he had rejected my love without apology. His courtship of Mary Clements proved the final signal we would never be more. There is no merit in clinging to false hope, but the heart is not pacified by logic, not even an assassin's.

Over the next day, I stared at my stores of poisons, unresolved. Selecting the perfect extraction was usually a highlight of a job, but for this mark, the prospect filled me with despair.

Did I want Haylan to feel pain or pass peacefully? Should it be quick out of love or drawn out as revenge for the torture my own heart had endured? Unable to make a selection, I logically considered my stores, one by one.

Amatoxin — I had recently used death cap mushrooms and doubted Haylan would willfully eat anything I served.

Strychnine, or the name I preferred, Saint-Ignatius' bean — After witnessing the drawn-out, ghastly death of the ring thief in the brothel last spring, I could not condemn my beloved to such suffering.

Hemlock — A worse death than the beans.

Wolfsbane — At least the act could be accomplished through simple exposure and not digestion, but I did not want my last memories of Haylan to be vomit filled.

Mandrake — Again, a consumption problem. And Haylan did not deserve the same fate as Baines.

Belladonna or camphor oil would have been good possibilities if my stores were not already depleted.

Of my remaining supplies that left potato poison or the apricot acid.

I stared at the two vials, hoping for divine inspiration.

Potato Poison induces a deep sleep, providing a peaceful death, but it is less potent and requires a larger dose.

The failed attempt on Lord Matheson tainted my opinion of an apricot extraction, but despite my bitter memory, it remained the best choice. Haylan's death would be painless and quick. He would slip unresponsive before convulsions began and then pass from an inability to breathe. I admit, I also wanted to redeem my previous failure with a successful use of the acid.

But I still needed a method of exposure.

Years ago, a Guild contact had written of grinding a powder so fine it could be blown into the target's face and inhaled for a more immediate effect. The concept avoided the complication of needing the magistrate to consume a tainted bite, and I liked the idea of the method's intimacy. I decided this was finally the mark to try the curious technique myself.

When the sun again rose, I faked a cold and dismissed Muriel. Knowing the intended target, I wanted to craft the purification myself. To grind the pits with care, to stir the crucibles with love, to pour my sweat and effort into one final gift for Haylan. Once Muriel tucked me into bed with a broth to her satisfaction, I convinced her to depart, suggesting a quiet cottage would foster healing sleep.

I waited a few minutes to ensure she had left and then leapt out of bed with strange vigor. I put my work smock over the nightgown and fastened the hedge bindweed flower pendant around my neck. After straightening the delicate charm in the hand mirror, my heart and head finally felt ready for the task.

Walking towards my workbench was a march of bewilderment. I remained eager to begin the process, but conscious of the solemnity of my work. The most attractive quality of the apricot seed acid became the meditative benefit of its preparation. Never before had I ground the pit meat so fine, or measured with such precision. I prepared a large batch to replenish my stores, and admittedly, I wanted to stall any way I could. Having started the extraction, I had accepted what I set out to accomplish but was not yet prepared for the finality. My stomach cramped every time I dwelled upon the intended mark.

While I watched the mixture bubble in the forge, my throat tightened as my mind turned to memories: the games we played as children, how he always knew where to find the year's best blueberry bushes. Haylan had escorted me in my father's funeral procession, holding my hand the entire journey. He had laid the first handful of dirt on the lowered coffin when my fingers refused to unfurl.

I choose to dwell on the good times. My mouth parched remembering his visits for afternoon sage water. My heart craved the way his eyes would gaze at me as if I were the only woman in the world. The charming dimple of his smile, how my body fit within his… He had a way of making me feel special. I just never became special enough.

Losing myself in the process, in concentration, in the magnitude of the task, the work calmed my anxiety. I toiled late into the night, unaware of the passing time. With diligence, I completed the purification and had a pan of powder drying in front of the hearth by morning.

Christmas Eve morning.

I should have been home, decorating the cottage with evergreens and brewing mulled mead. Perhaps Aselin and Edmund carried out those traditions in my absence. Likely they laid low, trying to blend in, which meant they would be preparing to attend midnight mass. Aselin hated church, but she understood it brought more attention if she did not attend. Edmund adored the ritual. I doubt he believed, but it allowed him to pretend they were a normal sibling pair for one night. There would be questions of my location, and I longed to know what lie they had spread. Enough had seen me carted away to spread rumors. Though perhaps, I was already old news and forgotten.

My heart also grieved for the lost potential within my apprentice. She had a gift that now wilted unnurtured. I wondered what she would do. She had tasted the sweetness of murder twice, and eventually, the craving would become overwhelming. The desire ran deep into her core, and without my guidance, I feared what recourse she might pursue. With unpolished skills, she would be caught if she attempted a mark. Her poison repertoire was limited. And God help her if she attempted to contact the Guild without a kill of her own.

Lost in my thoughts, my eyes stared at the flames of the hearth reflecting off the metal pan of powder. To be unaccompanied on Christmas is to be truly alone. There was no mass I could attend, no party in which I could partake. No one would give me a gift come morning nor would I experience the joy of giving. With no other way to keep vigil, I sang myself asleep as the last glowing embers faded in the hearth.

God rest you, merry gentlemen, let nothing you dismay.
Remember Christ our Saviour was born on Christmas-day,
To save my soul from Satan's power which long time had gone astray.

Chapter Fourteen

Despite my vigilant preparation of the magistrate's toxin, there was still the problem of unknown proportioning for a new method of exposure. I longed to go to the market and find another unsuspecting lad, but I could not risk drawing attention. If anyone recognized me, too many questions would arise that could not be answered. I took Kelton Darley to be a man of his word. If suspicion stirred, he would take the necessary means to protect himself. I lived because he deemed me a viable path towards his desire.

The smart choice would have been to rely on a known toxin and find an opportunity to solve the consumption dilemma. I could have waited until Haylan patronized a tavern, perhaps when he courted Mary Clements. There would likely be undesired casualties, and while I remained comfortable with that fact, the thought of such a murder did not satisfy the yearning of my heart.

This assassination had to be special, it was Haylan after all. I wanted to give him the best. I wanted our final moments to be intimate, just the two of us, to look into his eyes as he realized his fate.

Instead, I chose to decrease my plan's risk through testing. Given my past lesson, a human test subject was warranted. However, the prospect seemed impossible while living in isolation.

I pondered the dilemma for two days. Muriel asked me three times why I seemed so distant. She accepted the excuse of being deep in thought on the verge of a new breakthrough. The lie seemed to motivate her efforts; she loved being a part of something bigger than herself and prepared my requested compost with renewed vigor.

I did not know if Agnella agreed outright, or if Kelton ordered it so, but the Countess granted me space in her grow room. That evening, I intended to deliver the first pots. It was a welcomed distraction to my Haylan predicament. And the quicker I reestablished my garden, the more beans I would have for experimentation. The New Year was three days away, and the six-month deadline would be over earlier than I cared to admit. I wondered how my unique plants would fare in the miniature greenhouse. However, the prospect of the grow room also appealed to me since care of the plants would require my frequent visit to the estate. Muriel's simple-minded companionship grew mundane, and I welcomed any excuse to leave the confinement of my cottage.

Within the hour, we had two pots of belladonna and three castorbean plants prepared with compost soil and germinating seeds. It was a good first start. After donning my heaviest cloak, hat, and gloves, we made the short trek through fresh powder to the Earl's estate under the moonlight.

Muriel knew her way through the servant quarters and led us on a direct path. When we arrived, we found Agnella tending to a potted spike. The setting winter sun shone through the windows, casting a yellow haze around her radiant figure curiously unclothed in black. Instead, Agnella wore a rose-colored gown that matched the rouge adorning her pale cheeks. The fabric billowed loose around her frame, but even still, her pregnant belly could not be concealed. Upon entering, I dropped to a reluctant deep curtsey. Despite the ambiance, anger invaded my thoughts as I beheld my condemner.

"My Lady," I offered, wondering how I would be received.

Agnella turned to face me. It was the first time we had met since I had turned her into a murderer; the first time since she had betrayed me. She spoke with reluctance after a deep exhale, "I knew I could not avoid you indefinitely."

I dared not assume we remained on a first name basis. "My Lady, if it would please you, I can return another…"

"No," she interrupted with surrender. "There is no need. However, Mistress Sallay, if you would please give us the room."

Muriel eyed us both curious, stalling more than expected, but excused herself without further word after setting down the pots. I hoped the delay showed she grew less meek under my influence. Though the fact that the Countess knew the full names of each of her servants impressed me as a testament to her character. The singular display was enough to soften my ire.

"My Lady," I continued. "Thank you for the gracious use of space in your grow room."

Agnella waved her hand in dismissal. "Of course. It is the least I can do."

I nodded, contemplating her words. I appreciated the implied apology.

The highest shelf had been cleared for my pots such that they would be away from curious eyes and accidental contact. I folded my cloak and placed it on a nearby bench before retrieving a wooden step ladder.

"Do you blame me?" Agnella's soft words were unexpected, and she remained faced away from my direction.

"No, my Lady," I answered honestly. "I do not."

After a moment, she summoned the courage to turn, looking up at me on the ladder. "How could you not? I forsook you, Lavinia."

"You were scared and protected yourself," I offered. "Initially, yes, I did blame you. But I should have expected such a high profile…" I hesitated, trying to keep my words mundane in case the curious ears overheard. "That there would be an inquiry. If I had thought things through, I could have prepared you. In that way, I failed my patron."

Agnella looked at the plants and thought to hand me one but then remembered what they were and refrained.

"How is the Baron of Camoy?" I asked with genuine interest, curious to know if the greater good of love had been achieved through the act.

Agnella's smile gave more of an answer than her words. "I want to let things settle with Kelton's transition before I make a formal announcement."

"That news warms my heart. Truly. I cannot think of a higher ideal to sacrifice for than love." Grateful for the news, I returned her smile while stepping down from the ladder. "And the baby?"

She placed a gentle hand on her growing womb. "We have decided to announce the joyous news with the New Year."

"It will be a true blessing for everyone in the Shire."

For a moment, we became two women engaging in pleasant conversation. I dare say we both welcomed the respite of companionship, but the moment grew sour too soon.

Agnella nodded and after a pause, touched the silk of my navy skirt with apprehension. The fabric featured a thin grid pattern of off-white thread. Her words came hesitant and restrained. "It looks better on you than it ever did on me."

I was not convinced she meant the compliment, but the intent was genuine. She wished to show me comfort and appreciation, and that was what she could summon. I appreciated her efforts, nonetheless.

"Perhaps my Lady would enjoy a game of chess to pass the winter days?"

Agnella nodded. "I would indeed, but I am otherwise engaged. Another time perhaps?"

Her lie was apparent, but I understood. No wonder Haylan had seen through her like glass. "Of course."

My presence must have been a painful reminder of the things she had done. I had wondered how she fared and now had my answer. While she achieved her goals, she still refused to acknowledge the method.

"Thank you again for the shelf space, my Lady." I curtsied, retrieved my outerwear, and left Agnella to her plants.

The unmistakable sound of rustling paper drifted down the corridors which, at the late hour, were void of their usual murmur. Unable to ignore the curiosity, I diverted down the suspect hall leading towards Kelton's office. Akworth's rear was prominent through the cracked door as he bent over, searching through the Earl's desk. I bit my cheek, holding back a chuckle, and left the Baron to his late-night illicit inquiry. I had enough on my plate without being pulled into another of Akworth's ploys.

Over the crunch of snow on my way back to the cottage, the sound of approaching horse hoofs caught my attention. Kelton's same, nameless guard drove the barred wagon up to the rear estate door. The resurged memories gave me pause as he tied up the horses and winked in my direction before departing into the estate. Once he disappeared inside, I made haste towards my own cottage, more unnerved than I would admit. I wished to never lay eyes on that man again.

However, it dawned on me halfway home: I had a nearby source of easy test subjects. All I needed was the Earl's permission.

The next morning, I returned to the estate, but this time, through the formal receiving porch. I had arrived early in the morning, unsure how to request a meeting with the Earl. He had always come to my cottage when he desired an update on my progress, but now, I needed to call upon him. The footman regarded me with disrespect as I made my request for an audience, but he permitted my entrance into a small waiting chamber. I doubted he knew of me, and supposed few women came unaccompanied.

I took my place on one of the white upholstered chairs circumnavigating the bright room. An oil painting of the late Earl still hung on the far wall. I could not help staring into his grey eyes, so lifelike they seemed to speak from beyond. Thankfully, the likeness did not upset me, and I found the room a comfortable place to wait.

And wait I did.

I stared at the wood walls for so long the details of the leaf inlay design throughout the room seared into my memory. Out the window, the sun rose higher over the blanketed white hills. I wondered if Kelton actually remained busy or chose to make me wait as a reminder of my place. Though I dwelled within a cottage instead of a cell, I was a captive on the estate. I knew my station.

Throughout the morning, others came into the room and were called for their audience moments after arriving. It was possible they had appointments, but I harbored doubt. Now convinced of

Kelton's game, I intended to endure. I would not let him crack me, not now, not ever.

My rear grew numb and my legs restless. As hours passed, my stomach growled, and my mouth became parched. Suppressing the desire to fidget, my mind thought of Aselin. The poor girl could never sit still. Patience was not one of her virtues, and as the day wore on, I began to lose mine.

"Mistress Maud."

Hearing my name startled my trance. The sun had long past its apex when the attendant finally called for me. I looked towards him for reassurance in a moment of doubt. After his head nodded an affirmation, I stood, straightened my dress, and followed. With my body stiff from the long wait, it took me a moment to find grace.

I followed the attendant down a short hallway to the Earl's private office where he announced my presence. "My Lord Earl, Mistress Lavinia Maud to see you." He closed the door behind on his way out.

Alone with my coerced patron, I took slow steps towards Kelton who sat at his desk. I noticed the small oil painting of him and Agnella now sat in a place of prominence on a bookcase behind and recognized several baubles which had been relocated from his old office.

"You wished to speak with me, Mistress Maud?"

I remained standing in front of his desk, annoyed by his lack of invitation to sit. "Yes, my Lord. First, let me apologize if you found my request for an audience inappropriate or undesired. I did not know how else to contact you."

"Go on," Kelton gave the command without providing a future alternative. His face was long, and his figure slumped in the chair. I imagined it would take some time for the new Earl to grow accustomed to the demands of his title.

"I took a two-day rest from my research to prepare a plan for the Magistrate of Marfield per your order. Moryet knows what I am. He will not consume anything in my presence. Achieving discreet access to his food would be difficult without reaching out to former contacts.

"Instead, I propose delivering the poison through an airborne exposure described to me by my Guild. While not an option for your other desired mark, if I could discern the proper technique, you would have a new weapon in your arsenal. However, in order to work out the details, a full-scale test is necessary before any assassination attempt."

Kelton's sat forward in his chair with his curiosity peaked. "'A full-scale test?' You mean a practice kill?" The Earl awakened from his tedium. Without a doubt, I was the most interesting citizen caller that day. "Is that your customary procedure?"

"Yes, I always test new extractions before targeting a mark. I typically begin with small vermin and progress to larger animals. For high-risk targets, I have learned the hard way to test on humans first. In the past, I have tested on subjects in the market or local taverns. However, my current isolation makes such avenues difficult."

"Then what do you propose, Mistress Maud?"

I bit my lip for a moment, unsure how the Earl would respond. At the time, Kelton remained aloof towards me, and I was unaware of his own vicious desires lurking beneath. In hindsight, I wonder how much I provoked his suppressed fascination.

"If there was a prisoner sentenced to execution," I proposed, "perhaps they could be offered death by my concoction. I cannot guarantee the death would be quick or as painless as the gallows.

Certainly, the prospect has less pageantry than a beheading. Perhaps in exchange for the risk, if my extraction fails, their life would be spared. However, I assure you I have no intention of failure. It would tarnish my perfect record."

I held my breath looking down upon Kelton. The Earl tapped his finger on the desk in thought for a moment before standing with an abrupt motion that startled me. His eyes were wide with desire. "I like it."

I had expected to be granted permission, but not with so much enthusiasm. "Truly?"

"Indeed. However, I insist upon my presence to witness the administration." He licked his lips before offering a half-hearted explanation. "Someone needs to bear witness if his life ends up spared, and frankly I am curious regarding the extent of your capabilities."

"As you wish, my Lord." I did my best to hide my surprise.

"You say you learned the hard way to use human test subjects, Madam Maud?" I nodded before he continued. "Regale me." Kelton indicated to the chair in front of his desk.

The Earl poured me a glass of mead, and I told him the entire truth of my first assignment from the Baron of Camoy. How I took false service in the Viscount of Matheson's household, how the apricot acid was slipped into his goblet and my shock of seeing him alive that afternoon. Kelton hung on my every word, interrupting my tale only to ask further details or clarification questions.

With the story recounted, the Earl looked as satisfied as a child who had just received their favorite bedtime story, yet yearned still for more. "I assume you have many tales such as that one?"

"Yes, my Lord."

"Excellent!" Kelton clapped his hands together. "You shall come by each week and tell me another."

Once again, I was surprised but could not pass up the opportunity to brag and share my victories which had so often been private. "I would be honored."

That was the moment I began to understand Kelton had a personal fascination with my work. Perhaps his frequent visits to my cottage were motivated by more than eagerness of my progress. Though at the time, I underestimated the extent of his perversion.

Kelton nodded. "Very good. Bring your test poison to the rear door tomorrow at dawn. I will see a test subject is prepared."

I nodded and offered a deep curtsey.

"Of course, you understand there shall be repercussions." Kelton let the thought hang.

Try as I might, I could not follow his thought. "Repercussions?"

"If you fail, Madam Maud. If I have to free a man sentenced to execution due to the failure of one of your tests, there will be repercussions."

Kelton had waited for the last possible moment to decree such terms, and I resented being toyed with. Satisfaction supported his crooked smile, and a seed of doubt gave me reservation as I reevaluated the risk. I existed to provide my patron with such tools. Recanting my readiness to test would undermine my value. Worse, Kelton now anticipated a spectacle. I could not back out.

Swallowing, I kept my face as nondescript as possible. "I understand, my Lord."

With my nerves provoked, Kelton had won that round. But I vowed to win the game.

CHAPTER FIFTEEN

That night, I raced the remaining wax of a burning candle, frantically searching through the box of correspondence recovered from my cottage. Somewhere inside, lay a parchment I hoped had not been a figment of my imagination. One of the letters contained my contact's recount of administering a powder for inhalation. But which?

My eyes grew heavy scanning the letters. My contact's handwriting was a chore to read. It had never bothered me before, but in the moment of need, the scribble raised my anxiety during the frantic search. The overflowing box contained years of letters, piles of rumors, recipes, uncovered tricks — all cloaked in a written hand not native to English, all encrypted by a cipher, and all signed by the same signal phrase of the Guild: *Sola dosis facit venenum.*

Praise God, two-thirds of the way through the pile, I found the letter in which so much now stood at stake.

I double checked the powder had been prepared as described and the finer points of the exposure technique readied. After decoding the letter multiple times, I laid back on the floor and exhaled with relief. There was nothing further to prepare; I had remembered the details well. That fact felt both comforting and unsettling. I wanted to *do* something. I wanted a way to tip the odds in my favor.

Staring up at the wooden beams of my cottage ceiling, I accepted the truth: tomorrow, I would either succeed or succumb to unknown repercussions.

Repercussions.

What more could the Earl do to me? He kept me captive on his estate and condemned me to kill my beloved. I did not think he would hurt me, not when he needed me to kill Silas. Yes, he could employ another assassin — I knew of at least three capable in Marfield alone — but none other had proved their loyalty. Kelton was smart; he would not disregard the value of that trait, but intelligence also meant he could plan a vicious retribution.

Kelton's perverse smile haunted my thoughts every time I closed my eyes.

His threat echoed in my mind.

I reread the letter once more as the candle extinguished and condemned the room to darkness. Melted tallow now pooled on the floor and the wick vaporized without a trace. I dipped my finger into the hot puddle, delighting in the tingle before the fat hardened around my skin.

After stacking the deck to the best of my ability, the cards were now dealt.

Conflicted by an evil mix of anticipation and dread, sleep remained elusive. I passed the rest of the night with an eye on the horizon through my window. Ice had crystallized into a delicate pattern across the glass pane. The world was at rest except for me, and likely some man who had accepted my bargain. Whoever he was, I doubted my test subject was sleeping. In the morning, we would know whose risk would pay off, and God willing, I would prevail.

When the first light cast upon the snow-covered field, I gathered my supplies into a small satchel and made the short trek through to the Earl's estate. The barred wagon already waited in front of the rear entrance and knowing why flamed my innate desire.

The assassin inside suppressed the worries of the captive. I could taste the sweet moment I craved. After months of abstinence, I had the opportunity to kill, and my confidence returned with the notion. I was Lavinia Maud, personal assassin of the Earl of Gaulshire, the murderer of the Viscount of Matheson, slayer of the former Earl, creator of heinous concoctions. And now, I prepared to oversee a test of my own extraction, one that would elevate my craft to a new level.

I trudged my way through the foot-deep snow. With each step, my boots sank halfway up my calf as I held the hem of my skirt above the fresh powder. Through the small, cracked window in the estate's rear entrance, an unknown figure watched my approach and opened the door when I reached a few feet away. I should not have been surprised to see Kelton regarding me with hungry eyes. Fortunately for him, I shared his mood.

"I have never had a door held open for me by an Earl before," I offered, through my lashes.

He smiled. "It is the least I can do, Lavinia. I am looking forward to this morning's demonstration. A fine way to finish out the year."

He said my given name.

The syllables sounded strange from Kelton's lips, and the informality sent a chill of uncertainty up my spine. Out of respect and conservatism, I did not presume the same permission in return. "Yes, my Lord. As am I."

He smiled and led the way down a set of stone spiral steps to the cellar. Below, the air smelled stale, and without windows for ventilation, a light smoke scent permeated the space emanating from the torch-lined walls. The scent tickled my throat, and my coughs echoed into the darkness beyond the reach of Kelton's lantern.

The stairway opened to a wide hallway. To the left, casks of wine stacked to the curve of the buttressed ceiling. To the right, a second corridor separated two barred holding cells. One remained empty, and the other contained a single occupant. The man appeared to be in his late thirties, though age is a difficult attribute to estimate under layers of grime. His muscular frame stood proud as he turned in our direction.

"I am glad he appears to be well nourished." I realized I had failed to specify that requirement, but it was necessary for a proper test.

Kelton, as always, remained one step ahead. "Of course, the intended target is healthy so the test subject should be as well."

"You are wise, my Lord," I offered, impressed by the thought Kelton had applied to this task. Each audience with the Earl increased my intimidation. With each meeting, he revealed more of the monster concealed within. I did not blame him — we shared that similarity. But he tended to his desires conspicuously, which in a way, made him more dangerous. I licked my lips with the thought. If my heart had not been bleeding for Haylan, mayhap I would have found more in my patron, but thankfully I never allowed myself to be so persuaded.

I turned my attention back to the subject. "What is his name?"

The Earl shrugged, looking towards his guard with expectation. I followed Kelton's glance down the corridor to see the brute leaning against the wall.

The teeth from his sarcastic smile shined through the dim light. He gave me his usual wink that made my skin crawl. How I hated his arrogance. I wished I could have ignored the mannerism, but I at least I tried to hide my annoyance. Out of spite, I never bothered to learn the guard's name.

Kelton's guard answered the question. "His name is Ralph Glennon, my Lord."

"Roger!" The man in the cell exclaimed back. "For the tenth time, you fool, Roger Glennon!"

Kelton banged the lantern against the cell bars in warning, the crashing metal rang through the cellar and caught the man's attention. "What does it matter?" He spit the words toward the poor man.

"It matters a great deal," I offered with a hand around the iron bar. "Everyone deserves dignity in their final moments, regardless of the circumstances that brought death's hand upon them." I looked towards the man in a sense of awe. "In mere moments, he will meet our Maker, let his last contact with our souls be one of compassion."

Kelton scoffed, "Said by the one who asked to kill him."

"I said compassion, not clemency," I challenged, and to my surprise, Kelton backed down.

"Goodman Glennon," the Earl said with the slightest hint of spite in my direction. Seeing my nod, he continued. "You are sentenced to death for the assault of a virgin. I understand a last confession has been administered and you have accepted our offer of death by an experimental poison. Per the terms of the agreement, should the toxin fail to end your life, you will be exonerated. I swear this on my honor."

Roger laughed, looking at me, and then motioned towards the guard. "When he told me the Earl's potion mixer was a woman, I thought he lied to convince me to accept. Now that I see the truth, I am ever grateful I did." He walked to the bars, looking down upon me from his tall gaze. "Bring your best, wench. I am ready to walk free and perhaps have you next."

I returned his stare, my own eyes narrowing. His words did not even give me pause. I had grown immune to such perceptions of low expectation long ago, and I often exploited the common belief. However, I refused to let his slight linger unchallenged.

"On second thought," I offered, dripping with sarcasm as I stared at the condemned man, "I stand corrected, my Lord. It appears not everyone is deserving of compassion."

Taking my time for effect, I prepared the supplies from my satchel. My patron desired a spectacle, and I intended to provide one.

First, I donned a pair of black leather gloves and unfolded a small handheld fan. I remained silent, unwilling to squelch anticipation with an explanation. I then laid out a large square of damp linen on the ground. And after flipping through my journal to find the section devoted to the apricot acid, I inked my quill in preparation.

"My Lord, would you care to keep time for the sake of evidence collection?" I held the pocket watch out towards Kelton who drooled with eagerness to participate in any means. "If you will please, note the time of administration?"

Seeing Kelton's nod, I retrieved the small metal vial from my own pocket and held it up to the light of the Earl's lantern to pique my patron's curiosity.

"Inside is a powder refined from the meat of apricot pits. The substance is ground finer than I have ever purified. An airborne exposure should decrease the time-to-effect. However, the danger of this administration is that the poison *will* diffuse." My voice conveyed the seriousness of my orders. "My Lord, it is best you watch from as far as possible."

Kelton took a step back, and in response to my glare, took a few more.

Satisfied, I tied a piece of cloth tight around my face. After unfastening the cap of the vial, I dumped the white powder into the palm of my gloved hand.

Roger scoffed. "That is it? That tiny amount?" Despite the words of confidence, the subject's voice wavered to my delight.

Given the powder in my hand, I contained my laughter — if only he knew. Unwilling to make the same mistake again, I had filled the vial to the brim. My palm held three times the amount that had been poured into the Viscount's goblet, and inhalation is a more potent form of administration.

"If you would now please keep still," I asked my mark. Despite his attitude, he gazed fearfully.

"Do you have any last words?" Kelton's guard asked. In response to the condemned's silence, the guard gave permission with a nod of his head.

Outstretching my steady hand towards the mark, excitement flared through my body. I could taste the sweetness of a kill heightened by the unknown of experimentation. However, having a target encaged and waiting felt awry. The man was already marked for death, regardless of my participation. I missed the thrill of the chase, the dance of deception, the reaction of surprise. The killing felt sacrilegious, as if I degraded the act of murder.

No, the circumstance was not the assassination I craved, but it was the one available, and I vowed to enjoy it. Without further delay, I held my breath while a strong motion of the fan propelled the powder towards the mark's face.

I immediately stepped back several feet and wrapped the fan and gloves in the laid-out fabric to submerge and clean at home. Only when I could no longer hold my breath did I exhale and look towards my caged mark.

The cloud of powder had hit with accuracy. Ironically, the body's natural response to shock is a sharp inhale, which makes this method of administration all the more potent. The man had already begun violent coughs, but as the hacking grew less severe, my heart flared in concern.

"Please, God…" I muttered under my breath, watching motionless from nerves. For the first time since my arrival in the cellar, I thought of the unknown repercussions if I failed.

That was when his body began to stumble. His hand lost its grip on the metal bar, and moments later, his proud frame crashed against the stone floor.

The effects were not dwindling, he was falling unresponsive.

Relieved, I picked up my journal and began taking notes, recording the time of each progressive symptom from the watch Kelton held.

The Earl's eyes stared wide with fascination. His gaze did not stray from the spectacle before him. I noticed signs of the earliest convulsions, but Kelton did not gasp until they grew more severe.

Minutes later, the man laid lifeless on the cell floor.

"Time of death?" I called into the sudden silence.

Speechless, Kelton showed me the watch once more, and I recorded the time. After writing a few final observations, I closed the journal, lowered the cloth around my face and turned towards my benefactor.

"Was it well done, my Lord?"

Still staring at the corpse, all the Earl could do was nod. I assumed his mind struggled to process the reality of what his eyes had witnessed, though after a moment, he regained composure. "Indeed, Lavinia. Well done, indeed."

He broke his stare into the cell and transfixed on my face. I knew the light that sparkled behind his eyes: he had caught the bug of my murderous craving.

"We shall do this again soon, yes?" he asked in earnest. "The tasteless, odorless poison, how is it progressing?"

"I am working as fast as I can, my Lord." That is all I could say in truth at that time. In the few weeks of experimentation with the beans, I had yet to purify an extraction worth testing on even a rat. Of course, I was not going to tell Kelton that fact.

"Good," the Earl exclaimed. "Now come. Let us toast to a successful test."

No one could argue with Kelton once his mind had decided. So, despite it still being mid-morning, I found myself in Kelton's parlor partaking of a fine red wine.

Never before had I been treated to such celebration after a kill. In that moment, I reaped the benefits of my wealthy patron: dining on pastries, indulging my refilled goblet. His praise stroked my pride. His delight inflated my own rapture. Of course, every iota of fawning was warranted. I had proved a new method of exposure and demonstrated my capabilities. And God it felt good to kill again, after all that time. Even with the limitations, I savored the murder as much as the wine.

The Earl's cravings, however, had merely been itched. Only I could fulfill his gruesome desire and my pride was eager to oblige.

At his begging, I told the story of the only time I had made poison darts.

Getting a mark to consume a poison was not always an easy task — case in point, my dilemma with Haylan. Early in my career, the potential of poisoning from afar seemed a safer course. So, to test my curiosity, I dipped the tips of darts lifted from a tabling house into the concentrated juice from the berries of belladonna.

Late one night, I snuck into the mark's one-room house and readied my dart. The man had inadvertently witnessed the murder of my client's mark and needed to be silenced. I pitied my client's predicament and vowed to give him peace.

I was not the best shot, but I had practiced throwing darts for hours each day leading up to the moment. Focused on the man, I sighted down the dart's shaft. My hand rose and fell with each nervous breath. The miniature arrow wavered in my jittering fingers.

After a deep inhale, I held my breath, sighted true, and let the dart fly.

The dart overflew my target and sunk into his cat curled up on a blanket. The creature let out a heinous cry, jumped in fright and knocked over the man's goblet. Ale spilled everywhere, and as the mark turned in anger, he saw me. We both stared in shock, but I recovered faster and jammed a second dart into his jugular. The cat bounded a few paces before collapsing in the puddle of ale.

With the story recounted, Kelton's laughter filled the parlor. "I never did like cats," he exclaimed, before a long drink of his wine. Setting down the goblet, he sighed and then looked upon me. "Has anyone ever told you your eyes sparkle like jewels? They are the most unique olive color."

The unoriginal opening filled me with exasperation, but this was my ruthless patron and not some lad in a tavern or a mark. I responded coyly through my lashes. "I am not aware of many olive-green jewels."

"Likely because the Maker gave you the only two."

Regretfully, I blushed, despite my heart still belonging to Haylan. The unexpected reflex filled me with shame. Haylan deserved my absolute loyalty, especially considering my plans. And alcohol had incited my patron's complement, not genuine interest. But that day, I discovered there was more wit in Kelton's mind than for which I gave him credit. He proved a fine drinking partner, but he could not fill my longing. The Earl could not appreciate the subtleties of what I had accomplished with an airborne exposure. I wished for Aselin's companionship to share in the achievement. I longed for her inquisitive questions.

I missed everything about her.

As I savored the triumph, I felt empty inside. The bars, the subject's willingness, the controlled conditions — it had all tainted the ritual. I did not even feel the need for confession as the mark faced death anyway. Worse, the knowledge gained completed the necessary preparations for Haylan's assassination.

The poison proved ready, but I still questioned if I had the heart. Now, I no longer had an excuse.

CHAPTER SIXTEEN

I did not consciously pick the date, I just knew. Upon waking a few days later, my heart felt at peace, like the morning after a thunderstorm. I needed to seize the moment before rain fell once more.

Kelton laughed when I asked to borrow a pair of guard breeches, but obliged after I promised to tell the story in full detail on the morrow. Remembering how my skirt had rustled in the rectory, a man's attire seemed more practical. Haylan was not hard of hearing like the priest. After fulfilling my request, thankfully Kelton refrained from asking to assist. This job, more than any other, needed to be accomplished alone.

Muriel did not question my silence that day, she had grown used to me retreating into my thoughts on occasion. She also beamed when I released her early in the afternoon. It was a fair day and for the first time in weeks, more snow melted than fell.

Alone, in my borrowed cottage, I prayed. It may seem like a derogatory act before committing a murder, but I sought fair redemption. I prayed for confidence, luck, steady resolve, and forgiveness. I had forgiven Haylan for the fate that had befallen me as a result of his duty and hoped he would do the same.

The rest of the day passed as an incessant blur. I put sugar on my vegetable pottage instead of salt. I accidentally burned a page of my notes in the hearth with other discarded parchment. Fear and impatience consumed my every thought. In my weakest moments, I considered running away. I did not *have* to kill Haylan. I could flee the shire, start somewhere new. It was a naïve notion, but I indulged in the fleeting respite of daydream. And if I warned Haylan, he would only arrest me again.

I did have to kill him.

Any other option would be throwing away years of hard work. Advancement required sacrifice, and I was ready to prove my dedication.

In front of the mirror, I straightened Haylan's flower pendant around my neck. Once again, I admired its delicate beauty: feminine grace which contrasted the rest of my ensemble. The Earl's black breeches were large around my waist but held secure enough with a tight sash. I tucked my hair inside a stocking cap and hid my face with a thick scarf that would serve a dual purpose. With the borrowed dark jacket featuring the Earl's seal, I thought I passed for a young official messenger well enough at a quick glance. After verifying the metal vial and fan remained secure in my pocket, I donned leather gloves and set out towards the stable.

The disguise must have been convincing enough for the stable lad merely nodded with a quick greeting, "Good evening, boy."

Boy. I smiled under the scarf and grunted a short acknowledgment before preparing my own mount. I selected a brown chestnut steed that reminded me of Sullivan. He seemed mild tempered enough and did not fight when led from the warmth of the stable. Against the backdrop of the setting sun, we rode into Marfield.

Closer to town, several men passed me on their way home for the evening. Stores were closing their doors and crowds on the streets waned. Haylan's house was on the opposite side of the city from mine. Given my current disguise, I fought the strong temptation to ride past my cottage, but unwilling to take any additional risk, I refrained. My ruse had tricked a stable boy, but that did not mean it would fool people who knew me well.

Stars twinkled by the time I reached Haylan's cottage. Larger than my own, its façade comprised red brick with river stones around the front door. Haylan remained the sole occupant since his Grandmother passed the previous year, but Mary Clements likely had her eye on the dwelling. I could not suppress a smile at the thought she would never set foot in the house. My soul was also plagued from the sin of jealousy.

I approached from the rear, but even at a distance, I could see no light lit within the dwelling. My exhale of frustration appeared as a cloud in the cold air before me.

Haylan was not home.

I had prepared for the possibility, but my heart fell discouraged nonetheless. After concealing the mount in a patch of bushes a safe distance from the cottage, I began a reluctant yet dedicated vigil.

The night proceeded as soft snow fell from the heavens. Curled up in a ball for warmth, I rocked beneath the mount who also grew restless. Being an assassin was not always glamorous; it had miserable moments like all other professions. Cursed to wait, the bushes sheltered some of the wind, but the temperature dropped faster than I anticipated. My body shivered until my muscles were sore. I could not stop yawning, struggling not to surrender to exhaustion.

Where was Haylan? It was a Tuesday for God's sake!

The inside of my scarf became damp from my own breath making the garment worthless for warmth. I untied the knot, repositioned it over my face, and then tied it again. I repeated the cycle twice more before I mercifully heard the hooves of Haylan's horse coming over the hill.

Beaming, Haylan hummed some unknown tune which the night wind carried to my ear. For being late in the evening, he took his sweet time. Within the stable, Haylan brushed the beast's hair and fed it handfuls of oats, all while my teeth chattered with frustration. After my blood began boiling with impatience, Haylan finally closed the barn door and entered the house.

The moment had come at last.

Compelling my frozen body to move, warmth returned to my core. I had dreaded this moment for weeks, yet it passed with unexpected ease. I harbored no doubt, no second-guessing. Focused, I detached from the job which further eased my conscience. This was no longer about Lavinia and Haylan; I was an assassin, stalking my mark.

Standing behind the bushes, I brushed fallen snow off my coat while analyzing the situation. I advanced towards the house, targeting the side containing a small, singular window belonging to the guest bedchamber. Once I could touch the brick, I rounded the structure towards the front door.

Through the window, Haylan continued to delay in the rear kitchen, singing the same damn tune with a wide smile glued to his face. I watched him hang his riding jacket and hat on the stand near the back door and saw he wore his best Sunday doublet. My heart broke as I pieced together the clues. Over the following days, gossip confirmed my suspicions. Poet Clements had just accepted Haylan's proposal for his daughter's hand.

My heart also grieved for poor Mary. I would not be the sole woman mourning the loss of Haylan Moryet. In a curious way, it made me feel connected to the poet's daughter. We shared a strange sisterhood that could never be acknowledged. I longed to comfort her over the coming days, to find solace in companionship, together. But she would mourn with family. She would be able to attend his funeral.

I would suffer alone.

The repugnant smirk on Haylan's face fortified my jealous resolve. That, and the damn dimple. Proceeding, the flower pendant bounced against my chest as I reached the unlocked front door. Through God's grace, I made it into the house without being heard over the discordant song.

I positioned myself in a shadowed corner near the stairs leading up to Haylan's bedchamber. He would have to pass by at some point, and I would be ready. With the scarf secure, I dumped the contents of the vial into the palm of my gloved hand, unfurled the hand fan, and waited.

My eyes glued to my palm, willing my hand to stay stable. Inside, my heart felt like a trapped hummingbird, and I began to sweat under the wool jacket within the warmth of the house. I longed for a deep breath but dared not disturb the thick scarf given the contents of my hand.

The lights from the kitchen finally dissolved and footsteps approached my position. In the darkness with my borrowed black attire, I was near invisible.

My mind spun, calculating the distance to my target and constantly evaluating timing so as not to miss the right moment. Attack too early and the powder would not travel far enough, wait too long and Haylan would have turned his face away as he rounded the corner. The last seconds stretched on as I waited for my mark to be in the best position. Hold... Hold...

Now!

Relying on the glimmer of frail moonlight strands through the window, I fanned the powder with one hard stroke. The white cloud blew forward into his face. His hands waved in front of him frantic, batting the strange puff of air. Never before had I heard Haylan use such language.

Only when he started to cough did I emerge from the shadows.

Upon seeing my disguised figure, Haylan drew a dagger from his belt, but it fell through his already weak fingers.

"It will not be long now." My muffled voice carried into the darkness through the scarf.

The whites of his eyes grew wide as he fell against the steps, coughing with too much violence to respond. I did not think he had yet pieced together the identity of his attacker. I wanted him to know, so I gave him a clue.

"I am sorry, Haylan. I never wanted us to end this way. Though, I suppose we were always destined for such a confrontation. A magistrate and an assassin? It is almost too perfect."

"Lavin..." Haylan coughed, resting his head on the steps in fatigue.

"I want you to know I did not choose this."

His cough spattered blood upon the wood railing.

"You left me with no other option after the arrest," I continued, my own voice cracking. "I have to tie up loose ends and protect myself. I want you to know I struggled for weeks, many nights not sleeping. I knew what I had to do, but my heart would not permit it."

Haylan's eyes shut for a moment before he reopened them. I doubted he could see me anymore beyond the haze of a human outline.

My voice degraded to a near whisper. "I was happy for you and Mary and would have loved to see your children grow, to be like an aunt to them. This is not an act of spite or self-pity, it is simple self-preservation."

I longed to reach out and stroke his chestnut hair, to comfort him in his final moments when his heart must have been full of fear. But I could not risk potential contamination and reluctantly kept my distance.

"I love you, Haylan, despite knowing you would never return my love, even after everything."

Fighting through the struggle, he lifted his head one more time, facing me with eyes full of pain as he spoke his final words, "I know."

Haylan fell limp on the stairs and faded away.

I suppose part of me remained unwilling to acknowledge the truth. I stood still, waiting for him to stand once more, but his body convulsed until it came to a final rest. After several minutes, I lowered my scarf and began a solemn vigil. I watched his still frame late into the night, long after his breath exhaled for the final time. He looked so peaceful, despite lying prone on the stairs. I longed to give him a last kiss, to hold his hand one more time. Unfulfilled, tears streamed down my cheeks until I found the strength to leave.

"Goodbye, Haylan." I forced the whisper through a choked throat. After gazing at his fair face for one last memory, I departed into the night.

In a way, that night carried more intimacy than any moment from our ill-fated past. I assumed, all those years, Haylan knew of my love. Regardless, it was nice to hear it from his own lips. I was proud of him, of the way he died. He had accepted his fate and gifted me with last words of comfort without malice. Deep down, he loved me in his own way. I promised to carry on his memory. To never forget the sacrifice he made for me that night. In his honor, I never committed another assassination with the same method.

Upon returning to the bush, I found my mount asleep. I rubbed his cold muscles to reinvigorate them, and he woke with reluctance. We rode off towards the Earl's estate as the puddle of tears on my borrowed jacket turned to ice.

I never confessed my love for Haylan to the Earl, but he seemed to understand a personal sacrifice had been made. Despite my promise, he did not ask for the story the following evening, though I gave him an impersonal version of the tale a week later. Instead, we shared a bottle of wine in front of the hearth in silence. I appreciated his company and his compassion at that moment. But nothing, and no one, could ever fill the hole I had made inside my own heart.

They buried Haylan not far from my parents' grave. I watched the funeral from a distance. Mary Clements was beautiful, even clothed in black. She would have many more suitors and find love again. Since Haylan was a public official, the Earl sent a representative who partook in the service as well.

Aselin and Edmund also attended. There seemed to be a cloud over my former apprentice which filled me with relief. She clearly had not tried to continue untrained. Her face fell long, and her posture hunched. However she now passed her time was futile. No other hobby, no pursuit, no love, would ever fulfill her longing within. I understood she endured a special mourning of her own. Laying Haylan to rest was saying goodbye to another connection to me, to the life she longed for. Edmund put a gentle arm around her shoulder and held her close. He would not be able to understand, but he would provide what support he could.

I wondered if they thought I was also buried in the ground.

CHAPTER SEVENTEEN

At least the job was done.

I expected to feel relief, perhaps pride that I had summoned the gall. I appreciated the absence of apprehensive weight upon my shoulders. However, inside, I felt empty — no, not empty. I did not know how to describe it. Unsatisfied? I did not regret my actions, I only wished for a different fate.

Kneeling in front of the hearth, I made my confession with a crucifix in my hands. I allowed myself a day to mourn but the Earl's deadline loomed and so much time had passed already. With no further need or excuse to divert my attention, I poured my anguish into experimentation.

My standard processes for purifying a toxic extraction continued to fail with the castorbean. I tested increased temperatures, different levels of solvents and various boiling times. All combinations failed to produce a toxin that more than sickened a rat.

To her credit, Muriel tried her best to assist, but she lacked experience with such processes and her pace limited the number of combinations we could test in a single day. She sensed my anxiousness, and while I did my best to hide frustration, she internalized part of my stress into a self-inflicted guilt.

Unrelenting, Kelton pressed for results. He came by my cottage almost every other day, asking "when." Always *when*. Despite my best efforts to explain, he did not comprehend there could be no schedule. It could be hours or months before I cracked the bean's secret. To him, it should have been as simple as cooking a stew. All I had to do was make the poison... He either failed to understand or refused to hear my explanation that I did not yet know *how*.

And in my weak moments, I feared I never would.

February brought more of the same fruitless toil and winter. The afternoon sun poured through the kitchen window as I watched snowflakes fall through the blue sky in chaos, agitated by fickle winds. My mind had taken me elsewhere before the unmistakable sound of glass shattering brought me back with the suddenness of an axe. A piercing scream followed, echoing through the house. I ran to the workroom to see Muriel frightened, though fine. Shards of broken glass jar strew across the workbench. With the kettle in her hands, I pieced together the story.

"I am so sorry, my Lady," she muttered in fear. "I was being so careful, I do not know why..."

With a sigh, I silenced the poor girl's feeble apology. "It is alright, Muriel." I took the pot of hot solvent and set it on a stone. "The jars are getting too cold from the chill in here." Seeing her look of confusion, I continued, "When hot water is poured into a cold glass, the heat is not transferred uniformly and it..."

It was if a fire lit inside the fog of my head.

It is funny how inspiration can come from the most mundane sources. How often, the answer is found when we stop looking.

"Muriel." I turned to her with renewed excitement. "What if we should not be using heat at all? What if the chemical we are trying to purify is being degraded?"

I had lost her, but it did not matter.

Over the next week, I experimented with new combinations and heatless techniques. I discovered soaking the beans in a mixture of lye allowed the outside layer of the seed to be removed with tweezers. The painstaking, slow process required handwork with each individual bean. For hours on end, I hunched over the workbench until my back ached so deep I struggled to stand straight again.

I then mixed the uncovered beans with acetone and let them stew for various lengths of time before drying the contents near the fire. Curious, I hovered over the pans analyzing the extraction. The results produced a white powder that felt like flour between my fingers, fine and silky. But as I ran my hand through the pan, pain began to radiate through my arm. Curious, I brushed off the powder to see my fingertips stung bright red.

"Get the rats," I yelled with excitement.

"Mistress?" Muriel came running from the foyer with a broom in her hands.

"I think we have something. Fetch two of the trapped rats!"

I had made a poison of some sort, but could it kill?

That afternoon, each rat sat in its own cage, happily feasting on a specially seasoned dried tomato. One had been treated to a teaspoon of the powder, the other with two. Neither of them rejected the meal, which provided the first sign that the toxin might be tasteless as promised.

The Guild letters speculated the poison would kill slowly, but with an unknown time table, I checked on the pair hourly throughout the night. Each time they scurried around their cage without a care as if they somehow knew to spite me.

The next afternoon, I received revenge when one started to vomit.

I watched the creature mull around the cage in obvious pain, vomiting every few minutes in my own private show of ghastly delight.

Muriel came to check on me and looked at the sick rat. "How do you know when the medicine has worked?"

I shrugged. "The only way is to observe and learn. See how the one of the left is struggling more than the one on the right? That at least confirms the mixture is more potent with a higher dosage."

Muriel stared for a moment trying to comprehend what I had said. She also did not understand what fascinated me about two rats in a cage. With a shrug, she departed to carry on with the household chores.

On the morning of the fourth day, I awoke to find the left rat dead. It took a moment to realize the discovery was not a dream. Still huddled in my sleeping gown, I gazed at the motionless ball of fur with twinkling eyes and dutifully recorded the evidence with an unconstrained grin. I felt close but remained wary of declaring victory.

Through the wall, I heard Muriel enter and hang her coat by the door. After seeing the dead rat, the dim girl rubbed my back in sympathy. "I am so sorry, Lavinia. It looks like your medicine did not work again."

"No it…" Seeing her regard the dead creature with sadness was such violent contrast to my own elation that it gave me just enough pause to catch myself in time to correct my words. "No, it must not have worked," my words came out broken as I lied. "At least it is another observation to consider."

Muriel nodded, giving me an undesired hug from behind. "You will figure it out, Mistress. I know you will."

It took every ounce of restraint to contain my laughter until she walked out of earshot. What would she think if she knew she helped create a tool to kill, not heal? I longed to tell her, to see the horror develop on her face. But in the end, the secret manifested in a long-term amusement now that my efforts showed progress. Long ago, I had taken Edmund's innocence, I spared Muriel's as a gift of gratitude for her companionship.

After months of work, I had an extraction that killed a rat, but as I had seen before, humans proved a more difficult endeavor. Significant work still remained, but the development renewed my spirit.

And of course, the Earl had to visit that afternoon.

More focused than I had been in months, the last thing I needed was Kelton's distraction. From my workroom, my heart sank as Muriel welcome him inside.

"Lavinia? Oh, my Lord, she's having a rough day. One of her test rats died three days after she tested her medicine."

"Died?"

From the lift in Kelton's tone, I knew the exact expression plastered on his face. He did this strange thing with his eyebrows when he was excited. One shot straight up like an arrow, the other curved into a peculiar expression.

"Yes, my Lord. Do tread lightly with her today?" Muriel pleaded on my behalf.

"Of course, Mistress Sallay."

Kelton entered my workroom with a smirk so wide it must have pained his lips. I, in turn, wanted to gag from the tone in his voice.

"I hear a rat died, Mistress Maud?"

Nervous, I responded to his question by pointing. I had yet to clean the cage, unwilling to disturb the test subject while his partner still lingered.

Kelton picked up the cage and examined the dead rodent. Unamused, he turned with fascination towards the one who clung to the last strands of life. "How does death come?"

I tried to appear busy, writing in my journal to avoid the question I knew he would pose. I kept my answer as formal as possible, hoping my patron would take the hint to not disrupt my work. "Near the end, urine has a strong odor, and you can see the whites of the eyes are yellow. Death must come from organ failure."

Kelton persecuted the live rat without mercy, torturing it with a stick through the bars of the cage and enjoying the creature's unsuccessful attempts to flee. "Well, I would say it looks like progress."

"I did have a breakthrough last week, but one dead rat is not sufficient to claim success."

"Of course not, but a full-scale test would be decisive." His tone carried overzealous glee.

And there it was.

I turned towards Kelton for the first time since his unwelcome entrance. "My Lord, I know you are eager but these things take time and I am not sure it is potent enough for a man who…"

"There is one way to find out," Kelton interrupted me. "Is not there, Mistress Maud?"

I swallowed, trying to discern a way out. "I would hate for you to expend such effort when I doubt the extraction is ready for..."

Again, he cut me off. "It is no trouble at all. Shall we say tomorrow evening then?" He eyed me with the look of authority I knew better than to cross.

My stomach dropped.

"Wonderful," Kelton restored his coat. "I shall be expecting you after dinner." He did not even wait for a response before leaving.

When the door closed, I threw a metal ladle from the workbench across the room with all of my might. The utensil hit the wall with such force it dented the plaster before falling with a clang to the floor.

"Mistress?" Muriel ran to assist with whatever caused the ruckus. "Mistress, what happened?"

"Just get out!" I screamed, not even looking at her. "Now!"

She stared for a moment, freighted stiff with her mouth hanging open. Once my order processed, Muriel gathered her belongings and left so fast she put her coat on outside in the frigid wind.

I set down the quill and stared at the new dent in the wall. In the solitude, I regained control of my anger, wishing I never had lost my temper. Kelton had lit a match under the tinder that had been piling up inside; Muriel became an unfortunate casualty of the unstable emotion I had failed to tend.

I did not regret much from my life, but I did regret my outburst that day. Muriel could not help because I had kept her ignorant — purposefully of course, but she did not own that blame. Muriel served as a ray of sunshine through the worst winter of my life, and I knew how much I benefited from her companionship.

The next morning, Muriel reported for work without a word. The fact that she came at all indicated she had more spine than I gave her credit for. I had breakfast waiting on the table with a few molasses cookies she loved. I had taken them from the main estate the previous night after tending to the plants in the grow room.

"Muriel, I am so sorry," I spoke first and did not receive a response. "I am under more stress and pressure than I have told you and more than you would understand. Regardless, you do not deserve to be treated with such disrespect. I sincerely apologize for yesterday and beg your forgiveness."

Dropping her coat, she ran to me with a smile and a warm hug. Too often in my profession, I saw the worst in people. Muriel represented the best. I wished I could have been more like her; that I could have forgotten grudges instead of permitting them to fester and rot inside.

That out lash remained one mistake I regretted, but it was also one of the few I made right.

That evening, I treaded through the snow to the Earl's estate with my satchel full. Again, I had passed the previous night staring at the ceiling of my room, unable to sleep. My spirit bent with the constant pressure, and I feared I would soon break. The Earl had stolen all the joy from uncovering a new extraction, and for the first time, I headed towards an assassination in genuine fear.

I tried to settle my nerves by telling myself it *could* work. Yes, it *could* have worked, but it could also have cured the sweating sickness. Both outcomes seemed equally ludicrous. The extraction was not strong enough, not for a healthy male. I had spent my adult life perfecting my craft and every minute of that experience rang in alarm. Yet with no other option, I headed towards Kelton's test, forcing one reluctant step in front of the other.

Kelton again held the rear door of the estate open for me, except this time, I did not share his mood for playful banter.

"Why are you full of gloom, Lavinia? This should be a moment of triumph." Kelton led the way down the spiral staircase into the dark cellar with anxiousness I harbored for a different reason.

"My Lord, I also eagerly await that day, but I do not believe it has come. The extraction is not yet strong enough." I turned to him at the bottom of the steps with one last plea. "Please, my Lord. I beg you to postpone until it is ready."

"It has been four months, Lavinia." Kelton raked a hand through his hair in frustration.

"Yes, four of a six-month deadline."

"Is it not prudent to evaluate your progress?" Kelton posed the rhetorical question.

I exhaled, exasperated. I considered imploring him to test a goat, but Kelton had tasted the sweet satisfaction of poisoning a man and longed for a repeat spectacle. I knew only one act could calm such a craving. I understood his desire, though I had more patience.

Following Kelton deep into the cellar, the test subject's sniffles echoed through the hallway before my eyes laid sight on the cell. The man was in his upper forties and skinnier than the previously marked subject.

"His name is Oswald Stace," Kelton offered proud and freely before turning his attention to the captive. "Goodman Stace, you are sentenced to death for…" he looked towards his guard who once again kept post in the same spot down the hallway.

"Stealing chickens," the guard finished.

"Ah, yes," the Earl continued over the man's sobbing. "You have received a last confession and accepted my offer of death by an experimental poison." Kelton's words began to stumble. "It is obvious this fate is, well, understandably upsetting, so we will not drag it out longer than required." He then turned to me, keeping his voice low. "See? Compassion."

Kelton's toothy smile sickened my stomach before he continued to address the condemned.

"Per the terms of the agreement, should the toxin fail to end your life, you will be exonerated. I swear this on my honor." Kelton exhaled, clapping his hands together. "Alright, Madam Maud. He's yours."

I glanced at the man who wiped his nose on his brown linen sleeve. At least I would be setting free a thief, and one who I guessed had stolen for his own table. The man could not be blamed for being hungry. My heart did have a place for compassion. I hoped his suffering would not be too great before the ordeal concluded.

But in the back of my mind, my own prospects were of prime concern. Regardless what befell Oswald, I feared Kelton's repercussions would bring a worse fate. I had one shot to avoid whatever wrath Kelton would administer, so I shook thoughts of doubt from my head and focused on the task.

Per my request, two goblets of water waited on a table outside of the cell. One goblet had a white ribbon tied to the stem and the other a black. Since the Earl insisted on testing my unready, weak extraction, I planned to increase the proportion by saturating the liquid. With my back to the man to block his view, I retrieved the box of the white powder from my satchel and stirred several overflowing spoonfuls into one goblet until the first grains failed to dissolve. Other than the ribbon, the two goblets appeared indistinguishable; the toxin had indeed dissolved clear and odorless.

"Oswald," I called, turning towards the cell before holding out both goblets. "I would like you to drink from both glasses and describe what you taste."

Kelton leaned over my shoulder. "Do I not need a watch?"

I shook my head. "This toxin will run its course over several days."

Success or not, it would be a waiting game.

I turned back to the man with a nod of encouragement. "Go ahead."

He made the sign of the cross several times before accepting the goblets and examining them with insecurity. His hands shook with tremors so severe I worried he would spill the contents. In a moment of bravery, he closed his eyes and then sipped from one cup. His resulting look of confusion almost made the months of worried toil worthwhile.

"It's water?"

I sighed, restraining my frustration. "Yes, though could you please be more specific regarding its taste?"

The man looked back at the translucent liquid and tasted again before shrugging with confusion. "It's water. What more is there to say? It's not the most refreshing glass I have ever had, but it's fine."

"Alright." I gave up. "And the other then?"

He drank once more with a repeat response. "The same water?" He looked towards the Earl with a twinge of anger. "You promised me freedom if I survived a poison test. What game is this?"

For the first time all night, I smiled and enjoyed myself. Regardless of the potency, I had made a tasteless, colorless, and odorless poison. Once again, the accomplishment would be lost on my patron. I longed to tell Aselin...

I walked towards the bars, taunting the man as the poison assassin within me took control. "You are being tested, and *have* drunk poison." Picking up my journal and quill, I took a few notes to increase the stakes of the moment. After closing the book with a snap, I turned my attention back to Goodman Stace. "Now, if you please, hand me the goblet with the black ribbon."

He looked at the glass confused but compiled.

Sinister instincts kept my tone soft. "Drink the other, completely."

The man's lips quivered once more, his realization dawning a new understanding. Glaring at the blashy, tainted liquid, he closed his eyes, took a deep breath, and drained the contents before he could change his mind. After swallowing the last drop of toxin, he held the empty vessel upside down in defiant demonstration. "I do not feel anything."

"And you will not," I retorted. "Not for a while."

If at all...

The brief moment of triumph gave way with the reminder that my toxin remained too weak. I set down the journal looking at the man, my heart full of rare pity. "I am sorry, Oswald, but if this works, it will be a long, drawn-out death." The fear in his eyes gave away the obvious question he could not ask. "With luck, you will vomit and experience nausea. In days, your organs will start to fail. Beyond that? If I knew, we would not need a test."

I packed my belongings, leaving the untainted water on the table, and looked towards my patron. "I will be back tomorrow to check on his progress."

Kelton nodded. "How long do you reckon?"

I shrugged once more, hoping to give myself a long enough window that a miracle might occur. "Two weeks to be sure?"

"Two weeks then." To my surprise, for once, the Earl did not argue. However, his agreement made more sense as he played his favorite taunting tactic by calling to my back. "Two weeks or face repercussions, Madam Maud."

I refused to give him the satisfaction of acknowledging his call. Suppressing my shudder, I departed into the night towards my own dwelling of captivity.

Goodman Stace had prayed for his life to be spared. That night, I prayed it would extinguish. In two weeks, we would know which request God answered.

CHAPTER EIGHTEEN

Those two weeks were probably the longest in Oswald Stace's life. They were the shortest in mine.

I toiled endlessly to make the castorbean toxin more potent. If this test failed, I hoped to appease the Earl by being ready with another. My back ached from hunching over tiny beans, my fingertips burned from prolonged exposure to lye. I worked late into the night until my eyes failed to focus, and Muriel found me asleep at the workbench most mornings.

My cottage became a cluttered hazard of beans soaking in assorted additives, pans of toxins in various states of drying and caged rats subjected to poison. Muriel did her best to clean around the clutter without complaint, though one afternoon an unexpected, boisterous "God's wounds!" filled the cottage. I laughed at her expense, finding the girl in a puddle of lye, broken glass, and beans upon her washed floor.

With a hand over her mouth, Muriel's face turned redder than the dried tomatoes. "I am so sorry, Mistress! I apologize for my language, I do not know what has gotten into me."

I knew exactly what had influenced the girl and was proud to see a small piece of me reflected back. Keeping the thought to myself, I merely shrugged. "I will not fault you for using words in proper context."

But despite all the tests and variations, the extraction's potency remained the same. The singular piece of good news was how well my plants thrived in Agnella's grow room. As a result, I had a sufficient supply of beans for experimentation.

Agnella had reached her last trimester and celebrated with a formal announcement of engagement to Baron Akworth. The Baron insisted the news be spread before the baby's birth as a show of support for his widowed fiancé. Publicly, they both acknowledged the babe's father to be the late Earl, but in private, I believe they hoped otherwise.

I shook my head at the sight of them. No matter how convincing or consistent their lie, no one would believe their story if the thing came out a ginger. The public could count, and counting back nine months put conception before the Earl's death with time to spare.

If they harbored reservations over those facts, they did not share them. The entire estate focused on preparing for the birth of the child. I dare say even Kelton had baby fever, now that the title officially belonged to him. But my patron's coming sibling did not distract him from the experiment we kept in the cellar. And with the constant bustle upstairs, no one else noticed.

Goodman Stace started to vomit late on the second day. The symptom was expected, but part of me feared his body expelled the toxin. The following morning, he woke too nauseous to read the bible I had slipped him, and the pit in my stomach stalled its growth.

Maybe.

For a moment, I let myself relax, hoping I underestimated my toxin. But it seemed that one little thought jinxed everything.

Oswald's symptoms steadied, and on the fourth day, he began to recover. He called it a miracle, praising God with hymns and psalms. I did not have the heart to tell him he owed his "miracle" to my own predicted failure.

Kelton knew the test had failed but kept the man locked up for the remainder of the two weeks, forcing me to witness every living breath as a reminder of my defeat. Even though the clock had not expired, we both knew his focus had moved passed the man to his new subject of torture: me.

"Tick tock, Madam Maud," he whispered on day ten, as I passed him towards the grow room.

Kelton posted round-the-clock guards in the cellar, concerned I might try to poison the man again. The caution was unnecessary. I had nothing to benefit from pretending the toxin was ready. I feared Kelton's unidentified repercussions, but they would be worse if I failed with Silas. I did my best to maintain a strong front, despite the impending dread which compounded each day. Kelton alone knew what perverse desire would pacify his thirst, and anxiety of the unknown consumed me.

If the dread was not torture enough, I had lost my perfect record. No developed poison or high-ranking murder could reverse that damage. The repugnant chicken thief forever tainted my prestige, puncturing a hole in my pride.

The morning of the fourteenth day, I shoveled my stoop as Goodman Stace emerged from the estate towards a waiting coach. His hand shielded his eyes from the bright light of the sun before he fell to the snow laden ground, crying in a dramatic display of worship.

I rolled my eyes.

His coach departed towards the city when Muriel's sudden, perky appearance startled me.

"Mistress! Thank you." She squeezed her arms around me tight.

I looked at her bewildered, my nerves manifesting in a laughter of confusion. "For what?"

"The Earl said you begged him to give me a week off." She placed her hand over her heart as a tear swelled in her eye. "A full week, with pay."

I swallowed, feeling my heart invade my throat that grew too tight to say anything otherwise. My shoulders shrugged as I forced a smile. "It is the least I could do for your assistance these past months."

Muriel bounded inside, eager to finish the day's chores. Back at the manor, the Earl waved in my direction. I pretended not to see.

A week.

I had not considered his repercussion would persist for such a duration.

I stared at my journal for a good part of the day, unable to focus. I could not eat. I struggled to breathe. And when Muriel kissed me good-bye on my cheek, I could not feel a thing. My body fell numb with foreboding.

He waited until darkness fell.

I sat in front of the hearth, sipping a cup of warm cider that failed to provide the comfort I craved. The click of the front door latch was unmistakable over the low crackle of the fire. Part of me grew relieved. The waiting, the constant thought of what might occur, had become its own torture. But as his footsteps entered the cottage in a slow, infuriating rhythm, my body stiffened. Kelton was a master of mind games and knowing his strategy did not make me immune.

Staring into my cup, I listened to the floorboards creak under his approaching stride. I could not bear to face him, to do so would acknowledge the reality I wanted to ignore. When the steps stopped, I felt his breath on my neck and compelled from intimidation, I dropped to my knees.

"Please, my Lord." My trembling hands reached out to touch the fabric of his brown trousers in homage. "I stated the poison was not yet ready."

Kelton's cold fingers pushed a lock of errant hair behind my ear. "That is not my problem, Mistress Maud. We had a clear agreement." Kelton's voice stayed smooth as the silk handkerchief around his neck.

"For the first test," I whimpered, barely audible. "I did not ask for the second." I reached for any words, any defense that might save me from the unknown plight. "I am so sorry, my Lord! It pains me to know I let you down, that my inability brought you such dishonor."

Dissuaded by the plea, Kelton entangled his fist in my hair and yanked my head back, inducing a stinging pain through my scalp. Forced to stare up into his dark eyes, he leaned towards me, so close I could see his individual pores glisten with sweat.

"I believe you are sorry," Kelton whispered, menacing, "but for yourself more than my honor."

I flinched as his unexpected spit slid from under my eye over the curve of my cheek, leaving a sick slime in its wake. I knew better than to wipe it away as I endured his hot, whiskey-filled breath upon my face.

"Get up." Kelton's command came without warning.

He let go of my hair with a push that sent me to the floor. I struggled to untangle my feet from the layers of skirts before standing per his order, hunched and quivering.

The hearth blazed at my back while the Earl's anger inflamed before my eyes. At that moment, I learned the true extent of terror. I had anxiety when my father passed, leaving me alone. I was scared that night in the tavern with Baines, and I will admit, on a few jobs over the years. And I feared for my life the night in Haylan's gaols. But those emotions were shallow compared to the way my stomach now caved. I discovered how fear's black despair can be all encompassing. How the body can tingle stiff with foreboding.

Kelton fed off my angst, his predatory gaze flickered with anticipation. "Now undress, sirrah."

My eyes grew wide. My hands covered my chest in protection as my breathy voice appealed for mercy. "Please. My Lord?"

"This will take as long as you decide, Mistress Maud." His voice whispered, eerily calm. "Obey, and it will be over shortly. Fight me in any way, and the penalty will persist."

I could not.

Even with the threat, I could not bring myself to do it. I stood in front of him crying, hoping if I lingered he would change his mind. Instead, he slapped my face. After my head had recoiled, I looked at him through the blur of tear-filled eyes.

"Undress!" He screamed in a sudden escalation, releasing two weeks of anticipation in a single breath.

Feeling the volume of the command in my chest, I obeyed.

My hands shook, struggling to untie the lacings of my bodice. My legs trembled, threatening to collapse beneath me. Lowering the layers of skirts one at a time, the pile of clothes grew around my feet. I stood before him ashamed, clad in a thin shift which he motioned to remove as well.

I braced myself for the worst as I complied. Standing before him unclothed, I had never felt so small.

"Good." Kelton's voice returned to a calm tone. He slapped my arms covering my chest until I lowered them to my side. With an approving nod, his eyes examined my figure head to toe. "Now turn. Slowly."

My legs clutched together. My feet barely left the floor, shuffling during the rotation. Tears rolled down my breasts, tickling my skin. With my eyes cast down, I struggled to breathe. He examined the entirety of my flesh. Perhaps it was my own lack of creativity, but I had not expected this from Kelton. Perhaps it was my own naïveté, for I had never been in such a state before a man. My forced patron held my innocence in his hand, my virtue cracked like glass within his tightening grasp.

For the first time, I understood how my victims must have felt when they realized their fate. To know what is coming without any means to avoid the terror. I also knew, too well, the ecstasy that pulsed through Kelton's veins. Such an uncontrollable surge cannot be dissuaded, but I pleaded in vain anyways.

"Please, my Lord," I begged in a whisper. "Do not dishonor me."

When I completed the slow circle, the sting of another facial slap shocked me into a backward stumble. Unable to find footing, my body twisted, slamming into the stone around the hearth. A quick reflex stopped me from falling into the crackling fire, but not without my legs spreading wide as I came to rest upon the floor.

"*I* decide the terms of the consequence!" Kelton bellowed above. I scrambled, pushing my body away, but Kelton pressed towards me in response, "And you admitted yourself, you brought *me* dishonor." He grabbed my ankle and slid me back towards him as he kneeled over my disrobed frame. "So, why should I not?"

His grip around my leg ached as I swallowed, unable to respond.

After a beat, he laughed before mocking me. "But no, Lavinia, I will not deflower you." He grabbed a thick stick from the nearby pile of wood. "Though your fear is misplaced."

What occurred next defied my expectation. I also cannot say if it was worse than what I feared. The stick came down on my bare chest with such force it stole my breath. With the second blow, my scream burst through the cottage as he continued striking relentlessly: across my shoulders, into my stomach, over and over on my thighs.

When I could no longer attempt to crawl away, Kelton pulled me across his lap and struck my rear until I swore it burned with fire. Splinters from the stick penetrated my raw flesh. His insults resonated over the repeated crack of wood against my skin. My ears heard the words, but I refused to acknowledge his defamation.

Grabbing my breasts, he threw me to the ground, attacking my back. I curled into a ball, absorbing blow after blow until the stick relented first and cracked. The broken wood clanged against the back of the hearth from the force in which Kelton threw it into the fire. Accompanied by a scream of rage, he conceded to using his bare hands.

No matter how much I struggled, flailing and kicking, my meager frame could not match his strength. I could not get away from the barrage as he pulled me back in place by the knee. Blood stained the rug beneath me as he beat my body into the floor. The sweet, thick liquid coated my tongue.

Still, he persisted.

I retreated inside myself, determined to endure. Kelton's rhythm became predictable. My body tensed in anticipation of each strike until finally, the attack missed a beat.

I took an insecure breath as Kelton stood, shaking his sore hand. His chest heaved with deep, rapid gasps. He looked upon my uncurling body and ground the heels of his boot into my fingers. The other boot he pressed into my cheek.

"Plead for mercy, sirrah!" His wrath-filled hiss cut through my whimpers.

"My Lord…"

He yelled at a volume supported from the pit of his stomach, "Grovel!"

I wanted the pain to stop and thought of nothing else. Desperate, I would have obeyed any command if compliance ceased the attack. My words were muffled with my face pressed into the floor, but I groveled for my life.

"She is a worthless servant." I struggled to form each phrase that felt like a foreign language. "She failed you. She subjected her Lord to the shame of public failure. This retribution is just; it is a small taste of what she deserves."

"Go on." Kelton's order was void of mercy.

My tears stung the cut on my lip, and I tasted the salt. I dug deep to find the words he wanted to hear. Broken at the moment, I am not sure I did not believe them myself.

"She does not deserve your mercy but pleads for it anyways. She begs for the chance to serve you again, for the opportunity to right her wrong. Please my Lord. Please…"

"Good." Kelton kneeled over me, wiping his brow. "You promised me the ideal poison. Do not make me regret saving your life twice."

His eyes narrowed in consideration. Licking his lips, his fingers traced my sweaty neck before rounding my breast and lingering between my legs. His touch left a burning trail of violation across my skin. I wanted him off me, but the bulge within his breeches pressed harder against my stomach. My naked body abased upon the floor was simply too appealing. But his desires remained consistent. Standing with a second wind, the toe of his boot drove into my stomach, pushing me against the wall.

I no longer had the will or strength to resist. My body flailed with the blow like a pile of rags. Pinned between the wall and his foot, I coughed blood after one final kick. Every muscle in my body seemed ripped beyond repair. The last thing I remember was the room slowly spinning before a black tunnel swallowed my vision.

I woke on the floor, shivering.

The hearth had long extinguished, and I could not even smell smoke rising from the ash. Sunlight poured through the window, casting a blurred ray on my body.

I was not even sure I still had a body.

It hurt to breathe, to open my eyes, to lay on the floor. Every part of me was tender. Too tired to do anything else, I stared at the legs of an end table until the sun no longer shone.

I needed to find warmth.

My frail remains could not endure another night bare upon the floor. Somehow, I managed to force my mangled limbs into sitting. The room spun once more from the motion of my ringing head. I realized I could not fully open either eye and with what limited sight remained, I beheld the effects of what I had endured.

My body suffered more lacerations than I could count. Blood streaked down my skin from unknown sources. My thighs were

black and my arms a sickly yellow. My back seized with the slightest movement. But at least I was alone. With Muriel away for a
week, I feared Kelton might return and doubted I would survive
a second bout.

Gasping with each bolt of pain, I crawled through the cottage,
leaving a red trail in my wake. Several times my legs gave way
beneath me, and I crashed to the floor. With each fall, it became
harder to continue. I thought of my Lord Savior's final struggle
through Jerusalem. This was my own Lenten penance.

The ascent into bed looked more insurmountable than the
road to Golgotha. Instead, I pulled down a blanket, wrapped my
body in its warmth, and cried myself to sleep for another night.

The next morning I woke famished, but mercifully, still alone.

Despite the desire, I could not exist another day on the floor.
To heal, I needed to eat. I needed water. With a mountain of re-
solve, I sat back up once more. My God, how it hurt to breathe.
Leaning on the bed, I managed to my feet.

I should not have looked, but the call of the hand mirror on
the dresser grew too alluring to resist. I wish I could forget the
horror of the image reflected back.

My skin was too tender for clothes, so for the next day, I
stayed wrapped in the blanket, pulling the fabric tight around my
trembling body. Everything became a struggle. I finally coaxed a
small fire sufficient enough to warm a bowl of broth. The shaking
spoon spilled with each trip to my mouth, but I could feel the
nourishment flow through my body with a warmth of reassurance.

For the first time, I believed I would heal.

The third day was better. Since my skin remained too sensitive
for a bath, I managed to scrub away the caked blood with the pail
of water I made from melted snow. Slowly, my strength returned

and over the next days, I put myself, and the cottage, back together.

By the time Muriel's week of vacation concluded, I had scrubbed away the trails and splattering of blood, flipped over the rug by the hearth, and burnt the red-stained blanket. I managed to don a loose gown, but I could not hide the deep, facial bruises.

After hearing her anticipated question, I shrugged. "I fell off the ladder in the grow room, acclumsid. That far pot is too high of a reach, and I should have asked for help."

Muriel's eyes narrowed, comparing my appearance to the story I spun. "From the looks of it, you must have taken out half of the shelves on your way down."

"Thankfully, Agnella's bedridden now. I cleaned up the mess before anyone saw and repotted most of the broken plants. With a new babe to care for soon, I do not think she will notice the few that did not survive."

I relied on her simple mind to see truth in my tale.

Muriel looked at me once more but accepted the story. "Well, you should have sent for assistance or at least a wise woman." She placed a comforting hand on my shoulder, and I bit my lip, struggling not to gasp in pain.

"They are bruises, Muriel," I assured. "I will be fine."

Accepting my claim with reluctance, she looked beyond me, evaluating the state of the cottage with a sigh. "Well, we can cover bruises, but from the looks of things, it does not appear you have fared well on your own."

I dare say Muriel enjoyed the fact that my cottage was a disaster. Everything needed dusting, piles of bowls waited to be washed. A small basket of laundry had been left untouched from before her vacation. The disarray made her feel needed and truly, she was. Her company also helped me emotionally heal.

With Muriel's return, I was able to start dealing with what had transpired. Kelton had used me for his own entertainment. He had belittled me, reduced me to a whimpering rag doll. I wished I could have remained strong. I wished I would not have pleaded to him. While I could not change what occurred, I could control our interactions going forward — if I recaptured my inner strength. I longed for the rejuvenation of Holy Communion. My soul famished without mass but settled for prayer. I prayed for courage, for perseverance. I vowed to never let Kelton Darley make me feel small again. And on my knees, I resolved to use *him* to get what *I* always wanted. The days my body remained too faint to work became a gift; they forced me to use my mind. I considered every option which might provide an advantage during the last weeks of the deadline. More sure of the need than ever, I could not afford to lose any more time.

Kelton waited two weeks before returning to my cottage, and by the time he came, my request was rehearsed. He entered and carried on as if nothing had happened between us. The layers of powder Muriel applied to my face each morning concealed the last visible signs of the attack, my clothes concealed the rest. Kelton's eyes scanned my skin for bruises, and I enjoyed denying him that last wisp of victory. To his further dismay, I joined his game.

"Good morning, Madam Maud."

Biting my cheek, I managed through the pain of a curtsey in reply. "Good morning, my Lord. A pleasure as always."

His eyes narrowed in jest. "I trust you have been well?"

I smiled. "Perfect, my Lord. I have always found comfort in your generous cottage."

Kelton scoffed, picking up a jar of beans in examination.

"My Lord," I continued with a polished, gentle tone. "I assume you are here to check on the progress of your extraction."

"Indeed." He set down the jar to look towards me.

On account of Muriel, I closed the door to the workroom for privacy. "I do believe I am on the right track, but cracking the poison's secrets will require a regimented sequence of careful experiments. The variation of one element at a time. I simply cannot prepare all the tests myself. Mistress Sallay is a hard worker, but she is not experienced with these types of processes. I need someone who can work as fast as my own pace."

Kelton raised his eyebrows. "After everything, after my...convincing, you fear you will not make the deadline?"

I exhaled, remaining firm. "Alchemy cannot be rushed, my Lord." I stared directly at him. "A fist cannot transform lead into gold. However, leveraging the skills of my former apprentice could turn the tides in your favor."

Kelton stood silent for a moment, staring upon me in consideration. The vein in his temple visibly beat while his eyebrow furrowed before conceding. "Very well. When you are ready, take a horse and go see her."

My mouth fell open, surprised by his permission. For the first time in months, I felt I might meet the absurd deadline. Having won the small victory, my charm was genuine. "Thank you, my Lord."

Without a word, he nodded and left. He wanted to control me but wanted his poison more.

Kelton's permission rejuvenated my weak body and spirit. I yearned for Aselin's companionship, for her help with cracking the bean. I could not wait to tell her what had been accomplished and the status I sat on the verge of clutching.

Without a word of explanation to Muriel, I donned a cloak and headed for the stables. My teeth gritted, bearing the pain of mounting the horse, but it was well worth the suffering. On top of the steed, I felt free. My cloak billowed behind me as we laid fresh tracks on the trails.

For the first time in months, I was going home.

I had not decided what I would say before my own cottage came into view. Instead, I relied on improvisation, allowing wit to guide my mouth. Slowing to a trot, I tied the horse to my gate and walked up the path to my front door. The house looked much the same. It had been well tended throughout the winter months, and I was grateful to Edmund for his toil. The familiarity warmed my heart, and I caressed the door handle with appreciation. She was now mere feet away. My apprentice, my heir. With a deep breath, I readied myself.

Since it was my house, I did not bother to knock and walked through the front door. At the sight of my presence, Aselin's ceramic mug fell through her hands and shattered.

Chapter Nineteen

Aselin stared silent, frozen. I savored the moment, relishing her shock. I walked into the place as if I owned it — because I did. In my cottage, I was Master. Being back on top was another homecoming in addition to the physical return, even if the circumstances of the ascent were limited.

But Aselin's appearance restrained my delight. Her eyes ringed dark and lacked the spark which had first attracted me that day in the market. After her shock had waned, Aselin gave an awkward curtsey, remembering her place. "Master." With formality concluded, she ran over with a hug that threatened to knock me backward.

My body had healed over the last two weeks, but at that moment, my heart caught up. Aselin's elated reception proved I meant as much to her as she did to me.

"Everyone thought you were too ashamed to return after being arrested for harlotry," she spoke fast, touching my face in disbelief. "The stewsman confirmed the rumors you frequented the brothel. But I knew your true crime. I thought I would never see you again!" She touched my face in a mix of relief and skepticism.

With a gentle smile, my thumb wiped her tear. "You very nearly did not." I looked her over, amused to find her wearing one of my dresses.

"Aselin! Are you alright —" Edmund came running from the kitchen and stopped cold at the sight of my figure.

We gazed upon one another in a silent battle of wills. He would have been in charge of the house in my absence, but now, I was back. He knew his place and bent first.

Rising from his bow, Edmund's face turned white as if he had seen a ghost. In his mind, he had. "How? My Lady? I…"

I opened the drawer of the entryway table and forcibly placed Baines' goblet back in its proper place. With slow, menacing steps, I closed the distance to the boy.

"I took you into my household, Edmund. I cared for you and your sister for years, never asking for a coin in return. And how did you repay me?"

"Please… Madam Maud…" Edmund's eyes blinked, agitated. "When Haylan came asking, I got scared. I panicked."

"Lies." I pressed closer to him. "Did not you consider you could have been implicated as an accomplice? Did you ever think about your sister's hand in the act?"

"That is exactly what I did," he hastily defended. "I protected her by deflecting the blame!"

"No, Edmund." I exhaled, calming my voice. "I did."

I turned my back on the boy to face Aselin. "I was arrested for the murder of the Earl. Agnella and Father Eustace also gave me away. But I took full blame and covered your participation. The new Earl, Kelton Darley, offered me a post as his poison alchemist in exchange for my silent loyalty. I have been living on his estate since. My supplies were not impounded, they were delivered to me."

Her face twisted, contemplating the story as I paused with apprehension. My pride fell with the coming admission and unable to face Aselin, I focused on a knot in the floorboard.

"I had to plead for my life," I resumed with a choke in my throat. "Convince him I was worthy of his patronage. His mother's recommendation did not suffice, and out of desperation, I told him about the castorbean."

"Lavinia?" Aselin knew enough to understand.

"I have made progress unlocking the extraction, but I need a trained hand and mind to help me finish." I walked over to her, taking her hands in mine. "You cannot be happy with whatever façade of a life you have crafted in my absence. I know the desires you harbor and understand your thirst for ambition. I am on the verge of everything I have dreamed. My marks are now officials and peers, I have a full patron of prestige, but I am missing my apprentice. Come join me, Aselin."

The girl's eyes twinkled as if she had been awakened from a nightmare. Color returned to her face for what I assumed was the first time in months. I offered an edited version of my tale, but at that moment, I had given us both back our dreams.

"You did it." Aselin pulled back in awe. "Yes? Haylan died so unexpectedly…"

The memory still brought too much pain. "I did what I had to," I stated simply.

I turned and looked through the window into the front yard. The trees had grown. For a moment, I saw Haylan opening the hatch in the front gate. How many times had I waited for him through this very window?

Aselin's touch brought me back. "If anyone can understand, it is me." Aselin smiled in reassurance. "Of course, I will come. Of course, I will help."

"No!"

To our surprise, a masculine voice resounded through the hallway. We both turned in shock to see Edmund's fist clenched with fury.

"No," he yelled again. "You corrupted my sister once, and I stood idle. I will not let you do it again."

Ignoring my presence, Edmund's face relaxed with compassion as he walked towards his sister. "Ase, you promised me you had left those aspirations behind. I have warned you for years of the risk, and we have now seen that come true. Lavinia was arrested for murder, given up by her patrons. She got lucky this time, but how many times do you think she will be lifted out of the noose? Stealing apples in the market for our table is one thing. But this, being an assassin? It borderlines insanity." Spit flew from his mouth at the word, his once callow face set into the hard lines of a young man, standing tall. "It is a path towards living a lie, forever cowering in shadows. A life that teeters on a knife point and can be ripped away at any moment."

Aselin exhaled, entwining her fingers with his. "But it is a life of intrigue, of the highest ecstasies, accomplishing the impossible. A life that gives me control. A line of work that provides a freedom you take for granted and waste. Lavinia could have condemned me with her, but she covered my participation. She could have used me all those years, but instead, she patiently passed down her knowledge."

Aselin let go of her brother's hand. Her soft curls fanned from the speed which she looked back towards me. "I cannot pass a second chance to realize my goals. For all the reasons I agreed the first time, and so many more now, yes.

"But I also cannot abandon family," she continued. "Your invitation must extend to him as well. Edmund is right, he keeps me grounded and my arrogance in check." Aselin turned towards her brother. "I will leave you, Edmund, if you chose not to come, but I pray you will join me. I need your nightly talks, your voice of reason and restraint."

I folded my arms, challenging my apprentice. "You would risk the presence of someone who gave us up once already?"

"What was he supposed to say when Haylan presented such direct charges?" Aselin provided the defense I expected. "He did not speak unprompted."

"Fine," I agreed reluctant, though it was a small concession to gain my apprentice. Edmund could not pose a risk living with us in isolation, especially with the Earl in my pocket. "He may come too, provided he agrees to the same promise of silence."

I looked past Aselin to her brother. My approach pressed him backward against the wall.

"I understand why you gave me up." My sour words sought to unnerve the boy. My face pressed inches from his wide eyes. "But you have used your one absolution. Any hint of deception, any word from your meager tongue, and I will not be so forgiving." I stepped back, looking him up and down with a mocking glance. "The game is elevating, Edmund. You may find there is less use for pawns, especially ones who clutter the board."

The boy swallowed. "Yes, my Lady."

"You are lucky I value your sister, and that she values you. Your life depends on those facts not changing." I stared into his eyes, praying I was not making a mistake before departing deeper into my cottage.

Having provided my ultimatum, I turned my attention to logistics. Edmund scorned around the house, but he would not abandon his sister. We packed into the late hours and the following day, we loaded boxes into a borrowed wagon with a bed for

Edmund since the Earl's cottage only had two. I took time to inspect every inch of my cellar workroom, searching for any useful tools or notes Kelton's men may have missed. My efforts produced a few vials of potato poison, a jar of dried wolfsbane, and some random annotations — though none of which aided my current predicament. Still, I left my house with an advantage: Aselin.

The day the siblings moved in, jealously radiated from Muriel. She turned uncharacteristically cold at the first moment of introduction. I did not blame her, Muriel understood she was being replaced as my aid in the workroom, and that she would share domain over house chores with Edmund. To my disappointment, Muriel still lacked nerve and bit her tongue, unable to tell me off as I deserved.

My patron, however, had gall in abundance. As I expected, Kelton could not contain his curiosity and paid a visit the following day.

"This little cottage is becoming crowded, Mistress Maud." The Earl smirked.

"Better equipped to serve you, my Lord," I retorted with polite overtones. "My Lord Earl, may I have the pleasure of introducing my apprentice, Aselin Gavrell, and her brother, Edmund."

Kelton took Aselin's hand in a gesture of chivalry. "Madam Gavrell. Lord Akworth spoke of your unmatched beauty, but such a fine face must be seen to believe the account."

Aselin blushed.

I sighed.

My patron's infatuation with my apprentice grew old. Yes, she was blonde, well endowed, and fair — all features I did not possess. But I was the Master, the potion expert, the one who could give them what they truly desired beyond the feeble needs of the flesh. I wished my attributes were more openly valued. Yes, among many things, I was a jealous woman.

Aselin politely endured the fawning before Kelton's interest turned towards Edmund. "Mistress Maud, you did not state you would be bringing a male servant as well?"

I knew of one justification the Earl would understand, and I played the card without hesitation. "Edmund has been with me for years, it is a blessing to have him around the house for the tasks my woman hands are too weak to attempt."

Kelton looked the boy up and down. "Well, that is logical — as long as this new arrangement produces results." His eyes focused into mine as we both understood the unspoken threat. "I will hold you accountable."

I flinched, regretting I could not mask the fear he inflamed. "Of course, my Lord."

His face adopted his sickly smile while his finger ran the length of my jaw line. "Carry on then."

And we did.

For the sake of a peaceful home, I was relieved that Muriel and Edmund found companionship in each other. Edmund flourished, having someone else to talk to, and Muriel benefited from Edmund's life experiences. During the long winter months, I had tried to teach Muriel to stand up for herself, but it was Edmund who taught her to be strong around the opposite gender. A spark never developed between them, but they passed the time in each other's company.

Those two existed as background clutter while Aselin and I focused on the castorbean. Together, we poured through the evidence I collected, searching for any missed lead. During breaks, I told her about the airborne delivery method I had tested and the details of Haylan's murder. She knew of the six-month deadline, but I never disclosed the ramifications of the failed test. I never told another soul.

When no further insights could be gleaned from my journals, I began the entire process anew in demonstration. Nothing could be improved with the process to remove the bean's shell. Even if it could be done faster, the step did not affect potency, and we did not waste our time discussing the method. But afterward, the recipe became unclear. We painstakingly evaluated each step, pausing for hours to brainstorm refinements that might increase potency.

My spirit thrived from the hours of debate and discussion. The shared knowledge between our heads would have impressed any member of the Guild. We worked into the early hours of most mornings, consulting years of my journals, following hunches and experimenting. Despite the enjoyment, the long hours over weeks took their toll. We never spoke aloud of the deadline, though it loomed over our work. Each day, I was aware of the silent clock ticking.

It was late in the afternoon in early April that I finally solved the puzzle.

Aselin processed several jars of unshelled beans that had been stewing for days in acetone. She cracked open the fourth jar and poured the contents into a pan for drying. "This smells so strongly like fruit."

I will never forget that mundane remark. I nodded in reply. "It is the acetone still present."

Once again, inspiration came like the dawn.

"Aselin." Her name came out in breathy elation. "It is the acetone!"

I ran over to the hearth and took the jar from her hands, wafting the odor. "The liquid in here is still mostly acetone. What if all the toxin is in the particulate and not in the solution? What if the remaining acetone is diluting the poison!"

We both started laughing in joy, staring at the jar of clear liquid with suspended white flakes. Aselin complied with my order to retrieve a cheesecloth. With a steady hand, I strained the jar's contents over a metal pan, separating the precious solid toxin.

A day later, it dried to a white powder.

With Kelton's repercussions fresh in my mind, I could not bring myself to conjecture his response for not achieving the deadline. Apprehensive, my breath labored as I mixed a dried tomato with the results of the refined process. By my side, Aselin prepared a second tomato with a single teaspoon of the old purification for a separate rat. An uneasy silence fell upon the room as we watched both creatures poke at their fruit before nibbling away.

My hopes and prayers now manifested in two rats and two tomatoes.

The first day brought no visible symptoms, and I stared at the cages with bags under my eyes.

"Master." Aselin came up softly behind me. "Have faith. You seek a poison with a slow time-to-effect, there should not be any symptoms today."

I nodded with a small smile, finding faith in her truth. Aselin brought a fresh vigor to the workroom, unburdened by months of failure. I allowed her spirit to fill mine with encouragement.

Ultimately, the symptoms proceeded as before, but with the new recipe, they were magnitudes worse. And on the third day, I had my answer.

I have never been more elated to see a dead rat.

Outside, a spring sun melted the snow, and for the first time in months, I felt the storm clouding my own confidence begin to clear. I had extracted a powerful toxin though doubted it was fully purified. But out of time, the poison was as good as it was going to become within Kelton's deadline. The new purification proved more potent and killed my subsequent test goat, but I still did not know if it could kill a human. And once again, I faced a dilemma of dosage.

Saturating the victim's goblet still gave me the best chance to pass Kelton's test, though the setup did not satisfy the assassin within. I wanted to know the proportion curve. I wanted to know how much I needed to give Silas. To know how to tweak the dose to produce the longest delay in symptoms while maintaining lethal results.

Only one method would produce the detailed knowledge I craved. Driven by ambition, I took a risk and offered a counter-proposal to the Earl.

"Five subjects?" Kelton repeated my request with surprise before his eye began to twinkle. The possibility teased his desire.

"Yes, my Lord," I affirmed. "Last time, I saturated the water because the toxin lacked potency. I am confident such a high proportion will be lethal with my new formulation."

Confident was an overstatement.

"However," I lectured with false resolution, "it would be prudent to know at what dosage the poison is lethal. That will allow us to prepare a method of exposure for Silas which minimizes risk. I also hope a smaller dose will maximize the delay between administration and the onset of symptoms."

"To reduce the likelihood the death would be traced back to us," Kelton finished proudly.

He had stated the obvious, but I stroked his pride. "Exactly. Each of the five subjects would be given a different dosage, and we would observe how they fair. It would be best if each were as similar to the mark's age and weight as possible."

Kelton nodded. "Logical."

I swallowed, pausing, aware of the peril of the final request. "There is a catch, my Lord."

He did that annoying eyebrow mannerism as his voice chilled with deep resonance. "Go on, Madam Maud."

"As the dosage is reduced, the likelihood the result is lethal decreases. The dose makes the poison."

Kelton's irritation spawned instantly. "You are saying you cannot guarantee they will all die."

The edges of my vision blackened with the memory of his raged sweat dripping on my exposed body in front of the hearth. I shook my head and the memory away. "Not if we wish to understand the full range of dose."

"A clever way to provide yourself cover." Kelton stood, towering over me. "It seems you received my message loud and clear."

I sat still on the chair in his office, unwilling to acknowledge how deeply he had scarred me. I held my breath. This was the moment of truth as Kelton considered my proposal.

"Very well," Kelton conceded after not receiving the rise from me he hoped to incite. "I will consider the test successful if at least one of them dies and none of the five can detect the toxin. You promised me a tasteless poison."

My breath released, relieved. "I did, my Lord."

"I will contact you when we have your five subjects. Is that all, Madam Maud?"

It was not. I felt the inner itch rising like a tide of fire within my gut. He would not deny this final detail, and without remorse, I played my last card to win his favor.

"No." I paused, looking up through my lashes. "With respect, I suggest you do not release the ones who survive."

Having recaptured Kelton's attention, desire ignited in his eyes. "Oh?"

I rose, stroking his arrogance. "You, my Lord, are on the verge of assassinating a high-profile opponent with an unprecedented toxin that you alone possess. I am not concerned with Goodman Stace, but I advise that further knowledge of the poison's existence should be contained at all cost."

Kelton licked his lips as his wheels of perverse imagination turned. "Then what do you propose we do with the survivors?"

I could not answer that question. To kill for the sake of it violated my morality, but my recommendation did not waiver. Instead, I shrugged. "I leave that to your capable discretion. Though I would be happy to provide other toxins should my Lord desire."

Kelton waived his hand in dismissal. "There are many solutions." His face sparkled, distant with thought. After a moment, he returned to the present, "We shall not make it more of a dilemma than it needs to be. That is all, Madam Maud."

I departed, pleased to have a plan for execution. Surely one of the five would die, and with luck, the rest would characterize the poison. However, five test subjects meant I would need a larger supply the toxin than I had currently purified. Aselin and I set to work, and after I had explained the intention, her own eyes sparkled at the notion.

Aselin's words sped from her tongue, barely comprehensible. "With an array of test subjects in controlled conditions, we could define the potency curve for every toxin!"

"Settle down, Aselin." I shook my head, laughing before changing my tone. "Such thoughts occurred to me as well, though we will have to take our time. Unfortunately, my patron has a taste for dark merriment; I expect we will need to keep him entertained over the long term to ensure he does not satisfy his cravings in ways we would not desire."

Aselin's eyes narrowed, but I did not elaborate.

"In the meantime, we need to stay vigilant and replicate the process exactly. If this test does not prove successful…"

I left the thought hanging and after a moment started counting beans into jars of water for distraction.

My fingers grew stiff after hours of separating bean shells. The entire workroom smelled of acetone, forcing us to tie fabric masks around our faces and take frequent breaks to avoid intolerable lightheadedness. Muriel and Edmund sensed we remained deep in concentration and kept to themselves, restricting their interruptions to only when a meal was served. The cottage became a cluttered, organized chaos of beans soaking in glass jars on windowsills, pans of white powder drying near the hearth, and purified toxin waiting for vials in the hallway. Muriel took pride keeping the fire blazing, and Edmund upheld his promise to hold his tongue.

Despite my confidence, fear of failure robbed my sleep. I laid awake staring at the ceiling, night after night, trying not to wake Aselin whose bed we had set up in my room. In the worst moments, when I closed my eyes, Kelton's stick seized my mind. Twice, Aselin asked why I had tears in the middle of the night.

The first time I dismissed her concern with excuses of yawning. The second time I lied about missing Haylan.

Lack of sleep took a toll on my body, but it became a blessing in disguise. God works in mysterious ways. We often cannot see the bigger picture from our limited vantage points, nor understand that hardship can be disguised intervention. I did not know if divine influence or human weakness kept me awake that night, but the inability to sleep saved my life.

As I stared at the ceiling, a strange shuffle in the hallway caught my attention, followed by the distinct sound of a metal pan being pushed across wood. Every instinct rang in alarm. I made my way to the door with careful steps and opened it enough to peer into the hallway. Ten feet away, Edmund had his back to me, bent over the pans of poison with a bag of flour.

I controlled my anger enough to properly respond. She never would have believed me without bearing witness herself. So after placing a hand over Aselin's mouth, I woke her with a signal to remain quiet. Pulling her out of bed by the hand, I led her wary body to the doorway to witness her brother's act of contamination.

Aselin's mouth had dropped before she retreated back into the bedchamber. Now awake with alarm, she whispered in panic, "What do we do?"

Once again, I gave her a hand motion to calm down. Barely audible, I slowly dictated each word in emphasis. "Nothing right now. If he discovers we know, he could expose us before we can counter. We have no way of knowing how many pans have been contaminated, so confronting him now will not save any of the toxin."

I knew what needed to be done. If Aselin did not possess the gall, I would have done it myself, but I owed her the right to take the mark first. He was her own brother.

A single vial of the apricot poison remained from Haylan's assassination. Retrieving it from the nightstand, I placed it in her palm.

"He has now crossed us twice and cannot be trusted. This profession is risky enough without inside tampering. Complete commitment is the only way to contain risk." My eyes filled with sorrow, knowing too well the dilemma my apprentice now faced. I longed to shelter her but it was time for her to blossom. "Aselin, how committed are you?"

CHAPTER TWENTY

The next morning, when Aselin handed her brother a glass of cider, I knew.

For weeks, I delayed murdering Haylan, even contemplating means to avoid the kill. Aselin committed in one night.

If she had wanted intimacy, she would have picked a more private setting. Since she had chosen our breakfast, I figured I would offer my support and stay. Being Sunday, Muriel had the day off, and it would be the three of us, one final time.

Sitting across from Edmund at the table, my inner fire ignited with anticipation. Watching my apprentice carry out the lessons I had instilled offered more reward than adding to my own tally. She had made a quick, difficult choice, proving her decisiveness and commitment. I could not have been more proud.

Of course, I would not deny I was eager to witness the boy's demise.

Edmund always had an appetite that exceeded his frail physicality. Through a mouth full of bread with butter and sage, he mumbled his thanks before taking a sip of the cider to wash it all down.

My heart leapt.

Revenge is a sweet satisfaction. Edmund had been a bitter sub-ject since I learned of his testimony to Haylan. During many nights, I had dreamed of how I would kill him. Perhaps hemlock or St. Ignatius Beans. I wanted him to suffer, aware of death's imminent clutch and who had delivered the dark fate. But watch-ing Aselin in the act was more gratifying than my most vicious reveries. The identity of his killer would break his heart before it stopped beating, and I had a front row seat.

Aselin pulled out the chair next to her brother and watched him eat. Her face fell somber, savoring the final moments. We both processed the same calculation: when would he have con-sumed enough?

Aselin waited without a word as Edmund focused on his plate, the goblet was now a third consumed. Spooked by the awkward moment of silence, Edmund finally looked up, unnerved. His eyes bounced between his sister and me.

"What's going on?" His words mumbled through a full mouth of bread. His loaded spoon of waiting porridge stalled midway to his mouth.

"I am so sorry, Edmund." Aselin swallowed. "I want you to know I love you. I appreciate everything you have done for me over the years. I promise I will never forget your warnings and will always remain vigilant. I understand the risks I am taking, but only if there are no introduced variables."

Edmund set down the spoon, his attention now focused on his sister while he chewed like a cow. "Ase, you are making no sense."

She exhaled. "I saw you last night, with the flour."

His face finally dropped while Aselin continued.

"How do you think the Earl will respond if the toxin does not work? You diluted the powder to the point we cannot trust it."

"Lavinia's neck is on the line, not yours." Moist morsels of bread flew out of his panicked mouth before he finally swallowed. "And if the Earl loses favor with her then you will be free once more. Aselin, I thought you had put all this nonsense behind!"

What could she have said? I sat still, hanging on every moment of the unfolding drama.

Aselin shook her head, placing a hand on her brother's. "That line of thinking is why this is the way things have to be."

I had kept a close watch on Edmund out of curiosity for time-to-effect. He started to endure long blinks. He had to at least feel a fog in his head clouding his already dim intelligence. He sat at a table with two poison mistresses for heaven's sake. The fact he had not put together the pieces increased my amusement.

Edmund's eyes narrowed, unwilling to believe. "What are you saying, Aselin?"

She took the goblet and looked into the half-full glass. "I am saying, you have minutes left to live."

His eyes filled with panic, turning to me. "You!"

I shook my head with glee, baiting him. "Not me, Edmund."

Panic turned to disbelieving horror as he faced his sister. His eyes blinked longer. "Ase?"

Aselin's own eyes began to swell. "I am so sorry, Edmund. You left me no choice. You have been holding me back for years." She swallowed. "I want to know how far I can go."

Edmund tumbled off the chair onto the floor after losing balance. The chair tipped and rattled beside his body that fell limp. His mouth opened to speak, though produced no sound.

Aselin knelt beside him, brushing the hair back from his face to lay a gentle kiss on his forehead. Edmund reached out and took her hand with one final squeeze before never regaining awareness. I admired Edmund's courage; he had always placed his sister first, even in his final moments. My Haylan had done the same. The scene brought back a flood of memories I was not ready to endure.

I rubbed Aselin's back in solidarity for a moment and then excused myself to my chamber. Aselin cradled Edmund on the floor for hours, feeling the warmth leave his body. She did not regret her decision, we spoke of it later, but I knew first-hand surety did not make the act easier.

We were both now alone, without family in this world. We only had each other.

We buried Edmund in the back of my cottage. It was a hell of a job for the two of us to move his body onto the back of a horse and dig a hole in the middle of the night. The topsoil was wet from melted snow, but the deeper ground remained frozen. I admit, we dug a more shallow grave than we desired, but our arms could not support another shovel full.

Aselin confessed her guilt that we could not give Edmund a proper burial and headstone. We said a few prayers, but I too, recognized the inadequacy. Instead, later when the ground thawed, she planted an apple tree above his grave. Apples were his favorite fruits, though given how he had died, I found the choice curious. I never digested one of those apples… To each her own.

When we arrived back at the Earl's cottage the following morning, Muriel wondered where we had been. We had washed the dirt away at my cottage and had the foresight to bring a change of attire to cover our tracks. I told her that Edmund had received an opportunity to apprentice with a woodsmith in Yorkshire and that we had ridden the first hour with him to say good-bye. For her sake, I embellished the lie, describing how the opportunity had come sudden and unexpected. Still, hurt showed on Muriel's face, despite the message of regret we passed along on Edmund's behalf.

I did what I could, but frankly, I did not have time to deal with the emotions of a frail servant. The entire supply of the castor-bean toxin had been compromised. With no way to know which pans had been tampered with, I had to dispose of it all. My stomach ached at the sight of wasted poison, all that work — lost.

If Aselin ever mourned her brother, I did not notice. I believe she felt the pressure as well, and the experiment preparations kept us too busy to grieve. We searched the cottage for every last bean: any beans that may have wedged between floorboards or fallen behind the workbench. I scoured the grow room, as well. The majority of my potted harvest had been depleted during the last effort, and the small pile of recovered beans seemed inadequate. I had promised five test subjects and doubted Kelton would tolerate a decrease in that number.

But I only needed to kill one.

The burden of purifying an entire second toxin supply was demoralizing enough. With so few beans remaining, I could not afford a single error. Never before had I managed such stress. I made sure Aselin and I obtained a good night's sleep prior to beginning the process. She had always been a hard worker, but her focus sharpened with unnerving intensity. She had more on the line now, I suppose. We both did.

We corked the last vial of the extraction mere hours before Kelton paid a visit. He bought the same lie regarding Edmund we spun to Muriel, though he could not have cared less regarding the boy. I entertained my patron with a detailed description of the purification process, aided by visuals of each step. But, his attention quickly feigned, proving his interest with poisons laid exclusively in the results.

Kelton had selected Marfield's new magistrate himself: a puppet he controlled and kept in his pocket. Given the increased size of our test population, the gaols became the logical location for the experiment. The true purpose of Kelton's visit was to inform us all preparations were complete.

Before dusk the following day, the sound of the horse-litter splashing through puddles of melted snow persisted the entire trip into town. Aselin and I shared a coach with the Earl who, to our amusement, beamed with more giddiness than a young maid. His excitement manifested in unrelenting conversation, with which I did my best to keep up.

"I apologize for bringing ladies to the gaols," Kelton rambled.

After everything, that my patron chose that moment to treat me as a lady amused me. Though, Kelton was more pleasant when he got what he wanted.

"It is the ideal location, and I do not mind," I responded politely. "Are you not aware my father was magistrate before Haylan Moryet?"

Kelton looked befuddled before he broke out with laughter. "No!" He roared as I endured his delight at my expense. "So much for the apple not falling far from the tree, eh?"

I shrugged. "We both dedicated our lives to crime, just on different sides of the game."

Kelton insisted on hearing the story of how I had become a poison assassin, and I complied out of obligation. The tale passed the time and at least kept Kelton's endless banter contained.

My life had changed from the days of hunting marks in taverns and secret meetings with nervous new clients. I had not appreciated the quaintness of the early years of my career until everything altered. I felt the change as evident as the seasons cycling around me. I did not regret my new status, but I mourned the loss of what was. I wished I could go back and enjoy the early moments, instead of always fighting for the next progression. Ironically, we learn that wisdom after wasting so much of life.

The sterility of the upcoming test also did not help with my mood. Once again, I struggled with the notion that my caged rats were now human. I did not deny the necessity and remembered they already faced execution. My conscience settled as we arrived in front of my second childhood home. After all this time, I could almost see my father walking down the street, yelling at me to keep up. I am not sure what he would have thought of hosting such a test, but as a man of loyalty, he would have followed the desires of his Earl.

The new magistrate, Malcom Horner, came out to meet us. The crooked teeth of his half-hearted smile raised my guard, but I tried not to prejudge as he bowed.

"My Lord Earl," he began before turning to me. "Lavinia Maud, I presume? You have your father's resemblance."

"You knew my father?" I pried, surprised.

"Yes, Mistress. I was a boy in the justice's service back then, but my post gave me insight into his work as magistrate. Your father was a man of duty and dedicated to the job I hope to now fill with honor."

I warmed to him at that moment and found reassurance in my decision to stay in the gaols during the duration of the test. Since we had spent the effort to arrange a controlled experiment, Aselin and I decided not to waste the opportunity and prepared to spend long nights recording observations with minute detail. To my dismay, Kelton's guard insisted on remaining to assist.

With Malcom and Kelton's aid, all our bags and supplies were unloaded. Prisoners had been transferred to nearby towns and the staff was given a week's vacation while the gaols were "cleaned."

The empty halls contained an unnerving silence compared to the usual ruckus. However, the moist, musty air retained its unique aroma. The familiar odor filled my reassurance with each breath.

I feared witnessing each other might influence the test subject's individual reactions to the toxin. Therefore, five different cells had been prepared. I inspected each of the contained subjects and reaffirmed Magistrate Horner had done his job well. Each seemed to be in good health and near in age and weight to Silas.

With everything prepared to my satisfaction, I turned to Kelton. "My Lord, would you like the honor of determining which subject shall receive which dose?"

The opportunity to participate ignited the flame within his eyes. "The most severe crimes shall receive the lowest dose and presumably the most suffering."

"A logical decision." I nodded, having not expected my patron to choose a path of reason.

Kelton must have sensed my surprise. "Compassion, right Madam Maud?"

I smiled. "Indeed."

On the magistrate's desk, five pairs of identical goblets filled with water waited for my preparation. Aselin tied a black or white ribbon to each stem as I opened the container of the castorbean poison. It took seven small spoonfuls to saturate one goblet. Staring at the jar in my hands, my mind raced to estimate the remaining poison and decide how to best configure the experiment. Behind me, Aselin recorded the measurements while I counted aloud: seven spoonfuls in the first white goblet, then five, three, two and one.

With the poison depleted, my body tingled with nervous excitement. A year of my life had led to that moment. Truthfully, more than a year. The test served as the culmination of my career. I teetered on the cusp of everything I dreamed. This poison would set me apart from my peers, and I prayed it would earn me a fellowship with the Guild. Success would also seal my fate as the Earl's poison mistress. Everything rested upon the goblets before me.

Despite anticipation, a fragment of lingering doubt cast a shadow over the entire affair. I needed the poison to work more than I needed breath in my lungs. The Earl's pressure was a weight of bricks on my chest. If I failed, I might never leave the gaols. I, too, remained a condemned criminal, living by the grace of a capricious patron with a tantalized appetite for the gruesome.

But there was nothing more I could do. It would either work, or it would not.

I could not withstand the unknown any longer. After picking up the first pair of goblets, the one with saturated water, I nodded to Kelton. Unwilling to expose myself to further tampering, Aselin guarded the remaining goblets as the rest of us delivered the doses.

The first two subjects were both thieves. Unable to rank the severity of their crimes, Kelton flipped a coin, delighting in the notion that such a trivial manner decided a horrid fate.

As the first man sipped both of his goblets, I bit my lip so hard that my mouth filled with the sweet, copper taste of blood. When he stated they both contained plain water, I finally exhaled. If the saturated goblet could not be detected, I felt confident the poison remained tasteless with the new recipe. Now, it just needed to kill.

But before I could finish enjoying one victory, Kelton interrupted.

"Sir, if you had to guess, which goblet contains the toxin?"

The thief examined both goblets and with a shrug, holding up the tainted goblet with white ribbon.

Kelton glared at me. "Tasteless, Madam Maud?"

"Lucky guess, more likely," I said, though a wave of panic ran down my spine despite the odds.

The Earl gave a sarcastic shrug. "We will see."

To my relief, the second thief guessed as well, holding up the black.

The third subject was a rapist who maintained an irritating demeanor.

"I agreed to drink *one* experimental poison," the man stated, conceited. "These are *two* goblets."

"Which contain one poison," I sighed.

"So which *one* shall I drink?" The man shook the goblets in each hand as I sharply inhaled, fearing he might spill a single precious drop.

"Both," I snapped. "One contains poison, and the other does not. That is *one* poison."

Fed up, Kelton yelled at the man at such volume it reverberated through the entirety of the gaols, "You will do as you are told, or I will draw out your bowels right here with my bare hands!"

I did not doubt the Earl meant his words. The rapist did not either and drank the goblets without further delay. Of course, the damn man guessed the white.

The last two criminals were murders. The man who murdered his father picked the black before drinking the goblet with two spoonfuls of toxin.

With no more goblets to guard, Aselin joined us to deliver the last dose. As a reward for her efforts, she deserved to see the toxin consumed. Ending the grisly parade, Kelton led us to the cell of a man who had set his rival's house on fire. The wife and child had burnt alive while the father frantically tried to save them. Kelton's guard recounted that once the fire had been contained, the villagers found the babe's black corpse fused to the remains of his mother's breast. The heat had melted their skin. To die in such a manner... The father's helplessness must have crushed his soul. To think the convict deliberately caused those people to suffer such a fate — I did not understand how someone could be so full of evil.

After hearing the story, I hoped one spoonful of my toxin would not be enough. I prayed the arsonist would suffer a more vile death under Kelton's hand.

Adding to my enmity, the bastard raised the white goblet.

Before I even recorded the results in my journal, Kelton pinned me against the wall with his hand on my throat. I heard Aselin's gasp from somewhere behind my patron. The quill fell from my fingers and bounced on the stone floor. His crushing force radiated through my neck as I choked, struggling for breath.

"Three of five, Madam Maud." Kelton's tone caused me to shudder as he pressed his knee into my stomach. "Maybe I should make you taste your supposed 'tasteless' poison?"

My eyes filled with fear as I coughed. Prior memories flooded my thoughts, but this time, I kept my wits.

"Three of five is tasteless." My words were so breathy I am not sure if Kelton could not understand them or failed to follow my logic.

Kelton increased the force of his knee and lessened the pressure around my throat so I might speak. "What do you mean, sirrah?"

"There are two goblets. Each man had a fifty percent chance of guessing correctly. Since there were five subjects, it is equally likely to have three of five correct guesses as otherwise."

Kelton slapped my face which turned hard into the stone wall. "Do you dare to correct me, Mistress Maud?" Doubt flared in his eyes. He knew I had proven him wrong, but for his own pride, he could not admit it.

"No, never, my Lord. Each subject said they believed it to be water. They randomly guessed. I have not failed you, my Lord."

Kelton's eyes narrowed. "Not yet."

He backed away, and I used the wall to find my balance, my hand rubbing my throat as I regained composure.

Kelton turned toward Malcom. "Send a messenger when and *if* one dies."

Out of embarrassment, Kelton needed to leave to save face. We all watched the Earl's back depart with a sigh of relief. I met Aselin's stunned expression of concern and gave her a reassuring nod, coming to her side.

"Take note," I whispered in her ear. "Be sure to pick your patrons wisely."

Aselin's inquisitive stare was unfulfilled. "Master?"

I dismissed her prod and looked towards the magistrate.

"He has a temper, that one," Malcom muttered. "Maybe not the best fellow to have a poison mistress in his pocket."

For once, I could not argue.

Chapter Twenty-One

My father's honored gaols turned into a ghastly display of depravity lifted from my dreams.

To my delight, during morning rounds, the first thief complained his cell spun. Hours later, the signs of nausea were followed by vomiting. He refused his lunch, which bothered none of us, hoping it might reduce the repugnant mess. That night, Aselin noticed his ankles and legs began to swell, and despite having laid down for hours, his breath rate ran rapidly like a dog's panting. The next day, the pain in his abdomen brought tears to his yellowed eyes.

With each new symptom, my concern faded, allowing me to savor the display of suffering. The pace of the poison is indeed cruel. I generally prefer fast-acting extractions that provide immediate assurance of success. However, in this controlled circumstance, I reveled in the entertainment that persisted from hours into days. None of us could look away, awe-inspired by my heinous creation.

Aselin took a seat beside me to watch the thief moaning on the floor of his cell. "They are all vomiting now."

"Even the arsonist?" I asked.

She nodded, caught up in the spectacle before us.

For the first time since the experiment began, a true smile grew on my face. "See how he's grabbing his chest?" Aselin nodded in response. "I wonder if he will have a heart attack."

"Mayhap," Aselin responded in thought. "How much longer do you gather?"

I shrugged with a glimmer in my eye. "I do not know, but would you care to wager?"

Aselin turned to face me with the same gleam. Before long we had a pot of wagers from myself, Aselin, Malcom and Kelton's guard, with guesses on time of death for all five.

That evening, the thief slipped into a deep sleep. For the sake of record collection, we began checking his pulse every quarter of an hour. In the middle of the night, I could no longer find the weak rhythm. Even though he passed hours before I had wagered, jubilation burst through me as my shrill of excitement echoed through the gaols. Filled with abundant relief, I wept. The others came running at my ruckus to find Aselin and I embraced, jumping in tears of joy.

That was the proudest moment of my life, and I was glad to share it with Aselin.

Out of duty, Malcom sent a night messenger to Kelton who arrived the following morning. He found us gathered around the second thief who had fallen into a deep sleep at dawn.

"Care to join our pool, my Lord?" His guard asked.

I smiled. Even the oversized brute was enjoying the results. Of course, his question was unnecessary, Kelton could not resist the notion.

Over the next four days, each of the subjects succumbed to the same series of symptoms and eventually passed — even the arsonist. The result left me wondering how small of an amount remained lethal, but I did not dare suggest another test. I had enough observations to determine what dose would suit Silas and more importantly, I had proven myself to the Earl. My purse contained fewer coins, but my confidence surged. It was my moment of triumph, and I longed to share it with those who understood the enormity of the accomplishment.

Over the next days, I sat at a desk several times, fiddling with a quill. I wanted to take credit for the discovery to the Guild before anyone else unlocked the bean. But each time I stared at the blank parchment, failing to write a word out of an abundance of caution. As much as I craved accolade, the prudent course was to wait until the dust settled on Silas's coffin. Instead, I wrote of my experimentation with inhalation delivery of the apricot seed poison. At least I had something to contribute to the compilation of knowledge.

In the interim, Kelton's delight continued and was enough to pacify my self-pride. He was a man of fierce passion that outpoured in response to both failure and success. Of course, from my perspective, his positive intensity was less painful. Aselin and I returned home from the gaols to find two blue boxes with gold ribbons sitting on the table in the entryway. At the sound of our entrance, Muriel came running with her hands clasped in delight.

"The Earl said your medicine passed the test!"

Before I could prepare, her arms wrapped around me in a hug as tight as a noose.

I laughed, indulging in the moment. "Yes." I held her face at arm's length. "Do not underestimate your part in this endeavor, Muriel. You were there from the first trials in the workroom. Your efforts kept this house running so I could concentrate."

Muriel beamed with pride as Aselin stepped forward.

"Master, I kept your cottage while the castorbean plant was retrieved," Aselin interjected. "I was there at the *true* beginning."

I released Muriel and looked towards my apprentice with a patient smile. "Of course, Aselin. I do not need to recount your role. You know as well as I the long journey this has been."

Muriel distracted the exchange, gesturing to the boxes no longer able to sustain the suspense. "The Earl left these for the both of you. Oh, you must open them."

I shared my maid's curiosity and handed a box to Aselin before pulling the gold ribbon on the second to free the thin lid. Inside, under a burnt orange satin cloth, rested a diamond broach in the shape of an oval with spires protruding from the circumference. I gasped at the beauty of the gems. Holding the piece to the light of the window, we marveled at the reflected sunlight from the jewels' facets embedded in white gold. Muriel drooled with wide eyes while Aselin opened her box to find a matching piece.

My jealousy flared. I had been the mastermind behind the poison, my ideas perfected the extraction and *I* had sold the Earl on the notion. Though I knew why Aselin's gift was identical to mine. Despite all of my work and loyalty, I lacked the one thing she possessed over me: allure.

I was thin, my face well-toned. I kept my hair styled and carried myself with tall posture. But my face was not fair, nor my voice smooth as honey as Mary Clements. My locks were not soft blond with light curls, my chest not as voluptuous as Aselin's. The effect of those differences proved evident from the first meeting with Baron Akworth. The same male weakness appeared in Kelton when his eyes befell my apprentice. Aselin had the personality to reduce men to muttering fools and a hereditary advantage I could never match. The fact I could not even the playing field frustrated me to no end.

Thankfully, I learned to find satisfaction in my own self-pride. I also wallowed in Kelton's shower of appreciation that did not end with the broach.

That evening, Aselin and I received an invitation to dine with the Earl's family at the estate. We dressed in the finest gowns from Agnella's reject collection and ensured our matching brooches were prominent.

When we entered the dining room, Agnella's face read of jealousy. Her belly swelled under layers of light fabric that flowed free and unfitting. Her face was bloated and her hair cascaded down her shoulders untamed. Baron Akworth stared for a moment as we entered, catching himself in time to help his fiancé take her seat. Aselin's confident steps matched my stride into the room, and after a glared reminder, she fell to her proper place behind me.

"My Lord Earl," I acknowledged Kelton first with a curtsey and then turned to the others. "My Lady Countess, my Lord Baron." With formality concluded, I turned to Agnella. "My Lady, you look radiant and beautiful. I have no doubt your babe will be as stunning."

Agnella acknowledged my obligated flattery with a dismissive wave of her hand.

The dinner was a private affair with the five of us. Kelton sat at the head of table and Akworth at the other. The Earl gave me a seat of honor at his side, and Agnella took the opposite. That left Aselin next to me and to the Baron's side at the other end. Akworth clearly enjoyed the arrangement.

The small table seemed dwarfed by the size of the dining room. Despite multiple candelabras, the ceiling towered so high I could not see the fresco above. The walls featured an olive-green wash, trimmed with hand-carved, dark-stained wood. The entire stuffy, ornate ambiance did not appease my tastes, but it gave a fine aura for a formal affair.

The first course featured a stew, though, to my amusement, I noticed the entire table left the mushrooms on their plate. Boiled chicken followed with fritters, accompanied by polite, reserved conversation. Once our silver trenchers were bare, Kelton wasted no time proceeding with business, despite the remaining two courses. It seemed this dinner possessed an alternative motive beyond acknowledgment of my accomplishment.

Kelton began his speech with accolade, revealing to Agnella and Lord Akworth the clandestine tests that had occurred in the cellar and gaols. Akworth listened with intrigue, but Agnella's eyes grew wary. She either knew or assumed the Earl's intention. Kelton was her son after all, she must have been aware of the offensive desires that ran through her offspring.

Akworth seemed impressed by Kelton's description of my castorbean extraction. Having caught my eye, he raised his glass to me with a smile. Though the color drained from his face when Kelton revealed the intended mark.

"My dear, you must already know he cannot live." Agnella looked to her betrothed with more grace than I would have expected. Then again, this blood would not be on her hands. Mayhap that allowed her to be at peace with the notion.

Akworth swallowed his bite of roasted quail and removed the linen napkin from his shoulder. "Silas is not some meek buffoon like Tedric."

"Edward…" Agnella interrupted his sentiment with displeasure.

"Well, he's not," Akworth affirmed. "And what about his Uncle? Do you think Isabel's family will let such an act endure unanswered? They may have concealed the evidence, but we all know where she got the support for her treachery."

Kelton stood, pounding the table. "And does the Baron presume to think they are not also sitting around a table right now, planning how they might put Silas in my title?"

Agnella's soft tone lowered the tension in the room. "Silas has a birthright claim. It is only Tedric's proclamation that says otherwise."

Akworth exhaled, accepting the argument before him. He stared off distant for a moment, his plotting mind likely spinning. Sensing the tension decrease, Kelton retook his seat.

Akworth proceeded with the utmost caution, "My Lord Earl, how do you propose slipping this castor toxin to Silas?"

At that moment, I put together why Kelton had assembled this strange crowd for dinner. I turned towards the engaged couple, guessing my patron's intention. "Your wedding feast, my Lord." My eyes met Kelton's, and I knew I inferred correctly. "Silas will be obligated to attend. There will be plenty of food and commotion to pull off the job."

Kelton nodded. "With the right dose, Madam Maud's toxin will not show symptoms for several days, far too long for any connection to be made."

Akworth raised his eyebrow. "That is what we believed last time."

Kelton shrugged. "Marfield's magistrate has been bought, and if another cracks Agnella again, we already know who to arrest."

Their eyes befell upon me as I lost my breath. Another mark with another stipulation. My heart should have ringed with alarm, but it seemed, over the last year, I had grown accustomed to existing on the edge of a blade.

"That will not be necessary, my Lord," I spoke through a tense chest. "I will ensure Agnella is prepared. A servant's coif will help conceal my identity, though I cannot imagine my former circle of peers would overlap with the guest list. Your instincts brought me into your service for a reason. I can pull off this job without raising suspicion."

Appeased, Kelton raised his glass to me, and the table followed suit. Though I cannot deny the knot in my throat as I swallowed my wine.

My potted plants produced enough fruit to enable preparation of the castorbean extraction intended for Silas. With the rest of the plan set, I turned my attention to my budding garden in front of the Earl's cottage. I depended upon the relocated plants to replenish my stores and provide seeds for the following year. To my delight, the plants fared well in the untested soil, and the wolfsbane flowers were beginning to bloom. I cupped a delicate blue-violet bud in my gloved palm, more encouraged than I had been in months. Lost in the care of my precious plants, I could almost fool my mind into believing I was home. And with the poison development behind me, my own prospects bloomed as well.

One morning, the oppressive sun beat down as I weeded my circumspect garden. Only when Muriel appeared behind me, panting from her run, did I realize she was late.

"Mistress Maud." She arrived gasping for air, slurring her speech from excited haste. "It is time!"

"Muriel, you have to slow down." I took my maid's hand to steady her body. "Time for what?"

"The baby is coming." Her eyes lit with excitement. This is what Muriel wanted in life: a husband and a family. Today, she lived vicariously through the Countess. "I am needed at the estate. You will be alright?"

I laughed. "Yes, Muriel, I think we will manage just fine. Go!"

After a deep breath of preparation, she ran back through the grass field to the main estate.

That afternoon, we learned Agnella gave birth to a daughter, Margarette Nicola Paston. Aselin and I waited a few days before journeying to the estate to pay our respects. Of course, Muriel came as well. I bestowed a leather-bound book of rhymes upon the babe. With the watercolor illustrations, the work cost me over two months of Kelton's stipends, but I felt obligated to make a good showing.

The day we paid our respect to the child, Agnella's maid made us wait outside the nursery while the Countess finished speaking with her betrothed. Muriel attempted small talk, but Agnella's frustration piqued my curiosity, and I could not resist listening through the partially closed door.

"I am sorry, love," Agnella insisted with a tinge of annoyance. "I do not know. Tedric never said anything, and I have never seen such a ruby ring."

Akworth's scoff resonated even to my ears in the hall. "You are sure?"

"Quite!"

Through the door, I saw the Countess glare at him as I remembered my rescuer's words from the gaols in Matheson. Was Akworth still looking for that same mare head ruby? Yes, his thief had failed that job, but it made no sense why he would be looking in the Darley estate. And it was just a ring. Though everyone in the manor was uptight, bearing the stress of wedding preparations while caring for the newborn. More likely they discussed Agnella's

wedding band, but a ruby was a poor choice given her fair coloring. She needed something delicate to not distract from her
beauty.

Akworth resigned, kissing Agnella on the cheek before departing, and giving me a nod as he passed.

Agnella received us while seated in a rocking chair with a light
blanket. Her eyes showed fatigue, but her face radiated with pride.
At last, she had a daughter. Someone she could mold in her image,
who would not upset the delicate balance of inheritance.

With the Countess's permission, the wet nurse placed the child
in my arms. I cradled its tiny face in the crook of my elbow thinking I had seen more beautiful newborns, though aloud, I fawned
over the pink wiggling thing as expected. The couple had gotten
lucky, for her daughter had Agnella's coloring: the same olive skin
tone, hazel eyes and blonde hair. I stared at the face to discern if
any features came from Akworth over Tedric, but her features
were too small to tell. Many visitors must have made the same
examination.

The weeks before the wedding flew by with so many tasks to
manage. My attention divided between reports from Kelton's
servant who upkept the cottage I owned, overseeing the one I
borrowed, tending to the garden, replenishing my toxin stores and
planning for the upcoming assassination. Aselin and I were fitted
for servant attire in preparation for our roles during the occasion:
a navy bodice with a white, flowy chemise, a deep-green skirt with
a matching navy embroidered hem and a navy coif. Simple, yet
polished.

Muriel told me Father Eustace announced the upcoming nup-
tials at mass for three Sundays prior per tradition. It became my
own private countdown of anticipation. While Silas was not the

highest-ranking mark I had undertaken, he felt the most important. He would solidify my position with my patron and
represent the culmination of my efforts with the castorbean. The
entire population of Marfield looked forward to the grand affair,
but except for the betrothed couple, no one else shared my eagerness.

The Earl used the influence of his title, and the day before the
wedding, Akworth became *Viscount* of Camoy. While still out-
ranked by his bride, the new title appeased noble preconceptions.
And no one questioned why Kelton had not married off his
mother to increase prestige, given she was widowed with child. I
wonder if that had been part of Agnella's plan. She had played a
long-game and had played it well.

God bestowed the happy couple with a warm day. White,
puffy clouds covered enough of the sky to keep the worst of the
sun's heat at bay. Since Aselin and I planned to portray servants
for the feast, we excused ourselves from the ceremony with regret. Kelton agreed it was the prudent course. Frankly, I did not
miss having to stand through the whole ordeal anyway.

Through the window of the servant's kitchen, I saw the couple
depart for the church in separate horse-litters. As a new mother,
Agnella must have starved herself to fit in her gown. The light
blue dress featured velvet cuffs I found a bit heavy considering it
was a spring wedding, but the cut of the dress served her well —
especially the neckline that showed off her post-birth assets. Fragile white flowers adorned the fabric, and soft blue blossoms were
woven into her hair with gold strands. Muriel had asked if I might
contribute some of the white flowers from my garden towards
the effort. I laughed inside after she pointed to the hemlock blossoms, muttering a regretful excuse of not having any to spare with
the research ordered by the Earl.

Akworth wore a navy doublet from the same color family as Agnella's dress. The cream-colored hose under his tan breeches matched the fabric of his box pleated neck ruff. The light blue, navy and tan embroidery on the codpiece featured a pattern of tightly stitched gold thread.

By the time the guests returned, every spare inch of the table within the kitchen was filled with waiting, prepared trays. We had heard the wedding procession approach before their horses crested the hill leading to the estate. Salivating with anticipation, my mind focused on the small, silver vial in the pocket of my apron. Excitement beat in my chest like the drums of their march. Every sense heightened, my reflexes gleamed sharper. It had been far too long. The gaol tests had calmed my appetite but not satisfied my need. After months of preparation, the time had come.

At last, I was unleashed to stalk my prey and kill.

CHAPTER TWENTY-TWO

Attentive preparations transformed the ornate pretentiousness of the Earl's main hall into festive vibrancy. An array of richly dyed banners hung from the rafters: blues deeper than winter lake water, reds more vibrant than a Cardinal's cassock, yellows of marigolds and greens of fields wet with dew. The sight astounded my eyes, but I hid my delight, wanting to blend in with the judgmental crowd who expected nothing less. A rotation of musicians ensured ears were never void of celebration as well — if they could be heard. The volume of merriment grew so loud, guests had to shout to hear one another.

Though, no one would have it any other way.

Spiced mulled wine flowed in abundance, accompanied with ale for those who otherwise preferred. Platters of peacocks paraded from the kitchen with the birds' rainbow feathers adorning the dishes in an impressive display of savory precision. The scents of quail, goose, venison, sanglier, fish, and mutton all mixed together, enticing the senses of everyone present. Vases overflowed with nuts on long tables, waiting with stewed cabbage and oysters steamed in almond milk. Never before had I seen so many varieties of cheeses gathered on one platter. No expense had been spared with the array of fresh fruits and custards being passed around by servants.

As guests arrived, the staff ensured every hand stayed full of drink and food. My own platter consisted of berry tarts and small vessels of custard. I marveled at the grace with which the servers floated through the crowd despite the large trays balanced on their palms. I toiled to simply not spill.

At least my experience in Lord Matheson's household helped me blend in with the servants. Aselin stayed close by my side, trying her best not to be a bumbling idiot with the preparations. Thankfully, so many extra servants had been hired to assist that our misdirected efforts merged into the mayhem. The Earl's regular staff did their best to maintain patience, but frustration wore on each face. And with my hair pulled up under the linen headdress, the few servants who may have identified me were too busy to scrutinize.

While I recognized many of the shire's lords and ladies, they would not have cause to know a yeomen woman, such as myself. To my relief, House Lanton had declined their invitation, citing the young age of the children and the lack of a male to provide prosper escort for Lady Matheson. I never again wanted to look into the eyes of the Viscount's children and felt grateful I had one less thing to worry about that day.

But amongst the vibrant array of abundant wealth and splendor, it was a man dressed in plain black robes who piqued my attention. I often think of Kelton as a vile soul, but in truth, I harbored such a streak in my heart as well. And at that moment, it won out over common sense.

I tapped the old man on the shoulder and presented my platter. "Would you care for a tart, Father?"

The shock of Father Eustace's face made the risk worthwhile. I raised my eyebrows with a piercing stare, extending my arms and the platter further towards the priest.

"Lavinia? I…" The old man looked at the tray of tarts with a seed of doubt in his eyes.

The unspoken fear lifted my soul.

Father sputtered once more, "What are you doing here?"

"Making an honest living," I taunted, continuing to hold the platter. "Guests say you gave the couple a beautiful service."

My flattery remained unacknowledged as he thought through the dilemma. Father contemplated, too afraid to refuse but for good reason, fearing to indulge from my tray. After a moment, his shaking hand reached for a blueberry tart.

"An excellent selection," I complemented with satire. "Enjoy the feast."

I departed, filled with satisfaction from the unexpected delight. That moment alone made up for every minute I had spent in agony after his betrayal, deciding if I should permit him to live. Working my way through the crowd, I kept a curious eye on Father Eustace. When he thought I looked away, he discarded the tart on a random table's trencher. He never took another bite the rest of the evening.

When Agnella and Akworth entered, the room erupted into applause. They both beamed as he escorted her into the middle of the crowd. The musicians struck a fast-paced tune, and the newlywed couple led the dance. For all of Agnella's grace, her dancing struggled. Skillfully in response, Akworth gave her a strong frame and together, they floated across the floor. A few minutes later, the melody from the viol seemed to hang in the rafters before the musician's citole took over with a familiar percussive rhythm. The bride and groom led the crowd in an energetic galliard. Oh, and Agnella's wedding ring featured a large pearl, which much more suited her than a ruby.

Throughout their dance, I scanned the crowd, wondering which of the men was my mark. Kelton's description had been too common to be of any use, and no portraits of Isabel's family, nor House Vacher, remained in the estate. After a while of searching, I spotted the Earl of Gaulshire.

Even though the day did not belong to him, Kelton refused to be outshone. No doubt, he had retained the best tailor for himself. The red doublet and long coat with fur trim set him apart from all others.

"A tort, my Lord Earl?" I kept my eyes cast low, mindful of my cover as I presented my tray.

Kelton's eyes narrowed, his toothy grin overcame his face, overtly enjoying the role play. I chose not to let his reaction bother me.

"Why, thank you." He leaned in close to my ear and indicated in the correct direction. "There, in the maroon tunic with the fur collar and black breeches."

Spotting the mark, I nodded. "Thank you, my Lord." Our eyes connected for a moment before I departed to share the information with Aselin.

Once Agnella had exhausted herself with dance, Kelton declared the feast should begin. A thunderous applause erupted through the hall as lords and ladies found seats along the rows of wooden benches. Aselin and I watched Silas take his seat and made sure his table became our responsibility.

Silas had eyes so sunken they could not be read. His vacant glare gave me shivers. Once I did notice them, the grey irises staring back caused me to lose my breath for a moment. Rare eyes like that are unforgettable, and Tedric's face flashed within my recollection. This was indeed the late Earl's son. Otherwise, the rest of Silas's features were as strong as his brow, and the family resemblance manifested amongst the group. Aselin and I had done our research. By the positioning of each guest at their table, and the descriptions Kelton had provided, everyone's identities were clear.

The Vacher table remained quiet compared to the boisterous cackles of their neighbors. Agnella had been obligated to invite the House as Silas' uncle was a viscount in the shire. They, in turn, were obligated to attend in order to dispel the suspicion around their household. However, for that reason, no other guests cared to mingle with them. No one wanted them there, and I daresay, they would have preferred to attend a funeral. Social custom is a curious coercion. In the end, the Earl did not care if they received subpar service from two untrained women.

Regardless, we did our best out of self-pride.

"Are you enjoying the feast, my Lord Gesbury?" I refilled the goblet of ale of the Viscount, seated at the head of the table. My question seemed to interrupt his daydream.

"Oh. Yes, it is fine," he dismissed mundanely.

Silas's Uncle, Nicholas Vacher, the Viscount of Gesbury, has irises so dark they seem to be one with his pupils. His brows are always furrowed, and indeed, he has the chilling air of a traitor. Though, we tend to see what we want to in people. He too dressed in a deep maroon doublet, the color of his House crest.

The Vacher family maintained an isolated conversation, and Aselin and I did our best to remain invisible like well-trained serv-ants. However, my anticipation peaked. I could not help glancing at Silas, yearning for the moment I could execute my plan. My ruthless desire tore inside the cage of my chest, waiting to be un-leashed. I wanted to watch him willingly eat the poison I had literally shed blood perfecting. To savor the moment I achieved the promise made to my patron; a promise that seemed another life ago. Remaining patient became so much an endeavor it physically hurt.

Then to my relief, the posset course arrived. A tingle raced through my body, focusing my senses.

Aselin retrieved the reserved pot containing the specific curdle we had brewed ourselves. Cream boiled in whole cinnamon and four flakes of mace. All mixed with sixteen — no, eighteen — beaten egg yolks and only eight whites, a pint of sack, three-quarters of a pound of sugar, cinnamon, and in our pot, an overdosed portion of grated nutmeg. As the cream curdled over the hearth, the extra presence of spice had been evident in the aroma. Imperfect, but not offensive. However, the guests who received our posset would need sugar, and in abundance.

From the posset pot, Aselin poured the liquid and spooned curdle into separate bowls for each guest while I followed with sugar. We had begun the service ensuring Silas would be last and conveniently, I emptied the sugar vessel for the guest before him.

"I am so sorry, my Lord," I spoke with a show of nervousness. "I will retrieve some more sugar immediately." I curtsied and headed towards the kitchen before Silas could respond.

As I left, the Vachers grumbled of our poor service and in truth, I no longer cared. My head rushed with anticipation. My inner temperature rose causing my hands to grow so slick my fingers left prints upon the silver vial from the pocket of my apron. I poured the contents of castorbean toxin into the small dish, added a spoonful of sugar, and mixed the white powders before returning to the table with haste.

Poor service, poor food — it all fit the perception the Vachers wanted to hold of this wedding. With another apology, I spooned the laced sugar over Silas's bowl making sure to provide a sufficient dose. The test in the gaols had proved it did not take much, but the risk was so great. The rest of the sugar I temporarily concealed in a locked cabinet within the grow room and tossed down a garderobe after the feast.

While I stored the toxin, Aselin had one job: ensure Silas ate the pottage or take his order for an alternate dessert. Thankfully, the task required no effort on her part. With sugar, the dessert was quite enjoyable — we had verified ourselves. Our guests would never admit to such, but the majority of the bowls were clean. And while Silas did not finish the serving, Aselin assured me he had consumed enough.

An hour later, I eyed the Earl once more. Approaching his back with discretion, I whispered into his ear as I passed. "It is done."

He grazed his hand over my rear, and I turned back in time to see his sick smirk of heightened satisfaction. I recognized the look of desire in his eyes, awakened by our covert plot. But I had played my part and left him to find indulgence with another, assuaged by the knowledge the Earl could not publicly show interest in a wench without complications.

With the poison administered, I allowed myself to relax and enjoy the feast. My jubilation soared on par with the guests. After all, this party was for me, so that I might deliver the poison. And despite being relegated to a servant, I savored the duration with that mindset.

When the feast slowed, Aselin and I slipped away unnoticed before we would be tasked with chores for cleanup. My back ached, my arms throbbed from carrying trays of food I had craved to taste. My hair reeked of smoked meat, and my ankles swelled.

Aselin and I soaked our feet in buckets of warm water, enjoying a well-earned, lazy night in front of the hearth of the Earl's cottage.

Sharing a bottle of wine we lifted during our quick departure, I offered a toast. "To the cunning of two women who unlocked the castorbean, two yeomen who dare to remind nobles of their own human frailty."

"Hear, hear," Aselin laughed, raising her glass before turning sentimental. "But also, to one woman who had a vision and bravery to seize it. For her generosity to carry me along on her journey."

"Aselin…" I looked down for a moment with a tender smile. Touched, my eyes swelled, though I would have claimed exhaustion if asked.

"Truly, Lavinia," she continued. "I aspire to be like you. You challenge expectations and charge your own path. You are not afraid to take risks, and are being rewarded for your courage. I hope someday I am as successful."

I regarded my apprentice, my confidante, my friend. I had crafted her into an exquisite accomplice, a reflection of my own skill and ambition. I thought back to her first kill in the market, to the excitement harbored in her smile the day we met Akworth. She had grown, and as much as I wanted, I could not take full credit.

"You will be, Aselin." I reached out to squeeze her hand. "You will stand on the shoulders of my legacy and prevail to heights we cannot imagine."

I believed the words deep in my heart, I just never imagined the way she would bring my prediction to fruition.

The next few days became a waiting game. Each morning, Lord Akworth dispatched one of his spies to bring back news of

Silas's condition. We all waited with bated breath. On the third day, his informant returned with word that Silas had canceled a meeting with a tradesman on account of falling ill. I stayed anxious — confident, but anxious.

I was not alone. I saw Agnella accidentally cut through a stem of her potted bloom. Kelton passed me in the hall without offering mockery. Nerves also uncharacteristically ruffled Akworth. Claiming he lost his pocket watch, the Viscount frantically searched the estate. Unease lingered until news of Silas's passing reached the Earl's manor through an official messenger, two days later.

Kelton read me the message in the privacy of his office that afternoon. Inside, a ball of stress I carried dissipated like melting ice; my mind cleared of a fog I had not noticed before. Preoccupied with the relief, I still could not process my own accomplishment.

Though in truth, Silas's murder was a letdown.

I had toiled for this kill for years, and the distant death felt anticlimactic. Once again, I had been denied the pleasure of witnessing the vile consequence of my poison. I missed watching fear resonate from the mark, that instant they look upon me with an understanding of what I was, what I had done. Instead, Silas died on the other side of the shire, presumably surrounded by baffled physicians. How I wish I could have heard their theories.

Yet, I also worried about my own prospects.

I had completed Kelton's assignment and taken out his mark. How many targets could he have in mind? What were the ramifications if he no longer had a use for me?

And what alchemic challenge would now occupy my talent? It would be some time before I advanced the state of my craft with as giant of a step — if I ever did. What was there to pursue in place of the castorbean?

But Kelton already had answers for those questions.

"It appears my bargain with you has paid off in full." Kelton seemed rather pleased with himself. He picked up a blown glass paperweight from his desk and rolled the ball between his hands.

More of his graciousness could have been directed to me, but I patronized him out of duty. "Indeed, my Lord. Well done."

"To think that Lord Akworth pulled you from obscurity..." Kelton's voice trailed off, leaving me to guess the line of thought in his head.

Setting down the glass orb, the Earl's constant pacing kept my nervous breath shallow. Wary, I tried to keep the conversation flowing, "The Viscount is an excellent judge of character. He did marry the Countess, after all."

Kelton nodded. "Indeed."

Again, silence. I swayed on my heels, biting the inside of my cheek. When my unease had reached full height, Kelton continued.

"I enjoy having a poison mistress under my employ, but it is not lost on me that I coerced you into this position." Kelton finally sat and motioned for me to follow suit. "You have proven your usefulness and loyalty once again. I am not known for being the most gracious, though surely some sort of reward is entitled to such a poison Master."

I looked up at my patron, startled.

Master.

My cheeks warmed, blushed. My lips formed an unpreventable smile. To hear the title bestowed upon me by an Earl... *Me*, a woman, recognized as a Master in my own right.

Though I could not have agreed more with his words, my own came forth from obligation, "The privilege of serving my Lord is honor enough."

"Yes, yes. You have to say such things." Kelton waived his hand. The Earl took a breath and then looked upon me. "Master Maud, in reward for your service, I offer you your freedom. You may leave my estate and leave me behind, but if you do, you are not permitted to take on clients. You must understand, I cannot leave you equipped with such items without loyalty to my house. Otherwise, I have no guarantee of the allegiance of your next client. Therefore, your poison stores will be confiscated and you will be subject to the full extent of the law if I find you have pursued such paths again."

I swallowed. To have accepted such an offer would have been its own death. Kelton knew, and clearly, he had another option in mind.

I asked with hesitation, "If I stay?"

"I offer you a permanent position as my poison Master. You will continue to receive your stipend, though you may move back to your own estate if you desire. You may service other clients as long as you report all transactions to me. I expect you could be a wealth of information. But understand my interests and my marks take precedence above everything else."

I had waited a lifetime to hear those words: a genuine position in service to a noble. I felt the tingle of victory building inside, the disappointment of Silas's death on the verge of being compensated. My lips ached to accept, but I took a breath. Along the way, I had learned a few lessons from those around me.

"Double the stipend, and you have a deal, my Lord." I looked at the Earl, unblinking, calculating my next move should he decline.

Kelton's eyes narrowed, and I heard my heart pound in the perilous silence. I held my breath, afraid I had been too bold. Afraid I had incited my patron's wrath I knew too well. On the verge of withdrawing my request, Kelton nodded and accepted without complaint.

Mayhap, I should have asked for more.

Aghast, I chose to dwell on the genuine triumph. I held out my hand, trying to hold back my smile for the sake of business. "Then, my Lord Earl, you have yourself a loyal poison Master."

CHAPTER TWENTY-THREE

With my patron's blessing, I wasted no time moving back to my own cottage. It felt good to be home.

Muriel cried the day we left. I should have told her more fervently how much I valued her assistance all those months. But honestly, I did not fully appreciate her until afterward. Through the winter, my mind had been preoccupied with my own plight. Though, I believe she understood what she meant to me, despite my failure to express so in words. She had a way of reading people like that.

As a token of appreciation, I did gift her with a pearl necklace from my personal collection. I thought she could wear it someday when she wed. A month ago, news of her marriage did cross my path. Apparently, she wed a woodsmith from Belsay.

But being home put summer warmth into my spirit. From the comfort of my own writing desk, in the security of my home, I took a leap of faith and reported my discovery to the Guild. It took me three sittings, and several candles, to describe the process for refining the castorbean and record the story — well, as much as I would disclose. My hand throbbed by the time I documented the recipe in code.

Fixing my wax seal on the missive was a professional mile-stone. I remember sitting at the desk the night I finished, beholding the yellow parchment package with my heart full of pride and expectation. The letter contained more than a recipe, it served as my best chance to advance and earn my entitled pres-tige.

I accomplished what some believed to be a dream of wild folly. My report would start a cascade of letters sharing news of my claim. Given the significance of a tasteless, delayed poison, I had no doubt it would spread through the Guild with the rapid dissemination of a plague. Across Europe, poison makers would test my recipe out of doubt and spite, attempting to discredit my claim. When they found the process successful, my name would be known. Surely someday, a common alchemist will unlock the secrets of the castorbean, but the clandestine Guild of poison as-sassins will have known for generations. In that way, my memory will endure.

With news of my accomplishment now in route, I should have looked past Silas's assassination to the new world of opportunity before me. But like a lantern with dirty glass, the light I radiated obscured with unease. Lingering shards of unresolved guilt tor-mented my waking moments. I had hunted Silas as prey, without the excuse of a prior condemnation and without cause for retali-ation.

Only one cure existed for my self-inflicted wounds.

Kneeling in front of the church grotto, my heart struggled to find the peace it craved. Invocation to the Queen Mother's statue had temporarily stopped my bleeding, but the wound festered. I longed to hear the words, "You are forgiven." I craved the peace of confession. The unrelenting lure of the church steeple beck-oned behind me, looming in the distance. Trusting the new understanding between myself and Father Eustace, I could wait no longer.

Ah, it had been too long! Upon opening the church door, the sweet smell of incense burned my lungs with a pleasant sting. The Holy air enveloped me, sending my soul into exhausted ecstasy. But the act of blessing myself with water from the fount restored my sinful sorrow. I came with need. My rapid heartbeat matched the rhythm of the nun's straw broom scratching against the tile mosaic floor at the far end of the nave. Yes, I was nervous. What would I do if Father continued to deny the sacrament? What would he say in response to my sins? There was one way to find out. An hour remained for confession, and the booth beckoned.

On the other side of the confessional screen, Father's outlined shadow read a bible. His figure froze, recognizing the voice bidding him good evening. Silent tension hung within the small chamber, and I could taste sweet fear radiating from the priest. I suppressed my tantalized cravings, remembering the purpose of this confrontation. With a humble heart, I continued the ritual.

"Forgive me, Father, for I have sinned."

Again, Father Eustace did not respond.

"It has been several months since my last self-administered confession at the grotto, at least ten months since being granted the privilege of the proper sacrament."

Still, silence.

I wished he would respond. Anything. Being ignored was an insult to the rank I had been entitled by the Earl. Though, I had come this far and chose to continue.

"I confess the sin of murder. I am gravely sorry for these transgressions and the sins of my past."

The continued silence fostered frustration. Did he dare intend to ignore me? *Me*? The Poison Master of Gaulshire? Perhaps my warning had not been strong enough. I glared at the screen, determined to win the battle of wills. I would kneel all night if need be, waiting for the old man to bend to my will.

Wisely, he did not challenge my resolve.

His voice cracked weak, overwhelmed with dejection, but he complied. "You are forgiven."

That was all I needed.

Pleased, I resumed the ritual. "My God, I am heartily sorry for having offended Thee. I detest all my sins because I dread the loss of Heaven and the pains of Hell, but most of all because they offend Thee, my God, Who art all-good and deserving of all my love. Amen."

Having completed my contrition, my soul should have rejoiced. I should have felt the relief of a righteous hand lifting weight off my shoulders as I always had before. Instead, the fingers of insidious insecurity penetrated the mortar of my confidence. I felt a tangled web grow in my stomach like black ink spreading through water.

On account of my pride, I could not admit my unexpected insecurity. Confused and afraid, I muttered the few words I could muster as I stood, "Thank you, Father."

"Lavinia," Father Eustace stated with sullen sadness. "It is easy to repeat a sin once it has been committed. Our spiritual basis of comfort can become bent as our conscience is muted. It is not too late to escape the cycle. Even for you."

Father's words paused my exit as I contemplated the deeper truth. The murders under Kelton had felt wrong, killing the condemned. Were those too God's will? Did my lack of impunity validate Father's words? For the first time, I felt conflicted about my calling but could not admit insecurity. Without a response, I withdrew from the confessional.

As I walked home, Kelton's offer of freedom in exchange for retirement flashed through my mind, but my ever-present dark thirst lingered. God makes each of us in his image; was my desire not part of His creation? Father Eustace had also granted forgiveness, and I succumbed to the same logic from a lifetime ago: his grace represented Divine permission. I also pondered the considerable breakthrough I had contributed to my field. What is an inspiration, if not a whisper from God? How many lives might end by His will as a result of my toxin? Nearing the cusp of a turning point in my career, I felt compelled to see how high I could climb. To cultivate my God-given skill to the fullest extent of my capacity.

With my resolve intact, I turned to the logistics of my business. Being late in the summer, the roots of my poison garden at the Earl's manor entwined into the soil with too much maturity to transplant to the concealed garden in the back of my cottage. Therefore each week, Aselin and I made a trip to Kelton's estate to tend to our crop. The situation also provided an excuse to continue use of the grow room — a resource I loathed to relinquish. And since I remained under the Earl's formal employ, I used the visits to recount progress towards new extractions, the latest gossip from clients and their marks of interest. Kelton welcomed the weekly audience as a respite from the mundane necessities of governing the shire. With the relaxed atmosphere of our new arrangement, I daresay, I enjoyed them as well.

Between the Earl and Lord Akworth, a steady stream of referrals came to my door. I commissioned additional signal coins to support the growing distribution. The demand for my skills also taxed my stores of poison, but the good Lord provides, and somehow, I managed to keep pace. With the increasing number of marks, Aselin and I also became more precise in our dosage, allowing the stores to be stretched.

With so many requests, I had the privilege of being selective. Potential clients showered me with gifts, hoping I might accept their job over another. Each week, a new silk gown arrived on my doorstep, or a fine pot, a collection of rare spices, and occasionally a jewel. Sometimes a would-be patron's rationale appealed to my emotion, other times a particular challenge associated with a mark intrigued me. Sometimes the offered payment was just too generous to decline. And as my clientele grew in rank, my commissions prospered.

To handle the growing demand, I began letting Aselin select her own clients. Her first solo job targeted a man who had reneged on an arranged marriage agreement. The bride-to-be's father had worked for a year to raise the dowry, and in the last hour, the groom took a woman from another shire.

The family came to me in tears, and the story ignited our anger. Women have so many roadblocks against them from the moment they are born. With a reputation of a rejected match, I knew making another suitable pairing would prove difficult. The pain in her father's eyes broke my heart. This was a crime against women, but not one that could be brought to justice in a court of law. The story touched at the reason I had entered this profession: to hold the untouchable accountable.

I had saved Aselin from such a fate, and she recognized that fortune. She undertook the client with a passion equal to my own. I also pushed Aselin to be more independent. I gave her access to base ingredients but none of the prepared toxins, challenging her to make a purification herself. She recognized the long-term goal and dedicated herself to the task.

Of course, she selected hemlock.

"You will have to expand your arsenal someday." I rolled my eyes at the choice.

Aselin challenged, "Do you not deny the man deserves a painful death?"

She had a point. Without grounds to argue, I directed her to carry on.

Watching her methodical planning reminded me of my first assassinations. For days, she focused with an intensity that rivaled the most motivated scholar. At her request, I reviewed the final plans, and after an hour of prodding, I could not find a hole in the strategy. Even the contingencies proved well prepared.

On the selected night, I tied a cloak around Aselin's shoulders and gazed upon her with more love than I expected could be produced within one meager heart.

"Be careful."

She nodded, impatient. "Yes, Master."

This moment had always seemed years away. I sighed, knowing I had to let go. "Let me hear it one more time."

Aselin rolled her eyes but indulged me. "Trust your instincts, maintain a path for escape and always ensure deniability."

A lump formed in my throat which was fine, I could not find words that might hint at what I felt anyway. I gave her a last smile and sent her out the door to begin her career.

I paced the entire night. I thought my boots might wear a path in the floor in front of the hearth. Aselin had more protection than I enjoyed on my first jobs. She had the benefit of my hard-earned lessons. The potency of her toxin surpassed the weak concoctions I first used. But all of those facts could not subdue my worry.

In my anguish, I felt alone.

The house was quiet without Edmund. He would have been right there pacing with me — though fuming with anger. At least it would have been company and conversation would have passed the time.

Finally, the click of the wrought iron door latch flooded me with relief as her footsteps proceeded down the hall. I met Aselin at the entry way with outstretched arms to receive her cloak and handed her a cup of hot cider in return. I inquired only after she had taken off her boots to relax in the parlor. I knew the complex web of emotions running through her head; it would take a while for her to digest the experience. However, the light in her eyes spoke enough to quell my immediate questions. Her triumph felt like my own.

Suffice it to say, business steadily grew, and my patron remained pleased. The Lord above knows the tally as well as His Fallen Angel. But with all the marks, additional security measures were prudent. For a cut of my profits, Malcom deflected rumors and suppressed suspicion.

During one evening rounds, he overheard two prisoners discussing rumors of a suspicious murder in an alley. When the combination of their gathered speculation pointed towards a female poison assassin, Malcom ensured both prisoners were found dead with enough physical injury to insinuate their brawl was noticed too late. With such events, Malcom earned his place in my circle of confidence, and his office became a necessary destination during weekly errands.

"Good day, Magistrate Horner." I accompanied my greeting with an impressive clank of coins as I set the leather pouch with Malcom's cut upon his desk. It had been a good week.

He closed the office door before peering into the bag, his eyes lit with fulfilled greed, "It seems so, Master Maud."

Malcom unlocked a wood coffer with the key kept around his neck and placed the bribe within. It still caught me off guard to see the protective box hidden within the rear cabinet. My father and Haylan had kept it on a side table, but they had stored sensitive papers, not bribes.

I melted into an upholstered chair, appreciating the opportunity to get off my feet. The magistrate poured me a goblet of mead and sat on the corner of his desk.

"How is Kelton faring?" Malcom did not have the regular access I enjoyed and relied upon my visits for insight into our mutual benefactor.

Indulging before business, the mead tingled down my throat with satisfaction. "Stressed from all the disgruntlement of the King's recent tax."

Malcom smirked. "Kelton never struck me as one who would enjoy the business side of being Earl."

"No," I laughed. "That was clear from the first days." I rubbed my eyes, further slouching into the chair. "And what news have you?"

Malcom set down his own goblet and looked into his hands. Not hearing a response, I lifted my head out of the hand propping it up to regard the magistrate with concern.

"The rumors," he began, "they only continue to spread, especially now that Aselin's client list is growing."

"You said you have them contained?" I eyed him with a wide, piercing stare. Malice is more intimidating coming from an assassin, and I loved toying with those who knew the truth.

"I do!" He defended with an ardent tone, to my amusement. "They are, but you…"

"That is why I pay you, Malcom." I cut him off, sitting forward in the chair. "Do I need to find another?"

"No, of course not." Malcom held up his hand to arrest my thought. "I only seek to ensure you have awareness. Two nights ago, I received a report of a man in Blackhaven Tavern boasting about his rival's downfall. His drunken stupor rambled about hiring a woman, slipping toxin into the ale, bragging how he made the arrangements."

I knew the client he referenced. "And what did you do about it?" I pressed, lacking patience in my fatigue.

"By the time my man arrived, he was long gone. But if it happens again, we have enough witnesses who heard his confession. I will charge him with the crime."

I nodded satisfied before standing, ready to take the matter into my own hands if necessary. "Is there anything else?"

Malcom shook his head before pausing. The silence said more than his warnings. "It is getting harder, my Lady."

I exhaled. "I know." I looked at the magistrate for a moment before leaving. The risk would need to be addressed, but I needed time to strategize.

My journey home that night is the reason I remember the particular exchange. Bright orange leaves swayed above my head in the trees. Dusk blanketed the world, and my cloak billowed behind in the winds. The howling fall gusts had covered the sound of his footsteps behind me — at least that is what I chose to believe. It was more unnerving to think the man approached without notice, given the empty streets in the late hour, but I was tired and distracted. I naïvely enjoyed crunching the dried, fallen leaves under my boot when a man in a crimson robe placed a gloved hand on my shoulder.

Providing no justification, he guided me into the shadow of an alley. A velvet hood concealed his face, but I recognized the emblem embroidered in black on his chest.

The Guild.

If not for that symbol, I would have screamed, retrieving the dagger from my boot. Instead, my heart fluttered with pride. After all the years, they again made contact in person.

Alone in the narrow back street, his raspy voice filled the darkness. "It has been well done, Lavinia Maud."

My name never sounded so sweet as from his lips. I thought I might weep from joy, but out of dignity, I maintained composure. "Thank you."

He handed me a black lacquer box, and my hands shook with expectation. Having the necklace within my possession felt surreal, and I needed to see to believe. Rotating up the lid, my eyes beheld the onyx pendant: a polished black gem set into a silver representation of the Guild's seal. To anyone else, the necklace would appear an obscure, elaborate carving. Those in the know would recognize the design without question and bestow the respect owed to me: a Fellow.

"Congratulations on your ascension," he spoke once more. "We have high hopes for you."

Before I could respond, the man departed with as much mystery as he had appeared. I stared at the black box in my hands; the remaining proof the fleeting moment had not been a figment of my imagination.

My mind raced with the new possibilities open to me. The additional contacts I would now have access to. Secret recipes, a steady stream of rare herbs. Having received the recognition I deserved and craved, I wept overwhelmed.

Back at the cottage, Aselin stared at the pendant in shock.

"And he did not say anything else?" The onyx looked especially dark against her pale palm. "Did he mention me?"

I shook my head, holding my hand out for the pendant. "No, but I did send the letter of introduction last week. It will take time, Aselin. You will have to prove yourself."

She looked at her reflection within the gem as my waiting hand grew impatient. I took the necklace from her grasp, pulling the chain against her fingers. The gem was mine to marvel.

Within the solitude of my chamber, I propped my hand mirror against a book and took off Haylan's ivory hedge bindweed pendant. Removing the chain from my neck resurrected feelings I thought had been laid to rest. In truth, finally letting go of the item brought the closure I needed. In its place, the Guild's onyx hung prominently in the hollow of my chest. With the gem around my neck, I felt complete; as if my outside now matched who existed within. Years of promises I had made to myself, and my apprentice, were now coming true.

With my ascension, I focused on my own career, and admittedly, neglected my apprentice. When I returned from a job, more often than not she was away with her own assignment, leaving me to record my own observations in my journals. I missed our evening chats. I focused on the pendant and ignored the relationships that benefited me. With the protection of the shire's government and Marfield's magistrate in my pocket, I let down my guard. I trusted those men had my back. I never thought it would not be enough.

CHAPTER TWENTY-FOUR

The first hints of morning broke through the bedchamber window, prying my eyes awake. My feet had not yet touched the floor when Aselin departed the cottage, mumbling we were out of flour on the way out the door. I paid her no heed. Whatever motivated her that day had not blessed me, and I rather enjoyed the thought of having the house to myself. Once standing, I stretched, struggling to convince my body to release the last remnants of slumber.

It should have been a relaxing day. I intended to weed the herb garden and perhaps respond to a patron's request or two. I did expect one client to pick up a small pouch of aconite leaves that afternoon, which I still had to harvest. I wonder if the man ever found another source.

Outside, the wind howled, blowing tree branches into the side of the cottage. The air had a bitter sting, and I loathed the reminder of the upcoming winter. Fall had gone by so fast, and I had not taken the time to enjoy the warmth. The floor of my cottage also seemed to have soaked up the night's cold and now tortured my bare feet. My slippers had to be somewhere. In a daze of fatigue, the thought of hot broth called to me more.

I had placed a small pot over the hearth when a subtle knock rocked the door. Still in my nightgown, I wrapped a shawl around myself and walked to the front to answer the summons. My bare feet stepped on an unmarked, parchment letter that had been slipped through the crack. I opened the door in time to see a small boy running over the hills back towards town. Chilled wind blew dried leaves across the threshold, and I kicked them back outside with irritation before closing the door.

The letter was sealed with wax bearing no insignia or indication of the sender's identity. But with a number of hesitant appeals I received from would-be patrons, nothing seemed unordinary.

Ripping apart the seal, I unfolded the parchment:

You have been betrayed, flee!
- MMH

MMH. Magistrate Malcom Horner.

In an instant, I lost my breath. My hands shook. If Malcom sent the messenger, the note contained a dire warning. The rush of realization shocked me into productivity. Within minutes, I doused the fire, locked the door, and donned a simple tan chemise and green dress. I tossed a few poisons into a satchel with a flask of ale and rye bread before leaving the note on Aselin's pillow, unsure if she also needed to flee.

I ran around the cottage like a mad woman, fearful I would forget something important but wary of taking too long. With my cloak fastened around my shoulders, I finished the last lacings of my boots when commotion began outside. My heart fell.

I had not been fast enough.

Peeking through my bedchamber window, I did not recognize the men at the door, though I did not need to. Their drawn swords and barred wagon gave away enough. I counted four — more than I could ever hope to out-power and more than I could outrun. Perhaps one man could have been bought or bribed, but not a group. And four would not believe a lie. Without a better plan, I hunkered down silent, pretending I was away. It was a foolish notion but what else could I have tried? Frankly, it did not matter, the men never bothered to knock.

I bit my cheek in dread as the first crash of the axe splintered my door. I raced through my limited options, paying no mind to the tears warming my cheeks. Without another choice, I crawled through the house to the back door and closed it behind, afraid of making the slightest noise. If I could just make it through the back gate to the stable beyond the wall, maybe then I could out-run them on horseback. I knew the odds stacked against me, but the plan had to better than staying in place.

As it turns out, perhaps not. I took two steps into the yard before strong arms grabbed my torso from behind.

There had been a fifth man.

My scream echoed through the morning fog, muted by his hand as I kicked against the hold. I bit the man's finger so hard I tasted his blood. Seconds later, the others came around the cottage and together, they overcame my feeble frame with ease. Only after chains bound my wrists and ankles did I see the emblem on one man's doublet: House Vacher.

"Please!" I pleaded, out of breath. "I can help you make amends. We can avenge Silas."

My protests fell on deaf ears, same with my attempts to bribe. The men ignored every word and threw me in the back of the wagon without acknowledgment. As the horses departed, I crumpled with denial.

It had all happened so fast. I could not believe I was being carted off to the gaols, yet again. The cycle exhausted my will: carry out the patron's order, find myself arrested, then plead my case to a more power-hungry client.

The wagon took roads I did not recognize. We were not going into Marfield, that much I assumed given Malcom had sent a warning. We were not going to the Earl's estate either. Given the Vachers and Darleys declared each other rivals, that discovery was not surprising. As we turned south, I deduced we would be riding to Gesbury. With the new information, I tried once again to reason through my circumstance.

Who would have betrayed me such that Malcom would have known? Given I was in the hands of House Vacher, it had to be someone who knew the truth of Silas's death. That limited the possibilities to an exclusive list.

Kelton would benefit from an allegiance from House Vacher. Though, I assumed he loved having a poison mistress more than the loyalty of a minor viscount to the south. I also assumed the rift between the two houses was beyond repair.

Agnella could not have done it alone, even if she had a reason. She may have thought of the idea, but her stomach for such things remained weak. Akworth would have done anything for his love, but he had no reason to cross Kelton and was not positioned well enough to make a play for power. He had so many opportunities to cross me in the past, I could not think of a reason he would now.

Father Eustace remained too scared and preferred to refrain from politics.

To my knowledge, I did not have any disgruntled clients.

Of everyone, Malcom had the most to gain from such a deal. His loyalty to Kelton Darley remained only as strong as the flow of coins, and that sum could have easily been outbid. Perhaps the note had been penned out of last minute guilt. How would he, of all people, have come to know of my betrayal, unless he helped mastermind the plot.

I laid on the floor of the wagon unable to stomach the curious views of those we passed. I folded my cloak into a makeshift pillow and endured the trip, bouncing against the wood of the cart.

In truth, my betrayer did not immediately matter. I knew the identity of the man who had summoned me, and I prepared for negotiation by deducting ways I might assassinate Kelton. I had been in a similar situation before. Vacher would want revenge, and I knew how to give it to him. My own heart hungered for Kelton's blood as well.

The journey stretched on for hours without any word from my captors. Exhausted from thought and the lack of food I never had a chance to eat, I clutched my fingers around the onyx pendant and breathed deeply. Perhaps the Guild would look out for me now that I held the title of Fellow. I squeezed the pendant so hard my fingers grew stiff, and the carving left red marks in my palm.

With the high sun overhead, a small estate on the outskirts of Gesbury appeared like a mirage on the horizon. I watched the grey stone structure grow as we approached. Despite impressive upkeeping, the building's architecture gave away its age. Smaller than the Earl of Gaulshire's estate, the heavy architecture of large, plain stone blocks made the manor appear more foreboding. Though, perhaps I was biased from circumstance.

We took a long path that wound around the estate in a slow progression up the hill. The sound of dirt crunching under the wagon wheels challenged my tolerance already on edge with anxiety. I just wanted the sound to stop, for my body to stop being thrown around the wooden cart. Fie, I wanted someone to speak to me!

When the wagon halted, three men grabbed the chains and yanked me out. I laughed inside that they thought they needed three. More likely, they each wanted the honor of presenting me to the Viscount and settled for a fraction of the credit.

They dragged me through a hallway ending at a set of double doors upon which a guard knocked three times. After a moment, the door opened from the inside, and the men pushed me through to whomever waited. In response to my stumbled entrance, conversation in the room dwindled as every eye around the long, crowded table turned to me, the new trinket of entertainment. After gaining my footing, I stood tall. I had a role to play. I needed to convince this viscount I was worthy of a contract. I refused to let his gaze unnerve me and walked in with pride, my chains clinking against the floor.

Nicholas Vacher sat at the head of the table garnished for a feast. His dark eyes were unmistakable, and his brows were still furrowed in the same unnerving aura from the wedding. Vacher set down his goblet and stood, taking slow, deliberate steps towards me. In response to a subtle nod of his head, the Viscount's men once again restrained me before Vacher came too close. I took their anxiety as a compliment.

"You do indeed look familiar." His fingers cupped my chin as he turned my face to regard it from different angles.

The guards held my arms so tight they began to tingle from a lack of sensation. I stared back at into the Viscount's black irises, unsure what to say.

He looked over my shoulder towards the long row of judgmental eyes. "Is this the assassin?"

In response, a steady procession of approaching footsteps began from behind, echoing like a military drum. The room held its breath. I did as well, unwilling to turn around to spare my betrayer even a glance. Instead, my unwavering stare focused into the Viscount's eyes.

However, I could not ignore the approaching sound of swaying fabric, the undeniable rustle only produced by a skirt. The singular clue narrowed down the possibilities, and as the unknown witness rounded the group of guards to behold my face, my heart disintegrated.

"Yes, my Lord. This is Lavinia Maud, poison mistress of Gaulshire."

I did not need to look at my betrayer. I shattered, recognizing the voice.

CHAPTER TWENTY-FIVE

N ever would I have considered the possibility.

My eyes locked with hers, conveying words I could not utter. Her own cold stare back sent a chill through my limp body. Unable to bear my own weight, I hung from the guards who gripped my arms so tight their fingers dug into my skin. The world crushed down upon me such that I thought I would never breathe fully again.

My apprentice wore a red gown I had not seen before. Elaborate braids circled her head with a single spiral curl left loose against her cheek. Unable to read her etched face, I wondered if her heart hurt even a fraction of my own.

"Aselin…" I spoke her name in a near whisper, unaware of anything around us.

I never received a response.

As abrupt as everything happened, the men escorted me out of the hall. Behind my back, the crowd resumed their carefree meal in eased conversation.

What is there to say? The cellar reminded me of Kelton's estate: at least four small cells down a dark corridor with stale, moist air. My body shivered within moments of descending down the spiral staircase. Each of my breaths formed a cloud. After a quick discussion of which cell, the men released the iron restraints and left me to my misery in the selected room.

Once alone, I wept.

I wailed until my gut entangled, until my lungs could not cry out a single breath more. My body ached from being tense so long, my throat felt as raw as my heart.

I wondered how many nights she had laid awake in contemplation, if she ever second-guessed herself. I hoped the decision at least proved difficult, that somewhere deep, her bold heart harbored remorse.

When I calmed, I felt empty inside. A normal person would have felt anger, but how could I? What better way could she have demonstrated mastery of my teachings and carried on my legacy? She surpassed her master. She saw an opportunity for advancement and seized it with fervor. She simply played a better game.

I laughed. Edmund must have been rolling in his shallow grave, and soon his ghost would dance upon mine.

The previous times I had been incarcerated, I had clung to hope. This time, none existed. I found a calm peace in acceptance.

I knew Kelton would not come to my aid once again. I was not worth further angering Vacher and Kelton needed to maintain deniability with Silas's death.

Aselin would give strong testimony no one would be foolish enough to speak against. And since she harbored my skills, I could not hope to make a deal. What good was I to Vacher when he had Aselin in his pocket? The whole plot showed she had learned from watching me with Kelton and had taken the opportunity to seize the one thing she needed to secure her place: a demonstration of loyalty.

I was alone more than ever.

That night, I received the bowl of broth I had craved that morning. Having not eaten all day, and with the constant shivering, I slurped it too quick, forgetting to savor the meager meal.

Two a day, meals marked the passing time. I longed to know their schedule. There would be some sort of a trial, to make the accusation official, followed by sentencing. Not knowing how long I had to live became my biggest source of frustration. And after receiving my sixth bowl of broth, I grew impatient.

For hours, I paced between the walls of the small, windowless cell. I counted bricks. I found a few pebbles and tossed them into circles drawn with my finger on the dirt floor. I recited poems and psalms for the flies. I traced the mortar between the stones in endless laps around the confined room.

And I prayed.

I prayed for strength to endure what came. I prayed for mercy, forgiveness, and a calm heart. I prayed for Aselin, that she would have the strength to endure what she had undertaken. I prayed for her success to ensure my sacrifice would not be in vain. I prayed I had prepared her well enough and that she would find an apprentice of her own.

I admit, I also prayed for my soul.

I often contemplated why so many poisons have religious nicknames.

One Guild member once described these long, pale orange flowers along the Andes that are called "Angel's Trumpets." I assumed the nickname referred to the look of the blossoms, though if one consumes a fatal dosage, it is also the next sound you will hear.

There is a plant with linear, small white blossoms that goes by the name "Solomon's Seal." The name, of course, is after the ring said to have been engraved by God and given to the King directly from Heaven. For the impressive namesake, ironically the plant's toxin is so diluted a lethal dosage is impractical.

There is also wolfsbane, that goes by the names "Monkshood" and "Devil's Helmet." Hemlock which can be called "Devil's Porridge." And strychnine which, of course, is "Saint-Ignatius' Beans."

The castorbean is sometimes referred to as "Palma Christi." The plant has leaves as broad as a hand and from the greens, an oil can be derived with curing properties.

I have always been amused how the same plant can heal as easily as it kills. Not unlike humans. Father Eustace told me that God equips each of us with gifts and we must decide how to wield them. Perhaps, he was right.

There are at least twenty-five passages in the Bible which reference poison. One of my favorites is James 3:8, "But the tongue can no man tame; it is a restless evil, full of deadly poison."

Even mere words can poison our hearts, just as Aselin's had mine.

But sitting in the cell threatened to poison my spirit. With nothing to do except contemplate, I thought of all the mistakes I made that led me to those walls. The signs along the way I had missed. The trust I had misplaced. But my resolve remained firm. Long ago, I had decided I would go out in a blaze of pride. The days in that cell reaffirmed my decision. Not knowing when the judgment day would come, I tried to keep my dress clean and my hair tidy. I refused to appear the beaten criminal. With a piece of ribbon I broke off from my bodice, I tied my hair up in a polished knot and waited, my strength fermenting within.

And after the twelfth bowl of broth, they came.

I stood patiently as they clad my wrists in irons. I lifted my skirt to help the men bind my ankles. Wedged between two guards, I walked out of my cell with my chin high and my shoulders broad.

The same hall in which Aselin had given her betrayal had been rearranged for my trial. The Justice of Peace presided at the far end of the room from a table on a raised platform. I recognized him from the large mole on his nose, preceding his reputation. Vacher sat to his left, and to my surprise, Akworth to his right. Seeing the Baron's presence — the *Viscount*'s presence — rekindled my memory of the mare's head ring and I added one more line to my practiced monologue, eager to see his reaction. Throughout the proceedings, I learned the identities of the rest of my jury: the Magistrate of Gesbury and a young Baron serving as the Earl of Gaulshire's representative.

Five men before me. Five men who had decided my fate before I even stepped into the room.

The guards led me down the aisle between rows of spectators, they intended this to be an entertaining affair. I noticed Aselin seated on the right but did not spare her a glance. She had dealt this hand, but I intended to play it my own way.

The Justice banged a piece of wood against the table to quiet the room. I stood a few feet away from him but he shouted with such volume I longed to cover my ears. He did not speak for my benefit, but rather for the promised spectacle.

"Will the accused please state their name for the court."

I stared back at him, furrowing my brow. Waiting. Letting the silence grow uncomfortable. Forcing every lord and lady to the edge of their seat. I inhaled a breath for strength and for a silent prayer. The Justice stirred, his face tense with frustration, but I persisted in a statement this would occur on *my* terms. The moment he took a breath to speak, I cut him off.

"My name?" I spoke clear with the same volume, my words full of arrogant pride. "My name is Lavinia Maud, the poison Master of Gaulshire."

The Justice exhaled in no mood for my games. "You are standing trial today for the murder of Silas Vacher. How do you plead?"

This time, I responded immediately, "Guilty. Guilty with honor and no regret."

The room erupted into chatter as I beheld the man's eyes. The crowd came to witness the spectacle of a trial, and I had just destroyed their expectation.

Little did they know what I held in store.

The five men at the table conferred amongst themselves before the wood block restored silence.

The Justice continued, "This court has recorded a plea of guilty, but for the sake of the record, the evidence against the accused will be presented."

I sighed, unsurprised.

"My Lord Justice of Peace," Vacher responded, "I would like this court to hear the testimony of my witness, Madam Aselin Gavrell."

The Justice nodded and looked towards Aselin who stood.

"Madam Gavrell," Vacher started with a tone so politely sweet it must have gagged in his throat. "Would you please share your account from the night my nephew was poisoned."

"Yes, my Lord." Aselin nodded her head and then turned to the crowd. Her speech sounded rehearsed, and likely it was coached by at least a few of the men before me.

"I came to live with Mistress Maud as an adolescent. I was a beggar in the market she took in, and I was in no position to decline a free bed. When I followed her home, I did not know I would be entering such an illegitimate enterprise."

Her account, thus far, spoke true.

Akworth interrupted, "Madam Gavrell, what do you mean, 'enterprise'?"

Aselin beamed of innocence personified in her off-white dress. Her hair was pulled back in a pearl adorned snood I swore I had seen somewhere before. The window behind caused her aura to glow as I noticed the gold barrette gifted from Agnella in her hair. She relied on every ounce of her acting ability, and I did not discredit the cleverness of her performance.

"I would ask the jury to forgive the lewd nature of my testimony." Having received a nod from the men, Aselin continued. "Assassin business. Poison brewery. Manor of Sin. She cooked the toxins in her cellar and made us — my brother and me — cover for her deeds. My brother, God rest his soul, got in her way and drank an acid extracted from apricot seeds in his cider one morning."

The way she spun the truth proved Aselin had mastered my lesson: always ensure deniability. I recognized the irony. I had created the apprentice who now took away my last hopes for defense.

Vacher nodded. "And of Silas?"

Aselin licked her lips with another breath. "Venenated, my Lord. On the day of blessed union between the Countess of Gesbury and the Viscount of Camoy. You sat at the same table with your nephew that Mistress Maud serviced covertly in ruse. You ate from the very same pottage pot as the deceased, but she made sure he received sugar laced with her own concoction of extracted poisonous beans." Aselin covered herself with the sign of the cross and then looked down into folded hands.

"For what end, Madam Gavrell?" The magistrate spoke up. "What motivated the act?"

Aselin shrugged and then looked up through her long eye-lashes. "Only the Lord knows, but I can guess. Perhaps she wished to win the favor of your enemies. Perhaps she simply reveled in the ability."

And then, to top of her performance, she began crying.

"I am so sorry, my Lords. I am ever grateful to Viscount Vacher for rescuing me from her clutch of darkness. I wish I could have prevented the fate befallen on your nephew. I pray his soul rests in peace with our Almighty Father."

Kelton's representative stood up and offered Aselin his handkerchief. Through his support, she somehow found her seat. My eyes rolled from the ridiculousness of it all. Some of the crowd must have seen through the act. If they did, none came forward. I did not blame them, nor did I expect anything else.

The Justice stood, looking at the members of the jury. "Are there any more witnesses?" Receiving no indication, he continued, "Given the accused own plea and the testimony we have heard, does anyone on this jury wish a verdict of innocence?" Once again, the men shook their heads. "Then the court finds this woman guilty of the murder of Silas Vacher."

There it was. The cue for my moment of truth. No one will say I was not courageous for what I did next.

"Am I not allowed to provide testimony at my own trail?" My voice carried loud but still fought the volume of the crowd discussing amongst themselves and standing to leave.

The Justice looked to his left and right for a moment and then banged the wooden block to restore order. "You have already pleaded guilty, Mistress Maud."

"Yes, but I wish to plead more."

My words hung in the rafters of the stunned room now silent.

The Justice posed the question running through everyone's mind. "What did you say?"

"That is not all I am guilty of, my Lords." I stood tall, waiting for the room to settle. One by one, the crowd regained their seats.

Akworth sat motionless, but the sweat on his brow delighted me more than a spring rain. He feared what I might say.

Aselin looked up from her handkerchief with an open mouth, forgetting she should be faking tears.

The Justice struggled to find words at all. "Not all?"

"No, my Lord. Since this is my trial, after all, I wish to provide testimony such that when the historians and bards speak of the poison Master of Gaulshire — and they will — the account may be accurate and full."

The Justice gazed down from the dais dumbfounded.

Akworth coughed. "My Lord Justice, is this necessary?"

The men murmured at the table as I waited, still and composed. After a brief debate, the Justice addressed the room perplexed. "The accused has the right to speak."

Akworth's eyes were wide with concern, but his fear proved, after all that time, he did not know me. I was an assassin, through and through. I would not darken that honor at the eleventh hour by giving away my patrons. I looked towards Aselin who, God bless her, tried to sit still, but also harbored fear in her eyes.

Without invitation, I continued before I might be silenced.

"Despite the evidence presented, we are not here to discuss Mistress Gavrell or her brother," I began. "It is *my* account I wish to provide. Yes, I created my own toxins in my cellar. I tended to a garden of poisonous plants in my yard with love. I taught myself the alchemy and collected recipes over the years.

"It is my ingenuity which created an airborne toxin so powerful it slayed Magistrate Haylan Moryet the night he had proposed to his beloved.

"I perfected the tasteless, colorless extraction which killed Lord Silas Vacher. Beforehand, I tested that mixture on six prisoners sentenced for execution and crafted each grain of toxin in his honor. I infiltrated the wedding and serviced his table to gain access to my mark.

"I also infiltrated the household of Giles Lanton, the former Viscount of Matheson. While posing as a scullery maid, I polished his dinner vessels with camphor oil, causing the seizures from which he perished.

"Mushrooms, cultivated with my own hands, caused the death of Tedric James Paston, the previous Earl of Gaulshire.

"By my troth, one common female has shaped the politics and nobility of our shires. These are the nobles I have killed, but the yeomen and peasants who have also succumbed by my hand are too numerous to report here today. Cheating husbands, dishonest bankers, criminals, innocents, men, and even sometimes women."

My tongue tasted the sweetness of anticipation as I turned to directly face Akworth. "One of my favorite assassinations took place in a brothel where I recovered a ruby gem ring with a mare's head engraved on the side. I will never forget the sound of the thief choking on the St. Ignatious' Bean I added to his mead. I thwarted the plans of those above me in ways I will not comprehend, and in that regard, I shaped the tapestry of our history."

My eyes lingered, connected with Akworth's as he sat white, frozen like stone. The last laugh was mine.

I turned without warning, continuing my testimony.

"Twice, I have escaped the gaols to rise stronger. For years, I operated unrestrained, I chose who would live and die, and in my place, I leave a legacy behind."

I did not need to look at Aselin to know she would have heard my encouragement.

"Yes, you have now caught me. But the score is heavily in my favor. Nobles and peasants alike share a common frailty, and no title, no patronage, is immune to my poison.

"My name will be remembered for innovations and courageous acts. For how I refused to be disregarded due to gender and how I thrived in spite of it. The details of my life may be forgotten, but the name 'Lavinia Maud' will live on."

The room erupted in a chaos that could not be subdued by the Justice's wood block. Unable to restore order, he shouted over the crowd but could not be heard. I saw Kelton's delegate lean forward and address the Justice who scowled with reluctance, nodding his head with gritted teeth. With a final bang of the wood, he yelled once more.

"Lavinia Maud, you are sentenced to execution by beheading tomorrow at dawn."

Amongst the commotion, I saw Vacher shake Akworth's stunned hand with a celebratory air of accomplishment. But with the gasps around me, I did not care. My perverse smile lingered as two guards dragged me out of the courtroom, my heels scraping the floor. To my satisfaction, the room buzzed in my wake.

My moment in court had been everything I imagined. The look on Vacher's face... On Akworth's! All in attendance must have departed eager to spread my story. It would not be long until the news crossed the shire border. I hoped it would bring peace to Lady Matheson and encouragement for others to follow my legacy. And a beheading! My caste dictated I should have been hung, my neck snapped by unforgiving, rough rope. Kelton must have interceded on my behalf. Truly, it was a sentence worthy of my master status, and my patron's thoughtful gesture touched me. My radiant flame would blaze in final glory, shining inspiration upon a generation of assassins and poets alike.

But either way, I was nearly extinguished.

Alone in the cell, a melancholy acceptance smothered my joy. With my vow fulfilled, there was nothing left for me. No further clients to please, no more poisons to discover.

I knew exactly how the remaining hours of my life would transpire and the knowledge came with foreboding. I never guessed all the times I withheld awareness of their final moments from a mark, I granted mercy. It is a blessing not to know your last hour.

I paced with anxiety, trying not to think about tomorrow, waiting for Father Eustace to come receive my last confession.

I tried to concentrate on my prayers, but Vacher's deliberate reception of Lord Akworth after the trial nagged me like the flies contained with me in the cell, buzzing around my head. My former client's workings were no longer my concern, and I yearned not to waste my final thoughts on the man. I needed to prepare myself, my soul! But I could not. The way they had regarded each other, the personal nature of their contact... The puzzle infiltrated my mind, preventing the peace I deserved as a condemned woman.

Hearing the knock on my cell door, I stood with an exhale and straightened my dress. Despite everything between us, I vowed to be humble to Father Eustace; my final hours were not the time to be haughty.

"Come in, Father."

The door was opened, but not by the priest. Akworth slipped a coin to the guard who closed the door behind, leaving us alone in the cell. The delay enabled me to gain control of my shock.

"Akworth." My tone soured.

He scoffed, folding his arms as he beheld my sorry state. "So it was you." His laugh echoed through the stone room.

I swayed on my heels, insecure. It seemed I was on his mind as well.

The Viscount slowly walked towards the far wall and ran a curious finger across the dirt-laden, cold stone. "Do you realize, if you had not stolen that ring, none of this would have happened?"

I swallowed. "The ruby?"

"Yes." He smiled, examining the now black tip of his finger. "You are correct about one assertion, Madam Maud. You certainly 'shaped the tapestry of our history' in ways you cannot comprehend." His chest puffed as he turned to face me directly. "Yes — though I cannot fathom how you uncovered the story — I hired your thief from the brothel that night." His face fell sincere, but I saw through the false effort. "If you will indulge my curiosity: I always wondered, what happened to that ring?"

I owed Akworth nothing. Part of me considered remaining silent. But I had inconvenienced him, and I longed to know how. "I returned it to my client."

Akworth took a step forward. "Who was?"

I smiled, amused. "Lord Akworth, you of all people should know I will not reveal my patrons."

"Even if your client lied?" Akworth regained control of our exchange with a crooked smile. "At least now I know why my man never reported after the job. I had assumed Tedric caught him and discreetly silenced him."

Once again, my mind spun, trying to put together the pieces laid before me. "Tedric?"

"My thief stole the ring from Tedric, not your client."

Akworth resumed his pacing, drawing out the truth. I was sure he wanted me to wiggle like a worm on his hook, and I did my best to remain composed out of spite as he continued.

"Since I assumed Tedric remained in possession of the gem, I needed to gain access to his estate. When I discovered Agnella's veiled marital loyalty, I found my angle and made plans. Thankfully, I already had a proven poison assassin indebted to me."

His stare sent shivers through my wary bones. My dry throat had no words in response.

He continued, "With Tedric out of the way, I scoured the estate. After learning Kelton knew nothing of the ring, I assumed Tedric passed the knowledge to his true son. After all, the ring had been bequeathed to Tedric from his father, who had used the membership it represents to obtain his title. Once Kelton confessed his plans for Silas, I questioned the boy with haste before our wedding. He did not know either. In desperation, I confided in Vacher and to win his favor, I told him to seek out Aselin to avenge Silas. To my dismay, Vacher knew nothing of the ring as well."

Akworth smiled. "But now I know where it is. You may not give up your clients." Akworth's eyes gleamed. "But Aselin will. I will get the ring and the alliance I deserve."

My mouth hung open. My hand supported my wrenched gut. All the times I accused Edmund of being inconsequential, and I had been the pawn...

Akworth walked towards the door but could not resist twisting his dagger further. "You once told my wife you savor the cruel irony of poisons, I thought you would enjoy this last indulgence. Master Maud, you condemned yourself that night in the brothel."

I swallowed, still internalizing the story. My mind struggled to catch up. For the right price, Aselin would disclose my client, the one who had intercepted the ring. I wondered how much she remembered. But she had chosen to walk her own path now, and it was a dilemma for the living. I would not reveal my patron, not even for Aselin's benefit. But Akworth would use any means to obtain what he desired. For her protection, I sought to give my apprentice a final advantage.

"Viscount." My whispered word hung in the air until I earned his attention. "Watch after her, please? Promise me you will look out for Aselin in my absence."

His eyes softened, unable to comprehend. "You are concerned for your betrayer, at this hour?"

My faint words lingered between us. "Please, promise me?" After everything, he owed me that much.

Akworth took a deep breath and then nodded his head. "As long as our interests remain aligned, I promise."

It was the best I could hope for. With no further business to conduct, the Viscount knocked on the cell door and departed.

I wondered the true extent of Akworth's ambitions. I feared what revenge Vacher wished to enact with his new assassin. It took me hours to process the story, but nothing could be gained from regretting past deeds. Stealing the ring may have set the events in motion, but I did not grieve everything that had transpired. Even the darkest clouds have a silver lining. Consider that without Kelton's pressure, I might not have broken the castorbean and made Fellow. However brief my success, at least I achieved my dream.

My heart still mulled when I received the night's supper. I savored the last drops of chicken broth, swishing the salty liquid around my mouth. It was the last taste my tongue would ever relish.

Broth.

A meager last meal, though not unlike my Savior's final indulgence of bread.

Another knock on the cell door interrupted my licks of the bowl, and I turned in the direction with expectation. *Finally.*

"Come in, Father." The word escaped my lips with gratitude as the door opened. But yet again, the man who entered did not wear robes.

The guard looked down at his hands for a moment, regretting his words.

I pressed him not to try my patience. "What is it?"

"Mistress Maud," he muttered so low he was barely audible, "Father Eustace is unavailable."

My brows furrowed. "What do you mean, 'unavailable'?"

The Adam's apple on his throat quivered as the guard swallowed. "He will not be coming. That is all I know, Mistress."

My shoulders fell, my gut caved. I stumbled back, catching myself with a hand against the wall.

Could Father deny a convict their last confession? How far had the old man's morals fallen? To think such resentment settled in the heart of a priest. I had spared his life for heaven's sake!

My breath quickened, shallow. "Certainly, another priest must be available!" Anger rang behind my words while my eyes danced upon the guard with nerves.

"The Justice is trying," the guard defended, backing away from me. "We will keep you informed."

I bellowed with force from deep in my gut, "Tell him to try harder!" My voice cracked with the volume through a throat constricted with terror.

The guard did not respond and closed the door to my exasperated face.

The fact the man still feared me, despite being incarcerated, stroked my pride. My testimony must have reached his ears. But at the moment, I worried more for my soul than my legacy. What would become of me if I did not receive a last confession? The prospect burned my eyes with tears. My throat throbbed from wailing. I had not followed the Faith all those years to be condemned in the final hour. Curled into a ball in the corner of the cell, I wept for myself until the cold metal of the onyx pendant gracing my aching chest brought realization.

If I could not confess my sins, what was the point of waiting?

Fingering the gem with consideration, I wondered if the rumors were true.

I unfastened the chain and turned over the necklace. Utilizing a sliver of light protruding through the door jam, I forced my fingernail into a side seam of the pendant. The nail cracked, but the back of the jewel gave way. The silver back popped off to reveal a small dose of pressed, white powder. I cradled the toxin in the palm of my hand, satisfied I now had control of my fate.

I could end everything now, falling asleep peacefully in this cell. The little circle of powder could save me the embarrassment of being led through the city, the anxiety of facing the block. No crowd would mock me, no viscount would turn my death into a spectacle for sick revenge. It would be a more fitting death for a poison Master, and is that not why the Guild made such pendants? Without knowing what toxin it contained, I trusted the pill would yield the peaceful death deserved by a Fellow, the right I had worked years to earn.

The cell fell silent as I stared at the dose, my mind torn between the comfort it offered and the alarm of my conscience. My life was God's greatest gift but it never belonged to me. I was a steward, not an owner. God entrusted me to wield this body and the formidable talents contained by its flesh. I knew my life was not mine to end and faced with the prospect of no last confession, I did not need the taint of another mortal sin.

In an instant, I made my choice.

Restoring the silver back to the pendant, I fastened the necklace around my neck and stood. Emboldened with resolve, God rewarded my courage for that is when you walked through the door.

CHAPTER TWENTY-SIX

"And that is my story. That is how I ended up in this cell." With an exhale of conclusion, my heart feels lighter having told my tale. In front of me, the unfamiliar priest's silence is not unexpected as he lifts his eyes in slow motion to meet mine. I open my clenched fist to reveal the white, pressed powder dose.

The man's eyes grow wide to see the poison: a piece of physical evidence verifying my tale. He swallows. "It is clear, now, why Father Eustace refused to hear this last confession."

The man's shaky voice reveals his advanced age, but his eyes possess a depth of wisdom earned over the years. Still, it seems he does not know where to begin.

Father Thomas shakes his head while wiping his brow. "I wonder why the Good Lord, in his infinite wisdom, has chosen me to now bear this burden."

I smile in reply. "The Lord provides each of us with the gifts required to fulfill his plans."

"Indeed."

His search for words brings discomfort, but with nothing else to do, I wait, fidgeting in my chair as Aselin so often does. I had filled with relief to see Father Thomas arrive. The old man had traveled an hour through the rain to be with me on my last night. After meeting him for the first time, and spilling my life story to a stranger, I feel closer to him than people I have known for years. I hope he knows how much his presence means to me. And his fresh ears prove a blessing, untainted by history. I find myself grateful for Father Eustace's absence.

"Your skill," Father Thomas speaks, after deciding his strategy, "the 'God-given gift' you claim. What if your desires were your *hardship* to endure? God tests each one of us: some with wealth, some with ailments." His eyes bore into mine. "And others with skill and temptation. Did it ever occur to you that your test was to overcome the urge that pulls at your heart? One at which I think you failed quite spectacularly."

Passion fills the old man. His voice grows with power as he preaches. "You should have denied the devil's temptation and focused your heart on the Lord, Lavinia. You allowed ambition to poison your faith."

Once again, silence overtakes the small cell as the priest intends for me to contemplate. My heart grows heavy, blocking out the words I fear to hear. After several moments, he continues.

"Luckily, our faith teaches us it is never too late." The compassion in his voice is genuine as he takes my empty hand within his, kneeling before me, a sinner. "You are hours away from meeting your Maker. He alone knows what awaits you and the true love in your soul. But I have seen looming judgment so often bring revelations. And so I ask you, Lavinia Maud, do you renounce the Devil and all of his works?"

It is not the question I had been anticipating but one I welcome. There is no hesitation in my answer. "I do."

"Do you believe in God the Father, maker of Heaven and Earth?"

"I do."

"Do you believe in the Son, who died for our sins, whose mercy is endless?"

"I do, Father. With all my heart, I do."

"Then, Lavinia Maud, I will ask you for the final time in this mortal life. Are you sorry for the sins you have confessed this evening? Do you regret the decisions you have made and the lives you ended prematurely? Do you see how the cycle of sin prevailed in your life? How the Father's call remained ever present within your heart, but you fell into the Devil's temptation? If you could, would you now choose a different path?"

My throat swells. I cannot lie, not now. The full recount of my life reminds me of the success I achieved from years of effort dedicated to my craft. Of the independence I carved from a world that gave me none. The satisfaction I felt every time I watched someone suffer at my hand. The overwhelming achievement when I cracked the castorbean and the honor swarming in my heart when the Guild elevated my position. Facing my fate, I still overflow with pride from my accomplishments, and the onyx pendant shines brightly around my neck, even in the windowless cell.

But for the first time, I question my choices. With my mind and heart split in two, I give the one answer I can.

"I do not know, Father."

He smiles and squeezes my hand in response. "An honest answer, if I ever heard one. I believe there is still hope for your soul." With a glance towards my closed fist, he makes his request. "How about you give me the poison?"

I open my hand to stare at the pressed powder circle, the last means of control over my fate. If I hand it over, there is no further option. Shaking my head, I cannot condemn myself to the axe.

Father exhales, understanding. "Be comforted child, and be strong. Do not dread or fear, for the Lord God is with you in all things and wherever you go."

The familiar passage washes over me, and the poison becomes a weight in my palm. I know what I must do but lack courage. The priest slowly takes the toxic dose from my hand, and my fingers stay open, permitting the action.

"Well done, child," he offers before standing.

His indication sends a rush of panic through my veins. "Please." I reach out to grab the hem of his black robe. "Please, stay with me? I cannot bear to endure the waiting alone and the prospect consumes me with fear."

Compassion fills Father Thomas's eyes as he retakes his seat on the wood stool and opens his Bible. I exhale in relief. Together, we pass the rest of the night reciting prayers and reading God's word. He provides the comfort I am not sure I deserve.

And throughout the night, I reflect, listening to Father's voice recite the scripture. His words drone, providing restorative meditation. I do not regret my life choices, but I do regret not knowing what more I could have achieved. What other poisons could I have unlocked? What could I have accomplished with new access to the Guild? The unknown fills my body with remorse, reflecting on all the victories I might have obtained with the remaining years of my natural life. But such is not God's plan. My father said the brightest candles burn the shortest and I choose to find comfort in that thought.

Throughout the night, Father Thomas's voice never once falters. I take my turn reading, but he bears the brunt of the burden.

When the time arrives, I stare at the old man with so many emotions I cannot describe. With a last squeeze of my hand, he shows me he understands.

I have been wearing this dress for a week now, but do my best to straighten the dirt-laden, wrinkled fabric. I will face this moment with my head held high, though perhaps an iota more humbleness than I demonstrated at my trial.

One guard clasps irons around my ankles and wrists, a maid pulls my hair up into a white coif tied under my chin. Father Thomas lays his hands on my head for a final blessing before I am escorted away.

Everything feels surreal, as if a part of my awareness has already left my body. Nothing about this moment is natural.

Once we step outside, even the wind against my skin feels numb. My eyes take a moment to adjust to the rising sun, though my mind never catches up. The noise of the crowd becomes static in my ears, my surroundings are a blur of all five senses.

It all proceeds too fast: out of the estate, through the town streets. The crowds start to grow as we approach the square. All the eyes… The discomfort overwhelms my fear. I cannot process what is about to occur, the world around me feels like a dream.

Despite my whirlwind of confusion, I immediately recognize her pushing to the front of the crowd. How could I not? Swallowing my pride, I stop before her, and the guard escorts permit me one last moment.

"Aselin," I speak her name in a fragile whisper.

For the first time, I see the pain in her eyes and perhaps a small amount of shame.

If I do anything in my last living moments, I want to give her assurance. I wish I could embrace her, but my arms are bound, forcing me to rely on words.

"Aselin, I do not blame you. You did what I taught. You saw an opportunity and seized it."

A tear falls from her eye and my own swell in response.

"I love you like a daughter," I confess. "I want you to carry on my legacy. Make our recipes stronger, uncover new ones. Rise! See how high you can climb. And if God wills it, take your own apprentice to pass down our knowledge."

I lower my head to provide her access. "Aselin, I want you to have the pendant. You have beaten this Fellow fair, it rightfully belongs around your neck. Use it to whatever advantage you can gain. Ascend higher."

Her cold hands tremble against my skin as she unfastens the clasp. With pride, I watch her place the symbol around her neck. The stark contrast of the black onyx with her own fair coloring is striking, though well-suited. Taking a deep breath, she tips the pendant up to gaze into its black stone. Her eyes sparkle as mine did when it was gifted to me, but her words feel like a dagger.

"You played the game crippled by your peculiar sense of morality," she states, lifting her eyes to meet mine. "It limited you to mediocrity on both the fronts you hold dear. You were not righteous enough to please your God and not bold enough to let Him go to become the assassin you could have been."

Having said her piece, her face softens.

"But I have watched and learned. I will not repeat your mistakes. I will not hold back, and I *will* rise higher."

Perhaps my apprentice has a point but what could I say in response? I lived my life as best I could. Forcing a small smile, I finish what I need to say. "I forgive you, Aselin."

She takes me into a tight embrace before the guards push me forward with impatience. Looking back, I see her wipe her eyes. She plays a strong front but the moment of weakness touches me.

I recognize a few other faces in the crowd, but none which distract my focus from the wooden platform in the middle of the square. There it is. Seeing everything prepared focuses my mind on the thoughts I have tried to avoid. Each step closer becomes more labored. Each pace falls shorter. There, towards the place I would…

I cannot even bring myself to think it.

In the final moments, my strength caves, unable to support my breaking will any longer. Tears fill my eyes. I do not want to die. Not like this.

For the first time, I see it, the polished axe reflecting the last sunlight I will witness. There is a small chip near the edge of the iron blade. The man wielding the instrument has a mask around his face. I wish I could look into his eyes as he looks into mine. I wonder if the same anticipation for the kill flows through his veins which flowed through my own, so many times before. At least he appears strong enough; I pray he will make a strong blow.

What a disturbing need to pray for.

The guards push me forward, up the stairs of the platform. From the height, I see the full extent of the crowd gathered to harness my agony for entertainment.

Salty tears roll down my face to the wood block at my feet, stained with blood from those before me. Its curved indentation seems thirsty to absorb my offering. I wish I was not crying. I do not want witnesses to think I regret my actions or fear the next life. I do not want to be remembered this way.

The officials are speaking beside me, though I do not hear them. The crowd stirs and shouts, but my world is silent. My heart races, my throat clenches with pain.

They push me down on my knees and then my head to the block. The wood edge digs into the delicate skin of my neck. And there below, is the basket, waiting...

Will God take me? I try to recite His prayer, but my mind cannot concentrate. I just want it to end. The executioner takes his place to my side and lifts the blade.

Knowing death is imminent is a poison worse than anything I ever administered. Blackness percolates through every corner of my mind, consuming my complete existence. I just want it to be over.

Please, just let it all end. Please, just let it end. Please, just le...

Lavinia is gone, but her legacy continues...
Follow K.M. Pohlkamp for news regarding the sequel,
coming soon to Filles Vertes Publishing.

www.kmpohlkamp.com
@KMPohlkamp
www.fillesvertespublishing.com
@FillesVertesPub

APRICOTS AND WOLFSBANE

READING GROUP GUIDE

HISTORICAL INSPIRATION

Apricots and Wolfsbane was inspired by the life of Locusta, the notorious poison master from Gaul.

In AD 54, Empress Agrippina conspired with Locusta to murder her husband, Roman Emperor Claudius, with a batch of poisoned mushrooms in order to place her son, Nero, on the throne. While Locusta was subsequently imprisoned in AD 55, Nero sought to secure his throne by contracting Locusta to craft a poison to murder Claudius's son, Britannicus. When the concoction failed initial tests, Nero flogged Locusta with his own hands. Her second attempt succeeded. Upon Britannicus's death, Nero bestowed Locusta with pardons, lands, and lavish gifts. He also sent pupils to study with the poison master.

But all good things come to an end. In AD 68, the Roman Senate tired of Nero's rogue practices and the Emperor took his own life with a dagger before facing punishment. The Senate's attention then turned towards Locusta, and without protection from the Emperor, she was convicted with an execution sentence. Some accounts say she was raped to death by a giraffe and then torn apart by wild animals. [1] While that tale tantalizes the imagination, it is more likely she was led through the city in chains and executed by human hands.

For *Apricots and Wolfsbane*, Locusta's inspiration was lifted out of Ancient Rome and placed into two fictional shires of early 16th century England. During this time, a young Swiss-German physician and alchemist was working as a military surgeon while traveling widely across Europe.[2] While likely not part of a clandestine Guild, Paracelsus would go on to become the "father of toxicology" and coined the phrase, "sola dosis facit venenum" (The dose makes the poison).[3]

A NOTE ABOUT LAVINIA'S POISONS

Throughout history, women have used poison to provide independence not afforded to them by society. Poisoning was also one of the safest ways for a woman to end an undesired marriage. There were many known poisons widely available throughout Tudor England: belladonna, hemlock, arsenic, and wolfsbane, to name a few.

Literary license was taken with a few poisons within this novel. For example, strychnine was not isolated from St. Ignatius beans until 1818.[4] Ricin, which Lavinia develops from the castor bean, was actually discovered in 1888 by Peter Hermann Stillmark.[5]

However, a clandestine poison guild would have kept their recipes secret. The Guild provided a plot mechanism for Lavinia to have honed her craft and a means to a wide array poisons, perhaps some not commonly available. This is implied when Lavinia says:

"Surely someday, a common alchemist will unlock the secrets of the castor-bean, but the clandestine Guild of poison assassins will have known for generations."

REFERENCES

[1]Ramsland, Katherine. *The human predator: A historical chronicle of serial murder and forensic investigation*. Penguin, 2013.

[2]Joseph F. Borzelleca; Paracelsus: Herald of Modern Toxicology, *Toxicological Sciences*, Volume 53, Issue 1, 1 January 2000, Pages 2–4, https://doi.org/10.1093/toxsci/53.1.2

[3]Molyneux, Russell J., and Michael H. Ralphs. "Plant Toxins and Palatability to Herbivores." *Journal of Range Management*, vol. 45, no. 1, 1992, pp. 13–18. *JSTOR*, www.jstor.org/stable/4002519.

[4]Prat, S., Hoizey, G., Lefrancq, T. and Saint-Martin, P. (2015), An Unusual Case of Strychnine Poisoning. J Forensic Sci, 60: 816–817. doi:10.1111/1556-4029.12706

[5]Cummings RD, Etzler ME. R-type Lectins. In: Varki A, Cummings RD, Esko JD, et al., editors. Essentials of Glycobiology. 2nd edition. Cold Spring Harbor (NY): Cold Spring Harbor Laboratory Press; 2009. Chapter 28.

A Conversation with
K.M. Pohlkamp

What was the most challenging aspect of writing *Apricots and Wolfsbane*?

It is difficult to get every small detail of a time period correct within a historical fiction piece, but I sure tried - researching for hours and posting questions to Tudor English History boards. And while a novel for a modern audience cannot be written in Old English, I endeavored to give Lavinia's voice an historical feel. I wrote with a dictionary at my side to verify the origin date of words and used a few archaic phrases for color. I'm sure some period error has slipped through and I'm certain someone out there will let me know. It's alright.

Tudor England is my favorite historical period: the dresses were gorgeous, and the history is full of intrigue and scandal. Yes, I know renaissance festivals are not historically accurate, but I still look forward to digging my garb out of the closet each year and spending a day in a taste of another time.

WHAT WAS THE HARDEST PART ABOUT WRITING AN ANTI-HERO?

Lavinia is a cold-blooded murderer. There is no question about that. Yet for the reader to become invested in her story, they need to sympathize with her struggle, to empathize when her heart breaks – to cheer for her. It was a difficult balance to strike.

This is the reason Lavinia has a clear moral line: she does not murder children, she is loyal to her patrons - even at her own expense, and does not kill without reason. She describes each murder with finesse instead of the detail found in a horror novel. The fact Lavinia is remorseful after each murder also helps with relatability, even if her beliefs are misguided. Finally, Lavinia's longing for Haylan's love provides one conflict which will resonate with most readers, giving them an aspect of her life to personally connect with.

Lavinia has relatable weaknesses. She thrives with details and can reason through the most difficult purification. But she does not see the long game of those around her and fails to strategize appropriately.

Lavinia is also a reliable narrator, never lying to the reader. While she may be biased, she is also not a hypocrite. I did not think it was plausible for someone to truly thirst for murder and then completely comprehend the errors of their ways. This is why Lavinia does not fully embrace Father Thomas's final sermon to make a full reformation.

HOW DID YOUR OWN FAITH INSPIRE THE NOVEL?

I am Catholic, and while a story about a female poison assassin was weaving in my mind, my priest gave a sermon about how easy it is to fall into a cycle of sin and penance. Often we realize our actions are incorrect, and then feel guilt and performance penance. But after a while, the guilt wears, and it becomes easy to commit the sin again. Of course, my priest was talking about minor offenses, but as a matter of *reductio ad absurdum*, I applied this concept to a murderer.

I believe all is possible through Jesus Christ, but remorse must be genuine for sins to be forgiven. Lavinia believes she is truly repentant for her sins, but her repeated offense shows she is not. She uses Father Eustace's initial confession blessing to justify illicit desires. She closes herself to the truth she does not want to hear. At the end of the novel, Lavinia begins to comprehend her error, but I'll let the reader ponder if the revelation is too late.

WHAT WAS YOUR WRITING PROCESS?

I am a meticulous planner which dominates my process, beginning with extensive research for inspiration. I then develop lengthy spreadsheet outlines to work through pacing and strategize the best way to best tell the tale. (I am an engineer, after all.) When I'm ready, I start writing a piece in order, but about halfway through, end up writing the end and then filling in the middle. I find I constantly re-write the first chapter and could forever continue tweaking. I also am an avid fan of Twitter work-in-progress hashtag games, and if you follow me at @KMPohlkamp, you'll be treated to cryptic lines from new pieces.

Once I had an initial framework for the novel, *Apricots and Wolfsbane* wrote pretty fast. The manuscript was an unofficial 2016 nanowrimo project (National Novel Writing Month), and while I did not complete the piece in the month (I'm astounded by authors who do every year), I had a first draft by January. Editing is always the long slog, but it's rewarding to see a novel clean up, like a jewel being polished.

Finding time to write is a big challenge. As a mother with a full-time job, writing is my means of escape. Curled up under a blanket with my laptop, I can go anywhere. The best part of writing is the freedom.

WHAT DO YOU HOPE READERS WILL TAKE AWAY FROM *APRICOTS AND WOLFSBANE*?

First and foremost, I hope my readers are entertained by the tale of a female assassin. I hope they were caught off-guard by an unexpected plot event and stayed intrigued to the end.

But I would love if each reader took something away. Whether the reader relates to the feminist undertone, the twist on history, the morale lesson, or any other aspect, I hope this novel causes each reader to contemplate long after the last page.

QUESTIONS FOR DISCUSSION

1. In the end, do you think Lavinia comprehends her error in moral logic? Do you believe Lavinia felt completely absolved of her sins?

2. If Lavinia would have been released after meeting with Father Thomas, instead of being executed, would she have killed again?

3. In her younger years, Lavinia exacts vengeance on the man who merely bumped into her and made her drop flowers. Why does she not seek vengeance against Kelton?

4. Was Aselin's betrayal a surprise? What clues were there along the way?

5. In what way is Lavinia like her favorite poison, wolfsbane. How is Aselin like hemlock?

6. How would Lavinia's life have been different if she could have been named magistrate after her father? How did the limited choices available to women in the 16th century lead Lavinia to murder?

7. Lavinia's relationship with her faith could be viewed as a mechanism to disassociate herself from the act of murder. How was Lavinia's ability to justify her sin in the eyes of God a form of permission?

8. How would the novel have been different if Father Eustace gave Lavinia her final confession?

9. What will happen next? Will Aselin aid Akworth's search for the ring? Will she find success without Lavinia's guidance?

ACKNOWLEDGEMENTS

My dream was not to write a novel, but rather to have my novel *read*. The book in your hands is the culmination of perseverance and countless hours of toil at a keyboard. But you, having reached this page, fulfill my aspiration. Thank you for allowing me to tease your imagination, and I hope these pages gave you something in return.

I also hope you share Lavinia's journey with a friend - heck, how about all your friends? Word of mouth is the best marketing tool and I am eternally grateful for your support.

While an author develops an initial draft on their own, it takes a team to publish a book. Thank you to my husband, Jon, for tolerating nights at the keyboard and endless queries for opinions. Thank you to my friends and family who beta read those first drafts. To Kate Cowan at Broken Arrow Designs for the vivid cover art which brought a snapshot of my imagination to life. To Melissa Thiringer for deeply appreciated copy editing. To my children — this is what mommy really worked on after I kissed you goodnight, and someday when you're older, I'll let you read it. Thank you to my parents who encouraged me to always pursue what may seem impossible.

But my most sincere gratitude extends to Myra Fiacco, and Filles Vertes Publishing, for believing in an unknown author and her story. I am indebted to your support and editorial insights that brought out the best from my writing.

ABOUT THE AUTHOR

K.M. Pohlkamp is a blessed wife to the love of her life, a proud mother of two, and a Mission Control flight controller. Originally from Wisconsin, she now resides in Houston, Texas. She can be found at www.kmpohlkamp.com or @KMPohlkamp.

EXPLORE MORE TITLES BY
FILLES VERTES PUBLISHING